American *She-Wolf*

◊ ◊ ◊

JB
12/21

American She-Wolf

American She-Wolf

a novel

by
mike whicker

Copyright © 2021 by mike whicker

a Walküre imprint

This is a work of historical fiction

ISBN: 978-1-7356098-4-3

printed in the United States of America

American She-Wolf

For

My Family

American She-Wolf

Historical Note

The Western Allies intelligence communities displayed no qualms about bringing Nazis into their clandestine societies after WW II.

During the Cold War, both the CIA and British MI6 made use of Nazis (some who were boldly unrepentant). Records show both organizations went out of their way to recruit Nazi agents if the Germans could offer experience or expertise in working against the Russians. The CIA not only maintained a close working relationship with Reinhard Gehlen, but they also helped him set up shop. During the war, Gehlen served as the German Army's intelligence chief for the Eastern Front. With protection from the United States after the war, Gehlen assembled a large intelligence organization staffed with numerous ex-Nazis and known war criminals—at least 100 of Gehlen's operatives were former SS/SD officers or Gestapo agents. Gehlen's organization eventually became the official West German intelligence agency—the BND.

Records from the National Security Archive of George Washington University show that at least five associates of the notorious Nazi Adolf Eichmann worked for the CIA and 23 other Nazis were approached by the CIA for recruitment.

The roll call of former Nazis who worked for the British during the Cold War is long. Just one name is Horst Kopkow, an SS officer who during the war ordered the executions of approximately 300 spies (many were British and most were tortured before execution). After the war, Kopkow was arrested as a war criminal but ended up being recruited into the British intelligence fold in 1948. The British even faked Kopkow's death to deceive a war crimes tribunal.

The Soviets weren't ones to be left behind. The East German Secret Police they established after the war was filled with former Gestapo, SS, and SD agents.

Shield Maidens

(in Norse lore, fierce female warriors
who accompanied the Viking men into battle)

Part 1

Chapter 1

Can-Can

Paris, France
Friday, 22 June 1951

As the topless showgirls danced on stage at the Moulin Rouge, Erika Lehmann sat at a table with three Parisian couples. The world's most famous nightclub was busy tonight, as it was every night.

She had never seen the other people at her table before tonight and knew none of them. What brought her to this table was standard etiquette at the crowded Moulin Rouge. Guests were allowed to sit at a table with others if a chair was available.

The three young couples were quite pleasant. Erika sipped Champagne and engaged in lively banter with them in French for about twenty minutes before excusing herself to 'powder her nose.'

She left the large dining room and made her way up some red-carpeted steps. When she reached the top and turned down a corridor, a large man with a security label on his sleeve approached her.

"May I help you, Mademoiselle?" he asked in French.

"I have an appointment with Monsieur Holit," she answered in the same language.

"He mentioned nothing to me about expecting someone."

"He must have forgotten. If you ask him, I'm sure he'll remember."

He stared at the pretty blonde for a moment before saying, "Very well. Wait here."

He turned and walked down the corridor to an office door, passing other offices along the way. He knocked and heard a man inside say "Entrer." As soon as he opened the door he was clubbed over the head by the butt of Erika's pistol. He dropped to the floor like a sandbag. A small man with a hooked nose and eyeglasses sat behind a desk. Startled, he jumped to his feet.

"What is this! Who are you!"

1

"I'm the person sent to collect your racing form from the Maisons-Laffitte Racecourse."

"What are you talking about?"

"Let's not play games," she said. "I searched your flat. It was not there. You wouldn't keep it in a bank deposit box because you couldn't access it on weekends or after banking hours. Then it occurred to me, as the bookkeeper for the Moulin Rouge, what better place to keep it than stored in the massive safe behind you. If anyone else who can enter the safe found it, you could claim it was a souvenir you're keeping from a great day you had at the track."

"Mademoiselle, I assure you I don't know what you're talking about."

Erika shot him in his left arm with her .32 caliber, sound-suppressed Beretta Brevettata. He shouted in both pain and surprise as he fell back into his chair.

"Now for the other arm," she said as she pointed the weapon. "That will leave me two legs and if I don't have the form by then my next target will be your liver."

"Put the gun down!" he said in agony. "I will get it."

He grimaced as he turned to the safe. After dialing a combination, the door opened to reveal piles upon piles of French francs and smaller shelves stacked with paperwork. Holit dug to the bottom of a stack of folders and pulled out a horse track racing form. She snatched it out of his hand.

Holit became frantic. "How will I explain this to the club owners? When the security guard awakes, he'll tell them he was attacked."

"I know your bosses here know nothing of your activities. Fill me up a money bag of francs. You can claim you were robbed."

Erika fired another round just past Holit's head, it lodging in a thick cabinet next to the safe. "Hurry up!"

The man used his one good arm to quickly fill a bag with cash.

The security man began rousing. Erika walked over and kicked him in the jaw.

Gathering the bag of money, she placed the racing form inside and covered it with her shawl. Before leaving, she pistol-whipped Holit, leaving him as unconscious as the guard.

2

She walked the corridor and down the steps to the main dining room. The showgirls had started the Can-Can. Erika stopped to use the restroom before she calmly walked out of the Moulin Rouge and entered one of the string of taxis always lined up in front of the club on the Boulevard de Clichy.

Chapter 2

Asbach

Washington, D.C.
Three days later—Monday, 25 June 1951

Erika Lehmann now sat in Leroy Carr's office at CIA headquarters in a large complex of buildings on E Street in Washington. Carr was the Deputy Director of the agency—the second in command behind only General Smith, the Director. Al Hodge, Director of Counterintelligence and Erika's handler, was also there.

She handed over the racing form.

"Now," she said, "will one of you tell me why I was sent to Paris to retrieve a horse track racing form?"

Carr ignored her for a moment as he thumbed through several pages of the form.

"How was your flight home," Hodge asked.

"Not good," she answered. "I flew out of Paris Saturday morning and landed in a thunderstorm at the refueling point in Shannon, Ireland. The plane was delayed for four hours until the storm passed. Then the pilot had to alter his course across the Atlantic because of more storms, which extended the flight and made us refuel again in Newfoundland. We didn't land at Andrews Air Force Base until three hours ago."

"Anyone killed in Paris?"

"No."

Carr finally answered her question about the racing form. "This is a code book. The names of the horses are all code names for French politicians or other people of influence in France who support the Soviet drive to strengthen the communist party in that country. The odds on the horses reflect how much influence the men behind the names have in France. I'll hand this over to our cryptanalysis section. They'll crack it fast enough."

"Am I free to go?" Erika asked.

"Yes, take the day off," Carr said. "Al will delay your debriefing until tomorrow. We have another assignment for you, but it won't start for a few days."

"No down time?" she asked. "I just got back, Leroy."

Hodge interjected. "Lehmann, you were only gone for a week and you had downtime after the last mission."

"As I mentioned," Carr said. "The mission won't start for a few days, maybe not for a week. We're keeping our eyes on the situation."

"What's it about?"

"Let's get you debriefed about Paris before we start briefing you about your next assignment," Carr said. "Be here tomorrow morning at eight. Al will debrief you about Paris himself. A one-week mission with minimal enemy contact and no fatalities shouldn't take more a than a day for your report."

[that evening]
Erika sat at on a barstool in the Lili Marlene Café, a small pub not far from the Pentagon and the Arlington National Cemetery just across the Potomac River from Washington. She owned the café, having bought it with some of her inheritance from her deceased German father. The café supplied her the perfect cover.

Monday was normally the café's slowest day and tonight only four of the twelve tables were taken by dining customers. Several barstools sat empty.

The blonde CIA agent sipped on an Asbach brandy at the far end of the bar, away from others, as she talked with the bartender, Zhanna Rogova. Zhanna, nearly six-feet tall with short, jet hair and dark eyes always wore a neck scarf. She asked, "What did Carr have to say?"

Zhanna Rogova was also a CIA field agent and assigned to Erika's team of five all-female agents codenamed the Shield Maidens. Her job as bartender supplied Zhanna a cover. One of the other Shield Maiden's cover was as an instructor at the Naval War College in Providence, Rhode Island; one as a recruit trainer at Camp Peary, Virginia; and one was headquartered in Barcelona, Spain, posing as a Gypsy Flamenco dancer.

On some assignments, all five were brought together. On other missions it might be just two or three depending on the needs of the situation.

"You know Leroy and Al," Erika answered her question. "They're not going to tell us anything until they're ready. I have to debrief tomorrow about Paris."

Zhanna grimaced. "I hate those debriefings. If they'd let me into E Street with a gun I'd shoot someone during those debriefings."

Erika smiled, but she knew what Zhanna claimed was not out of the realm of possibility. During the war, Zhanna served in the Red Army and was known to the Germans as the Black Witch for her skill as a sniper and the number of kills she racked up. Near the end of the war, she was transferred to SMERSH where she became a cold-blooded assassin of 'Enemies of the State.'

"How did Ada do while I was gone?" Erika asked.

Ada was Adelaide, Erika's ten-year-old daughter. The child's father, a German SS captain died in combat.

"She did fine."

"She likes helping in the kitchen," Erika nodded. "I told her we'd go out for pizza and a movie tomorrow night."

At the other end of the bar, a group of three men burst out in uproarious laughter, apparently at a joke one of them told. One started shouting obscenities. Zhanna left Erika and walked over to the men.

"One of the tables has two children with their parents," Zhanna told the vulgar man. "We run a respectable place here. Watch what you say in here or I'll break your arm."

Chapter 3

Dragoş Luca

Washington, D.C.
Four days later—Friday, 29 June 1951

Erika felt guilty that she was away so much from her daughter, so she made the most of every minute they were together. Mother and daughter had enjoyed the past few days. They lived in a D.C. apartment but when Erika was away on assignments, Ada stayed at the Lili Marlene Café with Angelika, the café's manager. Angelika had a small studio apartment located upstairs off of the café's storeroom. Angelika was Erika's longtime German friend who she and Zhanna had helped escape last year from Soviet controlled East Berlin. Angelika was the only one at the Lili Marlene who knew Erika and Zhanna worked for the CIA. Bertha the cook knew nothing about their backgrounds, neither did either of the café's two waitresses.

Now, on Friday morning, Erika had been summoned to Al Hodge's CIA office along with Zhanna Rogova and Axel Ryker, another CIA field agent.

"Coffee is on the table," Hodge said from behind his desk.

The two women served themselves, pouring it into paper cups before retaking their seats. Ryker passed on the coffee and lit a cigar. Hodge pulled out three 8"x10" photographs of a man and handed one to each agent. The handsome and distinguished-looking man in the photo looked to be in his mid-forties. Hints of gray had started to invade his temples.

"His name is Dragoş Luca, a Romanian based at his villa on the Black Sea near Constanta," Hodge told them. "He controls over half of the poppy fields in Turkey. Makes his living selling opium among other things. The Russians not only leave Luca alone, but they keep a strong working relationship with him. He has significant contacts on practically every continent. Luca is also a weapons dealer and serves as a middleman for the Soviets selling weapons to Middle Eastern, African, and South American countries. The Intelligence Committee wants Luca put out of business."

"So, we're going behind the Iron Curtain again?" Erika asked.

"Yes. But we won't have to fly you in at night and land you in some farmer's field or drop you off by boat on the coast of the Black Sea in the wee hours. We've got a rabbit in the hat this time around. That Gypsy band Amy dances for is scheduled to play a series of concerts in Romania starting next Friday—a different city each weekend. Constanta is one of the cities. You two can accompany the band as stagehands, Amy's wardrobe mistress, or whatever capacity that seems legitimate. Amy will know what will work.

"The band's first booking is in Bucharest next Friday night where they'll perform for two nights. They'll be in Romania for three weeks. We expect they'll receive a grand reception at the airport. All the band members are Romanians who have gained international success. It will be like a homecoming. Dragoș Luca is a fan of the arts. He has a private box at the opera house in Bucharest where Amy's band will perform. With the publicity the band has as one of the best Flamenco groups in Europe, we think it's a sure thing that Luca will be at one of the performances. And as the richest man in Romania, you should get a chance to meet him in a receiving line or possibly a reception with some politicians or other big shots."

"What do you mean by 'we want him put out of business?'" Zhanna asked.

"We want capture and extraction, not assassination. We'd like to take him alive for questioning," Hodge answered. "There's a wealth of information he can give us about the workings of Soviet arms deals."

"And if taking him alive is not possible?" the former Russian assassin wanted to clarify.

"Then you will leave him be for now. We don't want to jeopardize Amy's cover. We've got too good of a thing going here with her—a member of a popular band that travels all over Europe and is even invited behind the Curtain on occasion. No single mission is worth sacrificing that."

Hodge continued, "As I mentioned, the concerts start next Friday. Amy and the band will fly out of Barcelona on Wednesday to give them time for rehearsals in Bucharest. That means Erika and Zhanna have to be in Barcelona no later than Tuesday so you can fly out with the band. Amy knows you're coming. We'll spend tomorrow here in my office. I'll give you more information on what we know about Luca. You'll fly out from Andrews Sunday morning. You should land in Barcelona Monday evening."

"What about the Fischer sisters?" Erika asked.

"Neither Stephanie or Kathryn speak Romanian or Russian. Amy is from Romania and you three speak Russian. There are so many Russians in Romania, or Romanians who speak Russian, you can get by with that language in the larger cities."

Ryker finally spoke. "If this man is not to be canceled, what is my role, exactly?"

The massive, 270-pound, scar-faced Ryker had served during the war as Heinrich Himmler's top Gestapo henchman. The brutish Ryker could snap a man's neck as easily as a chicken wishbone which he had proved on many occasions during his days with the Gestapo. He had worked with the Shield Maidens on several past missions because of his numerous contacts in Europe. Most of the women's missions took place in Europe because of the languages they spoke.

"You're going to Istanbul with me, Ryker," Hodge responded. "You and I will fly out for Istanbul on Wednesday. It's the closest I can get to Romania without being behind the Curtain. I'll set up shop there so I can supply help if the ladies need it for Luca's extraction. Axel, you'll remain in Istanbul with me unless Erika needs you. She's team leader."

"What is the extraction plan?" Erika asked Hodge.

"We'll brainstorm that tomorrow. Obviously, it will have to be something adjustable with options."

9

Chapter 4

Balik ekmek

Arlington, Virginia
Next day—Saturday, 30 June 1951

Unlike Monday nights, Saturdays were always busy at the Lili Marlene Café. Erika, Zhanna, and Axel Ryker had spent the day exchanging ideas in Al Hodge's office. Now they sat upstairs at a private table in the café's storage room eating dinner.

"Zhanna," Erika said. "Ada will stay with Angelika here in the upstairs studio apartment while I'm away. I told Angelika that you'd also be gone for a while. She'll handle the bar. When we brought her over from East Berlin a year ago, she spoke practically no English but now she can communicate with the customers when it involves café business like ordering drinks and meals. She'll be okay."

Zhanna nodded as she took a bite of her Jägerschnitzel.

"Axel, you should have no concerns being with Hodge. You won't have to operate in Germany."

Ryker was wanted in West Germany for war crimes. Only the CIA's intervention had kept Ryker from being united with a noose.

Her comment garnered no response from the ghoulish Ryker as he continued to eat.

Finally, Zhanna said, "Let's get in, get this guy, and get out without wasting a bunch of fucking time. If we can't extract, I say we shoot him despite what Al says. At least that will scatter his contacts and put a big hole in his operation. We'll claim it was self-defense. Al can't blame us for that."

"I agree with the crazy Russian," Ryker said.

"Don't call me crazy, you big goon!"

"You're as mad as a box full of hatters," Ryker said.

Zhanna pulled her dagger but Ryker was just as quick pulling his Walther PPK.

"Put the weapons away!" Erika demanded loudly. "We will all fulfill our objective to the best of our ability. That means extraction. If

10

circumstances along the way prohibit that, we'll adjust. If Luca has to be eliminated, then so be it. Despite what Al says, we're not leaving him unscathed and return with a failed mission. But our main objective going in will be to extract the man for interrogation. Axel, if all goes according to plan, you might not be needed. You can remain in Istanbul with Al and spend your time eating Balik ekmek and Turkish lamb."

She continued, "Axel, Al said you and he aren't flying out until Wednesday. Zhanna, have a bag packed and meet me at E Street tomorrow morning at 7:30. A car will drive us to Andrews Air Force Base. Al said a DC-4 will be on the tarmac ready to take off as soon as we get there. If we don't encounter bad weather or maintenance delays, we should see Amy in Barcelona on Monday evening."

Chapter 5

Tute

Barcelona, Spain
Two days later—Monday, 02 July 1951

Rain fell on Barcelona that afternoon, and the wheels of the DC-4 splashed down on a still wet runway at El Prat Airport at 6:45 p.m. The CIA plane had no special markings to distinguish it from any normal commercial aircraft. The only clue that it was not a profit-making flight was there were only four passengers aboard the 80-seat plane—two female CIA agents and a couple of men who worked as charge d'affaires for the U. S. Embassy who disembarked in Madrid before the plane flew on to Barcelona.

Erika Lehmann and Zhanna Rogova descended the steel ladder to the tarmac where a stunningly beautiful raven-haired woman waited. The women hugged and Amy Radu asked about their flight.

"It went well," Erika said. "No delays, but Zhanna and I are starving, Amy. The only food they had on the airplane was tuna salad sandwiches and potato chips."

"Then it's off to dinner for us," Amy said. "I know just the place."

After Erika and Zhanna showed their papers to a passport agent inside the terminal, Amy hailed a taxi from a row of six waiting for fares. The first driver pulled up and stopped, rolled down his passenger window, and looked at Amy.

"Are you Gypsy?" he asked her in Spanish.

"Si."

"I don't drive Gypsies. I don't want to get robbed." He drove off to return to the end of the line.

"What the hell was that all about?" Erika asked. Neither Erika nor Zhanna spoke Spanish.

"He's a Spanish Catalan," Amy answered in English. "The Catalans don't like Gypsies."

The next driver pulled up. This one asked no questions, got out of his cab, and loaded Erika's and Zhanna's suitcases in the trunk.

"Where to, Señoritas?" he asked in Spanish after everyone was crowded inside the small, rusting Opel that looked like it had already survived two lifetimes.

Amy said, "The O'Centollo Cantina and Marisquería on the Rosellón."

"Yes, I know that cantina," he said as he shifted the tired car into first gear and pulled away.

The back seat could only seat two so Amy sat in front. As the driver negotiated the streets of Barcelona, he kept glancing at Amy who sat beside him. Finally, he said, "You look like Amy Radu, the famous Flamenco dancer."

"Yes, I am Amy Radu."

"I can't believe it! I have Amy Radu as a passenger. You are my wife's and my favorite. We have seen you perform several times at Cordobes. My wife won't believe I drove you. Would you sign something for her? The fare will be free."

"A free fare is not necessary." Amy took a piece of paper from her purse. "What is your wife's name?"

"Luciana."

Amy wrote out something on the paper and handed it to the driver.

When they arrived at the cantina, the driver hustled out to retrieve the luggage. He tried to refuse payment for the fare but Amy insisted and paid him.

As the three Shield Maidens walked into the cantina, Erika said, "Amy, it seems like you've picked up Spanish quickly."

When Amy was assigned her current cover job, her Spanish was only so-so. Now, after being immersed in the language for some time she had learned a great deal.

"I wouldn't claim to be fluent; sometimes local jargon, slang, and vernacular are beyond me, but I can usually get by with normal day-to-day speech. In this cantina, the owner is a Hungarian Gypsy as is everyone else who works here—most are his relatives or clan members. I'm welcomed here and there will be no trouble. A couple of waiters speak fairly good English because they get a lot of British and American tourists. We'll ask for one of those so you two can communicate with him directly."

When they stepped into the cantina, Amy received a celebrity's welcome. The owner stopped what he was doing at the cash register and greeted her personally.

"Señorita Radu! Welcome back."

"Gracias, Lajos." Amy switched to English. "My two friends don't speak Spanish. Is Tamás working tonight?"

"Yes."

"May he be our waiter so my friends can speak in English?"

"Yes, of course," the elderly man said. "And I will have a table set up for you and your friends in the back where you'll not be disturbed by customers who recognize you."

"Thank you, Lajos. My friends just arrived in Barcelona and have not yet checked into their hotel. Do you have a place their bags can be stored?"

"Certainly, Señorita. I'll place them in my office."

The 'back' that Lajos had referred to was where certain locals played the gambling game Tute every evening, sometimes until three or four in the morning. The game was already afoot when the three women walked in. The four Gypsy men around the table all knew Amy and they exchanged greetings.

The table the women would share was farther to the back. A good-looking young man appeared in short order with two bottles of wine—one red and one white.

"Compliments of the house, Señoritas." Tamás handed out menus. A kitchen girl who had followed the waiter placed a cutting board on the table with several different cheeses, some grapes and figs.

"I'll return shortly for your orders," Tamás said in English.

"Thank you," Amy replied.

"It is my honor to serve you and your friends, Señorita Radu."

When he walked away, Erika kidded Amy, "I didn't know we'd be eating dinner tonight with Rita Hayworth."

Zhanna asked, "Why are there no labels on the wine? What do they do, make it in the basement?"

Amy said, "They own their own vineyards outside Barcelona. Wait until you try it. Gypsies know how to make wine. The water comes from an underground artesian spring. The wine is as pure as you'll ever drink. Also, this cantina is a marisquería. That means they specialize in fresh seafood. The Mediterranean is only a few blocks away. Lajos buys his seafood fresh from the fishmongers every morning. Any seafood you eat here tonight was swimming yesterday. You'll never find fresher."

"What do you normally get, Amy?" Erika asked.

Amy shrugged. "Everything is good here. If you want lobster, they are huge. They serve it on a large platter because it won't fit on a plate. But I normally order the combination offering. It comes with a nice filet of sea bass, scallops, huge prawns, clams, and mussels. You get a plate of olive oil linguini on the side.

That sounded good to Erika and Zhanna so three of those dinners were ordered when their waiter returned.

"Tell me Tamás," Erika said. "That card game those men are playing at that other table. Can anyone enter the game?"

Tamás hesitated. "Tute can take up to seven players at a table, but I have to tell you those men allow only Gypsies, and I have never seen a woman join them."

With her bright blonde hair and features that could have placed her on a Nazi Germany poster as the perfect Aryan woman, she surely did not fit in with the swarthy Balkan men at the table.

"Thank you, Tamás," she said.

◊ ◊ ◊

The seafood and wine were everything Amy had promised. Surprisingly, talk about the upcoming mission was avoided. They would all meet tomorrow for that.

When dinner ended, without warning the other two, Erika rose and walked over to the table of Tute players. "Does anyone speak English? Or perhaps German, French, or Russian?"

"I speak the English some," one of the men said.

"May my friends and I join you? I was told seven players is maximum. You have three empty seats."

"No. I am sorry, Señorita. Women are . . . how do you say? . . . bad luck at the table."

"Wouldn't you like to tell your friends you played Tute with Amy Radu?"

The man translated for the others. They all decided to ignore the hex and in a moment, the three Shield Maidens were playing Tute and smoking cigars in the backroom of the O'Centrollo Cantina.

Chapter 6

Huevos Rancheros

Barcelona, Spain
Next day—Tuesday, 03 July 1951

Erika and Zhanna shared a room at El Palace, an elegant, Gothic-style hotel only a few blocks from the sparkling blue Mediterranean, which they could see from their sixth-floor window.

El Palace had hosted many famous guests. Salvador Dali presently lived in the hotel's Grand Suite. A few months ago, the eccentric artist had asked that a horse be brought to his suite so he could study it for a painting he was considering. A fully grown horse wouldn't fit in the elevator, but hotel management managed to deliver a pony.

The hotel's guest list also included the infamous. Heinrich Himmler stayed here during his numerous trips around Spain for meetings with Franco both before and during the war.

As agreed upon last night, Amy knocked on their door at 8 a.m. They would discuss the mission over a room service breakfast.

"Any hangovers?" Amy asked. They had played cards until two in the morning.

"None," Erika answered.

"How'd you two do at the table?" Amy asked. "I won about 950 pesetas ($7)."

"I got behind early because I wasn't keyed in on the rules or strategy," Erika said, "but I won some of my money back near the end when I began getting the hang of it. I might have broken even by the end of the night."

Zhanna said, "I lost my ass to those butt-wipes—about $30. I don't know what that is in pesetas."

"It's about 3,800 pesetas," Amy said.

"Then fuck them and the camels they rode in one."

Erika and Amy laughed. "European Gypsies rarely ride camels, Zhanna," Amy said tongue-in-cheek.

"Alright," Erika said. "Let's order breakfast and get down to work. Amy, do you have any recommendations?"

"The Huevos Rancheros are very popular here."

"What the hell is that?" Zhanna asked.

"It's a traditional Spanish breakfast," Amy replied. "It has eggs, refried beans, tomatoes, onions, some mild spicy peppers and certain spices. You'll like it."

"Okay, get me that and tell them to bring me a barf bag and some fart pills so I won't be passing gas all day."

The room was in Erika's name so she called room service and ordered the meals. Because El Palace hosted many international guests, the desk staff and room service personnel weren't hired unless they spoke at least one other language besides Spanish. The girl she spoke to understood English.

"Okay, let's get down to business," Erika said. "Amy, how much did Al Hodge tell you about the mission? Did he mention the target, Dragoş Luca?"

"He mentioned the name and said this would be an extraction mission out of Romania. Other than that, he didn't say much about Luca. He told me you'd fill in the details. Al's main reason for calling me was he wants me to figure a way to attach you and Zhanna to the band for our upcoming Romanian tour. The band leaves for Bucharest tomorrow."

Erika said, "Dragoş Luca is Romanian but not a Gypsy. He's an international drug smuggler on a large scale, and he plays middleman for the Soviets with weapons deals to any country with the resources to purchase Soviet weaponry from handguns and rifles all the way up to rocket launchers and military aircraft. He won't be an easy target. He's a man the Soviets don't want to lose. Have you decided on what Zhanna and my roles will be with the band?"

"I do my own hair, but it would be normal for the dancer to have a hairdresser traveling along so that will be your job, Erika. Zhanna, you can pose as my wardrobe assistant."

"Good." Erika said as the knock on the door sounded. She opened and a spiffily dressed room service waiter rolled a cart into the room.

18

"We'll serve ourselves," Erika told him. "Gracias." She handed him a tip.

After the man left, Amy asked, "I assume Al supplied you with all the paperwork needed to enter the Eastern bloc."

"Yes," Erika said. "We have everything in order as far as paperwork is concerned."

"The first thing for now," Amy said, "is you learn the names of the band members like you've been friends for years. Communicating with them will be tough. Romanian is their mother tongue and all of them have picked up Spanish because the band has been headquartered in Barcelona for three years—long before I joined them. But as far as languages the band members speak, that's it except for Petru who can get by in Russian. As you know, none of them know anything about this is my cover job for the CIA." She handed both Erika and Zhanna a piece of paper. "They are all Gypsies from Romania, like me."

- Bull fiddle: Petru from Bucharest.
- Guitar: Viorel from Oradea.
- Cimbalom: Mitica from Arad.
- Violin: Cici from Transylvania
- Djembe drum: Nicu from Constanta.
- Accordion player: Raval, also from Bucharest
- Dancer/singer: Amy from Transylvania

"Cici is the only woman in the band besides me," Amy added.

Chapter 7

A celebrity welcome

Barcelona, Spain
Next day—Wednesday, 04 July 1951

At 9 a.m., the Barcelona Gypsy Romanian Orchestra and its entourage boarded a Turkish Airlines twin-engine DC-3 for the six-hour flight to Bucharest, Romania. Amy had introduced Erika and Zhanna to the group last night as her hairdresser and wardrobe mistress. Everyone in the band and entourage realized Amy was the reason for the band's recent soar in popularity around Europe and the Mediterranean. No questions were asked. A small stage crew of four men also traveled with the band so Erika and Zhanna were not the only non-musician members of the entourage.

The band would play three weekend concerts over the course of three consecutive weekends during its Romanian tour. At each locale they would play on Friday and Saturday nights. Their first engagement would be in Bucharest, the nation's capital and largest city. That would take place this coming weekend. The second stop would be in the next largest city, Constanta, located on the coast of the Black Sea. The tour would wind up with a final weekend in Cluj-Napoca, a city located in the heart of Transylvania.

Just after three in the afternoon, the Turkish DC-3 dropped out of the clouds and landed at the Bucharest Otopeni Airport. Reporters, photographers, and the Primar (mayor) of Bucharest along with other officials waited to greet the Romanian band that had brought prestige to their homeland. Flowers were handed to Amy and Cici by a young girl wearing traditional Romania festival attire complete with a garland surrounding her head, and a colorful dress with an apron. The Primar read a proclamation welcoming the band, then the reporters and photographers pounced.

◊ ◊ ◊

It took two hours for the band to answer questions and pose for photos for the newspaper people before they were able to maneuver their way to the taxi row. The four members of the stage crew remained behind to ensure safe delivery of the musical instruments, but Erika and Zhanna, as Amy's personal assistants, loaded into one of the four cabs needed to transport the band to the hotel.

The band didn't employ a manager. Those duties were handled by Petru, the bull fiddle player who founded the band three years ago. They checked into the Epoque Hotel near the Cişmigiu Gardens, the finest hotel in the city. The hotel manager had hired extra security for the band's stay to control any overly enthusiastic fans who might clog the lobby hoping to get an autograph or a picture with a band member.

Erika, Zhanna, and Amy would share a spacious two-bedroom suite. When they finally got to their room and tipped the bell hops, Erika said, "My goodness, Amy, I never thought there would be so much hubbub about a band arriving."

"It's not like this everywhere we go," Amy said, "but I was expecting this here. Romania has had little to celebrate since the war and the Soviet takeover. It's obvious the success of the band around Europe has Romanians excited."

"That sounds like an understatement from what I saw today at the airport," Erika said. "So, what's our schedule starting tomorrow?"

"The band will rehearse at the opera house twice tomorrow, with a brief, walk-through rehearsal Friday morning before the first performance that night."

Chapter 8

Dragoş

Constanta, Romania
Next day—Thursday, 05 July 1951

At his villa on the coast of the Black Sea, Dragoş Luca stood drinking tea on the veranda with three of his top henchmen. The waters sparkled before them.

"Did you get anything out of Costal?" Luca asked.

"Nothing," one of the men said.

"I want to see him," Luca stated.

The four men walked down to a cave-like subterranean floor where a bloodied man was chained to an overhead beam, his feet barely touching the ground.

"Are you ready to talk, Costal?" Luca asked the tortured man.

With great effort, the man replied, "I never betrayed you, Dragoş. I have always been loyal to you."

Luca turned to the others. "He might be telling the truth but we can't take that chance. Carve him up for fish bait and clean this place when you're done."

Two of the men grabbed chainsaws.

[that evening]
Luca now sat in his villa's dining hall with five other people at an Italian made black Marquina marble table that would easily seat thirty. With him were two beautiful young women who always seemed to be at his side when he wasn't engaged in business, along with the three male henchmen from earlier.

Servants had just taken away the dinner plates and delivered hazelnut Gelato in iced silver goblets topped with blueberries.

"Tomorrow evening," Luca said, "we'll take a trip to Bucharest to watch that Roma band from Barcelona perform. The one that's been in all the newspapers. Vasile, make sure the opera house knows I'll be

22

using my private box. Ion, you're in charge of security." Bucharest was only a two-hour drive from Constanta but Dragoş Luca didn't like wasting time. He told the third man, who always wore a yellow blazer, "Marku, have my plane ready."

Chapter 9

Djelem Djelem

Bucharest, Romania
Next day—Friday, 06 July 1951

Amy and the Barcelona Gypsy Romanian Orchestra had just finished their last rehearsal at the Romanian Athenaeum where they would perform tonight and tomorrow.

The Athenaeum was the pride of Bucharest with its neo-Greek portcullis under ionic columns, marble floors, red carpeted stairs, ornate and priceless frescos, gilded gold railings, and sparkling chandeliers. The structure had suffered some damage from German bombing during 1944 after the Romanian powers-that-be saw the writing on the wall about how the war was going to turn out for Germany and switched sides to begin cooperating with the Soviets. The damage was minor, however, and the building was restored within a year of the war's end.

When the band finished rehearsal, the four-man stage crew went to work helping the musicians care for the instruments and inspecting the sound system and talking things over with the building's stage lighting crew one last time. Amy's assistants, Erika and Zhanna, followed her backstage to her dressing room. This had not been a dress rehearsal so little needed to be done except lay out the dresses Amy would wear tonight.

"It looks like we have a sell-out tonight and tomorrow," Amy said. "At least that's what the house manager told Petru this morning."

"With the reception the band received when we arrived and all the publicity, that's not a surprise," Erika said.

Amy said, "When Al briefed us, he said this Dragoş Luca was a patron of the arts and had a private box here. I wonder if he'll show?"

"Maybe," Erika said. "If not, I would think he surely will attend the performances next weekend in Constanta where he lives."

Zhanna had not been focusing on the conversation. Instead, she wondered about the cover job she was supposed to be performing.

24

"What is a 'wardrobe mistress' and what the fuck am I supposed to do with these dresses?"

"You don't have to do anything, Zhanna," Amy replied. "I have a seamstress in Barcelona but she's eight months pregnant and couldn't make this trip. She and her husband don't want to take the chance the baby could be born behind the Curtain. If anything needs sewing, I can do that. I made all my clothes growing up in my clan's caravan."

"So what do we do now?" Zhanna asked.

"Now we go to lunch," Amy answered. "I need a hearty lunch because I never eat dinner before a performance. Dancing and singing for nearly two hours on a full stomach is not comfortable. The band always goes out for dinner after the show."

[that evening]

The performance nearly everyone in Romania had been waiting for was scheduled to begin at 8 p.m. People arrived early with 90 percent of the crowd in their seats by 7:30 with everyone seated before showtime. In Romania, it was considered the height of ill-manners to arrive late for an opera, symphony, a play, or any artistic performance. The Primar of Bucharest who had welcomed the band at the airport was there with his wife, two teenaged sons, and a half dozen of his top aides and their wives. Like the Primar, other movers-and-shakers of Bucharest occupied other private boxes that ringed the U-shaped auditorium. Not a politician, but the richest man in Romania, Dragoş Luca, sat in his private box with his two women and three advisors/henchmen. Three of Luca's private security detail that guarded his villa stood in the corridor outside the burgundy velvet curtain that led into the box.

The voice of the unseen Athenaeum Master of Ceremonies announced in Romanian over the PA that the performance would begin in five minutes and reminded the crowd that photographs were not allowed during the performance.

"Ladies and Gentlemen," the unseen man said. "Photographs will be allowed with the performers on stage after the performance."

25

All this was normal protocol for performances at the Bucharest Athenaeum so the performers and other patrons would not be distracted by flashing light bulbs.

Five minutes passed quickly. The voice came back as the lights dimmed in the auditorium and brightened on the stage.

"Ladies and Gentlemen. The Athenaeum is privileged to have with us tonight and tomorrow night fellow Romanians who have made quite a name for themselves around Europe and brought prestige to our homeland. Please welcome the Barcelona Romanian Gypsy Orchestra!"

The applause was loud. The band slowly walked on stage where their instruments awaited. Amy was the last to appear. She wore a slinky red dress, not at all fitting with something that would be seen on a Gypsy dancing around a campfire. Her hair was in a tight bun with a large rose above her right ear. She stepped up to the microphone and spoke in Romanian.

"Thank you all for the warm welcome. We are so happy to be back in our homeland. Before we start, please let me introduce the band.

"On bull fiddle is Petro." Petro waved to the applause. "Petro is from Bucharest."

"Playing the guitar will be Viorel from Oradea." More applause and Viorel waved, as would all of the band when introduced.

"On the cimbalom is Mitica from Arad."

"Cici will play the violin for you. She's from Transylvania."

"Our accordion player is Raval from Bucharest, and on djembe drum will be Nicu from Constanta."

"My name is Amy. I'll be dancing and singing for you tonight. Like Cici, I'm from Transylvania."

After the welcoming applause, the lights on stage went out, leaving it in total darkness. A minute passed and blue lights flooded the stage. The microphone was gone and Amy stood motionless with her hands at her side and her head bowed. Nicu, the djembe drum player, began pounding out a rhythmic beat with his hands on the solo drum. After a moment, the rest of the band joined in and Amy began stomping her feet with a red spotlight shining down on her, breaking the blue haze that enveloped the rest of the band.

The microphone was brought out when Amy needed it, and after an hour of singing and dancing popular Roma songs, Amy disappeared from stage for ten minutes while the band kept playing. In her dressing room, Zhanna helped her change and Erika took down her hair. When she reappeared on stage, the beautiful Gypsy was dressed in a tribal skirt of her clan, and an off-the-shoulder peasant blouse. The crowd erupted.

The band immediately picked up a fast arrangement, and with her hair now down, Amy whirled and whirled, whipping her raven-hair about wildly. The second half of the show was a tribute to not only the minority of people in Romania with Gypsy heritage, but to the country of Romania, as well. Amy ended the performance by singing *Djelem Djelem,* the unofficial but revered anthem of the Gypsy people. Although the vast majority of Romanians in the Athenaeum this night had no Gypsy roots, the crowd was on its feet with a standing ovation as the band joined hands and took its bow.

◊ ◊ ◊

After the autograph seekers and people who flocked on stage for a photograph with the band had been satisfied, Amy and the other tired band members finally got back to their dressing rooms. Amy was changing out of her tribal attire when a knock came on her door. Erika and Zhanna were in the room.

Zhanna answered the knock. "Who are you?"

The man took off his hat and spoke in Romanian. "My name is Marku. My employer, Dragoş Luca, is a patron of the Athenaeum and would be honored to take you and the orchestra out to dinner."

"I don't speak Romanian." Zhanna said in Russian.

The man switched to Russian and repeated his request.

"Fuck off," Zhanna said. "Miss Radu is changing clothes."

Erika quickly intervened in Russian. "Excuse my friend, Marku. We are Miss Radu's assistants. I'm afraid dinner after a performance is strictly reserved for the band and crew only. It's our tradition. Please tell Mr. Luca we appreciate his offer but we have to respectfully decline."

The man didn't look happy as Erika closed the door in his face.

"So, Luca did attend," Erika said, switching back to English. "Good. From Al's reports, Luca is not one to give up easily."

Chapter 10

Long-stemmed roses

Bucharest, Romania
Next night—Saturday, 07 July 1951

The Bucharest newspapers and radio stations had given the Friday night performance rave reviews and Saturday night's performance was just as successful. After the band finished signing autographs and posing for photographs on stage, they finally retreated to their dressing rooms. And like last night, a knock sounded on Amy's door shortly after she started undressing.

Tonight, Erika opened it.

"Zdravstvuyte, ya yam pomogu?" she said in Russian (May I help you?). She recognized the man in the corridor.

Since she spoke Russian, the man did the same.

"My name is Dragoş Luca. I am hoping to speak with Miss Radu."

"I'm Erika, Miss Radu's hairdresser. She's changing right now but I'll see if she's available."

"Thank you."

Erika disappeared for a moment, then Amy stepped up to the door covering herself with a dressing gown.

"Buna ziua," Amy said 'hello' in Romanian.

Luca removed his hat and switched to his native tongue. He introduced himself again.

"Miss Radu. My name is Dragoş Luca. One of my associates called on you last night to extend to you and the orchestra a dinner invitation. He tells me it is your band's tradition to dine together privately after a performance. I certainly understand that. However, I've read that your concert next weekend will be in Constanta. I have a villa on the Black Sea not far from that city. Will you and your band and entourage do me the honor of dining with me some evening next week? We will dine on my yacht as we take a cruise."

"What an exciting and very kind offer, Mr. Luca."

"Dragoş, please."

"Dragoş, it all sounds lovely," Amy said. "We arrive in Constanta on Tuesday."

"May I inquire where you are staying in Constanta?"

"To be honest, I don't know the name of the hotel. Petru, our bull fiddle player, serves as our manager and he takes care of those details."

"Very well," Luca said. "I have brought some flowers for you and your violinist. I hope you will accept them."

"Of course," Amy said.

Marku who had called on them last night stepped up and handed Amy a huge bouquet of long-stemmed red roses.

"Thank you," Amy said as she accepted them. "Cici's dressing room is across the corridor."

Marku turned and knocked on Cici's door.

Luca said. "I enjoyed your performances immensely." He handed her a card with a telephone number. "This is my private line. When you arrive in Constanta, please call me at this number so we can make the proper arrangements. Now I will bid you good night with the hope that I will see you in a few days."

Chapter 11

Constanta

Constanta, Romania
Three days later—Tuesday, 10 July 1951

The hotel in Constanta the band checked into Tuesday morning ended up being the Hotel Cherico on the Stefan Cel Mare less than a half-mile from the Black Sea. The location kept secret from the media, locals had not yet discovered where the band was staying so no throngs were present in the lobby and check-in went smoothly.

After getting settled in their suite, Amy, Erika, and Zhanna took their lunch in the hotel restaurant. Their waiter asked Amy for her autograph, but other than that they ate in peace.

"When we finish here," Erika said to Amy in English. "Call the number Luca gave you and let him know the band has arrived."

Amy nodded. "I'll suggest that tomorrow night would be a good night for his invitation. I'll put him off for a day so we don't seem too enthused."

"Good idea," Erika replied. "I wish the dinner was at his villa and not on his yacht. I'd like to get a look inside that place."

When they finished lunch, the three women went back to their suite and Amy dialed the telephone number Dragoş Luca had given her. A woman answered. She said hello in Romanian.

"Hello. My name is Amy Radu. Dragoş Luca gave me this phone number and asked me to call."

"He's here. Wait a minute, please."

In about a minute, Luca said, "Hello."

"Dragoş, this is Amy Radu. I promised to call you once the orchestra was in Constanta."

"Yes, Miss Radu. Thank you."

"Please call me Amy."

"Where is your group staying, Amy?"

"The Hotel Cherico."

31

"Excellent choice. I dine there on occasion. My yacht crew and caterers are on notice about the band's dinner cruise. Which evening is most acceptable?"

"Will tomorrow night work?" Amy asked.

"Of course. I will have cars at your hotel to deliver everyone to my private marina tomorrow night. They will be at your hotel at six o'clock. I know that's early but we'll make a night of it. This time of year is wonderful for swimming. The waters are very pleasant. Bring swimsuits if anyone wants to test the waters. Other than that, the dress is informal. I promise you and your people a wonderful evening."

"We look forward to it, Dragoş."

[later]

Al Hodge's and Axel Ryker's arrival in Istanbul had been delayed a couple of days because of problems in Korea to which Al had to help Leroy Carr attend. Finally, their plane touched down today at the Istanbul airport at 5:30 p.m. They reported immediately to the United States embassy. They would not be staying in an Istanbul hotel because the city, although in the NATO sphere of protection, swarmed with Soviet spies who would recognize Hodge by sight.

Chapter 12

Şom de Argint

Constanta, Romania
Next day—Wednesday, 11 July 1951

An ancient metropolis and Romania's largest seaport, Constanta traced its history back some 2,500 years. Originally called Tomis, legend has it that Jason landed here with the Argonauts after finding the Golden Fleece.

Today the sun shone in a cloudless azure sky. The temperature was already 85° Fahrenheit at 10 a.m. Erika, Zhanna, Amy, and Cici sat at a table on the walkway in front of a café three blocks from their hotel. Cici spoke no Russian, only Romanian and Spanish. Amy had to translate.

Cici was a young girl—Erika and Zhanna would be told she was 21. A small woman at about 5'3", the group's violinist had the look of the Roma—large, dark eyes and hair with olive skin. She didn't possess the stunning beauty of Amy Radu; most people would place Cici in the category of 'cute.'

The women decided on just pastry and Turkish coffee. Amy wore a wide-brimmed hat in hopes of not being recognized from all the newspaper photographs that had appeared almost daily for the past week. It seemed to work. They were not bothered by autograph hounds.

"Cici," Erika said. "Amy always announces at the performances that you are from Transylvania, like her."

Cici waited for Amy to translate.

"Yes," Cici answered. "My family was not a traveling caravan clan like Amy's. We lived in a small Gypsy village called Sucaegu. It's about ten miles west of Cluj-Napoca."

"The band's last performance is in Cluj-Napoca," Erika said. "I'm sure you're excited about that weekend."

Cici said, "I lost many of my family during the war when the Nazis swept through rounding up Jews and Gypsies, but I have an older brother who survived by fleeing into the forest. Yes, I am looking forward to seeing my home."

33

[that evening]

Dragoş Luca had invited everyone connected to the Barcelona Romanian Gypsy Orchestra. That meant in addition to the seven-person band, Amy's two assistants and the four-man stage crew had to be picked up at the Hotel Cherico. At five minutes before six o'clock, five sedans pulled up in front of the hotel entrance. The band members were gathered in the lobby when Marku entered.

The half-hour drive took them north of Constanta to a lavish villa resting on a cliff over the Black Sea. The cars did not stop at the estate: instead, they drove directly to Luca's private marina where eight boats of different sizes and for various purposes were tied up to docks. Sport fishing boats and speed boats lined up impressively, but all were dwarfed in size by an enormous, motorized yacht named the Şom de Argint that could cross oceans. (Amy told Erika and Zhanna the ship's name was Romanian for Silver Hawk.)

When the band members reached the bottom of the gangway, Marku said, "Please wait here everyone. Dragoş wants to welcome you personally."

Luca's henchman walked onboard and disappeared below. In a moment, Dragoş Luca appeared on deck and walked down the gangplank. He wore white cotton pants and a half-unbuttoned light-blue shirt, revealing a hairy chest and a gold medallion hanging from his neck on a thick gold chain.

"Welcome, everyone," he said. "My staff, the ship's crew, and my caterers have taken no shortcuts to ensure we have a grand evening. Please, follow me aboard."

As they walked, Luca smiled and commented to the women, "I'm glad to see you wearing light pants. The sea wind can cause ladies in skirts some distress."

Amy and Cici laughed at his joke. Amy translated for Erika and Zhanna. Because of the heat, all four of the women wore summer spaghetti strap blouses in various colors. Zhanna, of course, had on her ever-present neck scarf.

Luca led them down a flight of metal stairs and into a large entertainment area. A bartender stood behind a fully stocked bar. He had been ordered to wait until the guests arrived before serving. Luca spotted two of his other 'associates.'

"Ion. You may tell the captain he can now get underway. Vasile, inform the caterers to begin bringing out the food."

Ion nodded and disappeared on his way to the bridge. Vasile went to the galley. Luca signaled the bartender to open the bar.

No other guests seemed to be onboard except two young women who stood by the bar eyeing Amy and the three other women suspiciously. They both wore French two-piece bathing suits, with the bottom half covered with lace see-through sarong wraps.

The men in the band and the male stage crew were first to the bar as the ship's two massive diesel engines growled awake. The engine noise subsided when the ship pulled away from the dock. Finally, Amy, Erika, Zhanna, and Cici got their chance at the bar. Amy and Cici ordered Tuică, a favorite alcoholic beverage among Romanians, made from plums. Erika ordered the same. Zhanna ordered a double shot of Ketel vodka served neat.

At that moment, Luca joined them at the bar. "I should introduce you to two more of my assistants," he said, referring to the two glaring women. This is Crina and Sylvania." The two women moved close to Luca and placed their hands on his shoulders as if protecting their property. Luca glowered at them and they moved away like two sultry vampires scolded by Dracula.

The caterers relieved the awkward situation when the food was brought in. On a long table, they set up a huge, iced bowl of jumbo prawns along with trays piled high with steak and scallop kabobs. A prime rib roast was brought in with a chef to cut it into portions ordered by the guests. Alongside the medium rare roast was a large bowl of horseradish for guests to serve themselves.

"Dragoş," Amy said, referring to the food. "This is unbelievable."

"Nonsense, my dear. You honor me by accepting my invitation. You and your colleagues have brought honor and prestige to our beloved country. Later, we'll break out the champagne. From my villa, my staff brought to the ship a case of Dom Perignon in a rare 1933 vintage."

Zhanna quickly downed her double vodka and ordered two more from the bartender who spoke Russian. As she leaned on the bar, she said to the bartender, "You speak Russian well but with a Romanian accent. How is it you speak Russian?"

"I learned the language late in the war, after my town was taken over by the Soviets when the Germans retreated."

"Tell me about those two sluts that want to drape themselves around Dragoş."

The man blushed. "I'm just a bartender, madam. I know nothing about them."

Zhanna dropped the subject.

◊ ◊ ◊

An hour later the yacht was far out in the Black Sea. No land could be seen. Erika and Zhanna were now topside on the deck by themselves.

Zhanna tried to light a cigarette but the matches were extinguished by the wind before she got the fire close. She finally tired of trying and flipped the cigarette over the side.

Suddenly Dragoş appeared on deck and joined them.

"It looks like your orchestra mates are enjoying themselves below."

"I'm sure they are," Erika said in Russian. "How could they not? I wish now that I would have taken you up on your suggestion to swim, but I didn't bring a bathing suit."

"I'm sure we can find a solution, my dear. Sylvania and you look to be close to the same size. I'm sure she has extra bathing suits onboard. I'll have the captain stop the ship and announce a swimming party for those interested."

Twenty minutes later Erika had borrowed a swimsuit from an uncooperative Sylvania and Amy one from the smaller Crina. Both suits were in the French two-piece style. Zhanna and Cici did not take part. Unlike Cici, Zhanna was a good swimmer but there was always the neck scarf to keep in mind. It would come off within seconds of entering the water. A couple of the band members had brought swim trunks and joined in with Luca's two female assistants and Erika and Amy. From a small deck lowered near the stern that stopped just a foot over the waves, the swimmers entered the water with snorkel masks stored on the ship. Luca sent Vasile out on a powered skiff just in case anyone began struggling in the water.

Luca stood on deck with Zhanna watching the swimmers.

He said in Russian, "Amy's hairdresser, Erika, swims like a dolphin."

"She won several awards for swimming when she was a teenager. I understand her name was on a list for possible competition in the 1940 Olympics before the event was canceled because of the war." That was true, but Zhanna left out the part that Erika would have competed for Nazi Germany. "Do you have a way to light a cigarette in this wind?"

"Of course. How thoughtless of me. I have a special lighter. He pulled a gold butane lighter from his pants pocket and held it for her."

"Thank you, Dragoş."

He looked at her for a long moment. "You don't seem to be the type of woman to spend your life serving as a wardrobe matron. And I could say the same thing about your friend Erika, Amy's hairdresser."

"Why do you say that?"

"Neither of you look the part."

"And what is it we look like, Dragoş?"

"The Bulgarians have a group of highly-trained female frontline commandoes. It's a small group but they proved themselves remarkably effective during the war. Both of you look like you'd fit in with something like that more so than what you're doing now."

"Interesting," Zhanna said. "If I ever lose my job with the band, I'll call on the Bulgarians."

Luca laughed. They continued watching the small number of swimmers splash around in the waters of the Black Sea. Some clung to lifesavers. Erika had dived and had not resurfaced. This was noted by Luca. He got on a bullhorn in order to communicate with Vasile in the skiff.

"Vasile, find Erika, the blonde hairdresser. She dived and has not come up."

Vasile began patrolling back and forth in vain along the starboard side of the ship where all the swimmers had entered the water.

37

Erika was under the keel of the ship inspecting the two dead-in-the-water screws and rudder. Information that may or may not come in handy sometime. When she finished, she surfaced next to the ship for a quick breath and submerged again as she swam back toward the group. She came up under an unsuspecting Sylvania. Erika pulled down and off the bottom of the woman's bathing suit and, still underwater, swam away with it. Sylvania never saw who pranked her.

[an hour later]
The Şom de Argint was now again underway, heading out farther into the Black Sea. Erika's prank on Sylvania failed to enlist the embarrassing effect on her Erika intended. When swimming ended, Sylvania calmly pulled herself onto the platform and coolly walked past the male bandmembers and ship's crew who stared at her nakedness. She even stepped to the bar, serenely lit a cigarette, and ordered a martini before finally covering herself from the waist down with her see-through sarong.

Darkness had now fallen and everyone was on the open deck. The case of Dom Perignon '33 had been iced and delivered to the deck along with Irish crystal champagne flutes trimmed in gold. All the guests drank the expensive Champagne as they star-gazed. With no city lights to dim them, the stars and planets clustered the entire sky. Some seemed so close it was if they hung by strings to keep from falling to earth. Others farther away seemed to shout, "Here I am, Lord. I shine for you!"

Amy and Dragoş Luca stood alone on the bow, the other guests behind them on the deck.

"I'm glad you and your fellow musicians are enjoying themselves," Luca said.

"It's been wonderful, Dragoş." She put a hand on his arm. "We were not expecting this."

"Do you need any help of any kind?" Luca asked. "I'm in a position to help you if you ever encounter bureaucratic snags in Romania. I can also help financially if the band needs anything."

"We have not run into much red tape here in the Eastern bloc because we were invited by the powers in Bucharest, and the band is doing well financially. This allows us to stay in the best hotels. Petru handles all that but he seems content about our income. Our recent tours around the Mediterranean were performed in front of sold-out crowds, and we have a nice contract with the Cantina Cordobes Tablao Flamenco in Barcelona when we're not on tour."

"I will be at both of your performances here in Constanta on Friday and Saturday night, of course. I know of your band's tradition of a private dinner together after a performance, but tomorrow night is Thursday. May I take you to dinner? There is a restaurant I own here in Constanta. I'm sure you'd enjoy it. The dress is formal, I'm afraid, but I can send people to your hotel room to take care of all that."

"I have a formal evening gown, Dragoş."

"Then you accept?"

Amy knew her mission included finding out more about this man. Although he made her feel like a puppet on a string, she had to say, "Yes. Thank you, Dragoş."

"I will pick you up at your hotel at eight," he said.

At midnight, the Şom de Argint turned back on a course that led to its dock north of Constanta. It arrived and tied up shortly before 3 a.m.

Chapter 13

Stea Verde

Constanta, Romania
Next day—Thursday, 12 July 1951

Dragoş Luca sat eating a breakfast of cantaloupe and citrus fruits on his sunny veranda with Marku, Ion, and Vasile. Sylvania and Crina were not there.

"Ion," Luca said. "What's the latest on the shipment to Mexico City?"

"It was weighed yesterday," Ion said. "It came in at 295 kilograms of pure opium. Once it is cut in our facility in Mexico City and made into heroin that will be nearly seven million American dollars' worth that is marketable on the streets. Paying off the Mexican officials will cost us the standard 10 percent of our profit. It leaves from Antalya tomorrow."

Antalya was a city on Turkey's Mediterranean coast. Luca used that departure point so the freighters would not have to pass through the Strait of Istanbul where the chances were higher that the ships would be searched by NATO inspectors.

Luca then turned to Vasile. "Your report on the Russian arms deal."

"There has been a delay," Vasile replied. "The Syrians originally agreed to the price but are now trying to renegotiate. They'll pay the same amount of money, but they want three motorized rocket launchers included in the deal."

Luca swallowed some orange juice and said calmly, "There is a half-million American dollars in this for us and we basically have to do nothing other than act as a buffer between Russia and Syria. We don't have to deliver anything ourselves. I'll contact General Sukov this afternoon and suggest he take the deal. The Soviets are getting top dollar for the four T-34 tanks and small arms. Surely they can find three old rocket launchers from the war that are gathering cobwebs in some warehouse."

Luca switched subjects. "So, tell me. What did you think of last night and the Gypsy band?"

"I don't trust Gypsies," Marku answered quickly. "The Gypsies I've encountered in my life will stick a knife in you and take your wallet if given the opportunity."

Ion said, "It was an enjoyable evening, but I have questions about Amy's two assistants. Neither of them fit the part as a hairdresser and a wardrobe mistress. Did you notice the scars on the arms of the one named Erika? They are clearly knife and gunshot wounds. I wouldn't think being a hairdresser was such dangerous work. And then there is the Russian wardrobe mistress. How tall is she? Six feet? And she has the eyes of a killer."

Luca didn't mention the same thoughts had crossed his mind. Instead, he downplayed it. "Your imaginations run wild, my friends. This is a band invited to Romania by the government. The band made no effort to contact us. We contacted them and if you remember they turned us down that first night in Bucharest when I sent Marku to invite them to dinner. We have more concerns than to spend time worrying about this Gypsy band. I'm taking Amy Radu to dinner tonight at the Stea Verde. If I get stabbed, I'll let you know," Luca joked. "Marku, you'll be our driver and I expect you to treat Miss Radu with the ultimate respect. Understand?"

"Yes, boss."

"Call the restaurant this afternoon and tell them to have my private table ready at eight o'clock."

◊ ◊ ◊

Around that same time, Erika, Zhanna, and Amy sat together in their hotel suite.

"Tell me more about this dinner tonight, Amy," Erika said.

"There's not much to tell," Amy said. "Last night on the ship, Dragoș invited me to dinner at a restaurant here in Constanta he said he owns."

"When are we going down for breakfast?" Zhanna asked. "I'm starving."

Erika looked at her. "After all that food on the ship last night you're starving?"

"I didn't eat that much. The free vodka was better."

"We'll have breakfast after we're done here, Zhanna," Erika said before turning back to Amy. "What's your plan for tonight?"

"I'm not going to question him about anything that might seem suspicious," Amy said. "I don't want to blow our cover. We already know who we're dealing with and he has no reason to be cautious around us. If he mentions anything noteworthy that we might be able to manipulate for a capture and extraction, I'll let you know."

"It's obvious that Dragoş is infatuated with you," Erika said. "This might open him up. A man like that likes to impress people. We saw that last night."

"I'll keep my ears open and let him do most of the talking," Amy said.

A knock came at the door. Zhanna answered.

"Who are you and what do you want, baldy?" she asked the bald-headed, middle-aged man standing in the corridor.

He was taken aback by her rudeness, and said, "My name is Stovos. I own a local jewelry store and I have a delivery for a Miss Amy Radu."

Amy came to the door, identified herself, and accepted the wrapped package and thanked the man. "If you'll give me a moment, I get my purse."

The man shook his head. "Please, no tip is necessary. The gift is from Dragoş Luca. He has taken care of everything." He turned and began walking back to the elevator.

Amy shut the door and returned to the divan where she opened the package. Under the wrapping was a large, purple velvet jewelry case. Inside was a choker with diamonds of various sizes, many of a carat or more, along with a note from Luca:

I hope you will accept this gift and wear it tonight at the dinner that I so look forward to.

Erika inspected the choker. "This thing had to cost $10,000 at least. You could buy a nice house and a new car for what this cost."

"Fine," Zhanna said. "When we get back to Barcelona, Amy can buy herself a house and take us for a ride in her new car. Can we go downstairs for breakfast now?"

[that evening]

Marku, wearing his always present yellow blazer, knocked on Amy's door at five minutes to eight. She was ready. Her hair had been done that afternoon in the hotel's salon (not by fausse-hairdresser Erika). Her copper-colored silk evening gown revealed some cleavage without being bawdy and the diamond choker gleamed around her neck.

They took the elevator to the lobby where Luca waited. He was wearing an expensive, hand tailored Canali tuxedo from Italy. He smiled when he saw her.

"You look exquisite, Amy."

"And you look quite dapper, Dragoș."

He offered his arm. The hotel doorman opened the door. They walked out where a Rolls Royce Phantom IV sat at the curb waiting. Marku opened the back door for his boss and his guest, then got behind the wheel which was on the right side of the British-made car.

"So, where are we going, Dragoș?"

"A restaurant called the Stea Verde. It's not far, about a ten-minute drive. Marku will dine downstairs in the main dining area. You and I will dine at my balcony table that overlooks the Parcul Tabacarie."

Amy was aware of the city park with a large lake.

When they arrived at the restaurant, Marku parked at the curb directly in front of the entrance. The valet recognized the car and did not approach to move it. Marku opened the back door, Luca got out and extended his hand to Amy as she slid out. She took his arm and they walked into the restaurant, the door held open by Marku. The Stea Vera was of moderate size. The dining room looked as if it would seat about fifty people. The maître d spotted Luca and left his podium to great him and his guest.

"Mr. Luca," the man said in Romanian. "Your private table is ready. Our welcome to you and your charming companion."

"Thank you, Emilian," Luca said. "Let me introduce you to Miss Amy Radu. She is the dancer and singer for the much-publicized Roma band from Barcelona currently touring our country."

The man's eyes widened. "Miss Radu. You can be sure our chefs and staff will do everything in their power to make your visit tonight a memorable one."

"I'm sure it will be wonderful, Emilian."

Emilian turned and snapped his fingers. A handsome young waiter hustled over.

"Seat Mr. Luca and his guest at his private table," the maître d commanded. "Take their drink orders and have a bowl of stuffed olives delivered to their table immediately."

The young waiter bowed to the maître d and led Luca and Amy up a flight of stairs to a balcony with only one table that overlooked on one side the diners below and out the window to the other side the park and lake across the street.

Luca held the chair for Amy then he sat down. He told the waiter. "Bring us a bottle of Tuică for now. We'll order our drinks after Miss Radu decides on her dinner."

The waiter departed without speaking and in less than a minute returned with the bottle of Tuică and the bowl of huge olives stuffed with goat cheese.

"Thank you," Luca said to the waiter. "We don't need menus. Return in ten minutes. We'll be ready to order then. Try an olive, Amy. The restaurant brings them in from Israel. Our chefs here can prepare anything you want, from Romanian cuisine, to Turkish, Greek or Italian."

"This is not a huge restaurant, Dragoş. How many chefs do you have?"

"Four. I brought them in from the countries I mentioned. They all don't work together every night but today is an exception. They are all here for you."

"You flatter me, Dragoş. I'm a simple Gypsy girl. This diamond choker you sent me I will return to you. It cost way too much for a gift between friends who barely know one another."

"You can flatter me by keeping it. It will remind you of our friendship. Now, our waiter will be back shortly. What would you like to eat?"

"Definitely Romanian. I miss the food of my homeland."

44

"We'll take care of that tonight," he said. "May I order for us?"

"Please do."

When the waiter returned after exactly ten minutes, Luca ordered wine and meals of Samale (cabbage rolls), Mici (grilled meat rolls), and meatball soup. He also ordered a bottle of red wine. "This particular wine was imported from Yugoslavia. That country doesn't get nearly enough credit for its exquisite wines."

"Your restaurant must be doing very well, Dragoş."

"It makes a small profit, nothing to get excited about. My main business is shipping by sea. I own a fleet of freighters that ship goods to several continents. But all that is very boring. You are much more interesting. Tell me everything there is to know about the famous Miss Amy Radu."

She smiled. "You give me too much credit, Dragoş. My fame is limited. The only people interested in me are Gypsy Flamenco fans. Gypsies are still not liked by many. I have been insulted many times on the streets of Barcelona. Some taxi drivers refuse to take us as fares, and there are stores and shops where we are not welcome."

"Unfortunate," he said. "I have always thought the Roma are a fascinating people. They defend their own."

"Yes, they do."

They drank Tuică and sampled the olives until the meals and wine were delivered. A second waiter set a cart of various Romanian cheeses and breads beside the table as their main waiter opened the wine.

"Now, let's get back to you," Luca said after the waiters departed. "Tell me about your childhood."

She told Luca the truth. "My family and clan were travelers, unlike Cici our violinist who grew up in a Gypsy village. We spent much of our time in the Carpathian Mountains moving the caravan from small towns to other small towns, setting up camp in the forests nearby and entertaining the townsmen at night with gambling and dancing. Our clan witch told fortunes for a coin. Everyone in the clan contributed in some way. I was one of the campfire dancers. I would dance for a man and kiss him on the cheek for a coin. That's where I learned to sing and dance. We'd sell the men skins of wine or barter with them for flour and other goods. Of course, the wives of the townsmen didn't like their men staying out late in the forest with Gypsies. Usually after about a week, the women would complain to the town primar and we'd have to leave. But we'd come back in a year or so after visiting other towns. That's how we survived. Our men were good hunters and fishermen. Each night we would have a good stew of rabbit and squirrel. Sometimes the men would bring back a deer or a wild boar. What wasn't eaten that night would be preserved in kegs of salt. The fish we ate for breakfast, usually with some wild onions the women would collect as we traveled."

"Where is your family now?"

"As far as my clan, those who weren't rounded up by the SS in '44 scattered. I have no idea where they are. My immediately family—my parents and brother and sister—died in the gas chambers of Sobibor. The SS kept me alive to satisfy their needs. I managed to escape and spent the rest of the war fighting the Germans with a group of Polish resistance fighters."

Dragoş Luca didn't respond as most would with words of condolence and Amy was glad. She didn't want to hear empty words that could never bring her family back. Nevertheless, Luca was now even more intrigued by her. "Would you like to find any of your clan members who survived the war? If they are still in Romania, I feel confident I can assist you with that."

"Finding traveling Gypsies is an impossible task, Dragoş."

"Perhaps not. But it's your decision, Amy. If you decide yes, give me a list of names. How do you like the Samale?"

"They are delicious—and huge. One would make a filling meal. You're going to make me fat, Dragoş. Then Zhanna, my wardrobe mistress, will be complaining because I don't fit into my stage apparel."

He laughed and refilled her wine glass. "You mentioned Zhanna. Tell me about her and your hairdresser, Erika."

Now lies were necessary.

"They have worked for me for about a year—since the band gained popularity around the Mediterranean. I don't know much about their pre-war years, but I know Zhanna worked as a nurse for the Red Army during the war. Erika served as a Red Army translator for questioning of captured German troops. She was born in Bavaria so German is her native tongue, but she is a communist who was forced to flee Germany before the war. She ended up in Moscow. She speaks four languages fluently: German, Russian, French, and English."

"That's impressive. What languages does Zhanna speak?"

"Russian, German, and English. I'm afraid neither of them speaks Romanian."

Chapter 14

Final rehearsal

Constanta, Romania
Next day—Friday, 13 July 1951

Amy had to report to the Auditoriul din Constanta for a final, brief walk-through rehearsal with the orchestra at 10 a.m. Before that, at eight, she briefed Erika and Zhanna in their suite about last night's dinner with Dragoș Luca.

"As I told you," Amy said, "I did not question Dragoș because I didn't want to raise suspicion. We know our assignment—capture and extract. He did offer up on his own that his business was in shipping and that he owned a fleet of freighters. That's nothing we didn't already know from Al Hodge. However, he did ask me many questions. If the question concerned me, I told him the truth about my life growing up in the caravan, my family dying at Sobibor, and my fighting with the Polish resistance. At one point he asked about you two. I gave you your cover stories we agreed upon. He never asked about your last names. This surprised me. It's obvious he feels completely safe."

"Good," Erika said.

"He offered to help find any surviving members of my clan," Amy added.

"How did you respond?" Erika asked.

"I didn't. I'd love the help, but not from Dragoș Luca. I can't trust him. If he did manage to find some of my clan members he might hold them hostage if things break down."

Erika considered that Amy's personal business and moved on.

"I'm sure Luca will be at your performance tonight," Erika stated.

"Yes, he told me he'd attend both concerts. The one tonight and the one tomorrow night."

"I wonder what his plans are for the band's last stop in Cluj-Napoca?"

"I don't know," Amy said. "Many non-Gypsy Romanians avoid Transylvania. The old legends about that area persist to this day. Yet,

48

I'm sure a man with Dragoş's power and influence has no qualms about going anywhere in this country."

"Let's keep that in mind," Erika said. "Transylvania might give us an opening if you can lure him there. I'm sure we can depend on help from Count Lupei."

Part 2

Chapter 15

The offer

Constanta, Romania
Two days later—Sunday, 15 July 1951

The two concerts at the Auditoriul din Constanţa had been rousing successes like the previous week's engagement at the Bucharest Opera House. Dragoş Luca had attended both performances over the weekend with Crina on his arm. Sylvania was being punished for being rude to Amy and Erika during the Black Sea cruise. Luca had ordered her whipped on the bottoms of her feet so as to not blemish her beauty and then he confined her to her room at the villa. Ion took care of the whipping.

It was now Sunday and the performances in Constanta were over. The band would leave for Cluj-Napoca tomorrow. After last night's show, Luca personally came down to Amy's dressing room and invited Amy, Erika, and Zhanna to lunch today at his villa. He had ordered his Greek chef from the Stea Verde to report to the villa and prepare Papoutsakia and an appetizer of miniature Souvlaki.

Crina was at the table. After seeing what happened to Sylvania and having been slapped around herself by both Luca and his men for past minor infractions, Crina went out of her way to be sociable and welcoming. Luca's three personal henchmen were not present.

As always, a bottle of Tuică sat on the table. The alcoholic beverage made from plums was the most popular liquor among the vast majority of Romanians. Yet, it was practically impossible to get outside of this country.

"Before we leave Romania," Amy said in Russian for Erika's and Zhanna's benefit, "I need to buy a few bottles of Tuică to take back to Barcelona for the band."

"There is no need to purchase it, my dear," Luca said. "I have several cases in my wine cellar. A couple of cases will be my gift to the band."

"Again, Dragoş. You are too generous," Amy replied.

"It's my pleasure," he said. "Now, tell me about your next performance in Cluj-Napoca. You told me you are leaving tomorrow. I was curious why. Last week you didn't depart Bucharest for Constanta until Tuesday."

"Cici, our violinist, is from the Gypsy village Sucaegu not far from Cluj-Napoca. She wants a day or two to visit her village. She still has a brother there."

Luca nodded. "Completely understandable. I know how poor that small Gypsy villages are in Transylvania. I will make a donation in Cici's name to the village king. Do you need any assistance getting everyone and the instruments to Cluj-Napoca? I can have some men assist you."

"Thank you, Dragoş, but we're fine. We're taking the train to Cluj-Napoca. When we arrive, we're supposed to be greeted by people from the Primar's office. They'll take us to the hotel, and the Primar has arranged to loan the band three automobiles for our use."

Luca nodded. "Now, I'd like to talk about a proposal. I want to sponsor your band, and I want Erika and Zhanna to work for me as translators. I told you my business concerns shipping freight to various continents. I always need translators and I have none right now who speak English that I feel I can trust. Amy, this means you will have to find a new hairdresser and wardrobe mistress but how hard can that be? For this consideration, I can expand your band's performances to include South America, Latin America, and North America."

Amy paused. Erika and Zhanna looked at Luca.

"Dragoş," Amy said. "This is totally unexpected. All band business is up to Petru, not me."

"Tell Petru I personally guarantee the band's income will triple in the first year. You and the band will not regret this, my dear." He then looked at Erika and Zhanna. "Whatever the band pays you for your services for Amy, I will also triple."

"I'm in!" Zhanna exclaimed. "Now, can we get some vodka on the table instead of this shit made out of peaches?"

"Tuică is made from plums," Erika corrected her.

"Peaches, plums, whatever," Zhanna replied. "They both give me diarrhea."

Luca smiled. Crina rose, walked to a nearby cabinet, and brought back a bottle of Stolichnaya Elit.

"I know you'll need some time to talk things over with the band, Amy," Luca said. "I plan on attending your performances in Cluj-Napoca next weekend and I'll stay at the hotel where the band stays. Do you know which hotel that be?"

"Petru mentioned last night we'll be staying at the Hotel Beyfin."

"Very well. I will not intrude on the band's schedule in any way. I'll be there solely to answer questions if Petru or anyone in the band wants to speak with me about my offer."

Kitchen staff brought out the meals.

"What is this stuff?" Zhanna asked.

"Papoutsakia is stuffed eggplant, Zhanna," Luca answered. "The Souvlaki is normally referred to as Gyros in many countries."

Zhanna refilled her shot glass of vodka then said, "Looks good," as she dug in. With a mouthful of crab stuffed eggplant, she said, "Triple my salary, you say?"

Erika suppressed a smile. Zhanna was a wildcard and many times said the wrong thing, but sometimes her frank demeanor worked out.

"Yes, Zhanna. I'll triple your salary." Then Luca looked at Erika and continued to speak in Russian. "Zhanna will fit in perfectly in Transylvania as far as looks, but I wonder about you Erika. Amy told me you were born in Bavaria. With your blonde hair and German features you'll stand out. There is much resentment toward Germans among the Gypsies of Transylvania. I can offer you protection."

"Thank you, Dragoş," Erika said. "But I'm sure I have nothing to worry about being with Amy, Cici, and the rest of the band who are all Roma."

"Zhanna has already said she accepts my offer. What about you?"

"My friend Zhanna is very impetuous, Dragoş. For me, I'll need some time to think this over. Where would Zhanna and I be stationed?"

"In Antalya, Turkey. I will rent you two a suite at the finest hotel in that city. The flight to Antalya from Constanta is less than three hours. My airplane for your travel to and from Constanta will be at your disposal. Of course, the job will require a great deal of traveling to other continents and the accommodations on the freighters will not be first class. But when you arrive at your destination you will stay in an upscale hotel at no cost to you."

"Now let us finish our lunch," Luca continued. "I would never consider taking you and Zhanna away from Amy during her current tour. After the performances in Cluj-Napoca wind up, then you and the band can give me your decisions."

"What is this stuffed eggplant called again?" Zhanna asked.

"Papoutsakia," Amy answered.

"Is there any more of this back in the kitchen?"

Crina rose from her chair and went to the kitchen to have more brought out.

[that evening]

After thirty minutes of dropping coins into a pay telephone to route her call through Bulgaria and other connections to the American embassy in Istanbul, Erika finally had Al Hodge on the telephone.

"Lehmann," Hodge said from Istanbul, "you were ordered to check in four days ago." The irritation in his voice was evident.

"It wasn't possible, Al. Do you realize what it takes to make a telephone connection from behind the Curtain?"

"Alright, alright. Tell me what you have."

"Check out Antalya, Turkey. It looks like that is the port Dragoş Luca works out of."

"Antalya, okay," Hodge said. "What else?"

Erika didn't elaborate on the job offers for her and Zhanna. She needed time before that report. *"That's it, Al. How's Ryker doing?"*

"Ryker is Ryker. What else do you want me to say?"

"We're leaving for Transylvania tomorrow," Erika said. *"I'll get back to you when I can."*

"Wait a minute," Hodge said, but he heard her hang up. "Erika . . . Erika!" He slammed down the phone.

Chapter 16

Homecoming for Cici

Sucaegu, Romania
Two days later—Tuesday, 17 July 1951

The summer weather was pleasant but cooler in the higher elevations of Transylvania than on the Black Sea coast.

The band had arrived at their hotel in Cluj-Napoca yesterday evening. As promised, the welcoming committee awaited when their train arrived to deliver the band and crew to the Hotel Beyfin. Three empty sedans waited in the hotel parking lot for the band's use. Petru was given the keys.

Amy had told Dragoş Luca she would tell the band of his offer of sponsorship, so during dinner last night at the hotel, she told Petru and the other musicians. Most of the band and stage crew seemed enthused about both the money and performing in the Western Hemisphere, especially in the United States. Petru told everyone he would speak with Luca when he arrived. Erika, Amy, and Zhanna knew the tour would never come to pass if their mission to capture and extract Luca was a success, so they mostly remained silent during the comments.

This morning, Cici got the keys to one of the cars and took Erika, Zhanna, and Amy to her home village of Sucaegu. It was a short drive west, only about twenty minutes. Just outside the village, on the only dirt road that led to it, they were stopped by two shotgun toting men. Cici told the men this was her village and told them her brother's name before the men let them pass. The small Gypsy town was made up of colorful houses with dirt floors and many chicken coops, pigsties, and barns for sheep and goats.

With joy, Cici was reunited with her older brother. The people of the village—all Roma—had little interest in what happened in the outside world, so they had no idea that Cici now played in a successful and popular band that toured Europe. Amy, being a Gypsy, fit right in. As Luca had predicted, Zhanna pretty much fit in except for her height. The people had never seen a six-foot tall woman. Erika was another story. She drew the attention of all the small children who wanted to touch her blonde hair. She would kneel and let them touch.

They ate a humble lunch of chicken soup in Cici's brother's home and stayed in Sucaegu until late afternoon. Cici told her brother and the villagers she would return tomorrow.

By the time they got back to the hotel, Dragoş Luca had checked in, bringing Marku, Ion, and Vasile with him.

This was not the Shield Maidens' first mission in Romania. Erika, Zhanna, and Amy had been sent to this country once before, in early 1950. Later that evening, after dinner, Erika made a phone call to a castle in Transylvania outside the town of Zalău. The name of the castle was Castelul Lupului—Castle of the Wolf.

Chapter 17

Meeting up with Dragoş

Cluj-Napoca, Romania
Next day—Wednesday, 18 July 1951

This morning, Erika, Zhanna, and Amy met up with Dragoş Luca. He had called their suite last night and asked them to lunch, but Amy told him they would be spending much of the day in Sacaegu with Cici, so they met for breakfast in the hotel restaurant instead.

Luca handed Amy an envelope of Romanian leu currency worth around two thousand American dollars. "Please give this to Cici. It's for her village."

"Thank you, Dragoş," she said. "This will go a long way."

"Have you told your band about my offer?"

"Yes. They are very interested in hearing more."

"Good. I can speak to them any time. Perhaps at dinner tonight. There is a restaurant in this city that serves American-style steaks. I have never eaten there but it has a good reputation. The band might like it. Everyone's dinner with be my treat."

Amy said, "That sounds delightful. I'll let Petru know. Tonight would be good. Tomorrow, after rehearsal, Erika, Zhanna and I will visit a friend of mine who lives outside of Zalău and we've been asked to spend the night. I won't be back until Friday."

◊ ◊ ◊

After breakfast the women parted ways with Luca. They drove to a grocery store where they used some of Luca's money to buy staples for the people of Cici's village. When they returned to the hotel to pick up Cici, Amy told Petru about the dinner tonight. The four women drove to Sacaegu with the trunk of the sedan filled and weighted down with flour, sugar, and salt. They also bought candy for the children. The purchases took only a small portion of the money. Amy gave Cici the envelope to give to her brother for distribution.

[that evening]

Dragoş Luca had Marku reserve a private room at the restaurant named Cafeneaua Americană.

After the group arrived, the band and stagehands held no qualms about ordering the most expensive steaks and cocktails on the menu.

During the meal, Petru asked Luca if his offer to triple the band's income with expanding their tours was guaranteed, and he insisted it would have to be a written contract.

"Of course," Luca replied.

"We will talk this over and give you our decision after the performances this weekend," Petru told him.

"Very good," Luca said. "I told Amy I don't expect a decision before your tour of Romania is completed."

◊ ◊ ◊

When Luca and his men returned to the hotel, he gathered them in his suite.

"I want to know who this friend is that Amy and the other women are visiting," Luca stated.

"Probably another Gypsy village," Vasile offered, unconcerned.

"Amy mentioned that this friend was in the Zalău area," Luca said. "Zalău is about a ninety- minute drive from here but most of the roads are dirt and treacherous and wend through the wilds of Transylvania. It would be impossible to follow them in a car and not be spotted. Marku and Vasile, tomorrow you will give the women a couple of hours head start and then you'll go to Zalău. Take one of the photos of the women we took on the cruise and ask around town if anyone has seen or knows them. You're aware of Zalău. It's a decent size town of about 40,000 people and three quarters of them are not Gypsies so you shouldn't encounter problems in that regard. Just make some subtle inquiries.

"If Erika and Zhanna come to work for us, I will eventually have to tell them about our real business. It's time we learn more about them."

"What should we do if we happen to run into the women?" Marku asked.

"Just tell them I became concerned for their safety and you are there to offer assistance."

Chapter 18

A mournful lamentation

Zalău, Romania
Next day—Thursday, 19 July 1951

When Erika, Amy, and Zhanna arrived in Zalău they stopped in for a drink at the Slaughtered Lamb, a tavern they had frequented during the previous mission in Romania. It was mid-afternoon. They each paid for a glass of ale at the bar and found a table in the dark, rustic saloon. Zhanna also got herself a shooter of vodka.

"Any questions about how we're going to reveal our purpose to the Count?" Erika asked. "He knows we are CIA and we can trust him. In my opinion, the best plan is to be honest with him."

Amy and Zhanna agreed.

Erika had promised Count Sorin Lupei they would arrive by dinner time. Castelul Lupului was about an hour's drive east of Zalău over rough roads through dense forest leading to even higher elevation, so after the one drink, they left the Slaughtered Lamb.

Because the roads were dry and it was still daylight, the drive took 50 minutes instead of the normal hour. Erika pulled the car up to the front of the Gothic castle that would not disappoint any moviegoer as far as their expectations of a Transylvania castle. The massive edifice rose from the top of a hill on an estate of 18,000 acres, or 28 square miles, of heavy woodland, meadows, farmland, and grazing pastures that had been owned by the Lupei family for centuries.

On the massive, heavy wood front door, Erika banged the wolf's head knocker. Each woman carried a small suitcase for an overnight stay.

A spiffily dressed butler eventually opened. The door did not creak as in the movies. Everything at Castelul Lupului was well maintained.

"Hello, Geofri," Erika said.

The butler, who had worked for the Count for twenty years and before that, ten years for the Count's father, smiled. "Hello, Erika, Amy, and Zhanna. Welcome back to Castelul Lupului." He opened the door

60

wide and they stepped into a room that seemed as large as an airplane hangar. Tapestries covered the stone walls.

"It's nice to see you again, Geofri," Amy said.

"Thank you. The Count has looked forward to your visit since Erika called. We have a dinner planned that I'm sure you'll enjoy. I will have a maid show you to your rooms. The Count is presently not here but should return shortly. Dinner will be served at eight o'clock. This will give you all some time to relax and freshen up. Do you need help with your bags?"

"No, we can manage," Erika said.

"Very well," Geofri replied. He summoned a maid who led the women up a long winding marble staircase to their rooms. The castle had twenty bedrooms. The count rarely hosted guests so all the rooms had been sealed with the beds and furniture covered with sheets. Three of the rooms had been opened and cleaned and scrubbed this morning in anticipation of the Shield Maidens' visit.

[two hours later]

Markus and Vasile had struggled getting to Zalău. The combination of terribly maintained roads and lack of road signs that had dropped from neglect got them to the Transylvanian town an hour after they expected to arrive.

Finally in Zalău, they pulled into a gas station and asked the proprietor for some recommendations on popular restaurants and drinking holes. The old man told them about a café named the Mount, and a tavern called the Slaughtered Lamb. After getting directions, Markus handed the old man a five leu note and they drove off.

At the Mount, Luca's two men showed the two waitresses, the bartender, and the owner the photos of Amy, Erika, and Zhanna, with no results. They paid for their coffee and left for the Slaughtered Lamb.

[8:00 p.m.]

The three Maidens had changed into clothes more suitable for dinner and were seated at a long table in the castle's smaller dining room. A

61

maid had already delivered a bottle of Tuică to the table, which was opened and poured by Geofri who was now in full butler attire.

Count Sorin Lupei entered ten minutes later. He was a tall, distinguished-looking man of 43 years with a full head of dark hair only interrupted by silver temples. Because he knew his guests would not be wearing formal attire, he passed on a tuxedo in favor of a burgundy-colored silk smoking jacket. The Count spoke Romanian, Russian, and English. Since Erika and Zhanna did not speak Romanian, the conversation would be in English.

As he joined the women at the head of the table he smiled and said in a deep voice, "I apologize for not being here to greet you. I was inspecting one of the cabins located on the castle grounds quite far from here. It needs some care and I was there with my maintenance foreman. Tell me how you have all been. I believe it was a year-and-a-half ago when you first came to Castelul Lupului."

Although Amy had told Luca that they were visiting her friend, Erika had made the phone call because she was more acquainted with the Count.

"We're still alive, Count Lupei," Erika said. "In our business, that fact alone makes us happy."

The count smiled again and nodded his head. He knew they worked for the CIA.

"Erika, you said when you called that you needed my help. Let us get dinner started then you can tell me what it is you need from me."

Lupei looked at Geofri who stood dutifully nearby. Needing no further instructions, the butler disappeared to the kitchen. In a few moments an enormous prime rib roast was brought out by kitchen girls along with an assortment of roasted vegetables including mushrooms, carrots, and white asparagus. The prime rib was medium rare and a footman cut the women an ample slice. A teenage kitchen girl brought out Count Lupei's cut. It looked as if it had barely been cooked with blood running onto the plate.

"Later, after we finish our conversation and dinner," the Count said, "I will take you outside to reunite you with the children of the night."

[same time, Zalău]
Marku and Vasile sat at the bar in the Slaughtered Lamb. Darkness had fallen. They had ordered a drink and then asked the bartender to look at a photograph. Marku wore his signature yellow blazer.

"Do you recognize any of these three women?" Vasile asked. The conversation was in Romanian.

The bartender, who walked with a limp, looked at the photo.

"Who are you?" he asked.

"We are friends of these women and want to find them. We heard that today they might be in this area."

"My memory is not so good," the man said.

Marku pulled out a ten-leu bill and slid it across the bar.

"Now that you mention it, yes, I saw these women today. They were in here this afternoon."

"Do you know where they might be now?" Vasile piped in.

"Ah . . . let's see. I'm trying to think."

Markus slid another ten-leu note across the bar.

"They didn't say where they were going, but I know they are friends with Count Lupei. They were in here a year or so ago asking for directions to his castle. I remember them because of the one woman. We don't see that kind of bright blonde hair around here."

Markus and Vasile looked at one another. They and Luca were under the impression that this current Flamenco band tour was the first time Amy's hairdresser and wardrobe mistress had been to this country.

"Where is this castle?" Markus asked the barkeep.

"You don't want to go there unless you've been invited by the Count."

"Why?"

The bartender looked at them but didn't answer the question. "I'm done talking. Do you want another drink?"

"No, just directions to this castle," Marku said. He slid another bill to the man, this one a twenty leu note.

[at Castelul Lupului]
Halfway through dinner, Count Lupei had been briefed by Erika about the mission. Amy had told him about Dragoş Luca's interest in the band.

"Zhanna," the Count said. "You have said nothing."

"I have nothing to say," she answered.

Then the Count addressed them all. "I have heard of Dragoş Luca, of course. Any Romanian who reads a newspaper knows he is a very rich man who supports the arts in this country. I did not know of his business with drugs and weapons until now."

"The Russians keep his business secret because they use him for the weapons deals," Erika said. "For that, they give him a free pass for his drug smuggling operation."

"And our Romanian government, because they are under the Soviet thumb, have little choice but to go along," Lupei said.

"That's about it in a nutshell, Count Lupei," Erika said.

"And you're telling me your preferred plan is to lure Luca here to Castelul Lupului for capture and removal from Romania. Is that correct?"

"Yes, Count."

"I will think about this," Lupei said. "You all know I have little regard for our Soviet overseers and Romanian criminals who profit from collaborating with them, but it's my duty to keep the estate in mind, along with the families who depend on it for their livelihood."

[half hour later]
The gloom of the forest road that led to the castle forced Marku to drive slowly. The crescent moon did little besides cast lunatic shadows through the trees onto the road. The men saw gleaming eyes reflected by the car's headlights watching them from the forest fringe.

"This place is swarming with wolves," Marku mentioned.

"Just have your gun ready," Vasile said. "We'll stop before we get to the castle. Dragoş doesn't want us to encounter the women if we can avoid it. He just wants to know who Amy's friend is and we'll have a real surprise for him when we tell him the hairdresser and wardrobe woman have been to Romania before and know this Count. When we see the lights of the castle, we'll pull over and walk until we can see if the women's car is there. Then we return to our car and leave."

"I told Dragoş you can't trust a Gypsy," Marku said.

After creeping along for another half-mile, Vasile thought he saw some lights through the trees about 200 yards ahead. "Turn off the lights and pull over here, Marku."

The men got out of the car and walked just far enough up the road to where they saw the sedan Amy and her assistants had used parked in front of the castle. They immediately turned and headed back. They had gotten to within only a few feet from their car when a snarling wolf shot out of the forest and sank his teeth deep into Marku's left shoulder. Marku yelled in surprise and pain and fell to the ground. Vasile had his handgun ready and shot the wolf twice. He helped his injured comrade back to the car knowing he would have to drive. With a profusely bleeding Marku in the passenger seat, Vasile finally got the car turned around on the narrow road and headed away with a wolfpack in chase.

◊ ◊ ◊

Inside the castle, dessert had been finished and now everyone had a snifter of brandy in front of them. That's when everyone heard the two gunshots in the distance.

Count Lupei stiffened and sat up rigidly. He jumped out of his chair and ran outside and looked up at the moon. The three women followed him out. "The children of the night," he mumbled, then said louder, "One of you please tell Geofri to bring a car around immediately."

"I have the keys to our car parked right here," Erika said. "It will be faster."

The Shield Maidens and Lupei loaded in with the count in the front passenger seat. Since the only place to drive was down the road, Erika assumed that's where she should go but asked to make sure. "Tell me where to go, Count."

"Down the road," he confirmed. "The gunshots were not far away. A poacher on foot would never make it past the children of the night in the forest. He would have to have an auto."

The drive was short. Erika turned a hairpin curve and there in the headlights lay a downed wolf.

"Oh, God, no!" Lupei exclaimed.

Erika applied the brakes. The Count got out quickly and knelt beside the dead wolf. A wolfpack of a dozen feral wolves walked out of the forest when they saw the Count. The women were already out of the car and the wolves began snarling at them.

Count Lupei raised a hand and the wild beasts stopped growling. He pointed to the women and two wolves joined each woman at her side as protectors. This scene would be unbelievable and boggle the mind if the three women hadn't witnessed similar aberrations at Castel Lupului 1½-years ago.

Zhanna spotted something on the ground not far from the dead wolf. She walked over and picked it up with her two protectors remaining by her side. It was a 4-inch square swath of yellow material. She held it up to show Erika and Amy.

Erika said, "Count, we know who this wolf attacked. It was one of Dragoş Luca's men."

"I will listen to no more tonight," he said sternly. "Please return to the castle and do not follow me. You'll be safe. No children will bother you."

He picked up the dead wolf, walked off the road, and disappeared into the forest. The rest of the wolfpack followed him. Before the women returned to their car, they heard from the forest the Count singing a mournful lamentation.

Chapter 19

Backstage

Castelul Lupului, Transylvania
Next day—Friday, 20 July 1951

It was at breakfast before the Maidens saw Count Lupei again.

Amy told him they had to leave to return to Cluj-Napoca this morning for an afternoon walk-through rehearsal in preparation for the concert tonight.

Lupei ignored her and asked, "Are you sure it was one of Dragoş Luca's men who was attacked last night?"

Erika answered, "There is no doubt, Count Lupei. A henchman of his named Marku always wears a yellow blazer that exact color. We have never seen him without it. Luca knew we were visiting a friend in the Zalău area. It's obvious that he had some of his men follow us here. That was unexpected on our part and we apologize."

"It has made my decision an easy one," the Count said. "I will cooperate with you in your quest to apprehend Luca and put a stop to his wicked dealings. Geofri and I will attend your performances tonight and tomorrow night in Cluj-Napoca. I'll let you ladies work out a way I can meet this man so I can invite him to Castelul Lupului. Where are you staying in Cluj-Napoca?"

"The Hotel Beyfin. Luca and his men are also staying there," Amy answered.

"I'll have Geofri reserve us a suite there for tonight and tomorrow night," the Count said. "Geofri is an excellent driver. We'll check into the hotel sometime this afternoon. The reservation will be in my name. Call on me when you can."

[later that morning—Cluj-Napoca]
Last night, Marku was bleeding from his shoulder to the point Vasile knew he would never make it back to Cluj-Napoca alive, so Vasile drove to the only hospital in Zalău. There, Marku's wound was cleaned and

iodine applied before being stitched up. His left arm was put in a sling and he was given his first rabies shot.

They finally made it back to the hotel in Cluj-Napoca and reported to Luca's suite. Ion was there.

Luca looked at the weak Marku and his sling. "What in hell happened to you?"

Marku collapsed on the settee.

Vasile said, "He was attacked by a wolf on the grounds of Castelul Lupului. But we're here for our report. Amy's friend is Count Sorin Lupei, the estate's owner. But get this, boss. We found out this is not Erika's and Zhanna's first trip to Romania. A bartender in Zalău told us they were there a year or so ago and visited the Count."

Luca stared at Vasile for a long moment. Finally, he said, "A Count? There aren't many of those left in Romania. I never heard of him. Ion, call one of our government contacts on our payroll in Bucharest and inquire about this Count." He paused again to think. "Amy told me she has to return here for a rehearsal this afternoon, and with the concerts they will be in Cluj-Napoca for the rest of the weekend. We have to find out the last names of Erika and Zhanna so I can have my Soviet contacts run a background check. I'll contact the port of entry people at the airport in Bucharest where the band arrived and get these two women's last names."

Marku bemoaned, "I have to go through twelve more rabies shots."

"Shut up, you fool," Luca sneered. "You should have shot the damn thing before it reached you."

[that afternoon]

After having already given four performances in Romania, rehearsal this afternoon was an abbreviated one where a few songs were played mainly for the benefit of the theater's sound and light crew.

Dragoş Luca attended the rehearsal along with Vasile. Ion was back at the hotel running a check on Count Lupei. Weak from blood loss, Marku also remained behind at the hotel. When the hour-long rehearsal ended, Luca invited Amy to sit with him for a moment.

"Did you get to see your friend?" Luca asked.

"Yes. It was a nice visit," Amy replied. "You mentioning that gives me an idea, Dragoş. He is coming to the concerts this weekend. I invited him to call on me in my dressing room tonight after the performance. Why don't you also come see me. I'd like to introduce you two to each other."

"I would welcome meeting your friend, my dear."

When Luca and Vasile left, Amy went backstage. Erika and Zhanna waited in her dressing room.

"Naturally, he's acting as if he knows nothing about where we went," Amy told them. "He doesn't want me to know he sent his men to Zalău to find us. Vasile was with him, but Marku, his normal driver, was not."

"I can see why," Zhanna said. "That wolf probably took a big chunk out of his ass. Hopefully, it bit his dick off."

"I invited Dragoş to visit us backstage after the performance tonight. I told him I'd like to introduce him to the Count."

"Good work, Amy," Erika said. "That eliminates our problem of getting those two together. By the time we get back to the hotel, Count Lupei and Geofri should be checked in. I'll call on the Count and tell him about tonight."

◊ ◊ ◊

When Luca and his men returned to the hotel, everyone gathered for Ion's report on Count Lupei. Even the weak Marku wanted to be there.

"That Count is a real Count," Ion said. "His name is on the Register of Nobles in Bucharest. He's one of only eleven Romanian Counts on the official registry that are still living. He owns a huge estate outside Zalău and wields considerable influence in Transylvania. That's all our contact in Bucharest could tell me, but that has to be the place Marku and Vasile visited."

"Vasile and I told you that was the estate," Marku said to Ion impatiently. He then turned to Luca. "Boss, there is something not right about that place. Let's drop this whole thing and return to Constanta. We don't need those women."

Luca grumbled, "You sound like some ignorant Transylvanian peasant woman who still wears garlic around her neck to fend off vampires. I know we don't have to have them, but that's all changed. We're not dropping anything until we find out who Erika and Zhanna really are. They are our concern, not spooks from ridiculous old folktales. If we're being set-up, those two women must become corpses."

[that evening]
The theater in Cluj-Napoca wasn't as large as the opera house in Bucharest or the civic auditorium in Constanta, but it was a beautiful venue with a balcony sporting gilded gold railings. A massive crystal chandelier dropped down from the vaulted ceiling which, like the Sistine Chapel, was hand painted. Instead of Michelangelo's biblical themes, this ceiling depicted famous battles from Romanian history, including one of Romanian hero Vlad III and his victories over the Ottoman Empire in the 15th century. Vlad III was more commonly referred to in Romania as Vlad the Impaler for his trademark of impaling enemies on stakes, or Vlad Dracula since he was the son of Vlad Dracul who ruled Wallachia, a region of Romania.

Dragoş Luca, along with his bodyguards, Vasile and Ion, took seats in the balcony where Luca preferred to sit if the venue had no private boxes. Count Lupei and Geofri had seats on the main level in the front row, just a few feet from the stage.

When the curtain rose, the applause was substantial. Amy thanked everyone and waited for the clapping to subside. As she always did; Amy introduced the band members and where in Romania they hailed from. Each received a warm welcome, especially Amy and Cici who were from Transylvania.

The lights in the theater were dimmed and on stage brightened. Amy stomped, twirled, sang, and wildly manipulated her skirt for nearly two hours, under lighting that switched from red, to blue, to gold. She left the stage twice for costume changes. While she was off stage, the band continued the performance by playing Roma instrumentals.

After the final song, the band members took their bows and left the stage to a standing ovation. The crowd shouted loudly for an encore. Eventually, the Barcelona Romanian Gypsy Orchestra returned to the stage and Amy sang Lule. It would be more than an hour later before the band members left the stage after they met with fans who refused to leave without a photo or autograph.

Finally back in her dressing room, Amy sat down in the chair facing her vanity mirror.

"I'm bushed," she said to Erika and Zhanna.

"I can see why," Erika rejoined. "It was a great performance by you and everyone in the band, Amy. But don't take a nap yet," she joked. "I'm sure the Count and Luca will be knocking shortly."

Erika was right. It wasn't ten minutes before Dragoş Luca knocked on the door and was let in by Zhanna. He was alone. Vasile and Ion had been ordered to wait for him in the car.

"Yet another outstanding show, Amy," Luca said. Amy had not yet changed out of her last costume—her tribal skirt and off-the-shoulder peasant girl blouse.

"Thank you Dragoş," Amy responded. "You are always so kind with your comments."

"Kindness has nothing to do with it, my dear. The truth speaks for itself."

Another knock came. Zhanna again opened the door. Sorin Lupei stood there in his tuxedo with the colorful lanyard and medallion around his neck that denoted he was a count. In his left hand was a cane with a solid silver wolf's head handle. It was a cane he didn't need for walking, but each of the eleven remaining counts of Romania had his own unique cane that depicted something from the family history. The canes were expected to be seen with the counts at public events.

Amy came to the door. "Please come in, Count. I have a friend I'd like you to meet." She led him to Luca. "Count, this is my friend, Dragoş Luca. Dragoş, this is Count Sorin Lupei of Transylvania."

The two men shook hands.

"It is my honor to meet you, Count Lupei," Luca said.

71

The Count gazed back at Luca with the eyes of a predator. "No. I am honored, Mr. Luca. Everyone in our beautiful homeland has heard of you and your great contributions to the arts."

"Thank you, Count. Coming from you, that is indeed a high accolade. Yes, the arts are my passion. Amy tells me you will be in Cluj-Napoca for the weekend. Would you honor me by accepting an invitation to lunch tomorrow? I would suggest dinner, but I know neither of us want to miss the orchestra's final performance in Romania here tomorrow night."

"I accept your kind offer," Lupei said.

"Wonderful. Amy told me you're staying at the Hotel Beyfin. Since we are all staying there. I think the hotel restaurant would be convenient. Feel free to bring your entourage."

"I don't travel with an entourage," the Count said. "Only my butler accompanies me. Yet, he prefers to avoid such gatherings and is happier to eat in our suite."

"Very well," Luca replied. "I will also bring none of my associates with me. However, with your permission, I would like to invite Amy to join us."

The Count nodded. "That would be delightful."

[an hour later]

Amy, Erika, and Zhanna were finally back in Amy's hotel suite.

"Did you see the look in Count Lupei's eyes when he met Luca?" Erika asked the other two women.

Zhanna, the former Russian assassin, responded first, "I saw it."

"What did it tell you, Zhanna?" Erika asked.

"It tells me that the Count has no intention of helping us capture that rat bastard, Luca. He's going to turn Luca over to the wolves if he can lure him to the grounds of Castelul Lupului."

Erika, the Shield Maiden team leader, nodded then looked at Amy.

"I say Luca should get what he deserves," Amy said. "Let the Count's children of the night have Luca."

"We'll have a lot of explaining to do to Al Hodge," Erika said.

"It won't be the first time," Zhanna replied.

72

"True," Erika said, "but I think Al is right. We can do more damage to his operation if he's taken alive and subject to interrogation. If our mission were an elimination, we could have done that in Constanta. Amy, you're the only one invited to the lunch tomorrow. You know how to proceed. We want to get Luca to Castelul Lupului. Let's get that done first. If that succeeds, I'll talk to the Count about how important it is to capture and extract Luca instead of simply killing him."

Chapter 20

Invitations

Cluj-Napoca, Transylvania, Romania
Next day—Saturday, 21 July 1951

Dragoş Luca was already seated in the Hotel Beyfin's restaurant when Count Lupei and Amy entered. He rose from his chair as they approached.

"Thank you for coming, Count Lupei and Amy." As it was lunchtime, a maître d was not yet on duty. Luca held the chair for Amy.

"Thank you, Dragoş," she said. After she sat down the two men took their seats. She wore a conservative brown dress, one a businesswoman or a schoolteacher might wear.

Despite it being lunchtime, the tables were still covered in snow-white linen table clothes with gleaming Waterford crystal glasses and china. Sterling silver utensils embossed with the hotel's name sat ready in their proper lineup. A waiter delivered menus and took drink orders.

"Gentlemen," Amy said as she opened her menu. "I won't be ordering any alcohol because of my performance tonight."

Amy ordered a Greek Gyro and a glass of lemonade. Dragoş Luca ordered a Gibson martini and a veal cutlet. Count Lupei ordered a Romanian shepherd's pie and a bottle of Czechoslovakian lager. "The Czechs make good beers," Lupei said. "Some claim they are comparable to many German beers."

"I agree," Luca said. "I have cases of various Czech beers in my wine cellar in Constanta. Mentioning Constanta, I would like to extend an invitation to you, Count Lupei, to visit me at my villa there. It would be a high honor for me if you were to accept."

Luca had beaten Lupei to the punch.

Luca then addressed Amy. "My dear, your last concert in Romania is tonight. When is your next engagement?"

"The band has four weeks off before we return to the Cordobes Tablao Flamenco in Barcelona for a two-week engagement. The Cordobes is more or less our home venue. In late-August we leave for a

74

three-week tour to cities in Morocco—Tangier, Casablanca, and Marrakesh. One weekend in each city, not unlike our tour here in Romania."

"If you have four weeks before you have to be back in Barcelona, then you can stay here in Romania for a week or so," Luca said.

"The band's airplane flies out Tuesday," Amy replied.

"The band doesn't have to miss its plane. They can still fly home Tuesday. It would be so nice for me, and I'm sure for Count Lupei as well, to have you and your two assistants join us. I will gladly pay for your tickets to fly you back to Barcelona later."

Maybe this was not a bad idea, thought Amy. It would give them more time to dissuade the Count from what the Maidens knew was his plan to kill Luca.

"I would love to stay in my homeland for a while longer, Dragoş," Amy said. "If the Count accepts your invitation, I will be happy to stay."

Luca looked at Lupei. "Count, it looks like it's up to you. The only thing I can add is that I promise you a wonderful time in Constanta. I have accommodations at my villa that a man of your stature deserves and expects."

"I accept your kind offer, Mr. Luca. As long as you agree to let me return your hospitality at Castelul Lupului after my visit to Constanta."

"I look forward to that," Luca responded. "May I suggest Tuesday to arrive in Constanta. I am returning tomorrow, but I'm sure Amy will want to be at the Bucharest airport on Tuesday when her band members depart. I will have a driver pick up Amy and her two assistants. Bucharest is only a two-hour drive to Constanta. For you, Count Lupei, I will have my private airplane pick you up here in Cluj-Napoca on Tuesday and fly you to Bucharest. Sedans will be waiting for all of you at the airport to take you to my villa."

"Very well, Mr. Luca. It will be just me and my butler. I'm afraid I must limit my visit to a two-night stay."

Luca would have asked the Count to address him as Dragoş but he knew that would be out of place. Nobles did not refer to commoners by their given names unless that commoner was a trusted and long-time friend or employee.

"Whatever you say, Count," Luca said. "Again, I am honored. Now that everything is settled, all we have to do is look forward to the performance tonight."

Dragoş Luca considered everything had worked out perfectly. He had succeeded in delaying their arrival in Constanta for three days. By then his Russian colleagues should be able to tell him who Erika and Zhanna really were.

Chapter 21

A Mosin-Nagant 91/30

Cluj-Napoca, Transylvania, Romania
Next day—Sunday, 22 July 1951

The Barcelona Romanian Gypsy Orchestra played its last concert in their homeland last night to another standing ovation and calls for an encore.

This morning, Erika and Zhanna gathered around the coffee table in Amy's suite. Amy had already briefed her two Shield Maiden sisters on the lunch with Luca and Count Lupei the previous day, and the Count's trip to Constanta.

"I wonder why Count Lupei accepted the invitation," Erika said.

"Luca beat him to the punch," Amy said. "Luca invited the Count to Constanta before the Count got the chance to invite him to Castelul Lupului. In Romania, the Count refusing an offer of hospitality just to offer his own in return would be considered a slap in the face. In our favor, it works both ways. Luca had no choice but to accept the Count's counteroffer to visit Castelul Lupului. Under those circumstances, the Count handled it perfectly."

"You said we'll stay overnight in Luca's Constanta villa," Erika said.

"Two nights," Amy answered.

"Good," Erika said. "That will give me time to search the place. In the meantime, we need weapons. I'll contact Al Hodge in Istanbul. He can have Ryker deliver them to somewhere on the Black Sea coast while we're in Constanta."

[nearly the same time]
Dragoş Luca was on the telephone with one of his many contacts in the Soviet intelligence services—the MGB. The names on the visas of Amy's two assistants when the band first arrived in Bucharest was Erika Tanzer and Zhanna Antonova.

"We have nothing on an Erika Tanzer or a Zhanna Antonova," the MGB major told Luca. "It looks like they are clean."

"They can't be clean, you fool!" Luca shouted into the phone. "Did you give General Kulikov the photographs of these women I sent you?"

"Must I remind you that the General is not at your beck and call, Comrade Luca? And neither am I. You operate at our discretion."

Having been put in place by his Soviet overlords, Luca said, "Major, just get the photos to the General. This is important for both of us."

[that afternoon]

With a telephone call again routed through Bulgaria, Erika finally reached Al Hodge at the U.S. embassy in Istanbul.

"Al," she said. "I'm calling from a pay telephone. I don't have much time. We need our handguns and extra ammo. Zhanna also wants a Mosin-Nagant 91/30 sniper rifle with a P/U scope and at least three extra boxes of 7.62x54mm rimmed cartridges. Can you have Ryker deliver everything to the coast somewhere near Constanta Tuesday night?"

"Now hold on a minute," Hodge said. "First, tell me what's going on."

"We're doing our mission. We're not going to be able to extract a man like Dragoş Luca if we're unarmed." She went on to tell Hodge about the mutual invitations between Luca and the Count.

Hodge checked his map. "There is some deserted coastline 18 miles south of Constanta, the same place you were dropped off on your previous mission to Romania. Do you remember how to get there?"

"Yes."

"Ryker will be there just before midnight on Tuesday. Make sure you or one of the Maidens are there when he arrives. He will then join you on your mission."

"What?!" Erika exclaimed. "Ryker's presence will serve no purpose other than put Luca on more guard."

"Then don't introduce him to Luca in Constanta. Send Ryker directly to that Count's castle. It's not up for discussion, Erika."

Erika thought for a moment. Maybe Hodge had simplified things. "Okay, Al. Instead of Ryker delivering the weapons to Constanta, send him directly to Castelul Lupului. We can't capture Luca in Constanta, anyway. He's too well guarded. He has men with him wherever he goes and quite a few more that patrol the villa grounds. This will save us from having to hide the weapons. Zhanna's rifle would especially pose a problem."

"Alright. When are you returning to the castle?"

"Thursday."

"At least that gives me enough time. I'll have to send Ryker to Vienna and fly him into Romania under the radar to Oradea. There's nothing but hilly terrain around Zalău. Oradea is the closet Transylvanian town to Castelul Lupului that has outlying open fields a plane can use to land without being spotted by townspeople. Ryker will be there at the castle with the weapons by the time you get back there. I'll pick up stakes here in Istanbul and relocate to Vienna. You can reach me at the Hotel Imperial."

Chapter 22

Paella, Gazpacho, Jamón, and Churros

Constanta, Romania
Two days later—Tuesday, 24 July 1951

Earlier this morning the band members and crew traveled by train to Bucharest where Amy, Erika, and Zhanna saw them off. The Turkish commercial airliner had been approved by the Soviets to fly to certain cities outside the Eastern bloc with passengers who held the proper paperwork. This plane would make a landing in Barcelona. Amy had told Petru and her other band members that she would follow them soon, promising everyone that she would definitely return to Barcelona before the band's next commitment to perform at the Cordobes Tablao Flamenco in August. She hoped that would be true.

As he had promised, Dragoş Luca had a large sedan with driver waiting at the airport to pick up the three women. The driver was Vasile. He greeted the women and loaded their bags in the trunk.

At nearly the same time, Luca's private airplane with the pilot and Ion aboard sat down on a dry landing strip at the Cluj-Napoca airfield to pick up Count Lupei and Geofri. The Count and his butler made them wait for two hours, but they finally arrived at the airport and boarded Luca's plane to Constanta.

◊ ◊ ◊

The Shield Maidens were on their way to Constanta by car and the Count and Geofri by plane when Dragoş Luca received a telephone call to his villa.

"Dragoş, this is Armen."

Soviet MGB General Armen Kulikov was the head of the Russian Ministry of Security for Romania. Luca normally dealt with the general's assistant, the major he had spoken with the other day. It was unusual for Luca to receive direct contact from Kulikov who was calling from MGB Romanian headquarters in Bucharest.

"Yes, General," Luca said. "It's a pleasure to hear from you."

"You won't think so after you hear what I have to say. Major Pashkov showed me the photos of the three women you inquired about. I recognized one immediately. She's someone who would be recognized by many Russians who served on the front lines during the war. The one I'm referring to is the tall, dark-haired women wearing the neck scarf in your photos. Her name on her Romanian entry visa, Zhanna Antonova, is false. Her real name is Zhanna Rogova. She was awarded the Hero of the Soviet Union medal by Stalin himself for recording over 300 kills as a Red Army sniper. The German's called her the Black Witch. Later in the war, Rogova became an assassin for SMERSH. She is now employed by the CIA."

Luca sat dropped jawed. This was a major embarrassment for him and he knew there could be repercussions from the Soviets.

Kulikov continued. "We don't know yet who the blonde woman is in the photograph, but we will find out."

"And the name Amy Radu?"

"That is her real name. She's a Flamenco dancer from Barcelona. Or at least we know nothing else about her at this time."

"General, all three of the women will be arriving here in Constanta shortly. I will of course have Rogova eliminated."

"You'll do nothing of the kind!" Kulikov thundered. "First, I want to identify the blonde woman—this Erika Tanzer. The MGB is taking this over from this minute forward. You'll do nothing until I get back to you. Treat them cordially as your guests and give them no indication you know anything about Rogova."

After Kulikov hung up, Dragoş Luca steamed. Amy had told him Zhanna served as a Red Army nurse during the war. That meant that Amy was either in with the CIA on some plot or had been played the fool by the American agency who had succeeded in getting Zhanna imbedded undercover in the band as a wardrobe mistress without Amy knowing. Then what about the blonde hairdresser? Amy told him Erika was a German disgruntled with the Nazis who served the Red Army as a translator for German POWs undergoing interrogation. Was that also a lie on Amy's part, or had she been duped a second time?

[that evening]

All of Dragoş Luca's guests had arrived at his villa by mid-afternoon and were settled into their lavish rooms by maids followed by tough-looking men who carried the luggage.

Now, at dinnertime, everyone sat in the villa's main dining room with a floor to ceiling window that served as one entire wall looking out onto the Black Sea. First brought to the table were two bottles of Tuică.

"Your presence graces my home, Count Lupei," Luca said.

"Since your invitation, I've looked forward to this," Lupei responded. "It's been quite some time since I've been to the coast."

Also at the table were the three Shield Maidens, Geofri, and Luca's two mysterious female companions—Crina and Sylvania. Luca's three personal henchmen, Vasile, Ion, and Marku were also present. Marku had regained his energy from the blood loss but still wore the sling on his left shoulder. Erika couldn't help but notice Count Lupei eyeing Marku, his sling, and his new yellow blazer.

Conversation tonight would be in Russian. Everyone understood that language except Amy. Knowing this, they would repeat what they said in Romanian for her benefit.

"Marku," Erika said. "It's obvious you've injured yourself. I hope it's not serious."

"I fell down some stairs on the yacht a few days ago while carrying some supplies aboard. I'm fine. The sling comes off in three days."

"I'm glad to hear that," Erika said. Everyone knew he was lying. The Count kept staring at him.

The host changed the conversation. Luca said pleasantly, "Enough about my clumsy friend. I hope you enjoy the meal tonight, Count. In honor of Amy and her orchestra's great success with the concerts in our country, I had my chef prepare some Spanish favorites. Amy, my dear, I know you've surely had the offerings in Barcelona. I just hope my chef's versions measure up."

"I'm sure everything will be wonderful, Dragoş," Amy replied.

Five bottles of wine were delivered first and the corks popped open by a footman. Maids then delivered platters of Paella, White

82

Lobster Gazpacho, Jamón, and Churros. Enough to feed twice the number of people at the table.

"What is all this shit?" Zhanna asked.

"Zhanna!" Erika said sharply. "Don't be rude. You always ask that with something new and then when you eat it you like it."

The exchange between the two women was noted by Luca, making him even more keen to find out who this blonde hairdresser was who could reprimand a SMERSH assassin.

"Please help yourselves," Luca told everyone. "I didn't want to decide for everyone what to eat so I told the kitchen staff to not serve everyone the same thing. Count Lupei, I don't expect you to fill your own plate. Vasile will gladly do that if you'll tell him what it is you want."

"No need, Mr. Luca," the Count replied. "Geofri will take care of that." Lupei told Geofri want he wanted and Geofri dished it up.

After the guest of honor was taken care of, everyone else began putting food on their plates.

"Count Lupei," Luca said. "I'll say once again that you honor my house by your presence, and I look forward to your kind invitation to visit you at Castelul Lupului. I'm sorry to admit my visits to Transylvania have been few over the past few years, and very brief, so I'm looking forward to spending some time there."

"I look forward to your visit, Mr. Luca. I also extend my invitation to your men here at the table and the two lovely ladies."

Erika smiled as she ate. Count Lupei had nailed Luca into bringing the men at the table to Castelul Lupului. It would be ill-mannered if Luca refused. Now, she had to convince the Count to not kill Luca.

Chapter 23

Give my regards to Zhanna

Constanta, Romania
Next day—Wednesday, 25 July 1951

Two hours after breakfast, Erika, Zhanna, Crina, and Sylvania went for a joy ride on the relatively calm Black Sea in one of Dragoş Luca's speedboats. Sylvania manned the helm. After a half hour, they reached a small island barely rising out of the water. Sylvania guided the boat slowly to the bank. Crina jumped out, waded through knee-deep water to the shore, and tied the boat up to a withered elm tree.

They had brought towels. Each woman laid their towel on the sand, removed all their clothes, and lay down under a bright sun. Zhanna left on her neck scarf.

"Crina and Sylvania," Erika said. "I'm curious. How did you meet Dragoş?"

"At a nightclub in Bucharest about a year ago," Crina answered. That was true but the Soviets had actually set up the meeting. The two women's charms that night had worked and Luca invited them to his villa where they had stayed ever since. The drug lord/weapons dealer had no idea the women were MGB agents with orders to report in regularly on Luca's activities. Both women had recognized Zhanna Rogova immediately upon meeting her, but after Luca had Ion whip the bottom of Sylvania's feet, neither of the two women told Luca what they knew.

◊ ◊ ◊

Amy had to skip the boat ride. Luca had asked her to remain behind. The two now strolled the villa's gardens.

"So, your fantastic tour of Romania is over, Amy," Luca said as they walked. "I was told I'd get your band's decision on my offer at the end of the tour."

"The band accepts, Dragoş, and everyone is excited. You do understand that we must fulfill our next two contracts—two weeks at the Cordobes in Barcelona and then the three-week tour in North Africa."

"Of course, my dear. I would never expect you to renege on a commitment. I will have my attorneys begin drawing up our contract. When you return to Barcelona after your tour in Morocco, one of my attorneys will fly to Barcelona and the paperwork can be taken care of at that time." Then Luca got to what he really wanted to talk about.

"As you know, Erika and Zhanna will then work for me as translators. I hope that losing them will not cause you distress."

"I can't say I won't miss them, Dragoş. They are good at what they do, and we've become friends. But I would never think of standing in the way of someone leaving the band for a job that pays triple what we are paying them."

Luca nodded. "I'm curious about Erika. When she changed into a bathing suit the night I took the band on the cruise on the Şom de Argint, I couldn't help but notice the scars on her arms. They looked like knife and gunshot wounds."

"She told me she received those wounds fleeing Nazi Germany as she made her way to the Red Army front lines."

"I see. Well, that explains it. And what about Zhanna? I have never seen her without a neck scarf."

"Neither have I, Dragoş. I assume she just likes neck scarves. Many women do."

He didn't believe a word she said. If it were up to him, he would eliminate the women immediately, but he was hamstrung by General Kulikov who had ordered him to do nothing until the MGB office in Bucharest had established exactly who Erika Tanzer was. Luca operated his lucrative but illegal operations with impunity only because of Soviet protection. He knew he best not cross them.

"I haven't seen the Count and Geofri since breakfast," Amy said as they walked past a long row of beehives.

"The Count told me that he and his manservant wished to go into downtown Constanta this morning to pick up gifts for his maids, footmen, and kitchen staff. The count mentioned chocolates, which are apparently hard to come by in Transylvania. I had Vasile drive them."

"That's very kind of you, Dragoş."

[later]

After dinner, Count Lupei kept Luca busy with talk in the villa's study. This was a request made to the Count by Erika. She needed time to search the villa.

Luca and the Count sat in the study drinking Scotch and smoking expensive Cuban cigars. No one else was present.

"Tell me, Count Lupei. Being a count has to come with an esteemed ancestry. Your last name in Romanian means 'wolf' and your estate Castelul Lupului means 'Castle of the Wolf.'"

"There are many wolves in Transylvania, Mr. Luca. The grounds of my estate are quite large so it goes without saying that some wolves are occasionally seen on my property. They keep the deer and boar population at reasonable levels, and occasionally they will take a lamb from one of the shepherds that I allow to graze their flocks on certain areas of my property. As far as my surname, I was born with it, as were my father, grandfather, and several more generations. I'm sure that applies to you as it does most people."

"Of course," Luca said.

The Count exhaled a puff of the cigar and looked Luca in the eye. "I look forward to your visit to Castelul Lupului, Mr. Luca, and my opportunity to repay your kind invitation to Constanta."

◊ ◊ ◊

While Count Lupei kept Luca sequestered in his study, Erika searched the villa. She found a room in the bowels of the mansion where it looked like people had been tortured. Chains hung from iron rafters and there were remnants of blood on the rock floor.

She finally made her way to Luca's private quarters. She pilfered through cabinet and desk drawers being careful to return everything to its place. So far she had found nothing of interest. As she continued her work, she heard a noise behind her and spun around. Sylvania stood in the doorway.

Erika drew her dagger from its sheaf on her lower leg. It was the one weapon she had been able to smuggle into Romania.

Sylvania looked at Erika and the dagger.

"Put the knife away," Sylvania said. "You won't find what you're looking for in the villa. Everything is on Luca's yacht." Before she turned to leave the room, Sylvania said, "Tell your friend, Zhanna Rogova, that I hope she enjoyed our boat ride today. By the way, Dragoş knows who Zhanna really is. He doesn't know who you are yet but it's obvious you're Zhanna's leader. That means you're CIA. I didn't tell Dragoş that I recognized Zhanna when I first saw her. He learned it from my and Crina's boss at the MGB. I will also not tell him that I found you in here tonight."

Chapter 24

Running with the wolves

Constanta, Romania
Next day—Thursday, 26 July 1951

Erika had told Zhanna and Amy about her encounter with Sylvania last night, and that she and Crina were MGB. Sylvania had kept her word to not tell Luca about catching Erika searching his room, and now the CIA team sat having breakfast with Luca, his men, Sylvania, Crina, and the Count and Geofri. Luca's guests would be leaving this morning to return to Castelul Lupului.

"Again, I want to thank you for your hospitality, Mr. Luca," Count Lupei said. "I have enjoyed my stay on the coast. I look forward to being your host at Castelul Lupului."

"Thank you, Count. I will arrive on Saturday. My intentions are to bring Ion, Vasile, and Marku with me as well as Crina and Sylvania with your permission. If that is imposing, my associates can stay at an inn in Zalău."

"I wouldn't hear of it," the Count replied. "We have more than enough rooms for everyone at the castle."

"My airplane for your return to Transylvania is at your disposal," Luca said. "It seats ten passengers, but I understand there is no place to land around Zalău."

"No, there is not, but if your plane will drop us off in Cluj-Napoca, I will call ahead and have a footman there with our small passenger bus. On Saturday, when you and your people arrive in Cluj-Napoca, Geofri will be there to pick you up in that vehicle."

[that evening]
The Count, Geofri, and the three Shield Maidens arrived at Castelul Lupului two hours ago and had already eaten dinner when a small Piper Cub painted black swooped in just above the treetops and landed in a

remote pasture near Oradea, a Romanian town just across the border from Hungary.

A large man emerged from the plane, grabbed a duffle bag, and walked away as the pilot turned the plane around for takeoff.

The man walked for 45 minutes until he came across a farm. In the dark, he knocked forcefully on the door. It took a second, even harder knock that rattled the windowpane before a porch light came on and the door opened. An old farmer stood there with a shotgun pointed at a horror of a man with multiple facial scars and wearing a black porkpie hat cocked to one side.

"Who are you and what do you want?" the man said in Romanian.

"Do you speak Russian?" the horror asked.

"Yes. Now what do you want?" The man tightened his finger on the trigger.

Axel Ryker saw this and smiled grotesquely. "You will sell me the truck in front of your barn."

"It's not for sale. Go away."

"I will give you five times what that rusting piece of shit is worth. You can buy a much better truck." With a lightning move, Ryker snatched the shotgun out of the old man's hands and barged into the room.

The farmer's wife had been hiding and listening. She appeared suddenly and said frantically, "Tiberiu. Sell him the truck. Do you want to die?"

"Your wife is wiser than you, old man," Ryker said. "How much is it worth and how much petrol is in the tank?"

"I . . . I think I could get about two hundred leu for it," the old man stuttered. "The tank is about half full."

"Do you have extra petrol in your barn?"

"Yes, we do," the wife said quickly before her husband was caught in a lie.

Ryker pulled a wad of bills from his pocket and thumbed off 1000 leu. "Fill the tank and I'll be on my way."

◊ ◊ ◊

It took Axel Ryker two hours to reach Zalău in the sputtering, cloud belching truck. Then it was another half hour ascending the mountainous roads east of Zalău before he reached the road that entered the grounds of Castelul Lupului. Ten minutes later, a nearly full moon allowed him to see Erika Lehmann running through a meadow to his right with three wolves running alongside her. He stopped the truck and tried honking the horn which didn't work so he reached out the window and fired a shot in the air. Immediately, other wolves appeared on the road, snarling and blocking the way.

Erika ran to the truck with her bodyguards, saw it was Ryker, and entered the truck on the passenger side.

"Ryker, firing a gun around here might get you killed, you should know that."

Ryker had been on the previous mission to Romania and had seen strange things at Castelul Lupului.

"Surely not," Ryker smirked. "I have always had a fondness for dogs."

Erika ignored his snide reply. "I assume you have our weapons."

"No, Hodge sent me here on holiday. Of course I have them, Sonderführer."

Sonderführer was Erika's rank in the German Abwehr. She had ordered Ryker to not call her that dozens of times. He persisted just to annoy her.

"Let's just get to the castle, smartass," she said.

"Your friends are blocking the way, but I will gladly run over them." Erika held her hand out the window and the wolves moved aside.

Part 3

Chapter 25

Wild boar

Castelul Lupului, Transylvania
Next day—Friday, 27 July 1951

After breakfast, Count Lupei and Geofri went for a walk through the castle's vegetable gardens.

"Count, when Luca and his people arrive tomorrow, the wolves will sense immediately that the killer of one of them is in the passenger bus," Geofri said. "They will never let the bus proceed even though I'll be driving."

"I've already considered that, my old friend," Lupei said. "I'll ask Erika to be on hand at the entrance of the road at the bottom of the mountain. Erika has the She-Wolf in her. I sensed it during her visit last year. The children of the night are in her hazel eyes. You can pick her up at the bottom of the road. If she's in the bus, her brothers and sisters will let the bus pass."

Lupei added. "This Ryker who arrived last night will also have to be guarded. There is something black inside him. The children will feel that."

[same time—Constanta]
Dragoş Luca was on the telephone with MGB General Kulikov.

"Dragoş, what is your plan for your visit to the Count tomorrow?" Kulikov asked.

"Myself and three of my top men will stay at the castle. I'll also have five more men, including an expert sniper that will stay at an inn in Zalău, the nearest town." (He didn't mention Sylvania and Crina, thinking Kulikov knew nothing about them).

"You do understand that you are to take no action without my permission. As I told you, the MGB is taking over this case."

91

"I understand, General. I'm just being cautious."

"We found out who this Erika Tanzer really is," Kulikov said. "Her real name is Erika Lehmann. She was the Nazis' top spy during the war. Her Abwehr codename was Lorelei. She now works for the CIA. Zhanna Rogova is one of her teammates."

"General, I don't understand why you won't allow me to take these people out," Luca said with irritation. "The remote wilds of Transylvania would be the perfect place to end this problem."

"Obey, your orders, Dragoş. The problem will be handled but not on a Count's property. We are trying to build good will with the Romanian people. They hold their few remaining counts in high regard. The women must return to Bucharest for a flight back to Barcelona. We will have people at the airport to make the arrests. Both women will be sent to Moscow for chemical interrogation. If they survive that, Rogova will then be hanged for treason. If Lehmann survives interrogation, she will then be offered to the Americans as trade bait for some of our agents captured in the United States. The Americans won't know they've traded for a mindless vegetable until it's too late."

[that evening]

The three Shield Maidens, Axel Ryker, and Count Lupei had just taken seats at the table in the castle's smaller dining room. Everyone at the table spoke English so that would be the language used tonight.

"Tonight," the Count announced, "everything we dine on comes from the grounds of Castelul Lupului—wild boar, the vegetables, and the wine."

"It sounds delicious, Count," Amy said. "I didn't realize the castle grounds had vineyards."

"They are located on a hill near the eastern border of my property. I house an elderly couple and their two grown sons and wives in a farmhouse and pay them to take care of the vineyards and make the wine."

As if on cue, a footman appeared with a large silver pitcher and poured everyone a glass of a dark red wine.

The Count raised his glass. "I believe in America that a common toast is 'Cheers.'"

"Cheers," everyone said and took a sip except Axel Ryker.

"The wine is delicious, Count," Erika said. "Please give my compliments to the family you mentioned."

"Mr. Ryker," Lupei said. "I noticed you didn't return the toast or try the wine."

"I want to know what it is I'm supposed to do here," Ryker grumbled. "I delivered the women's weapons as ordered. If that was my only purpose, I want the Sonderführer to allow me to leave."

"You're not going anywhere, Ryker," Erika frowned. "Dragoş Luca and his henchmen will be here tomorrow. You might be able to serve some purpose. And show the Count the respect he deserves."

Count Lupei said, "It's alright, Erika. However, I feel I must place you in the position of protecting Mr. Ryker from the children. He must not be allowed to leave the castle unless he is accompanied by you, Zhanna, or our friend, Amy. Transylvanian Gypsies understand the children of the night and I have introduced the children to Zhanna. Mr. Ryker will be safe if he's with one of you."

The massive, 270-pound musclebound Ryker laughed. "I need no help in snapping a wolf's neck."

Count Lupei glared at him. "If that were to happen, Mr. Ryker, I would be very displeased. Much can be learned from beasts."

Luckily, the uncomfortable conversation paused as dinner was brought out. After everyone was served, Count Lupei said, "Erika. I received a telephone call from Mr. Luca this afternoon. He plans on arriving in Cluj-Napoca late tomorrow afternoon. By the time Geofri gets them here it will be after dark. You'll have to greet him at the entrance of the road to the castle. The children of the night will never let them proceed unless you are there."

Erika nodded. "I will be there, Count. Please understand that our mission is to capture Luca, not to kill him."

Count Lupei took a sip of wine and said nothing.

Chapter 26

Laphroaig

Transylvania, Romania
Next day—Saturday, 28 July 1951

Dragoş Luca's sniper and four other men had traveled to Zalău yesterday and checked into the Slaughtered Lamb which also served as a small inn with six small bedrooms on the floor above the tavern.

Now the passenger bus containing Luca and his entourage driven by Geofri neared the road to Castel Lupului. A large pink moon led the way. Marku's shoulder sling was now gone.

Wolves howled in the distance. Marku leaned over and whispered to Luca. "I'm telling you boss. There is something not right about this place."

"Don't start that again," Luca answered sotto voce so Geofri couldn't overhear. "Have you never heard a wolf howl? Our problem isn't the wolves but the two CIA agents—maybe three if Amy is in this with them."

"What is the CIA after, Dragoş?" Vasile asked softly. "You?"

"I don't know. They did not approach me in Bucharest. I approached them. Perhaps the Americans have some business with this Count. Counts have access to people in upper government. He might be supplying the Americans information. That's what we have to find out for my report to Kulikov."

They finally turned onto the road to the castle. After going around one curve, they saw Erika standing in the middle of the road. She was clearly recognizable in the headlights. Geofri stopped the bus and opened the passenger door with a lever.

Erika circled around and got in. "Dragoş, the Count asked me to meet you here and welcome you."

"Thank you," Luca said. "That's most kind of you and the Count."

As they started off, the head beams reflected pairs of gleaming eyes watching from the forest fringe.

◊ ◊ ◊

Dinner was long over by the time Luca and his entourage arrived at Castelul Lupului. They were shown to their rooms by the staff and given some time to settle in. Geofri asked everyone to meet the Count in the library in an hour, as the study was not big enough to comfortably seat Luca and his entourage, the Count, the three Shield Maidens, and Axel Ryker.

In a room of cherrywood walls camouflaged by shelves of books on every wall, the group took seats on one of the several sofas that encircled a low table made of oak that was roughly hewn by an axe.

"I am quite proud of this table," Lupei announced. "A man and his son who farm some of my grounds presented this to me as a Christmas present a few years ago."

"It's a fine addition to this wonderful library, Count Lupei," Dragoş Luca said. "Also, I want to thank you for having Erika meet us at the bottom of the mountain."

"Think nothing of it," Lupei said. "I wished to ensure your safe arrival. Have you eaten dinner?"

"Yes, Count. We ate in Cluj-Napoca before your butler picked us up."

"Nevertheless, I will ask Geofri to have some cheese and bread brought in."

"Don't get up, Count," Erika said. "I'll let Geofri know."

"Thank you, my child," the Count said. "Please also tell Geofri we'd like some cigars and cigarettes from my study, and a bottle of Laphroiag."

The Count continued as Erika left the room. "Mr. Luca, I have not yet introduced you to another of my guests. This is Axel Ryker. He was born in Lithuania (true) so he speaks Russian fluently. He and I became friends a few years ago when we met in Cluj-Napoca (false)."

"Any friend of the Count is a friend of mine, Mr. Ryker," Luca said.

The scar-faced Ryker didn't reply or react, other than to stare at Luca and his men.

Erika returned and retook her seat. Just a few minutes later, Geofri led a footman and a maid into the room. They set the bread and cheese, a humidor of cigars, a smaller humidor of Turkish cigarettes, and the Scotch on the axe-carved table.

"Ladies, please help yourselves first," the Count said. Crina and Sylvania helped themselves to the bread and cheese. Zhanna took a cigar from the humidor and poured herself a double Scotch. Erika and Amy took some cheese. Along with that, Erika grabbed a cigar and Amy a cigarette. Luca's men and Axel Ryker bypassed the food and went straight for the cigars and expensive Scotch.

"How are you able to get Laphroaig, Count?" Luca asked pleasantly.

"I have a confrère in Czechoslovakia—Prague to be exact—who deals in liquor. He comes across a case or two of Laphroaig on occasion and contacts me."

Lupei moved on. "Mr. Luca. My invitation to you and your people will extend for as long as you wish to stay. I'm honored to have such a great supporter of the arts in Romania at my home."

"Thank you, Count. You flatter me."

"I must ask one thing," the Count added. "If you or any of your people step outside the castle, you must be accompanied by Erika, Zhanna, or Amy."

"I don't understand, Count. Why is that?"

"Just a precaution. I ask that you humor me, Mr. Luca. Now, with that aside, since we didn't have the opportunity to welcome you tonight with a feast, we will do that tomorrow night."

Ion was Luca's man that sat closest to Axel Ryker. Heinrich Himmler's former top Gestapo henchman noticed Ion staring at him. Ryker took a long draw on his cigar and blew the smoke in Ion's face.

Chapter 27

Timisoreana

Castelul Lupului
Next day—Sunday, 29 July 1951

After breakfast, Zhanna, Crina, and Sylvania went for a walk in the forest. Even at morning and under a bright sun, the canopy of thick trees added a gloom to the forest floor.

"Geofri said at breakfast that a storm might move in tomorrow," Crina said as she stepped over a large fallen birch branch. In another tree, a screech owl silently followed the women's progress.

"Let's avoid small talk," Zhanna said. "You asked me to walk with you. Erika told me you know who I am, yet you have not told Luca. Why is that, and what do you want?"

"We are here to help," Sylvania replied. "Luca knows who you and Erika are and that you're with the CIA. The MGB general that is Luca's Soviet overseer told him."

Zhanna stopped and looked at them. "You are MGB?"

"Dragoş Luca needs to die," Crina said. "He has had many people killed with no evidence that they betrayed him. All it takes is a whim on his part. Then there are the countless deaths from his narcotics over the years. He doesn't know we are MGB. We might be next just because we know too much about his business. We are sirens; we are not trained field agents like you. Our orders are simply to report his activities to our superiors. If something were to happen to him here in Transylvania, Sylvania and I could not be blamed."

"Our mission is not to kill, Luca," Zhanna said candidly. "We're on a capture and extract mission."

"Then let us help you with that," Sylvania said.

"We don't need your help," the former SMERSH assassin retorted. "You said yourself that you're trained only as sirens. Stay out of it and you'll stay out of trouble."

"I think you do need our help," Sylvania added. "Crina and I can give you information you need. For example, Luca has five men stationed in

Zalău waiting for orders. One is an expert sniper that Dragoş hires occasionally."

The Red Army's former elite sniper gazed at Sylvania. "What's his name?"

"We don't know. He speaks Romanian and Russian but with a Polish accent. The other four men are bodyguards from Luca's villa in Constanta. None of them hesitate when it comes to pulling a trigger."

"Back to the sniper," Zhanna said. "What does he look like?"

"Medium build. Brown hair. A small scar on his chin. But the main feature that makes him stand out is he has one gray eye and one green eye."

Zhanna mumbled to herself, "I can't believe he's still alive."

"What was that?" Crina asked. "Do you know him?"

Zhanna shook off memories and returned to the present. "Never mind. It's not important. Erika is team leader. I will tell her about your help and we will protect you. Consider us friends, but if you betray us, I will personally slit your throats."

"You can trust us," Crina said.

"I hope so for your sakes."

Sylvania was curious. "Last night in the Count's library, he referred to Erika as his 'child.' The Count can't be more than ten or fifteen years older than Erika and he didn't call you or Amy that."

"It's because of Erika and the Count that we can walk safely right now," Zhanna said.

The two other women were bewildered. "What do you mean?" Sylvania asked.

"Never mind," Zhanna said. "Just hope you never have to find out."

[that afternoon]

Erika, Zhanna, and Amy sat on a stone portico high over the ground outside Erika's room. Zhanna had filled them in on her conversation with Crina and Sylvania.

"They are sirens," Zhanna added. "They are in way over their heads and they know it. They're scared and want Luca dead to protect themselves. I told them we would protect them if they continue to keep their mouths shut about us to Luca. It doesn't look like they know Amy is one of us."

"Good," Erika said. "That means Luca doesn't know or he would have mentioned Amy when Crina and Sylvania overheard him discuss with his men that you and I are with the CIA."

"That's all fine and good," Amy said. "But knowing you and Zhanna are CIA means he's on guard and that makes everything much more difficult for our assignment. Having those five men in Zalău proves that. Zhanna, did they tell you anything about the men?"

"Only that they're staying at the Slaughtered Lamb. The women don't know their names. All they know is that four of them are Luca's men who protect his villa and the fifth is a freelance sniper who Luca hires from time to time. They didn't know his name either, but I asked for a description. He's a Pole named Jaro Banik. He was a great sniper and fighter for the Polish resistance during the war. We met once when the unit I was attached to at the time entered Poland. He and I shared drinks together one night around a campfire. We ended up spending the night together in my tent."

Erika and Amy looked at her but said nothing as Zhanna lit a cigarette.

After a moment of thinking, Erika said. "The men in Zalău are worthless to Luca. They won't last long if they enter the castle's property. The wolves will ensure that. Zhanna, tonight you and Ryker will go to the Slaughtered Lamb after the Count's welcome dinner for Luca. These men in Zalău won't know Ryker but this Jaro Banik will know you, which will give you and Ryker credibility when you tell them you represent the Count and extend to them an invitation to dinner tomorrow night. They have no way to contact Luca other than to call the castle. That would be risky on their part as Geofri will answer the telephone. Luca knows this and has probably ordered them to not call the castle under any circumstances. Tomorrow night the wolves will have them.

"Once the men in Zalău are taken care of, we'll have to address Marku, Ion, and Vasile. After that, we extract Luca. That's if I've convinced the Count to let Luca live. I'm not sure if I have."

[that evening]

Dinner had been a lavish affair held in the castle's expansive main dining room despite it being much bigger than necessary.

It was ten o'clock by the time Zhanna and Axel Ryker were able to leave Castel Lupului. After the one-hour drive to Zalău, they arrived at the Slaughtered Lamb at just after eleven.

Ryker entered first. The banter of the locals in the pub went silent as the large, scar-faced man wearing a porkpie hat stopped just inside the door and looked around. He ignored the staring customers and went up to the bartender.

"I'm looking for five men, not locals, who are supposed to be staying here. Where are they?"

"Information comes at a price," the barkeep said.

"It will cost me nothing," Ryker glared. "Are they here in the pub or upstairs?"

Fully intimidated by the gruesome Ryker, the man stuttered, "Four of them are sitting at the last table. I don't know where the other man is who was with them when they arrived."

Ryker looked at the table of four men, who like everyone in the bar were gazing at him.

"Give me a beer," Ryker demanded.

The Slaughtered Lamb served only one beer—a Romanian beer called Timisoreana. The bartender poured Ryker a pint. Ryker put the necessary coin on the bar then walked toward the men's table. Without asking, he grabbed an empty chair from another table and wedged it in amongst the men.

"I was told by Dragoş Luca that he has five men who work for him staying here. That has to be you. Where is the fifth man?"

One of the men said, "Who the fuck are you?"

"My name is Ryker. I represent Count Lupei."

The men stared at Ryker and said nothing.

"I asked you a question," Ryker said. "Where is the other man?"

The same man, obviously the leader, replied, "If I were you, I'd get the fuck out of here."

Ryker took a swig of beer and grinned. "Bravely spoken."

At that time, Zhanna walked in. As planned, she had delayed her entrance to give Ryker time to find the men if they were in the pub. She walked over to the table. The four men recognized her from her visit to the villa in Constanta, but they knew her only as Amy Radu's wardrobe mistress. She saw that Jaro Banik was not at the table.

"Hello, gentlemen," Zhanna said. "I see you have met my friend. We've been sent here by the Count to offer you an invitation to dinner at his castle tomorrow night."

The men relaxed a little bit.

"Mr. Luca told us there were five men. Where is the other one?"

"He's in his room," the leader answered.

"Is there a room number?" she asked.

"No. They have no room numbers here. His room is the second door to the right in the corridor at the top of the stairs."

"Thank you."

Zhanna walked up the stairs and knocked on the second door to the right. In a moment, a dark, ruggedly handsome man in his mid-30s with one gray eye and one green eye opened the door.

"Hello, Jaro," she said.

"Zhanna. I've been expecting you. It's wonderful to see you. Please come in."

Chapter 28

Jaro

Zalău, Romania
Same night

The rooms at the Slaughtered Lamb were little more than cubicles the size of a jail cell. Zhanna sat down in a creaking wooden chair. Jaro Banik had no other place to sit other than on the bed.

"Would you like to go downstairs for a drink?" Banik asked. "Or I have a bottle of Luksusowa here in my room."

Luksusowa was a potato vodka made in Poland.

"The vodka would be fine," Zhanna said.

Banik produced a bottle and two coffee cups from a tiny end table near the bed. "Forgive me for the cups. These rooms are rather spartan, as you can see. They won't allow glasses to leave the bar area."

He poured her a drink. "See, a double. I remember, Zhanna. How is your neck scar. Does it still give you trouble?"

"I've learned to live with it." She removed her neck scarf to reveal a hideous 1½-inch wide purple and red scar that completely circled her neck—a rope burn after being captured and hanged by the German SS in fighting outside the Korsun Pocket in 1944. Luckily she was cut down in time by her Red Army comrades who retook the village as the execution was taking place.

"Damn SS," Banik said. "My only regret is that I wasn't able to kill more of them during the war."

"What do you know about me, Jaro?"

"I found out two years ago from the East Germany Stasi that you had survived the war and were now CIA. Dragoş Luca does not know I know this, and the four men with me do not know about you and I will not tell them."

"Jaro. I came here to warn you. Abandon Luca. Leave the country. Do not step on the grounds of Castelul Lupului."

"Zhanna. Luca is paying me handsomely. When I am paid for a job I always see it through. People like Luca know this. That's why they hire me."

"Jaro. I'm pleading with you to not enter the castle grounds. It's a dangerous place for anyone not cleared by the Count to be there."

"Why? How many men does he have for security?"

"He has no security men."

"You're not making sense, Zhanna."

"An associate of mine is downstairs right now inviting your four comrades to dinner at the castle tomorrow night. Do not come to that dinner, Jaro."

"Obviously, you're telling me the four men will be canceled tomorrow night."

"Leave the country, Jaro. That is my wish for you, and my advice."

"I'm sorry, Zhanna. I have already told you I always complete a job once I've been hired. Who is your friend downstairs? Erika Lehmann? I know you are part of her team. The Shield Maidens have become quite well known within the Eastern bloc intelligence communities."

"*His* name is Axel Ryker," Zhanna said.

Banik looked at her for a moment. "Are you talking about the Gestapo investigator?"

"Yes."

"My God. How many Nazis do the Americans employ and protect. Ryker should have been hanged for war crimes years ago."

"The British and the Russians also took many Nazis into their folds after the war," Zhanna reminded him.

"True. Let's go downstairs. I have never met Ryker. You can introduce me as one of your old comrades from the war. But before we leave, I want you to know that the one night we spent together will always be a cherished memory for me, Zhanna."

"I also remember it fondly but those were different days, Jaro. Back then, on the front, one never knew if he or she would be alive the next night. Respite had to be taken when it presented itself. Please think about what I've said. I've come here to talk to you because I want to avoid this coming down to the two of us trying to kill the other."

◊ ◊ ◊

Ryker and Luca's four men at the table had borrowed a deck of Tute cards from the bar. Ryker had no problems fitting in with these men. They were all killers. As the game progressed, the competition grew more aggressive.

The man sitting next to Ryker grumbled, "Ryker, you were the dealer for this last hand. You couldn't have gotten that draw without cheating."

Ryker noticed out of the corner of his eye the man pulling a dagger from his ankle under the table. Ryker grabbed the man's wrist with his vise-like grip and squeezed until the man shouted in pain. Ryker took the dagger from the man's hand and deeply sliced his right index finger.

Zhanna was descending the stairs with Jaro Banik when the dagger incident occurred so she never got the chance to introduce Banik to Ryker. It was time for the two of them to leave the Slaughtered Lamb and return to Castelul Lupului.

Chapter 29

The pendant

Castelul Lupului, Transylvania
Next day—Monday, 30 July 1951

After breakfast, Erika, Zhanna, Amy, and Axel Ryker gathered on the portico outside Erika's room. Both Zhanna and Ryker had given their reports on last night at the Slaughtered Lamb.

"Axel," Erika said. "It's unfortunate that I can't send you anywhere without trouble happening. But if Luca's man pulled a knife on you, I understand your reaction this time. Any of us would have struck back."

She then looked at Zhanna. "Do you think this Jaro Banik will take your advice to stay away?"

"No," Zhanna said.

"Do you want him to live?" Erika asked.

Zhanna shrugged. "If possible."

"Once the men drive onto the Count's property they're doomed," Erika said. "The Count's guardians will finish them off before they've driven a quarter of a mile on the castle road. To save Banik we'll have to intercept the car before it reaches the road to the castle. Luckily there is only one road they can take from Zalău. Axel, tonight you will fell a tree that will block the entrance to the Castelul Lupului road. They will have to stop there to remove the tree. We'll be there waiting for them and eliminate the four men. Zhanna, how do we tell which one is Banik?"

Zhanna thought for a moment. "I'll be hidden with my Mosin-Nagant rifle. I will shoot out a couple of the car's tires so they can't drive away. When the men know they're under fire, they will all get out of the car and seek refuge in the forest. As soon as they exit the car, I'll shoot Jaro, but with a wound shot that will only make him fall to the ground. This will tell you all which one is Jaro. If by chance Jaro is not with them, I will shoot out one of the car's windows to signal you."

Erika thought, *It would so much easier if they didn't have to try and spare Banik. The Count's children of the night would take care of the men.*

105

But she had to respect Zhanna's wishes. Her Russian friend had always been there for her.

"Okay," Erika said. "This afternoon I'll fill in Count Lupei. As far as Dragoş Luca is concerned, he won't know he lost his Zalău backup henchmen." She then looked at the sky. "Clouds are moving in. Perhaps Geofri's weather prediction of a storm later today was correct."

[that evening]

Thunder rumbled in the distance as a steady rain forced the windshield wipers into service on the Russian-made Volga sedan. The car was nearing the road that led to Castelul Lupului.

When the sedan reached the castle road it was forced to stop because of a large, fallen spruce that blocked the turnoff. Suddenly the men in the car heard two gunshots in rapid succession and two of the car's tires went flat.

"We've been set up!" the driver shouted.

Thinking they had been invited to a dinner by Luca and the Count, they had left all their weapons in the trunk. Staying low, they flew out of the car to retrieve the weapons.

Because of the storm, visibility was poor. Zhanna had to use her scope, but the taillights of the vehicle were still shining and the scope allowed her to see the men as they frantically retrieved their guns and rifles from the trunk. There were four men; Jaro Banik was not one of them. As she was hidden in the forest to the right of the car, Zhanna exploded the passenger-side door window with one shot—her signal that Jaro Banik was not among the men.

The four men ran into the forest, two to the left and two to the right. They were dead within minutes at the hands of the team. The bodies were dragged out of the forest and loaded into the car. With two flattened tires, Ryker still managed to drive the car a quarter of a mile to a cliff. He got out and sent the car and bodies over the precipice.

Back at the place of the attack, Erika, Zhanna, and Amy stood dripping with rain as they waited for Ryker to return. Suddenly, another Volga drove up and stopped. Jaro Banik got out of the car.

"I heard the gunshots and I'm sure Luca's men are dead," Banik said. "Thank you for warning me, Zhanna."

Amy aimed her gun at Banik, ready to pull the trigger. Erika placed her hand on Amy's to lower the weapon.

"What are your intentions, Jaro?" Zhanna asked.

He looked at Erika and Amy and said nothing.

Zhanna said, "I spared you tonight, Jaro. I cannot do it again."

"I told you I always fulfill a commitment, Zhanna. My contract with Luca stipulates that I protect him. None of his men were mentioned so what happened here tonight is of no concern to me. I will return to Zalău and leave you in peace." He handed Zhanna a package.

Against the objections of Amy, Erika allowed Banik to turn his car around and head back on the road to Zalău.

Ryker showed up a minute later.

"Let's get back to the castle," Erika said.

They had parked their car a couple of hundred yards up the castle road. Ryker, with his bull-like brawn dragged the fallen tree off the road so it wouldn't be there in the morning. The group walked to the car. All were drenched to the bone. The muddy uphill road proved slow going, but they finally arrived back at Castelul Lupului.

Everyone went to their room to change out of wet clothes. Zhanna opened the package Jaro Banik had given her. Inside was a silver necklace with a snarling wolf's head pendant, along with a note:

Zhanna. I have heard the legends surrounding Castelul Lupului.

Chapter 30

Roaring brook

Castelul Lupului
Next day—Monday, 30 July 1951

Dragoş Luca had no idea he had lost four men of his backup crew in Zalău as he finished his Baclava at breakfast. All of the Count's guests sat at the table.

"My dear Count," Luca said. "This morning, my three men and I would like to take a stroll and see some of your magnificent countryside."

"That is fine, Mr. Luca. But remember that I insist you be accompanied outside the castle for your protection. There are many wild beasts on the grounds of Castelul Lupului. Wolves and wild boars roam day and night. Wild boars can especially be unpredictable. Romania also has the largest population of bears in Europe outside of Russia. We spot bears often."

This threw a major monkey wrench into Luca's plan. He wanted to talk to Vasile, Ion, and Marku alone.

"I'm sure we'll be fine, Count Lupei," Luca came back.

"I must protect my guests, Mr. Luca. It has to be this way."

"Very well, Count. I would never go against the wishes of my gracious host." Luca would have to talk privately to his three men later.

◊ ◊ ◊

Two hours later, Luca and his men walked in the forest with Erika Lehmann. Because of Erika being at their side, Luca could not discuss the business with his men that he had planned. Yet maybe he could get something from this.

Their walk took them to a stream swollen from last night's torrent. Although only 20-feet wide and shallow, the extra water caused the creek to roar down the mountain, the cold water bubbled like a witch's caldron as it crashed against boulders jutting from the stream bed. It looked unwise to attempt to cross on the slippery rocks so the group moved away from the stream to avoid the musical cacophony of nature.

"Erika," Luca said. "I'm anxious to have you and Zhanna in my organization as translators."

"We both look forward to it, Dragoş."

"I'm sure you'll miss Amy."

"Yes. We'll miss the entire band," she said. "But you offered us jobs and pay that would be foolish to turn down. Amy and the band understand that."

"I want to ask you, Erika. Why does the Count consider us safe out here in the woodlands if you accompany us? I wouldn't dream of considering Crina or Sylvania for such responsibility."

She had to make up a quick lie, "The Count told me some of the safer places to walk in the daytime."

"I see," Luca replied. "I have business awaiting me in Constanta, Erika. I can't stay here much longer. I have to leave on Thursday. I'll take you and Zhanna with me. You'll begin your work when we arrive back at my villa." Luca, of course, knew they were CIA. It was time to force their hand and find out exactly what it was they wanted from him. "I also need to send Vasile and Ion to Zalău tomorrow. I will inform the Count at dinner tonight."

"The Count will insist that your men are accompanied," Erika said. "Zhanna and I will go with Vasile and Ion."

"There is no need for that. We'll be in cars," Vasile said.

"It doesn't matter," Erika replied. "If the car broke down on the castle property, the Count would be concerned about your safety."

"That's absurd," Ion grumbled.

"I'm not sure it's absurd, Ion," she said. "See what the Count has to say at dinner tonight. The decision is up to him as your host."

[that afternoon]
Erika, Zhanna, and Amy were now at the bank of the same unruly, overflowing stream that raced impatiently down the mountain. Unlike this morning, the women crossed the water, jumping from ancient

stone to stone. On the other side, they continued their walk into the thick forest.

The wolves of Castelul Lupului were far from domesticated pets. The women were spotted by hidden, feral eyes but the wolves kept their distance, as they had done that morning when they saw Erika escorting the men.

"Amy," Erika said. "It's clear that Dragoș Luca does not know you are CIA so I kept your name out of the conversation this morning. He wants to send Vasile and Ion to Zalău tomorrow. This is a problem."

"It certainly is," Amy said. "He'll find out four of his men are missing. I knew it was a mistake to not eliminate that Polish sniper last night."

"Jaro is still our enemy, but he will tell Vasile and Ion nothing," Zhanna argued.

"And how do you know that?" Amy asked.

"Because he told me he wouldn't."

Erika took back the debate. "Before dinner, I will inform the Count on these developments. He'll tell Luca that he insists that Zhanna and I go with his men to Zalău. We have to make our move soon. Luca told me he's returning to Constanta on Thursday."

[that evening]

Dinner tonight was held in the castle's smaller dining room, which was still big enough to seat twice the guests at the table. Crina and Sylvania, looking very lovely, were seated bedside Dragoș Luca but never uttered a word unless spoken to directly.

Tonight's dinner was a whole pig with an apple in its mouth that had been slowly spit-roasted over hot coals for 16 hours. The Count had purchased the pig from one of the farmers on his land. The abundance of summer allowed an impressive array of vegetables and fruits as accompaniments. Bottles of Tuică and Castelul Lupului wine sat on the table for the diners to serve themselves. A footman appeared and started slicing up the pig.

"What a feast, Count Lupei," Luca said. "I salute you."

Everyone raised their glass to the Count.

110

"Think nothing of it," Lupei said. "I have told you before that it is my honor to have under my humble roof such an esteemed patron of the Romanian arts."

"You flatter me again Count Lupei," Luca said. "I regret to tell you that on Thursday morning, I have to return to Constanta for business concerns. Since Erika and Zhanna now work for me, they will go with me to Constanta. In the meantime, I want to send Vasile and Ion to Zalău tomorrow to pick up a few things."

"That's fine, Mr. Luca. Erika and Zhanna will accompany you for your safety going and returning to the Castelul Lupului grounds."

"Such a kind offer, but I assure you my associates can drive themselves, Count."

"I disagree that they can do that safely, Mr. Luca. Erika and Zhanna will escort you. As your host, those are my wishes."

Chapter 31

Ciorbă de Perisoare

Transylvania, Romania
Next day—Tuesday, 31 July 1951

Ion and Vasile joined Dragoș Luca in his room at Castelul Lupului. "It's obvious that we're being held prisoner," Luca said. "That Count claiming Erika or Zhanna has to accompany us at all times to protect us is bunk. It has to be Erika's doing and she's talked the Count into going along with it."

"I'm not so sure, boss," Marku bemoaned. "I've been attacked by one of the wolves. I know you don't like hearing me say this, but there is something not right about this place."

Luca looked at Marku with irritation. "Erika and Zhanna are CIA. We know that. It's finally clear what their goal is—capture me. The reason I'm sending Ion and Vasile to Zalău today and not you is because of your whining."

Luca turned to Ion and Vasile.

"We will take advantage of the two women going along with you to Zalău. General Kulikov doesn't want anything unfavorable happening on the Count's property. Take the two women to Zalău. Introduce them to the Zalău team and keep things casual. By the time you're ready to return to the castle it will be nighttime. Pick a secluded spot somewhere on the road from Zalău, eliminate the women and drag their bodies into the forest before you get on the Count's property."

"What will you tell the Count when the women don't return with us," Vasile asked.

"I'll tell him nothing," Luca scowled. "I'm sick of this Count. Your story will be that the women chose to stay in Zalău for the night. With the two CIA women eliminated, he has no firepower to protect him. We'll return to Constanta tomorrow. Vasile, find a way to speak to one of our Zalău men in private. Tell him to have everyone at the castle tomorrow morning at eight o'clock, including that expensive sniper I hired. We'll depart for home then. We won't wait until Thursday."

[late that afternoon]
The sedan provided by the Count was driven by Ion. Vasile sat in the front passenger seat. Erika and Zhanna rode in the back. They had been driving for almost an hour and were nearing Zalău. The banter had been friendly.

"Zhanna and I have been to the Slaughtered Lamb," Erika said to the two men. "They serve a very good sour meatball soup. I think the Romanian name for it is Ciorbă de Perisoare. Is that right?"

"Yes," Ion said. "It's a popular dish in our country. I look forward to trying it there if you say it's good, Erika. Ciorbă de Perisoare is not a dish that everyone makes correctly. I've been told it's hard to get the spices right, but if they do, it's delicious."

Erika said, "Vasile, you told us a few minutes ago that we will be meeting up with five of your friends who also work for Dragoș. Why didn't you bring them to the castle?"

"Mr. Luca thought it would be taking advantage of the Count's hospitality. He already brought along me, Ion, Marku, and Crina and Sylvania to the Count's home. He allowed these other men to come to Transylvania to see the beauty of the countryside."

Knowing the men were dead, Zhanna said, "I look forward to seeing them." She started to laugh but Erika quickly nudged her. Zhanna had met Luca's men Sunday night when she and Ryker visited the Slaughtered Lamb, but neither Ion nor Vasile knew about the trip.

They arrived at the pub an hour before sunset. Luca had given Ion money to pay for everyone's dinner and drinks. They found a table for four and sat down. A girl who could not be over 16 years old walked up and asked them for their drink orders in Romanian.

"Do you speak Russian?" Ion asked her. "The two ladies with us don't speak our language."

The young girl replied in Russian "Da."

"Good," Ion said in Russian. "I will be paying for drinks and dinner tonight. The ladies will order first."

"Bring me a bottle of vodka and a glass," Zhanna said.

Erika ordered a brandy.

Ion ordered a bottle of Tuică for the table, then he and Vasile both ordered gin neat. "Also, we'll each have a bowl of Ciorbă de Perisoare. My friend Erika tells me it is very good here."

The young girl wrote down the orders, nodded, and walked away.

"So," Erika said to the men, "where are your friends?"

"They are rooming upstairs," Vasile answered. "I thought they would be here in the pub but that doesn't matter. We'll have the waitress inform them we're here after we eat. This will give us more time to talk. Erika, you seem especially close to the Count, but we were under the impression that he was Amy's friend and this was your first visit to our country."

"Why the Count has taken a liking to me is also a mystery to me, Vasile." She skirted around the comment that they thought this was her first trip to Romania.

Ion joined in. "All these legends about Castelul Lupului, how did they get started?"

"I don't know," Erika said. "All the strange stories the locals believe are ridiculous, of course."

The waitress delivered the liquor. Zhanna, who was easily bored, had pretty much ignored the conversation. She poured herself a double vodka, downed it with one gulp, then poured another.

"Does anyone have a cigarette," she asked.

Ion pulled a pack of Lucky Strikes from his blazer jacket. "These are American," he said. He held his lighter for the six-foot Russian Amazon with hair and eyes the color of a raven's breast.

The waitress delivered the soup in one large ceramic vessel and spread bowls around the table for everyone. Also included was a large loaf of Tara Paine, a common farmer's bread in Romania, and a bowl of goat cheese for a spread. The loaf was not sliced. A knife was included for the diners to cut what they wanted.

Small talk continued as everyone ate.

"You were right about the Ciorbă de Perisoare, Erika," Ion said. "The soup is very good."

The waitress came around again for more drink orders.

Ion looked at Zhanna's bottle of vodka which by now was almost empty with Zhanna showing no effects.

he told the young girl

"We'll take another round for everyone," he told the young girl.

When the waitress returned with the drinks, Ion said to her, "We have five friends who are lodging here in the rooms upstairs. Would you be so kind as to tell them we are here?" He handed her a ten leu note.

The young, parttime waitress knew nothing about the lodgers upstairs and had never met them but was quick to accept the substantial tip.

"Da, ser," she said in Russian. (Yes, sir.)

The four at the table were finishing up their dinner when Jaro Banik walked downstairs and joined them, sitting down on a chair he moved from a nearby, empty table.

"We'll need a bigger table when the others come down," Vasile commented. "In the meantime, ladies, let me introduce you to Jaro Banik. Jaro, this is Erika and Zhanna."

Erika and Zhanna shook hands with Banik.

"A larger table won't be necessary," Banik said. "I'm the only one here right now."

"Where are the other four men?" Ion asked.

Jaro Banik looked at Zhanna then answered Ion's question. "I think they went on a stroll around town. We didn't know you were coming."

"Ion, why don't you drive around and find them," Vasile said. "It shouldn't be difficult. This town isn't that big and the men will be walking the streets."

"Very well," Ion replied. "I'll bring them back here."

After Ion left, Erika said, "Let's hope your friends are found, Vasile. If they've ducked into another pub, it might be very late before they return."

Vasile, thinking Jaro was with him, had heard enough and addressed the women. "We know you two are CIA. Are Amy and Ryker members of your CIA team?"

"Yes," Erika answered.

"What is your end game?"

"Our assignment is to capture and extract Dragoș. We have no interest in you or Ion. You don't have to die like the other four men if you leave here tonight and never return to Castelul Lupului. As soon as Ion returns, pack your bags and flee to wherever you wish."

"When did you kill our associates?"

"The night of the storm."

"That's unfortunate. Dragoş will not be pleased. I'm afraid you have things twisted, Erika. Ion, and I *will* return to the castle tonight but you and Zhanna will not. Jaro will report to the castle tomorrow morning. Amy and Ryker will be eliminated by that time and the Count will have no protection."

"You're making a big mistake," Erika warned. "I answered your questions truthfully and I'm giving you a chance to get away with your lives."

Vasile chuckled. "That's very thoughtful of you. I'm afraid I cannot offer you the same consideration. I have a gun aimed at you under the table. Please be so kind as to hand over all your weapons to Jaro."

Zhanna said, "I'm not handing my weapons over to anyone, shithead. I'll stick that gun you have under the table up your ass and empty the magazine into your colon."

"You have your answer, Vasile," Erika confirmed.

Vasile scowled. "Jaro, you have a sound suppressor on your handgun. Shoot the Russian below the table."

"Very well," Jaro Banik said. He fired one shot but it was into Vasile's belly. "We have to get him out of here quickly," he said to Zhanna and Erika. "He'll be spurting blood in a moment."

Erika told the waitress (who had seen nothing) that their friend had too much to drink as Jaro and Zhanna put one of Vasile's arms around their shoulders and dragged him out of the pub. Vasile was still alive and groaning when he was thrown into a trash receptacle in the alley beside the Slaughtered Lamb. Jaro finished him off with a sound suppressed shot between the eyes and then they covered the body with garbage before returning to the pub.

"We got our friend a taxi," Erika told the young waitress. The girl was busy at another table and thought little of it. She had seen drunks escorted out before. The two Shield Maidens and Jaro Banik returned to their table to wait for Ion to return.

"Why are you helping us, Jaro?" Zhanna asked.

"I'm not," he answered. "My contract with Luca is to protect him, not his men. The agreement also says nothing about I'm required to kill

CIA if it's not necessary. I don't want to harm you, Zhanna, but I will keep my agreement to protect Luca. Hand him over to me. He can return to Constanta then I've kept my bargain. There, I'll receive the second half of my payment and then disappear. You, Erika and your CIA team should leave this country at the first opportunity."

"Our team has never abandoned a mission, Jaro," Erika said.

"And neither have I. Even though I work freelance, those who employ me know of my reputation and determination. That's why they pay the high rates I demand."

"I know you, Jaro," Zhanna said. "You can deny it all you want but you did help us tonight. There has to be a reason. What is it you want?"

"I want to enjoy a bottle of Tuică as we wait for Ion to return. We will cancel him, and then I'm hoping you'll take me with you to Castelul Lupului tonight. I've heard the legends and I know I'll need an escort."

The women stared at him. Erika finally decided this would at least be a way they could keep an eye on the Polish assassin.

"What are you going to tell Dragoş Luca about his missing men?" she asked.

"I'll tell him that they are all dead—killed by the wolves."

"And what purpose would that serve? If you believe the legends, you must know that you and Luca can never leave the property without the Count's permission."

"I understand that," Banik said. "But it's my job to be with my client."

"Zhanna," Erika said. "I'll leave this up to you."

Chapter 32

Return to Castelul Lupului

Transylvania, Romania
Same night—Tuesday, 31 July 1951

The bottle of Tuică was almost empty when Ion finally returned to the Slaughtered Lamb.

"Where is Vasile," he asked as he sat down at the table.

"He became impatient with the wait and is driving back to the castle," Jaro countered. "He left about a half hour ago."

"Where are the other men, Ion?" Erika asked. "Didn't you find them?"

"No, I didn't find them," he said curtly.

"Vasile ordered me to wait here until you returned," Jaro said. "Then we are all supposed to return to the castle."

Ion was suspicious. "That doesn't sound like something Vasile would do—leave here without the rest of us, I mean."

"Nevertheless, he did," Jaro said. "We are leaving now. The bill has been taken care of. If you wish to stay here, that's up to you."

"No, I'll go with you. Dragoş will want a report from both me and Vasile."

◊ ◊ ◊

It was well past midnight when the sedan driven by Erika and containing Zhanna, Jaro, and Ion turned onto the road leading up the mountain to Castelul Lupului. About a half-mile up the road, and well onto the Count's property, Erika pulled the car to a stop.

"Why are you stopping?" Ion asked.

"You're getting out here," Erika said.

"What are you talking about?"

Erika quickly pulled her pistol and aimed it at him. "Get out of the car."

To Banik, Zhanna cautioned, "Stay in the car, Jaro."

118

The Russian got out of the car and dragged Ion out onto the road where she disarmed him.

"If you can run quickly enough and avoid the forest," Erika said to Ion through the window, "you might make it back to the Zalău road."

Ion would enjoy no such luck. The car that abandoned him had yet to round the next curve before the women and Jaro heard Ion's screams as he was being ripped to shreds by the children of the night.

"So the legends of Castelul Lupului are truth," Banik said.

Zhanna replied, "You should not have come here, Jaro. I tried to warn you."

Chapter 33

A walk at night

Castelul Lupului
Next day—Wednesday, 01 August 1951

Last night after arriving at the castle, Jaro Banik filled in Dragoș Luca about everything in front of Erika and Zhanna. This morning, Luca ordered Crina and Sylvania to take breakfast in their rooms. Everyone else sat around the table in the small dining room. Breakfast was ham and poached eggs on Tara Paine bread, but Luca and Marku weren't hungry.

"My men have been murdered and now I'm your prisoner, Count," Luca said.

"That is correct, Mr. Luca," the Count replied after he took a sip of coffee. "All except the part that your men were murdered. They received justice."

"How can a Romanian cooperate with the American CIA in good conscience? Yes, I know that the three women here are CIA."

Count Lupei looked at Luca and laughed. "I would ask you why a Romanian would be in bed with the Soviets. The Americans didn't invade our country and mistreat so many of our people. Your Soviet friends did."

The Count then looked at Jaro Banik. "Mr. Banik, last night Miss Rogova told me you fought for the Polish resistance against the Red Army during the war."

"That's right," Jaro replied.

"She also told me you are not one of Mr. Luca's established men, only having been hired recently as a bodyguard."

"Yes, and I will fulfill that role, Count."

Lupei smiled. "I admire a man who insists on doing his job. I have no reason to detain you. You were not among Mr. Luca's men when one of the children of the night was killed. You may leave whenever you wish. My butler, Geofri, will drive you to Zalău."

120

Dragoş Luca cut in. "Count, are you saying that this all about one goddamn wolf being killed? You have to be insane."

"Be careful what you say, Dragoş," Amy said.

"I'm not interested in any of your advice, Gypsy. You're just another traitor."

Erika started to read Luca the riot act when Count Lupei held up his hand.

"Never again insult one of my guests, Mr. Luca," the Count said sternly.

A nervous Marku said, "I tried to warn you about this place, boss."

"Shut up!" Luca yelled.

Axel Ryker, who said nothing but listened with amusement, finished his breakfast and lit a cigar.

Zhanna looked at Luca's untouched plate. "If you're not going to eat that, asshole, hand it over." She reached over and took his plate.

"What happens now, Count?" Luca said cynically. "Am I to be thrown to your wolves or killed by these CIA agents as my men were?"

"Erika has convinced me that the worst thing that can happen to you is that you be taken to the United States where you will pay for your crimes, and where your organization and cooperation with the Russians in weapons smuggling will be revealed to the international press. Geofri has unhooked the telephone and hidden it. You have no way to contact your Soviet partners, and it goes without saying that you cannot leave Castelul Lupului grounds without my permission. Until then, you are free inside the castle. We will hold meals as usual. You and Marku can join us or take your meals in your rooms if you prefer. If you wish to stroll outside the castle grounds, you must be accompanied by Erika. She is among the very few over the centuries who holds the mark in her eyes that allows her to command the children of the night. Zhanna and Amy can also escort you because my children have seen them walk with Erika."

[an hour later]

Jaro Banik and Marku gathered with Dragoş Luca in his room.

"It's obvious we're dealing with a lunatic who's in cahoots with the CIA," Luca said.

"Lunatic or not," Banik said, "it's obvious that I can't get you off this property without my sniper rifle, which is in my room at that inn in Zalău. I'm going to have to accept the Count's offer to have me taken to Zalău."

Luca nodded. "Let's get this done as soon as possible. I also want that Count, the CIA women and that Gestapo goon dead, along with Crina and Sylvania. I feel those women betrayed me."

"That is not our agreement," Banik said. "I'm getting paid to protect you. I will kill only those who stand in my way of satisfying the contract."

[that evening—after dark]

Erika, Zhanna, Amy, and Axel Ryker held a meeting as they walked through one of the many deep forests of Castelul Lupului. That afternoon, Geofri had driven Jaro Banik back to Zalău.

"It was a mistake letting Jaro go," Zhanna said as they made their way under a bright moon. "We should have had the Count detain him until after we extracted Luca."

"For once I agree with the Russian," Ryker said. "He should have been thrown to the wolves with Luca's other man you brought back from Zalău the other night."

Erika said, "Jaro Banik was released because the Count told him he could go. I cannot overrule the Count's wishes."

"Zhanna," Amy asked. "What is Jaro's plan?"

"I don't know," Zhanna answered. "All I know is that Jaro is very good at what he does and will be back. Somehow he will find a way."

Erika said, "We'll get Luca out of here as soon as we can. Geofri had to cut the telephone line. I'll have to go to Zalău tomorrow to call Al Hodge. He's in Vienna now. I'll tell him we need a spirit plane as soon as possible."

Chapter 34

Shepherd's Pie

Zalău, Romania
Next day—Thursday, 02 August 1951

Luckily, Erika caught Al Hodge in his room at Vienna's Hotel Imperial just after he returned from lunch.

"Lehmann. Why does it always take you so long to check in? I never know if you're alive or dead."

"I'm calling from a telephone booth in Zalău, Al. I didn't call before because I didn't have anything to report."

"Why are you calling from Zalău?"

"Dragoş Luca is in our custody. The Count disconnected the castle telephone so Dragoş Luca can't call out. We're ready to extract Luca. We need a spirit plane here as soon as possible."

"I'm sure you realize that there's no place to land a plane on the Castelul Lupului mountain, nor in the Zalău area. We had to land Ryker outside Oradeo, that's a three-hour drive from the castle."

"There are farms scattered about on the eastern edge of the Count's property. I spoke with the Count this morning. We can use one of those fields. We'll set up some burning oil pots to lay out a runaway the pilot can clearly see. When can you have the plane here?"

"Saturday night," Hodge answered.

"Not until then?"

"Erika, there is planning and logistics that go into this. I just can't pull a pilot off the street and tell him to fly behind the Iron Curtain, land in a farmer's field, and bring back the bad guy. Leroy will have to clear everything through the Pentagon for an extraction from behind the Curtain. Then I have to sit down with the Air Force in Munich. Who's with you right now?"

"Zhanna and Amy. Ryker's back at the castle keeping an eye on Luca."

"I'll relocate to Munich. Call me Saturday morning at our embassy there and I'll let you know if things are set for that night."

"Okay."

After ending the call, the three Shield Maidens loaded into their car and headed to the Slaughtered Lamb.

"Do you think Jaro will be there, Zhanna?" Amy asked.

"I think it's likely. He has no reason to be concerned with us. If our intentions were to kill him, we could have done that the other night on the mountain road when we dragged Ion out of the car. There is a creed, even among snipers and assassins."

The nighttime business enjoyed by the Slaughtered Lamb was still a few hours away. Half the tables were empty. Erika and Amy chose one while Zhanna walked up the stairs to Jaro Banik's room.

Working was the young waitress. Erika ordered brandy for herself and a double shooter of vodka that would wait for Zhanna. Amy ordered the house red wine which inn owners bought from Count Lupei's winery.

Zhanna came down shortly.

"Jaro is not here. The door locks are so ancient it's an easy matter to enter with a skeleton key. His things are still in his room including a Mosin-Nagant sniper rifle similar to the one I use except his has a different scope."

"Okay," Erika said. "We'll wait for him and offer him one last chance to clear out."

It would be a while before Jaro Banik returned. The women enjoyed their drinks and talked of other matters.

"Amy," Erika said. "If all goes well, next week you'll be back in Barcelona with the band."

Amy nodded. "Yes, if all goes well. I'm sure you're anxious to get back to your daughter, Erika."

"Yeah, I am. I've been thinking of moving Ada and me to an apartment in Arlington. We're not that far away in D.C. but it would be more convenient to be closer to the Lili Marlene."

Erika owned the Lili Marlene Café in Arlington. The German-themed bar/restaurant didn't earn a lot of money after all the bills were paid, but at least it didn't lose money and it gave Erika the perfect cover job. She had made Zhanna the head bartender, providing her a cover job, as well.

"But," Erika added, "Ada likes her school in Washington and is doing well there. She enters the sixth-grade next month so I haven't made a decision yet."

"Zhanna," Amy asked, "how about you?"

"What about me?"

"Do you like your job at the Lili Marlene?"

"Sure, I like it. Erika saved me from dishwasher jobs in greasy spoons where Leroy Carr always placed me. I like running the bar at the Lili Marlene."

Erika asked Amy, "What are you going to tell the band when you get back to Barcelona about the lucrative deal with Luca falling apart."

"I'm going to tell them that Luca is having problems with the Soviet overlords in Bucharest over some other matter and that the deal is delayed until he works all that out. We have engagements at our home cantina, the Cordobes, and the concerts in Morocco for late-August are already booked. The band will be fine without Dragoş Luca's patronage."

Suddenly, Jaro Banik entered the pub. He immediately spotted Zhanna and the two other women. He walked to the bar, bought a drink, and headed their way.

"May I sit down, ladies?"

"Please do," Erika said.

"I thought I might see you all here soon," he said, "but I wasn't sure. Anyway, it's a pleasure to see you all, especially you Zhanna. I'm sure that by now you have searched my room."

"I see that you are still using the American M84 scope," Zhanna said. "The Russian-made P/U scope is better."

"It's all about what one gets use to, Zhanna. The Americans made weapons airdrops to the Polish resistance and the M84 scopes were commonly included and were all we had. An M84 takes some time to adjust, but once it's targeted in, I found I have success with it."

Jaro flagged the waitress and ordered everyone another round of drinks.

"I'm hungry," Zhanna announced to everyone.

"So am I," Jaro agreed. "I've eaten nothing since breakfast and have been walking around this town all day. I've found that the Shepherd's

Pie here is very good. And why wouldn't a lamb and vegetable pie be good coming from a place called the Slaughtered Lamb?"

The waitress was again called over for their orders.

As they drank, smoked cigarettes, and waited for the meals, Erika said, "Jaro, you have no way of helping your employer as long as he is on the Count's property. We waited for you to return here today so we can tell you one more time to save yourself. Zhanna doesn't want you killed. Please pack up your things and leave Transylvania tomorrow."

Amy added, "Dragoş Luca's fate is sealed. Don't sacrifice yourself needlessly for a man like him."

Banik looked at Erika and Amy, took a puff of his cigarette, then looked at Zhanna. Their eyes met. Zhanna knew right then that Jaro Banik had no intention of defaulting on his contract with Luca.

[later that night at Castelul Lupului]
Under a waning but still gleaming silver moon, the Maidens, Ryker, and Count Lupei stood atop the pinnacle of the castle's keep. In the distance, the wistful howling of wolves seemed to serenade the earth's satellite.

"Zhanna," Erika said. "Go ahead and tell the Count what you told Amy and me in the car coming back from Zalău."

"Jaro Banik is not leaving," Zhanna declared. "I could see it in his eyes."

"Since you will be flying Luca out from my property and not have to take him to Oradeo," the Count said, "the man has no chance to survive if he enters the grounds of Castelul Lupului."

The Count paused for a moment before adding. "He has only one chance. He has spent a night at the castle. All of you need to check carefully to make sure none of your clothing is missing—something you have worn recently that the maids have not yet washed."

126

Chapter 35

The perfect choice

Castelul Lupului
Next day—Friday, 03 August 1951

The Count had ordered Dragoş Luca and Marku to take their breakfast in their rooms. Everyone else met the Count in the smaller dining room. Amy revealed to everyone that one of her unwashed blouses was missing.

Count Lupei said, "Amy is the perfect choice. If he stole something of Erika's, the scent would draw the children to him as she herself can do. For the rest of you, your safety has been ensured so the children avoid you. And Amy, as a Gypsy, already has a level of respect. The Roma and the children of the night are both outcasts that have shared the mountain lands of Transylvania for centuries. Zhanna, your acquaintance is a knowledgeable and dangerous adversary."

Everyone looked at Zhanna.

"I searched Jaro's room at the Slaughtered Lamb and came across no women's blouse," Zhanna said. "He must have it hidden someplace else. Jaro will know that we will attempt to extract Luca as soon as possible. He will not wait. If I had his assignment, I would come tonight."

[Zalău]
Jaro Banik sat cleaning his disassembled rifle. Nearby was a package he had asked the bartender to store for him at the bar. Inside the brown paper package was Amy Radu's unwashed blouse.

[later that morning—Castelul Lupului]
Zhanna Rogova also sat in her room cleaning her disassembled Mosin-Nagant 91/30 sniper rifle that Axel Ryker had delivered when he brought the women their weapons.

Part 4

Chapter 36

An offer from Jaro

Zalău, Romania
Same day—Friday, 03 August 1951

"Zhanna," Jaro Banik said. "There is no need for us to be at odds."

It was two o'clock in the afternoon. Zhanna had asked Geofri to drive her to Zalău for one last opportunity to talk Banik out of trying to rescue Dragoș Luca. The two sat in the bar at the Slaughtered Lamb. Geofri waited outside in the car.

Banik continued. "Join with me. You and I can make exceptionally good money if we were a team—more than perhaps you can imagine. You can be safe from the CIA behind the Iron Curtain."

"The Soviets have a price on my head, Jaro. The CIA offers me refuge."

"They do that only because you offer them a service. They will abandon you in the blink of an eye if they think they no longer need you. And you don't have to stay in the Eastern bloc. You can live anywhere in western Europe if you wish. I know you like Paris. We'll work together as full partners."

"Jaro, I know you are coming tonight."

Banik sighed. "Of course you do because you'd do the same."

[that night]
Because it was summer, darkness didn't fully descend on Transylvania until about 8 p.m. An early dinner was held at six o'clock. Again, Luca and Marku had been ordered to take their meal in their rooms.

As the group ate, Zhanna told them that Jaro Banik would not be deterred.

"As long as Luca and his man remain in the castle," the Count told them, "they cannot be rescued regardless of Jaro Banik's protection with Amy's scent."

"Axel," Erika said. "You'll position yourself at the top of the castle keep where you can see for a long distance. If you see anything suspicious, fire a round in the air. Zhanna, Amy, and I will be fanned out in the forests nearby."

[same time]

As Dragoş Luca and Marku sat eating their dinner in Luca's room, Luca said. "The Polish sniper I hired will be coming for us tonight."

Marku stopped chewing. "How do you know that?"

"Because the night he stayed here at this God-forsaken castle he managed to slip me a note and this weapon." Luca showed Marku a small, double-barrel .32 caliber derringer that would fit into the palm of a hand. "He wants us to make our way out of the castle at eleven o'clock and run into the forest to the west of the castle. He will be waiting."

"We'll never make it," Marku frowned. "The wolves."

"Marku, if you want to stay here and end up in prison in the United States for the rest of your life, that's up to you. Me, I'll take my chances with the damn wolves. Banik will be armed with his rifle. He was one of the best snipers during the war. Even these wolves of our strange Count cannot survive a well-placed bullet."

[10 p.m.]

Jaro Bank hid the sedan in the forest fringe on the Zalău road before he reached the mountain road to Castelul Lupului. He got out, threw some fallen pine boughs over the car for camouflage, gathered his weapons and began the trek to the castle on foot. He had cut Amy's blouse in half and had both pieces dangling from his belt buckle.

At the same time, in the forest surrounding the castle, Erika, Zhanna, and Amy had spread out in the woods. South of the castle, Erika walked with four wolves. To the east, Amy was alone, but unbothered by the Count's children of the night. Zhanna, also ignored by the wolves, patrolled quietly to the west, her severe Red Army sniper makeup blacking out her eyes like a ghoulish mask.

North of Castelul Lupului needed no such guarding as the castle sat on a thousand-foot-high precipice with a roaring mountain river at the bottom of the gorge.

[a few minutes before 11 p.m.]
Banik had made his way to a point in the forest where he could now see the castle. He would have preferred a half-moon. Tonight's waning three quarter moon would give him better vision, but that would apply to both sides. He would have to stay in the shadows. He had been ignored by the wolves as they picked up Amy's scent.

Inside the castle, Dragoş Luca knew it was time to act. With a frightened Marku behind him, they left Luca's room and descended the stairway. On their way to the castle's front door, an unsuspecting maid suddenly came out from the kitchen area. Luca grabbed her around the neck from behind and held the derringer to her right temple. "If you scream, I'll blow your brains out. I'd hate to do that. These marble floors are exquisite, and brain matter and blood require significant cleanup."

Luca kept a tight grip on the terrified maid as he and Marku left the castle. With the hostage still in tow, they ran into the forest to the west where Banik had told Luca in his note to go. Axel Ryker, standing on the castle keep parapet, saw what was happening below and fired a single gunshot into the air.

Luca and Marku, slowed by the maid, hadn't run more than 100 yards when Banik stepped out of the shadow of a large oak.

"I did not tell you to bring a hostage," Banik said harshly. "She will just slow us down. Release her."

"I'll do no such thing," Luca countered sternly. "She might be needed."

"What do you think that gunshot was for? Scaring pigeons? The CIA Shield Maidens have been signaled. Release her or I'll abandon you to your fate. She can make her way back to the castle on her own."

Reluctantly, Luca released the woman and she ran back toward the castle. Banik took one half of Amy's blouse and handed it to Luca.

"Tuck this into your belt. It will confuse the wolves and keep them at bay."

"What about me?" Marku blustered.

Banik looked at the underling. "I'm sorry, Marku. My contract with your boss does not include that I protect you." Banik quickly drew a Bowie knife from its scabbard on his belt and stabbed Marku just below his ribcage, puncturing a lung and his heart.

Luca looked down at his dying henchman, and said only, "Regrettable. Now how are we getting out of here, Banik?"

"Separately," the Pole replied. "I have a car hidden in the forest near the Zalău road but it's camouflaged and you'll never find it. I have a boat in the gorge river below the castle. You will make your way down the cliff and use the boat to get you off of Castelul Lupului property. The cliff is manageable if you take your time. The moon will help you see. I will remain here and hold off the CIA to give you the needed time, then I will escape with my car."

"That boat better be there, Banik."

"It's there," he shot back. "You better be in Constanta when I get there to collect the rest of my fee or you'll have more than the CIA to worry about. Now get going. The women will be coming around soon. Take this." Banik handed Luca a German-made Luger.

Luca took the handgun and left, running toward the cliff located about 400 yards away.

◊ ◊ ◊

As the Fates would have it, Zhanna Rogova was the closest Maiden to Jaro Banik's location, although she didn't know that. The only signal any of the women had that something was happening was the single gunshot into the air by Axel Ryker from the castle's keep. That gunshot told them nothing else and gave them no direction.

Zhanna, with her blacked-out eyes and carrying her Mosin-Nagant rifle, moved gingerly through the trees, staying in the shadows as much as possible. She knew how skilled Jaro Banik was as a sniper.

Suddenly, a rifle shot cracked the silence and a piece of bark from the maple tree Zhanna hid behind shattered and flew away.

Zhanna shouted into the forest, "Thank you for the warning shot, Jaro."

In the distance, she heard Banik yell back. "You're welcome, Zhanna. I don't want to kill you."

From the sound of Banik's yell, Zhanna estimated he was about a hundred yards away, about the length of a soccer pitch or an American football field. That was close. She knew Banik had made sniper kills during the war from a quarter of a mile away. He could have easily taken her down in the slivery-blue light of tonight's moon.

Erika, Amy, and Ryker heard the rifle blast west of the castle but Erika was concerned about diversions and told Amy earlier to keep to her ground. Erika would also hold her ground unless more gunshots were heard. Ryker, who had not been assigned an area, descended the keep and ran out of the castle in the direction of the rifle shot. The muscle-bound Ryker, who was anything but a long-distance runner, would take time to find anyone. It now all came down to a cat and mouse game between the Second World War's best Polish sniper and the Red Army's best sniper.

Through the macabre forest the two snipers worked their way from shadow to shadow. As she had done during the war in the summer months, Zhanna stopped to remove her shoes and socks. This would give her more sensitivity to fallen twigs and small branches she didn't want cracking under her feet.

This circling for position went on for about 15 minutes. Suddenly from the east came the noise of someone running through the woods. From their hidden positions, both snipers used their scopes to see the hulking Axel Ryker lumbering in their direction.

Zhanna knew this was her break. Jaro Banik would surely shoot Ryker. She quickly scanned the area where she suspected Banik might be and saw his rifle pointing Ryker's direction from behind a tree. This shift exposed Banik's left arm as it held the rifle and Zhanna quickly took her shot. The bullet ripped through Banik's bicep. He dropped the rifle and fell to his knees. This exposed him further and Zhanna's next shot passed through his abdomen.

She sprinted toward him.

When she arrived, he was still alive but coughing blood. A bleak expression was etched on his face. She picked up his rifle and tossed it behind her.

"Jaro. Where is Dragoş Luca?"

He said nothing.

"I tried my best to avoid this, Jaro."

He looked at her and muttered in pain, "Zhanna . . . I'm glad it was you."

Then he died.

Chapter 37

An unhappy Count

Castelul Lupului
Next day—Saturday, 04 August 1951

Last night, after the team found Zhanna, everyone spread out to find Dragoş Luca. After two fruitless hours they had found nothing other than Marku's body. It was as if Luca had vanished into thin air.

Zhanna insisted that Jaro Banik's body be buried properly and not left to the ravens, boars, wolves, or bears. Amy returned to the castle and brought back a couple of shovels. Banik was buried where he died.

Now, over breakfast, the team and Count Lupei discussed the situation.

"We have to decide what to do with Crina and Sylvania," Erika said. "They helped us and I promised them we would protect them."

"That will be up to you and your team, Erika," the Count said. He was very unhappy that Luca had escaped.

"What happens now?" Amy asked Erika.

"Al Hodge told me to call him this morning to check on the spirit plane. I'll have to tell him to cancel the flight because Luca escaped and we want to remain in Romania for now to track him down."

"Knowing Al," Amy said, "I don't envy you that phone call."

Erika nodded. She wasn't looking forward to it either. "Count Lupei, can Geofri get the phone hooked up?"

"No. He had to rip the wires from the wall. It will have to wait until Monday before he can get a telephone repairman here from Oradea."

"Then I'll call Hodge from Zalău. Zhanna, Amy, and Axel, you can go with me and we'll check the Slaughtered Lamb. I don't expect to find Luca there. He's not a fool, but we need to check anyway for protocol's sake during debriefings when this is all over."

[same time, Zalău]

Dragoş Luca had many cuts and bruises from the difficult descent down the steep incline to the river. A small jon boat was tied up to the bank as Banik had promised. A rough ride down the swift river took Luca off Castelul Lupului property and to within a mile of Zalău.

He dared not return to the Slaughtered Lamb knowing that the CIA people would surely check for him there. Luckily, he had stuffed his pockets with money. The sole car dealership in town was a small operation that sold only used cars. He purchased one and left Zalău behind.

[one hour later]

The Slaughtered Lamb had not yet opened for the day, but the bartender and kitchen cook where there preparing for opening and the front door was unlocked. The team barged in.

"We're not open yet," the bartender told them.

"You're open now for us," Zhanna announced sharply. She was wearing the wolf pendant that Jaro Banik had given her.

Erika went into the telephone booth and closed the door. Ryker stood guard at the front door to make sure no one else entered. Zhanna approached the bartender. "Which room upstairs did Dragoş Luca stay in?"

"He's not here," the man said.

Zhanna drew her dagger and glared at him. "I didn't ask you that."

Faced with the six-foot-tall Russian with death in her eyes, the man stuttered out, "The fourth . . . the fourth door on the left."

Zhanna had her skeleton key but having the correct key would be faster. "Give me the key to the room."

He quickly retrieved a key from a drawer below the bar and handed it over.

Amy stayed downstairs to help Ryker monitor the place as Zhanna went upstairs. The Russian trashed Luca's room as she searched for any information or items that might provide a clue. She found nothing but clothes, personal toiletries, and a half empty bottle of Tuică.

Downstairs, Erika finally reached Al Hodge at the American embassy in Munich after diverting the call through the U.S. embassy in Istanbul.

"Erika," Hodge said from Munich. *"Everything is set for tonight with the plane. Have the oil pots lighting the farmer's field by eleven o'clock. The plane will be there by midnight."*

"Cancel the plane, Al. Dragoş Luca escaped last night."

"What!"

"We'll find him, Al. Just give us some time."

"You told me there was no way he could escape from that Count's castle!"

"Quit shouting," Erika said. "I was wrong."

"No shit!"

"Give us another week, Al."

"You're not getting another minute, let alone another week. Your mission is over. Listen to me very carefully, Erika. The airplane will be there tonight as planned. You and your team will be on it. If you're not, you and everyone on your team is suspended and will be reevaluated for service. You know what that will mean for you all, but especially for Rogova and Ryker."

Erika knew of the consequences for Zhanna and Axel. She paused for a moment.

"Are you still there?" Hodge asked. *"Did you hear what I said and do you understand your orders?"*

"I heard you, shithead. You're making a mistake, but we'll meet the plane. We'll be bringing two other women with us."

"Who the fuck are they?"

"They're Romanian nationals who helped us and we promised them protection." She didn't wait for another harangue. In frustration, she slammed down the receiver so hard it cracked the cradle.

[that evening]

The team sat for their last dinner at Castelul Lupului. Crina and Sylvania were not ordered to eat in their rooms, so they were also at the table.

"Count Lupei, I figured out how Luca escaped," Erika said. "This afternoon after we returned from Zalău I was looking down the mountainside north of the castle. Wanting to know if a descent was possible, I tried it. When I reached the river, I found a rope tied to a tree on one end with the other end in the water. Obviously, a boat had been tied up there. Jaro Banik outsmarted us, especially me. I accept the blame."

"No blame needs to be accepted, my child," the Count said. "And I apologize if I seemed irritable at breakfast this morning. If I can be of any service to you in the future, don't hesitate to contact me."

"Thank you, Count."

◊ ◊ ◊

The oil pots marking the landing strip where ablaze when the black Lockheed 10-seat Hudson with no markings set down in the farmer's bean field near the eastern border of Castelul Lupului property. The Count had told the farmer he would be compensated for the damage done to the rows of beans affected.

The team, with Crina and Sylvania in tow, ran out of the forest and boarded the plane. Besides the Air Force pilot, a co-pilot/navigator was onboard. The pilot revved the plane's two engines, turned it around, and took off, barely clearing the treetops as it began the 4½-hour flight to Munich. They would have to fly under the radar as the blacked-out Hudson passed over Hungary. Only when they reached Austria could the pilot increase altitude, turn on the running lights, and finish the flight to Germany.

Chapter 38

Erika's hometown

Munich, Germany
Next day—Sunday, 05 August 1951

Al Hodge and the team sat in a conference room at the American consulate. Crina and Sylvania were confined to their rooms on Hodge's orders.

"Okay," Hodge said. "Before we get down to the business of Dragoş Luca, tell me about the two women you brought back with you."

"I already told you, Al," Erika said with annoyance. She was still fuming about Hodge canceling their mission. "They were planted in Luca's operation by the MGB. They helped us with information about Luca. If we left them in Romania, their days were numbered. Either Luca would find them and take his revenge, or the Russians would ship them to a gulag for helping the CIA."

Hodge sighed in exasperation. "Alright. The CIA doesn't want to get the reputation that we abandon foreign assets who cooperate with us. I'll send them to Washington and Leroy can decide what to do with them. They can go on the same plane that takes all of you except Amy back to the States. I told you, Erika, that we can't sacrifice the perfect cover we have for Amy just to nail Dragoş Luca. She'll return to Barcelona and rejoin that Flamenco band."

"Al, if you would have given us a few days like I requested, we would have located Luca," Erika said.

"Forget it," Hodge declared. "There's an Air Force DC-4 taking a general and his staff back to the States on Tuesday. You, Rogova, Ryker and the two Romanian women will be on it. I'll get a smaller plane to take Amy back to Barcelona that day. I'll be here in Munich until Thursday for reasons that are none of your business, then I'll fly back to D.C. on a commercial flight. Zhanna, let's hear what you have to say."

"Fuck you, Al," Zhanna replied.

"That's what I thought you'd say. You know you'll have to undergo extensive debriefing about a failed mission when you get back to the States. All of you will. Axel, do you have anything to say?"

The impossible-to-intimate Ryker shrugged. "I obeyed orders from Erika, who you named our field leader. I am not concerned with debriefings. I will add that I agree with Erika. We could have hunted Luca down."

"Amy?" Hodge asked.

The beautiful Gypsy replied, "I agree that we could have found Luca. His operation is still intact and he has no reason to think he has to flee from Romania. That is my home country. I know it well and I know Luca. I would lay odds that he's already back in Constanta. Maybe even at his villa being protected by extra security supplied by the Russians. If not in his villa, he's probably holed up in a penthouse he keeps reserved at a luxury hotel in Bucharest, or on his yacht sailing on the Black Sea. We could have found him."

"You might have, or you might not have and wound up captured by the Soviets," Hodge said. "So far, your affiliation with the Flamenco band that was a guest of the Romanian government has protected you. That's over now with Luca and the Ivans knowing you're CIA. Roaming around Romania would be much more dangerous now, and if you're captured that would be a much bigger disaster for the CIA than a failed assignment. The mission is cancelled."

Erika asked, "Are we trapped in this embassy until Tuesday, or may we go out? This is my hometown."

"You may go out for a few hours tomorrow," Hodge answered. "But remember what I told you on the phone when you called me from Zalău, Erika."

She knew he was referring to the dire warning he delivered about Zhanna and Axel if orders were not obeyed. Their protection would be revoked. Erika had not told either of them about this, but it was her job to protect the team.

"We'll be on the airplane Tuesday, Al."

Chapter 39

An old friend of Karl Lehmann

Munich, Germany
Next day—Monday, 06 August 1951

Every Shield Maiden and Ryker had been to Munich before. Some, especially Ryker, numerous times during the war. But Erika showed them personal places, like the apartment building she lived in with her father when she was a teenager.

She took them to the Hofbräuhaus for dinner. The world-famous beer hall took up an entire block of the Platzl. They took a table outside in the courtyard beer garden and ordered beer from a buxom Bier Fräulein decked out in a blue and white dirdl that revealed quite an amount of cleavage.

"Next month when the Octoberfest starts—it starts in September and ends in October—we'd never get in this place without waiting for hours," Erika told them.

Zhanna bummed a cigar off of Ryker.

"Have you ever thought about purchasing your own cigarettes and cigars?" Ryker asked Zhanna as he handed her one.

"Why would I do that when I can get them free from assholes like you?"

The Bier Fräulein delivered the beers that were brewed on-site. She placed a giant, one-liter glass stein called a Maß in front of each of them. Before she left, Erika ordered an assorted sausage platter for the table that would feed four and included a large bowl of sauerkraut and another bowl of green beans.

As they drank their beer and waited for the food, no one mentioned Dragoş Luca or the failed mission. Nobody wanted to talk about it.

"Amy," Erika said. "It looks like you'll be keeping your promise to the band to return to Barcelona before your next booking."

"Yes. We start a two-week engagement at our home cantina this coming weekend, then we begin our tour of three cities in Morocco—Tangier, Casablanca, and Marrakesh. The venue we're performing at in

Casablanca is Rick's Café. It started up about three years ago and is named after the café in the Humphrey Bogart film. They have capitalized on the famous movie and apparently it is doing quite well, especially among tourists."

"Is anyone interested in some gambling?" Erika asked. "It's illegal here but I know places that cater to American servicemen that the Army MPs ignore." Erika was mainly thinking about trying to cheer up Zhanna, who had been bogged down in the doldrums since killing Jaro Banik.

"Is there a time that Hodge wants us back at the embassy?" Amy asked.

"When we checked out this afternoon, he told me to have all of us back by dark, but I'm not paying any attention to that. I told him we'd be on that plane tomorrow. That should be enough for him."

Everyone was game for the gambling.

◊ ◊ ◊

Erika banged hard on the steel door to a closed-for-the-day auto repair shop on the Truderinger Straße. It took two knocks on the alley door before a man opened a small, sliding window in the door—much like the security windows in the American speakeasies during Prohibition.

The man said nothing. Only his eyes and part of his nose were visible.

"We're here to see Helmut," Erika told the eyes and nose. "Is he here?"

"Maybe he is, maybe he isn't. Who are you?"

"Tell Helmut that Erika Lehmann and some friends want to gamble."

"Go away."

"The only person who will be going away is you if you don't deliver my message to Helmut."

The eyes stared at the three women and a monster of a man. "I'll be back." He then slammed the access window shut.

They waited for about two minutes before the tiny window reopened.

"Erika! I can't believe it."

"Hello, Helmut."

The man shut the window, unbolted the door, and invited them in.

"These are friends of mine, Helmut," Erika told him. Then to the team she said, "This is Helmut Kormann. He and my father were friends."

Kormann was 55 years old with horseshoe hair—bald on top with a ring of graying hair on the sides and back of his head. He wore thick spectacles and sported a well maintained, pointed goatee.

"Helmut, from the security, I assume you still have your games going in the back room."

"Yes, but Monday is our slow night, Erika. There are about a half-dozen American G.I.s back there and only three or four locals."

"That's fine," Erika said. "We came just for the fun."

"I miss your father and your gracious mother, Erika. Karl and I were very close for twenty years. I'm so glad to see you. You look well."

"Thank you, Helmut. I remember how close you and my father were here in Munich before the war—before we were forced to move to Berlin because of my father's work for Dr. Goebbels and the Propaganda Ministry."

Kormann led them through the garage and past numerous cars up on blocks. They reached a door marked 'Hausmeister' and entered. Inside was not a small janitor's room with mops and buckets, but a large room that contained three poker tables, a craps table, a Roulette wheel, and two pool tables. As Helmut had explained, there were only nine men testing their luck—six American servicemen and three German locals. A bartender had set up a small, makeshift bar on a metal worktable. A keg of Augustiner beer was iced down in a large drum and various liquors and paper cups sat on the table. It definitely wasn't Monte Carlo, but it would do.

Kormann told the bartender that the drinks for Erika and her friends were on the house tonight. The burly bouncer with the eyes and nose who originally answered the alleyway door stood nearby. Ryker pushed him aside. "Get out of my way, Schweinehund."

Chapter 40

Sandwiches in Ireland

Munich, Germany
Next day—Tuesday, 07 August 1951

The tires of the four-prop DC-4 lifted off of the terra firma of Germany at noon. Onboard was a two-star Army general Erika had never seen before and his staff of four lower-ranking officers. With Erika was Zhanna, Ryker, Crina, and Sylvania. This left plenty of room to spread out in the 80-seat airplane. The military men gathered in the front rows; the CIA team took to the back seats.

Erika, Zhanna, and Ryker had made numerous trans-Atlantic trips since starting work for the CIA directly after the war. It was a long, tiresome flight that normally took around 30 hours when the refueling and maintenance check in Shannon, Ireland, were factored in. During the return flight to the States, they would pick up six hours of time zone changes, but that only affected their wrist watches, not the length of the flight.

The stop in Shannon usually took two hours. The CIA contingent debarked to get something to eat inside the terminal. The general and his men stayed onboard except for a First Lieutenant who was sent into the terminal to buy some sandwiches and take back to the plane.

The First Lieutenant ended up standing next to Erika at the lunch counter. He was a rugged 6'1" with dark eyes. When he took his Army cap off inside the building it revealed a shock of unruly brown hair.

"I saw you on the plane, of course," he said. "May I buy you a cup of coffee?" He spoke with a type of dialect that sounded Southern.

"If you wish," Erika said. She kept her chicken salad sandwich and handed the big bag of more sandwiches to Zhanna who stood beside her. "I bought everyone an extra sandwich for the flight later on tonight. Half are chicken salad and half are peanut butter."

Zhanna took the bag and joined Ryker and the MGB women at a table.

Erika and the Lieutenant took a seat at a different table. She saw his name tag read 'Hatfield.' "Where are you from in the States, Lieutenant Hatfield?"

"West Virginia. Please call me Shirl."

"I'm Erika. Your last name is Hatfield and you come from West Virginia. Isn't that where the Hatfields from the famous Hatfields and McCoys feud took place?"

"There and in eastern Kentucky where the McCoys mostly lived. But yes, I am a descendant of *those* Hatfields. Devil Anse Hatfield, the leader of the Hatfields at that time and heavily involved with the feud was my great-uncle."

"Fascinating," Erika said. "And now you are on a general's personal staff. That must be exciting for you."

"Don't be too impressed, Erika. My job is not very glamorous. As a First Lieutenant I'm the lowest guy on General Worden's totem pole. I have a captain, a major, and a Lieutenant Colonel in front of me. That's why I'm the gofer for sandwiches."

Erika smiled at his humor.

"Tell me about you," he said. "I see you and your associates are traveling on an Air Force plane. All of you must serve the U.S. government in some way."

"We woman are translators for State Department officials when they travel to Europe. We translate at NATO conferences—things like that. The large man with us has a job in State Department security. He helps protect diplomats when they travel to political hot spots."

Hatfield turned around and looked at Ryker who sat with the women several tables away. Ryker caught the Lieutenant looking at him and glared.

Shirl Hatfield turned around and commented to Erika, "That guy sure looks like he has the physical tools and disposition to be security."

Erika replied, "Yes, he certainly does, doesn't he?"

"How long will you be in the States?" Hatfield asked. "And will you be around the Washington area? Don't answer that if it's confidential. I just thought maybe we could meet up again. Perhaps next time for dinner."

"It's not confidential, Shirl, but I really don't know. Sometimes the State Department doesn't give us much notification ahead of time. There have been trips I didn't know about until the night before we were to fly out. Are you going to be in D.C. for a while?"

"At least for a month," he answered. "General Worden has a stint at the Pentagon for at least that amount of time."

"I own a small eatery and tavern in Arlington called the Lili Marlene Café. It's not fancy but we serve good food and drink at reasonable prices. It's easy to find. It's on South Nash Street, just a few blocks south of the National Cemetery."

The great-nephew of Devil Anse Hatfield said, "The Lili Marlene Café on South Nash Street. Got it. I'll be there, Erika."

[same time—Barcelona]

Amy arrived in Barcelona and took a taxi to the El Palace Hotel. She checked in, then after the porter dropped her bag in her room, she found Petru and a couple of other members of the band in the hotel bar. They were glad to see that their main attraction had returned in time for their engagement at Barcelona's Cordobes Tablao Flamenco this coming weekend.

[four hours later]

The sun had sunk behind the western horizon. Ireland was well behind them. The only thing below the DC-4 now was the dark waters of the Atlantic Ocean.

"Who is the lieutenant from the general's staff you were talking to in the Shannon terminal?" Zhanna asked Erika quietly. Crina and Sylvania were asleep in their chairs. Ryker, two rows ahead, puffed on a cigar. As before, the military men sat far away in the front of the fuselage.

"He bought me a cup of coffee and asked for a dinner date in D.C. Apparently the general will be working at the Pentagon for at least a month. I don't want to go out with him. Instead of accepting a date, I told him to stop by the Lili Marlene some evening for a drink."

Zhanna nodded. "Yes, when someone does what we do, it's best to stay at arm's length with relationships. Love is meant for others. Not women like us.

Chapter 41

New territory

Washington, D.C.
Next day—Wednesday, 08 August 1951

In her six years of working for the CIA since the war, Erika and her Shield Maidens had never failed a mission. Sometimes they used unorthodox procedures and did not always follow their precise orders, but in the end they had always delivered on the overall objective one way or another.

So this was new territory for her and the others as they sat in Leroy Carr's office at CIA headquarters on E Street in Washington. It was mid-afternoon. Carr was the Deputy Director—the second man in charge at the CIA. He had cars with drivers wearing black suits who looked like undertakers waiting for them when the DC-4 sat down at Andrews Air Force Base just over an hour ago.

"Al has kept me updated throughout this entire affair," Carr said to them all. Erika, Zhanna, and Ryker were there. Crina and Sylvania had been driven to a local CIA safehouse as soon as they stepped off the plane.

"The two Romanian women will be taken care of," Carr continued. "Abandoning foreign assets is not wise and will not help us in the future."

"Al said basically the same thing, Leroy," Erika said.

"He said it because he knows it's true. If an intelligence organization of any country gets the reputation of abandoning foreign nationals who help them, they will be hard pressed to get others to cooperate in the future."

"What are you going to do with Crina and Sylvania?" Erika asked.

"I'll find them something. I would wager the State Department can use a couple more Romanian translators, but they have to learn English first. We'll have to send them to school at Fort Huachuca in Arizona where they teach English to foreign nationals."

"Now," Carr continued. "About the mission. All three of you will go through debriefing. For a failed mission, plan for at least a week of interrogations. You will debrief for six hours every day for as long as it takes. Starting tomorrow, be here at E Street from eight o'clock in the morning every day until two o'clock in the afternoon. You will all have different personnel questioning you in separate rooms, of course."

"And during our time off?" Erika asked.

"Return to your cover jobs. Erika and Zhanna to the café in Arlington. Ryker, since you have to be here every day for at least a week, you can't leave for Philadelphia. Take a room at the Mayflower Hotel. When the debriefings are over and I've read the reports, we'll sit down and talk about the future of the Shield Maiden team."

[45 minutes later—Arlington, Virginia]

School for the year had not yet started. Erika knew her 10-year-old daughter would be at the Lili Marlene Café. Angelika Egermann, Erika's friend from Germany and the café's manager, had a small studio apartment above the café and Ada stayed with her when Erika was out of town.

Erika told the taxi driver, "Sir, you're driving too slow. Here's five dollars, please speed up." She was impatient to be reunited with Ada. Five dollars was a massive tip and the driver suddenly transformed from driving like Grandma Moses to driving like Lee Wallard, the winner of this year's Indianapolis 500. Finally, they arrived at the café.

Erika found Ada standing on a box washing dishes in the kitchen.

"Mutti!" Ada yelled when she saw her mother. Erika rushed to her and they embraced for a very long moment.

"How have you been, my darling?" Erika asked the child.

"I am fine. I've done a lot of dishes to help. I like helping you, Mutti."

Tears welled in Erika's eyes. Adelaide—Ada was her mother's pet name for her—had been born in the spring of 1941 after Erika's fling with a German SS captain.

Only after the long embrace and multiple kisses with Ada would Erika turn to Angelika and Bertha, the café's cook. But when she did, she greeted them warmly with more hugs. The failed mission haunted her, but she was glad to be back at the Lili Marlene.

[later—the Lili Marlene Café]

By six o'clock that evening, things were back to normal at the café. Zhanna Rogova had donned her apron and now tended bar. Axel Ryker, because he could not return to his home in Philadelphia until debriefings were completed, had come in for dinner.

Wednesday nights were not as busy as weekend nights, so tonight there were four empty tables in the small, 12-table café. Erika sat with Ryker.

"Axel. Is Rose coming to D.C.?"

"She and our son will be here tomorrow, along with the nanny. I reserved a large suite at the Mayflower."

In a story that proves that sometimes truth is stranger than fiction, the former Gestapo henchman married a rich American heiress—Rose Bristow—two year ago. They now lived on her father's palatial estate outside of Philadelphia. The estate included not only the mansion but several lake houses, one of which Ryker and Rose lived in. The estate also included a landing strip and hangar for the Bristow's private airplane.

"I know you'll be glad to see Rose and your boy," Erika said. "How old is your son now?"

"A year and a half," Ryker answered. The only time anyone saw the grisly Ryker soften a bit was when he was around his wife and son. According to Rose, Axel was a loving husband and father.

"Be sure and bring them by the café," Erika said. "I'd love to see them again."

151

Chapter 42

Godmother

Constanta, Romania
Next day—Thursday, 09 August 1951

Since returning to Constanta from Transylvania last Saturday, Dragoş Luca had doubled security surrounding his villa and spent nearly two full days in General Kulikov's MGB's office in Bucharest explaining the past week and the CIA's plan to capture him.

"You never should have put yourself in that situation, Dragoş," The general had told him.

"The Gypsy band was a guest of the Romanian government, General. How was I to know the women were CIA. You didn't know either until Zhanna Rogova was eventually identified and by then it was too late."

"Regardless, we're now aware that the Americans know about you. Your operation is in danger, my friend."

"I can take care of this," Luca said. "I know where Amy Radu will be for the next several weeks. I have the band's schedule. They're in Barcelona for the next two weekends and then begin a three-week tour in North Africa. Morocco to be exact. I can turn the tables on the CIA. If I were to capture Radu, it would give us bargaining power. The weak Americans are notorious for never deserting one of their captured field agents."

Kulikov took a drag on his cigarette and thought for a moment. "Very well. But you're on your own with this Dragoş. I cannot help you with manpower and if it all goes awry the Soviet government will disavow ever knowing about your dealings in drugs or weapons. As far as we're concerned, the only thing we'll admit is that we were aware of you only as a rich Romanian and an aficionado of the arts."

"I will take care of this, General."

◊ ◊ ◊

[that evening—Arlington, Virginia]

Rose Bristow and her baby sat with Erika. The baby had been born with a Cleft palate which had been repaired when the child turned one. Only a small scar on his upper lip remained.

Axel was at the bar getting their drinks from Zhanna. He returned with three bottles of Warsteiner Dunkel, a dark lager imported from Bavaria that Angelika had recently brought in. The Lili Marlene sold popular American beers, but Angelika thought a German-themed café should offer at least one German beer.

After Ryker sat down, Rose said, "Erika, Axel and I would like to talk to you about something. Axel tells me you're Catholic. So is my family. We'll be getting our baby baptized this Sunday at the church my family attends. I know we have waited a long time and this is late notice, but Axel couldn't decide on a godmother. The godfather will be my brother, Stephen. Axel has finally decided. We would be honored if you stood up as the godmother. Our boy will be christened John Axel Ryker. Axel wanted him to have the surname Bristow, but the Catholic Church will not allow that. The father's surname must be used."

Erika said, "I don't know what to say. I'm flabbergasted. Of course I will stand up for your son. It will be my honor." She was amazed that Ryker had chosen her. They had butted heads so many times in the past. She looked at him. He looked away and took a large gulp of his beer.

"Thank you, Erika," Rose said. "Philadelphia is only a one-hour flight away. I'll have our plane here Saturday afternoon and we'll all fly out together. You can spend that night at the estate. Again, thank you so much. Bring Ada and invite Zhanna or whomever you wish. I'll call my mother tonight." Then Rose chuckled, "You know my mother; she won't let an opportunity to have a gala reception after her grandson's christening pass her by. Expect the Philadelphia mayor and his wife to be at the church along with other bigshots."

Erika didn't doubt it. Rose's father, Archibald Bristow, was one of the richest men in America, having amassed his considerable fortune in the shipping industry. He was a major stockholder in several train and ocean-going shipping conglomerates. He was a powerful man and the political powers-that-be went out of their way to stay on good terms.

"I assume appropriate church clothes will suffice," Erika said to Rose.

"Yes, no formal attire will be needed," Rose affirmed. "I'm so excited!"

◊ ◊ ◊

An hour later, the Lili Marlene received two surprise guests. Crina and Sylvania walked in with a CIA bodyguard. Al Hodge had approved the visit to let them know the safehouse was not a prison. His move was not philanthropic. The CIA thought these two beautiful MGB sirens might serve the CIA in that role in the future. Of course, neither Crina nor Sylvania were aware of that.

Speaking little English, they were relieved when they spotted Zhanna at the bar. They knew they could speak Russian to her. Their CIA watchdog separated himself from them and began playing darts.

Erika excused herself from Ryker's and Rose's table to join the women at the bar.

"Erika and Zhanna!" Sylvania bubbled in Russian. "Crina and I are so glad to be in the United States. Thank you so much for keeping your promise to not abandon us in Romania. Crina wants to see New York City. I want to see Hollywood."

"Yes," Crina said. "I want to see the Empire State Building and the Statue of Liberty."

Zhanna ignored their enthusiasm and asked, "What are you drinking?"

Both said martinis. "Three olives, please."

Zhanna walked away to fix the drinks.

"I'm glad you came," Erika said to both women. "Have you started your interrogations yet?"

"We start tomorrow," Crina answered.

"Let me give you a tip. Foreign assets such as yourselves need to be completely honest and reveal everything they know. The CIA interrogators will know if you're covering up anything or not being totally forthright. You can't fool them. If you want to remain in the

United States and someday see New York City and Hollywood, be completely truthful when answering the questions."

"Yes, we will, Erika," Sylvania replied.

The two Romanians had tunnel vision when they entered and had not spotted Axel Ryker. Crina looked around the bar and finally saw him at a table with a woman holding a baby.

"I was hoping we'd never see that monster again," Crina said, then asked Erika. "Who is that unfortunate woman sitting with him?"

"That's his wife and baby and you'd be wise to watch what you say. Axel is a member of my team, as you well know."

"I'm sorry, Erika," Crina apologized. "I meant no offense."

Crina's faux pas was forgotten as Zhanna delivered the martinis.

"Enjoy your drinks and your time at the Lili Marlene Café, ladies. Come back anytime," Erika said before turning to the bartender. "Their drinks tonight are on me, Zhanna."

Chapter 43

Amy whirls

Barcelona, Spain
Next day—Friday, 10 August 1951

The Barcelona Gypsy Romanian Orchestra had completed a brief rehearsal this morning at the group's home cantina, the Cordobes Tablao Flamenco. They would open at the cantina tonight. Now they sat backstage eating lunch they had ordered from a favorite eatery located down the street.

The conversation was in Spanish.

"It was nice seeing our homeland," said Raval, the accordion player. The others agreed.

"It was bittersweet for me," Viorel said. He was the guitar player. "My family was swept away by the Nazis so in many ways it was sad for me to see the old places."

"Amy, will you miss Erika and Zhanna?" Nicu, the Djembe drummer, asked.

"Sure, we had gotten to be friends. But no one can blame them for taking a higher paying job with Dragoș Luca. Until I find their replacements, Cici is going to help me with my hair, and a waitress here at the Cordobes will help me with my wardrobe quick changes during the performances."

"Speaking of Dragoș Luca," Petru mentioned. "He said he'd send an attorney to Barcelona to discuss his proposal to sponsor us and get us work in North and South America. What's the latest on that, Amy?"

"I'm afraid all that is on hold for now, Petru," Amy answered. "It seems Señor Luca has encountered some serious business dealings he must first address."

"Does that mean he's backing out?" the cimbalom player asked.

"I don't know, Mitica. I'm just telling you what he told me."

Most of the group were disappointed.

Cici said, "I was so hoping to perform one day in the United States."

"We don't have to have Luca's backing," Petru said. "We are the most popular Roma band in Spain and the Mediterranean. We make a good living. If we all stay together, one day we will perform in the United States. I promise."

That night, the Cordobes Tablao Flamenco was standing room only as it was whenever the Barcelona Gypsy Romanian Orchestra performed. On stage, Amy stomped and whirled.

[that evening—Arlington, Virginia]

Al Hodge dropped by the Lili Marlene this evening. Every table and bar stool were occupied so Erika took him upstairs after he got his Bourbon on the rocks from Zhanna. "I hope you choke on an ice cube," Zhanna had told him.

A small area of the floor over the café was taken up by Angelika's studio apartment. The bulk of the space was the storage room where a table sat for private conversations.

As Erika and Hodge sat down at the table, she said, "It was nice of you to let Crina and Sylvania out of the safehouse last night, Al."

"I don't want them to think they're prisoners. This afternoon, after their morning interrogations, I had a couple of men drive them around Washington on a quick tour of the sites—they drove by the White House, the Capitol building, Lincoln and Washington Monuments, and the Jefferson Memorial."

Erika smiled. "What's the real reason, Al. You're going to recruit them, aren't you?"

He was honest. "Maybe. It depends on how they do during their questioning. That will continue for several more days. If Leroy decides they might be of service to the United States, we'll send them to Arizona. They can learn English at Fort Huachuca. That will take some time, of course. Probably a year. But if and when they can function well with English we'll consider bringing them in. In the meantime, they can enjoy the great Mexican food in southern Arizona."

Erika changed the subject. "Axel's and Rose's son is being baptized in Philadelphia Sunday morning. You and Leroy are invited."

"What church?"

"The Cathedral Basilica of Saints Peter and Paul. Mass starts at ten o'clock. The diocese bishop himself will pour the water. Afterwards there will be a celebration at the Bristow estate."

"We'll be there," Hodge said.

Chapter 44

An offer from Archibald

Philadelphia, Pennsylvania
Sunday, 12 August 1951

Yesterday afternoon, the Bristow family's 12-seat, twin-engine Cessna and their personal pilot picked up Rose and Axel, their baby and nanny, and Erika and Zhanna in Washington and flew them to the Bristow estate where Erika and Zhanna spent the night in the sprawling mansion.

Today, the Philadelphia Basilica was packed for the ten o'clock Mass. This was normally the case, but today even more guests had come for the Rite of Baptism for Archibald Bristow's only grandchild. The mayor and his wife were there, along with several city councilmen and state legislators. Even a U.S. congressman and his wife crowded into a pew. Al Hodge was present, as were Leroy Carr and his wife Kay.

After the Catholics in attendance received Holy Communion, the baptism began as one of the several priests on hand called the mother and father and direct participants to the altar.

Rose and Axel stepped forward with Rose's brother and Erika Lehmann. Erika carried the baby.

The bishop joined them at the font. Other priests led the prayers for the Catholics in the church to renew their baptismal vows, then the bishop took over.

Erika held the baby over the font as the bishop poured water on the child's forehead and said in Latin, "I baptize John Axel Ryker in the name of the Father, the Son, and the Holy Spirit." Then in English he said to the congregation, "Let us welcome this new child of Christ."

Everyone, Catholic or not, clapped.

After the baptism, all the invited guests drove to the Bristow estate west of the city. Archibald Bristow had a limousine and driver waiting in front of the church for the bishop and priests who took part in the ceremony.

When the guests entered the mansion's Grand Hall, Rose and her mother were there to greet them. A table was set up near the entrance where a female caterer handed each guest a crystal flute of expensive French Champagne. Other dapperly dressed caterers, male and female, circulated over the hall's pink Tennessee marble floor carrying silver trays of hors d'oeuvres and kabobs. A string quartet set up in the far corner quietly played Beethoven's *Ode to Joy.*

All the illustrious guests took a back seat to the real star of the show—John Ryker. Envelope after envelope containing money was handed to Rose even though the guests knew that the grandson of Archibald Bristow needed the money as much as King George of England needed another crown.

Al and Leroy stood with Erika.

"I never thought I'd live to see the day that I attended the baptism of the son of Axel Ryker," Leroy said.

"I never thought *Ryker* would live to see this day," Al countered.

Archibald Bristow walked over.

"Thank you for standing up for my grandson, Erika. Axel and Rose couldn't have picked a better godmother. And thank you for coming all the way from Washington, Leroy and Al." The powerful Bristow cooperated with the government when his influence served a purpose and he knew they were all CIA along with his son-in-law.

"It's an honor to be invited, Archibald," Leroy said.

"Erika, do you need anything for your café I might be of help with?" Bristow asked.

"Archibald. You've done so much already," she replied.

Last spring, at Rose's request, her father paid to totally refurbish the café's rundown restrooms with new floors and fixtures. In the kitchen, he also replaced the old four-burner stove with a brand new six-burner, the refrigerator, water heater, and the dishwashing sink.

"Nonsense, my dear. You are now my grandson's godmother. We consider that family. Rose tells me there's a building attached to your café that's for sale. If memory serves, I think Rose said it was a hardware store that went out of business and is sitting empty. The logical thing to do would be to buy the building so you can expand the number of tables in your café. We can build a couple of apartments on the second floor of the add-on building. One for you and your daughter, and one for your colleague Zhanna, who I understand has been living with you and your daughter at your apartment in D.C. and sleeping on your sofa. Is that correct?"

"That's right," Erika said, "but we're getting by fine, Archibald."

"Next week," Bristow said, ignoring her, "I'll send some of my real estate people to have that building inspected and appraised. Then we'll make a fair offer to the owners. If it's been sitting abandoned for a while, they'd be foolish to turn down a fair offer. Once the legalities are out of the way, I'll send a construction crew to begin work."

Bristow changed the subject. "Leroy. Where is your lovely wife, Kay?"

Carr chuckled. "I always lose her in crowds. Kay is much better at mingling than me."

Erika said, "Kay's near the statue of Achilles talking to the mayor and your wife, Archibald."

"Okay, Miss Eagle Eye," Hodge said. "Where's your buddy, Rogova?"

"She's back near the musicians with a flute of Champagne in each hand trying to avoid interaction as she usually does. That's Zhanna."

Chapter 45

More surprises for Erika

Arlington, Virginia
Next day—Monday, 13 August 1951

In the late afternoon, Erika sat at a barstool in the Lili Marlene talking to Angelika and Zhanna. She had told them both about Archibald Bristow's plan to expand the café.

"What do you think, Angelika?" Erika asked.

In English, but with a heavy Berlin accent and her sentences arranged in German grammar, Angelika said, "Wonderful, I think it would be. Why do you ask, Erika? Perhaps you do not the same way feel?"

"I'm just thinking about Ada. She likes her school in D.C. She's doing well there and has made friends. During my school days I had no roots, going from grade school in Germany to different high schools here in the United States, then back to Germany for college. I did a little checking on the local public school here in Arlington she would attend. Tomorrow I'm going to drop by a Catholic school. I would have gone by both schools today but the debriefings about Romania take up most of Zhanna's and my day. I'll be glad when the damn things are over."

"Someone should play the violin for you," Zhanna said. "I grew up in a state-run orphanage in Leningrad where I was locked in a box the size of a doghouse overnight if I broke a rule. When I had to pee, I was forced to go in my pants. Ada will be fine, Erika. Kids that move around during their school days end up being better at adapting when they become adults. Talk to your daughter and see how she feels about it. She loves being here because she thinks she's helping you. What Bristow offered is pocket change for him. Don't screw things up. When the time comes that we can no longer serve the CIA as field agents, they'll put us on the shelf. We'll all need a decent income when that happens. If that is to come from this café, we'll need more business."

Erika didn't reply, but she knew her enigmatic Russian friend was right.

[that evening]

One surprise after another for Erika continued when Shirl Hatfield showed up tonight at the Lili Marlene. He didn't see Erika but recognized Zhanna behind the bar and approached. The raven-haired, six-foot-tall woman with the neck scarf was easy to remember.

"Hello," he said. He was dressed in civilian clothes. "You probably don't remember me but I was on the plane with you and Erika that brought us all back to the States from Munich."

"I remember seeing you," Zhanna said. "You're a lieutenant."

"That's right. My name is Shirl Hatfield. I'm glad to meet you." He extended a hand. "What's your name?"

Zhanna ignored his hand. "Why do you want to know my name?"

He took his hand back. "I'm just trying to be polite. Erika invited me to stop by. Is she here?"

"Maybe."

Now the great-nephew of Devil Hatfield was getting fed up. "Are all the bartenders here as friendly as you?

"No. I'm the friendliest, asshole."

Hatfield chuckled. "While you decide whether Erika is here or not, I'll take your best Kentucky Bourbon on the rocks."

Zhanna liked his feisty attitude. She poured him a Maker's Mark. "That's 75¢. Give me a dollar. That will take care of the drink and my tip. Erika is upstairs sweeping the storeroom. Go through the kitchen and have a young girl named Ada take you up."

Erika was using a broom and dustpan to sweep the storeroom floor when Ada led a man into the room.

"Mutti," Ada said. "Aunt Zhanna sent this man up here to see you."

"Shirl," Erika said. "What a surprise!"

"I don't know why it's a surprise, Erika. You invited me to stop by your café."

"Yes I did, didn't I. I guess I assumed you would not come. Anyway, welcome to the Lili Marlene."

"I already got quite the welcome from your bartender. She made me feel like I'd be lucky to get out of here alive."

163

Erika grinned. "I see you've met Zhanna. She's a bit overprotective of me on occasion."

"I won't disagree with that."

She smiled again, then turned to her daughter, "Ada. Thank you. You may go back to helping Bertha now."

"Yes, Mutti. I have dishes to wash."

When Ada departed, Hatfield said, "That is one delightful young lady. Your bartender could take some tips in etiquette from her."

Erika laughed. "I'm afraid Zhanna will never change her ways. She's friendly to customers until they start asking questions. But thank you for the compliment about my daughter."

"Ada is your daughter?"

"Yes. Her name is Adelaide. Her father died a few years ago."

"I'm sorry, Erika."

Erika laid it on the line. "Shirl. I come with baggage. I'm not talking about Ada, who is my blessing from Heaven. I have other baggage you'll want no part of. You deserve better. Let's go downstairs and have a couple of drinks and a good time. Then we'll part ways. Believe me, it's in your best interest to forget about me."

"Your plan for tonight sounds perfect, Erika. But we will not part ways after that if it's up to me. I don't care about whatever the baggage is that you talk about. May I take you out to dinner tomorrow night?"

Chapter 46

Carilli Ristorante

Constanta, Romania
Next day—Tuesday, 14 August 1951

Dragoş Luca met with the captain of his ocean-going yacht. They sat on the veranda of Luca's villa overlooking the Black Sea smoking cigars in the afternoon.

"Begin preparing the Som de Argint for a lengthy voyage," Luca told his captain.

"How long will we be at sea?" the captain asked. "I need to know so I can ensure adequate fuel and provisions are onboard."

"We'll be sailing to Morocco and dock in Casablanca. We will be there for a week or ten days."

"Casablanca. That would be the Al Meena port. When will we depart?"

"You have plenty of time to prepare," Luca said. "We'll be leaving in two weeks."

"How many passengers?"

"Myself and ten of my men."

The captain nodded. "I'll make sure the ship and crew are prepared."

[that evening—Washington, D.C.]
Against her better judgment, Erika accepted Shirl Hatfield's invitation to dinner. He picked her up at the café at half past six o'clock.

"Would you rather go to a steakhouse or an Italian place?" he asked as he drove back to the bridge that crossed the Potomac.

"I haven't had Italian in a while."

"I know a good place. It's a small mom and pop run by a couple from Naples. It has only eight tables but on a Tuesday night we shouldn't have trouble getting one."

Hatfield drove to the Foggy Bottom neighborhood of D.C. and parked on the street as close as he could get to a restaurant named Carilli Ristorante. When they entered there was one table available.

"I was almost wrong," Hatfield said. "I didn't think it would be this busy on a Tuesday."

"That means it serves good food," Erika commented.

A young woman wearing a black dress greeted them and led them to the sole empty table. Plates and silverware were already resting on the red and white checkered tablecloth. She handed them menus and said she'd return in a few moments for their orders.

"She's the daughter of the couple that owns and runs this place," Hatfield told Erika. "She's their only child. Her parents do the cooking."

"You must come here often, Shirl."

"Not really that often—maybe once a month when I'm in town, and that's only for about half the year. A friend of mine, another lieutenant, is stationed at the Pentagon fulltime and comes here at least once a week. He told me about this place and about the family."

They picked up the menus. "Do you have any favorites you'd recommend?" Erika asked.

"To be honest, I'm a spaghetti and meatballs guy. I really haven't tried much else on the menu."

When the young woman returned, Erika ordered the rigatoni with hot Italian sausage, Shirl his spaghetti and meatballs. He also ordered a carafe of the house red wine and a plate of fried peppers and sauteed mushrooms for the table.

"I'm certainly no wine expert," he admitted, "but I think the house wine is pretty good here."

"I'm sure it will be lovely."

"You probably know a lot about wines, Erika. Traveling around the world as a State Department translator, I'm sure you eat at state dinners and fine restaurants."

"Yes, we do, but that doesn't make me a wine expert. We don't get to order. We eat and drink what is put in front of us on those trips. We're not told the brand name or vintage of the wine unless the host diplomat or official decides to mention it during the meal."

"Well, if you ever want to know anything about Hillbilly moonshine, I'm your man."

They shared a laugh.

The dark-haired daughter of the Carilli's delivered the wine first and then brought out the food. She also placed a basket of garlic bread sticks in the center of the table.

"Everything looks delicious, Shirl."

"I hope you like it. This is just a little, out-of-the-way place but I've never had a bad meal here."

"Many times those are the best places," she replied. "Especially if they're family owned. These small restaurants have to rely on word-of-mouth advertising and the family knows the importance of customers spreading a good word. That's what brings in more business."

"Your Lili Marlene Café seems to be doing alright, Erika."

"Alright is a good way to put it. We're at least making a small monthly profit now after bills and salaries are paid. The first six months or so after we opened that wasn't the case. We operated in the red."

Conversation slowed as they began eating. Finally, Hatfield asked, "How do you like the food?"

"It's very good, Shirl, and the wine is nice. Good choice."

"Tell me about your daughter—the wonderful young lady I met last night."

"Ada is ten. She was born in Switzerland in 1941, during the war."

"I heard her call you 'Mutti.' That's German for 'Mommy' isn't it?"

"Yes, I was born in Germany and I'm teaching her that language."

"You were born in Germany? I don't notice an accent."

"I spent my high school years here in the United States. My ability to speak fluent German, and English without a German accent is what got me the job at the State Department. I can also translate Russian and French, but I have an American accent when I speak those two languages."

"That's impressive," Hatfield said. "Since General Worden spends a lot of time in Germany, I've picked up some German, but it's what I'd call 'tourist German.' I can communicate with taxi drivers in Germany, shopkeepers, waiters, and ask directions on a street, but that's about it. I'm certainly not fluent. Maybe you can teach me more."

Erika had planned on this being their first and only date. "Shirl, I told you yesterday that I have issues you shouldn't have to deal with. You need to find yourself a nice West Virginia girl."

Part 5

Chapter 47

Tenacity is what she meant

Barcelona, Spain
Two days later—Thursday, 16 August 1951

When at its home cantina, the Barcelona Romanian Gypsy Orchestra held full rehearsals three days a week because each weekend they changed some songs and Amy some of her dancing so the act wouldn't become stale for their regular fans, some of whom came to the Cordobes Tablao Flamenco every weekend to see them when the band was playing in town.

After rehearsal today, Amy and Cici went for coffee at the O'Centrollo cantina where Amy had taken Erika and Zhanna to dinner. Run by Gypsies, they knew they were welcome here. That was not the case at some restaurants in Barcelona. Even though most Spaniards had dark hair like the Roma, most Gypsies could be identified by their chestnut complexions. And in the case of the band members, it was especially easy to recognize them as Roma. They all spoke Spanish but with a Romanian accent.

"Are you looking forward to our tour in Morocco, Amy?" Cici asked.

After this weekend's performances at the Cordobes, the band would depart next week for Africa.

"Yes, I've never been there."

"Neither have I," Cici replied. "But I'm excited about it. What do you think we'll do after the tour?"

"I assume Petru will bring us back here until he can land us another tour. The Cordobes always wants us. If you could choose a tour, where would it be, Cici?"

"The United States is number one. If not there, then at least to South America."

Amy smiled. "I knew you'd say the United States. Like Petru said, if the band stays together, maybe someday we'll all make it back to the

169

States to perform." The band had been to the United States once before when Bernice Bristow, Rose's mother, hired them for a social event at the mansion. That's where Amy met them and is how she became a band member when she danced at the event. But that visit was only for three days and the band had no time to see any sites or experience American culture because of rehearsals.

"Why wouldn't the band stay together?" Cici asked.

"I don't know. I hope it will, but things can happen. Mitica just found out his wife is pregnant. Maybe he wouldn't want to travel that far away from her or take her on a long journey in her condition. Gypsy cimbalom players are not easily replaced, especially ones as expert as Mitica. He's the best cimbalom player I've ever heard, Gypsy or not."

Amy saw the downcast look in Cici's face.

"Forgive me, Cici. I'm being a croaker of doom and that's not my intention. We will all keep our hopes up that someday the band makes it to the United States."

[that evening—Arlington, Virginia]

Erika and Angelika met upstairs at the Lili Marlene. Zhanna was downstairs tending bar.

"Angelika," Erika said. "Rose called me from Philadelphia this afternoon. An agreement has been reached between Archibald Bristow's representatives and the owner of the property next door. The closure documents were sent to Archibald for his signature. Rose said blueprints will be drawn up and sent to us to look over and make any adjustments we want. The blueprints will include the first floor used as an extension of the café. On the second floor there will be two apartments, a two bedroom for me and Ada, and a one bedroom for Zhanna. That will leave a little bit of space on that floor for another storage room."

"One never can have too much storage area," Angelika said with her heavy German accent. "This is wonderful, Erika."

"Rose asked if you would like to have your studio apartment enlarged."

"No, my living quarters are adequate. Making my apartment bigger would only cut down on the storage area we have now."

"You're the perfect manager, Angelika."

"Work like this is all I know, Erika. I did it for twenty years at my Lili Marlene Café in Berlin. You rescued me out of East Berlin and purchased this café for me to manage. I owe you more than just being a good manager. I owe you my life."

"You owe me nothing, Angelika. Zhanna and I owe you thanks for hiding us when the Soviets were looking for us in East Berlin. Okay, when the blueprints arrive, we'll look them over and you can make any adjustments you want. Everyone who works for Archibald Bristow works quickly. I imagine his architects will have the blueprints to us soon."

"I went into the building next door on Monday when the . . . what is the word for someone who sells property?"

"A realtor."

"Yes, the realtor, was showing the building to Mr. Bristow's people. I think we could add about twenty more tables, which would give us thirty-two and leave room for a stage. If we eliminate the stage, we can have more tables, but with a stage we can bring in entertainment on the weekends and maybe on certain weekdays like Wednesday or Thursday. We have to increase our number of customers to have this generous offer from Mr. Bristow pay off for the café."

"Alright, Angelika. You're in charge of the café extension. Do what you want. If I ask for any changes to the blueprints it will only be about the apartments upstairs."

"Have you told Ada that you and she will be moving from your apartment in Washington?"

"Not yet. I don't like taking her from her school where she is doing so well, but after thinking it over, I'm sure Ada won't mind. She loves working here in the kitchen."

"Ada will do well at any school she attends, Erika. She has her mother's tennessee."

She had meant to say 'tenacity.'

Chapter 48

Preparing to leave

Barcelona, Spain
Four days later—Monday, 20 August 1951

The Barcelona Romanian Gypsy Orchestra completed its two-weekend contract with the Cordobes Tablao Flamenco this past weekend.

Now, on Monday, the band members and the four-man stage crew were packing up their clothes and the band's instruments and gear. They would leave for Morocco tomorrow morning. Instead of flying, which would get them to their first stop in Tangier in a couple of hours, they had decided to take an ocean liner to enjoy a leisurely cruise on the Mediterranean Sea. The liner would take about 26 hours to reach Tangier, but they would travel through the Strait of Gibraltar. None of the band contingent had ever done this and they thought it would be exciting to pass through the famous strait where one could see two continents. The continent on the starboard side would be Europe, then they could simply walk across the deck to the port side and see Africa.

Even with the additional travel time as compared to a flight, they would still arrive in Tangier Wednesday morning. That would leave adequate time for rehearsals and for the crew to address any stage issues.

[same day—Constanta, Romania]
Dragoș Luca had not yet replaced Marku, Ion, and Vasile, his longtime henchmen/advisors who were now dead. Yet he had placed in charge a man named Cezar to head the ten-man team that he would take with him to French Morocco. Cezar had been in charge of the villa's security team for six years.

Luca was now meeting in his villa with Cezar and the captain of Luca's ocean-going yacht.

"Cezar," Luca said. "I told you I wanted your ten best men. Do you have them prepared?"

"Yes, sir. And we have the weapons and equipment we will need already onboard the Som de Argint."

Luca turned to the captain. "How far is the voyage to the port in Casablanca and how long will it take us to get there?"

"It is 2,525 nautical miles. If we sail at 22 knots, we can be there in just under five days."

"Very well, we'll leave Thursday," Luca told both men. "That will put us in Casablanca next Tuesday. The band starts its tour this weekend in Tangiers. We will bypass that city. It's too near the Strait of Gibraltar and it's swarming with British servicemen. On the other hand, Casablanca is mostly just French or Berber locals and American tourists."

"Captain," Luca continued. "We have to be concerned with Amy Radu or any of her band members recognizing the Som de Argint if they were to be in the area of the dock in Casablanca. They have all been onboard."

The captain took a moment to glance at a chart he brought with him. "We can drop off you and the men in Casablanca, then we can move the ship to Rabat. There are adequate docking facilities there and it's only 55 miles up the coast."

"Very well," Luca said. "That will be our plan. Stay docked in Rabat. I have associates in the Moroccan underground who purchase our product. I will contact their Zaeim—the head man—and have him supply us with automobiles. Communication there has to be addressed. The locals speak Berber, Arabic, or French. Some in Casablanca hotels and restaurants speak English because of all the American tourists. I'll ask the Zaeim to give us drivers that can translate in Russian. It's doubtful he will have any that speak Romanian. After we capture the Gypsy, it's only a one-hour drive to Rabat. That will be faster than sailing the ship back to Casablanca to pick us up."

[same day—Arlington, Virginia]

The blueprints had been delivered on Friday. Erika and Angelika checked them over. Erika asked for no adjustments as far as the upstairs living quarters and extra storeroom were concerned. Angelika thought the stage downstairs was a bit too small and asked for it to be enlarged.

Today, Erika and Angelika sat talking to Jerry Drucker, the owner of Drucker Construction, whose company had remodeled the café's restrooms last winter. Archibald Bristow hired Drucker Construction quite often for construction projects on the eastern seaboard. This job was a small one; Drucker's company built multi-story office complexes, apartment buildings, and even remodeled skyscrapers, but whenever a project was needed by Bristow, big or small, Drucker always took charge himself to ensure the finished product would please the shipping magnate who never squabbled at Drucker's bid. They worked together with mutual respect.

"Alright," the tough as nails union employer said. "I've been sent the edited blueprints. Mr. Bristow wants this job done as quickly as possible and with top quality. I'll have a large crew here tomorrow. We'll convert the attached building first so we don't disrupt your business. After that's finished, we'll knock out the wall separating the present café from the extension. My men will be working around the clock. All I need from you broads is to just stay out of our way and keep everyone else out of our way."

"Okay, Mr. Drucker," Erika said. "All of us broads will stay out of your way. How long do you think it will take?"

"With the big crew I'm bringing in, and working around the clock, I'd say a week at the most, probably five days if we don't run into any plumbing problems with tapping the two new apartment bathrooms into the café's current sewer connection."

Chapter 49

Leroy is sidetracked

The Mediterranean Sea
Next night—Tuesday, 21 August 1951

The Italian ocean liner was now halfway to Tangier. The Barcelona Romanian Gypsy Orchestra would arrive in the Moroccan city tomorrow around noon. Amy stood alone on deck at midnight. A sliver of a pink moon hung high over the starboard bow. Far out to sea, there were no city lights to camouflage the breathtaking heavenly spectacle above her of shimmering, iridescent stars that filled the sky and seemed to be there for just one purpose, to glorify their Creator. The Gypsy raised her hands and prayed for the moon and stars to their Father, as she and her caravan clan had done in Transylvania every clear night when she was a youngster.

[later—that morning in Washington, D.C.]

Al Hodge sat in Leroy Carr's office at the CIA's E Street Complex.

"Al, I have to go to Korea. More problems there. I'm flying out Thursday. I'm not sure when I'll be back. I hope I'm not gone longer than a couple of weeks."

"What are the problems this time?" Hodge asked.

"There have been leaks. Our CIA station chief in Seoul suspects that at least one or maybe even two of our Korean assets are moles working for the communists in the north. While I'm gone, messages and communications to me here at E Street will be forwarded to you. You take charge. If anything comes up that you need the Director's okay, just go to him. He knows I'm putting you in charge of my day-to-day business."

"Is there anything pending I need to be aware of, Leroy?"

"Nothing that you don't know about. You already know that most of our problems right now, besides Korea, are in the Middle East and South America."

"Okay." Hodge said.

"The two Romanian women you brought back have completed their interrogations. They'll leave tomorrow for Fort Huachuca. The Shield Maidens and Ryker still have a couple of days to go with their debriefings. The reports will be on your desk when they finish. What's the latest on them?"

"Amy and that Gypsy band are on their way to Morocco for a three-city tour," Hodge replied. "She called before she left Barcelona." Amy was under orders to inform Al whenever she left Barcelona, including where she was going, dates, and where the band would be staying. "As far as Erika and Zhanna, they haven't been arrested yet for beating someone up or stealing a boat for a joy ride."

Carr chuckled. "Well, at least that's some good news."

"Get this, Leroy. Archibald Bristow bought the building next door to Erika's café as a gift to her for being his grandson's godmother. He's even picking up the tab for a total remodel job so the café can expand its number of tables. When it's completed, Archibald is also going to pay for some advertising for the café in the Times."

Carr shook his head in amazement. "There are a few guys out there with a whole lot of money, Al."

"Yeah. You and I need to become railroad and freighter tycoons," Hodge said whimsically. "You can handle the ships. I'll take the trains."

[that evening]

Crina and Sylvania walked into the Lili Marlene Café at ten minutes before seven o'clock, driven there by their CIA safehouse watchdog, who once again let them have their own space. He walked over to one of the pinball machines, dropped in a dime, and began playing as he kept an eye on his charges.

Angelika tended bar. The two Romanian women had learned one sentence in English and Sylvania used it. "Excuse me, do you speak Romanian or Russian?" The Romanian accent was extremely heavy but the words were understandable.

"No," Angelika said. "I speak Deutsch und English," Angelika answered. She knew the English word 'and' but still slipped up on occasion and used the German equivalent. "You were in here the other night. You want to see Erika and Zhanna. Zhanna's on break. They're both upstairs."

Crina and Sylvania didn't understand a word except for the names Erika and Zhanna. They gazed blankly at Angelika. The German realized this and held up a finger to signal them to wait for a moment. Angelika went into the kitchen and brought out Ada. "They don't speak English or Deutsch, Ada," Angelika said. "Take them upstairs to your mother."

Ada smiled sweetly and waved at the two women to follow her.

At the top of the stairs, Ada led the two women into the storeroom.

"Mutti, Miss Angelika told me to bring these two ladies to you."

"Thank you, Liebchen. I know these ladies."

Ada departed to return to the kitchen.

"Have a seat," Erika said in Russian.

The Romanians sat down next to Zhanna who was smoking a cigarette.

"You're late," Zhanna said. A safehouse guard had called the café that afternoon to tell them the two women had requested a trip to the café and that they would be there at 6:30. It was now 7:00.

"We just arrived," Sylvania responded. "The man who drives us had to park the auto two blocks away because of all the trucks on this street."

"Someone is remodeling the building next door," Erika replied and left it at that.

"Erika, we are so excited," Crina beamed. "Tomorrow, Sylvania and I leave for a place called Ass-azonia where they will teach us English. We will be there for some time, but a man named Mr. Carr told us that after we learn English we might be offered a job at the American Department of State as Romanian translators."

Erika new the real reason Leroy Carr was sending them to Fort Huachuca. He had his eye on sending them back behind the Curtain as CIA assets.

"That's good, Crina," Erika said. "I'm happy for you and Sylvania."

Chapter 50

Erika receives the news

Washington, D.C.
Three days later—Friday, 24 August 1951

Al Hodge sat behind his office desk at E Street reading various reports and communiqués. After an hour of doing such, he came across a message from Romania. It was sent by the CIA's Romanian mole in lower government in Bucharest. In Romania, any seagoing vessel that left Romanian waters had to apply for permission from the communist government and include all stops, dates, and when the ship would return to its home port. The communiqué relayed the information that the captain of Dragoş Luca's yacht had applied for permission to sail to Casablanca and Rabat in Morocco. The application was approved quickly because of Luca's standing with the country's Soviet overlords. Hodge checked the dates. They coincided with Amy Radu's date to be in Casablanca with the band. Luca's yacht had set sail yesterday.

[that evening]
Hodge walked into the Lili Marlene shortly before six o'clock. Zhanna was of course behind the bar. Erika was helping the café's two weekend waitresses deliver food and drinks to the customers at the tables.

Al approached Zhanna.

"What do you want, shithead," she said.

"I'm here to talk to Erika, smart ass."

"She's busy. Do you want a drink or are you going to stand there with your thumb up your ass?"

"Rogova, I hope you know that you're a pain in the butt. Give me a Maker's Mark on the rocks."

Zhanna went to pour the drink and returned. "That's two dollars," she said.

"You try and do this to me every time I'm in here. I know that drink sells for 75¢. Here's a buck." He laid a dollar bill on the bar.

"Okay, you cheap bastard." Zhanna snatched up the dollar bill. "Don't expect any change. The extra quarter is my tip."

Hodge ignored her as he saw Erika walk out from the swinging doors to the kitchen with two plates of food for customers.

Five minutes later, Hodge and Erika were upstairs seated at the storeroom table.

"It looks like the men next door are still working this late," Al commented. "I thought union construction workers knocked off at five."

"Archibald is paying for three shifts so it can be done quickly. They will even work around the clock this weekend. They started Tuesday. Yesterday, the owner of the construction firm told me they should be done Monday—Tuesday at the latest."

"I'm happy for you, Erika. I mean that."

"Thanks. What brought you here, Al? You usually don't come by unless there's more of a reason than to have dinner."

"That not true," he contested. "I've brought Mary here three or four times for a meal since you opened last year with no other agenda than having dinner."

Hodge lost his wife to cancer in the late-30s. Mary was a waitress who worked at the Hamilton Diner—a popular Arlington eatery best known for its 24-hour breakfasts. Al and Mary dated occasionally.

"That's true, Al. Sorry."

"I do have something to talk to you about this time, though. Amy and her band arrived in Tangiers on Wednesday. They're performing there tonight and tomorrow night."

"I know that, Al. Amy told me her schedule."

"Then you'll know that next weekend the band is playing in Casablanca. I found out this morning that the captain of Dragoş Luca's yacht applied for permission in Bucharest to sail to Casablanca and Rabat. According to the log, the ship left yesterday and makes a stop in Casablanca during the time Amy and her band will be in that city."

Erika gazed at him with her wolfish, hazel eyes that could seem yellow at times, depending on the light. "When do we leave?"

"I have to stay in Washington this time. Leroy will be in Korea for a couple of weeks. While he's away, I'm handling his daily business. You,"

Zhanna, and Ryker will be in my office at nine tomorrow morning for a briefing. You'll fly out Sunday from Andrews. I'll get you a DC-3."

"It should be a DC-4," Erika maintained. "They're faster."

"I'll get you a four if I can, but they're not always available. The State Department and military have first crack at fours. If you leave Sunday morning, taking into account refueling and maintenance stops, even a three can have you in Morocco by late Tuesday. Tell Zhanna about the briefing tomorrow and make sure she's there. I'll inform Ryker; he's still at the Mayflower because his debriefing about the failed Romanian mission isn't over yet."

Chapter 51

Tangiers

Washington, D.C.
Next day—Saturday, 25 August 1951

Erika Lehmann, Zhanna Rogova, and Axel Ryker were brought into Al Hodge's office by his secretary at 8:55 a.m.

Hodge pointed to a table along the back wall. "Coffee and cups are over there. Help yourselves."

Erika and Zhanna poured themselves a black coffee into a disposable paper coffee cup. Ryker passed on the coffee. He sat down in one of the chairs and lit a cigar.

After everyone took a seat, Hodge said, "Okay, this is what we know now about Dragoş Luca's schedule. The information comes from a Romanian national who fought the communists with the Romanian underground during the war. He now has a job working in the lower echelons of the Romanian government in Bucharest. He has no love for the Soviets and now works for us as an asset. We pay him, of course. Although he's lower level, he's privy to non-classified information such as flight logs and sea-going vessel logs.

"According to the asset, Luca's yacht will dock in Casablanca briefly on Tuesday, then sail to Rabat and tie up there. Rabat is only 55 miles up the coast from Casablanca. I couldn't requisition an Air Force DC-4, Erika. You all will fly out on a DC-3. Your stops for refueling will be at Saint John's in Newfoundland and another in Shannon, Ireland. Then the plane will fly you to the Canary Islands. The Canaries are only 60 miles from the Moroccan coast and the islands are a Spanish colony. If we land you there, we won't have to deal with the authorization demands of the Moroccan airports—information Luca might be privy to. I'll make sure our transport people have a launch in the Canaries ready to take you to Casablanca."

Hodge continued. "You decide on which hotel to stay at in Casablanca when you get there. Just remember that Luca will surely stay at one of the best hotels. I had our people in research look into this.

The two most expensive and swankiest hotels in Casablanca are the Sidi Maarouf Hotel and the Hotel La Casablanca. Amy and the band are staying in the Sidi Maarouf. Luca won't want to stay there and take the chance of running into her or a band member in an elevator or the bar. I'd guess he'll stay at La Casablanca. Luca will most likely have men monitoring Amy's hotel. You don't want to be seen there, so avoid both those hotels. Find a cheaper place to stay. Any questions?"

Erika asked, "Is Amy aware of this?"

"Luca doesn't arrive until Tuesday. Amy is scheduled to check in with me tomorrow. I'll tell her then about Luca and that you, Zhanna, and Axel are heading her way."

"Will the launch that takes us from the Canaries to Casablanca be at our disposal after we arrive. What if we have to go to Rabat?"

"The launch will dock at the Al Meena port in Casablanca and remain there for your use. There are sleeping quarters on the launch for the pilot and navigator. They'll remain onboard and be there to take you up or down the coast. Don't forget that Morocco is a Muslim country. You and Zhanna will need to dress moderately and wear head coverings in public."

[that evening in Tangiers]
The Barcelona Romanian Gypsy Orchestra was performing for their second night at the Gaeat Madinia—the civic auditorium in Tangiers. Last night was the band's first night in this city and the 1,000-seat venue was about three-quarters full. Word had gotten around and tonight the place was packed with standing room only.

Amy stood onstage under a spotlight singing the Gypsy song *Dacă aş fi o mierlă* (If I were a blackbird.)

Chapter 52

Al talks to Amy

Andrews Air Force Base, Maryland
Next day—Sunday, 26 August 1951

The construction work on the expanded café wouldn't be finished until tomorrow or Tuesday so Erika and Zhanna never got to see the finished project before they had to leave.

The two women and Axel Ryker boarded a twin-engine DC-3 at Andrews at 8:00 a.m. and took off into a light drizzle. Each brought along a dagger and a handgun, and then a weapon of their own choosing. Erika brought along a sawed-off shotgun, Zhanna her Mosin-Nagant sniper rifle, and Ryker a Thompson machinegun.

Other than the pilot, copilot, and navigator, they had the 25-seat plane to themselves. A large cooler of various sandwiches and soft drinks was aboard for them and the crew to access when they wished.

When the airplane climbed above the rain and headed toward a rainbow on its flight to Newfoundland, Ryker asked, "What are our priorities? Are we doing this to rescue the Gypsy or are our intentions to finish the job we started and capture Luca? We might have to choose between the two."

"We're not sacrificing Amy just to capture Luca," Erika retorted. "He's not worth it. Even Carr and Hodge agree. Amy's safety comes first, then, we'll talk about securing Luca. That will depend on how things are going at the time. We have to be flexible."

"It would be so easy to just kill him," Zhanna said firmly, still wanting her revenge for being forced to kill Jaro Banik. "I could be stationed on the roof of a building across from Luca's hotel. When he steps outside, one trigger pull and problem solved."

Erika responded, "If he kills Amy, then he dies. Otherwise, we'll work toward capture."

◊ ◊ ◊

[one hour later—Washington, D.C.]

One thing Al Hodge liked about Amy Radu was that, unlike her Shield Maiden leader, Amy reported in on schedule. The two were on the phone.

"Did it take you long to make your phone connections from Africa?" Hodge asked.

"Yes, nearly an hour."

"Where are you calling from?"

"A café three blocks from our hotel."

"Good. What's the latest from Tangiers?"

"We finished our performances last night," Amy answered. *"We're packing up tomorrow morning and leave for Casablanca in the afternoon. Instead of flying, Petru chartered a bus. Casablanca is only a four-hour drive. The bus can take us and the equipment directly to our hotel. This way we won't have the annoyance of getting instruments and other stage equipment from an airport. We should arrive around dinnertime."*

"Okay, Amy. There are some significant developments. Dragoş Luca is on his way to Casablanca on his yacht. He's scheduled to arrive sometime Tuesday. I see no other reason for him to go there when he knows you'll be there other than to undertake something bad. Erika, Zhanna, and Ryker flew out from Andrews this morning and will arrive in Casablanca sometime Tuesday evening. They will stay at a different hotel, but Erika will contact you when they arrive. Keep on your guard about Luca, Amy. Surely he has brought men with him. We don't know how many."

"Thanks for the heads up, Al."

Chapter 53

A surprise for Dragoş

Casablanca, French Morocco
Two days later—Tuesday, 28 August 1951

Al Hodge had nailed it when he guessed which hotel Dragoş Luca would stay in.

The Som de Argint docked at the Al Meena port in Casablanca at 5:30 p.m. Sedans sent there by the local, corrupt Zaeim were waiting to drive Luca, his men, and their equipment to the Hotel La Casablanca.

When Luca and his ten-man team debarked from the ship, the captain immediately pulled away from the dock and headed to Rabat, 55 miles north on the African coast.

[that evening in Casablanca]
The telephone in Amy Radu's hotel room rang. It came just in time, as Amy was getting ready to walk out the door to meet Cici and Mitica in the hotel bar.

"Buna ziuna." Amy said hello in Romanian, thinking the call was most likely from one of the band members.

"Amy, this is Erika. Did Al Hodge talk to you?" Erika spoke in English.

Amy switched to that language. "We talked Sunday. He told me about Luca coming to Casablanca, and that you, Zhanna, and Ryker are on your way."

"We are," Erika confirmed. *"We were scheduled to land in the Canary Islands this evening, but a lightning storm over the Bay of Biscay forced the plane down in Lisbon. That's where I'm calling from. We have to wait out the storm. That means we probably won't be in Casablanca until sometime tomorrow. I just got off the phone with Al. Stay away from the Hotel La Casablanca, Amy. Al confirmed that Luca and his men checked in there about an hour ago."*

"The Hotel La Casablanca. Thanks for the information, Erika."

Amy hung up.

185

"Amy . . . Amy!" Erika shouted into the phone then banged the receiver down hard on the cradle.

"Dammit!" she grumbled in frustration.

Zhanna and Ryker stood near to Erika in the row of red-painted, wooden telephone booths lining a long wall in the Lisbon terminal.

"What's wrong?" Zhanna asked.

"Amy is going to confront Dragoş Luca tonight."

[same evening]

Luca took all of his men to dinner tonight at the posh Hotel La Casablanca's main dining room. The waiters were Berbers who all wore full-sleeved, white djellabas—a sort of baggy dress that fell to the ankles and could be worn by both Berber men and women.

"That Gypsy band begins playing Friday at a place called Rick's Café," Luca said to the group during the meal. "They also perform on Saturday. After the Saturday performance is when we'll move in on the traitor to our country, Amy Radu. Capturing her alive is preferred, but if that's not possible, eliminate her. We'll take no chances that one of our own Romanian countrymen continues working for the American CIA."

"She's a Gypsy, not a pure blood Latin Romanian," Cezar said. "What else can you expect from a Gypsy?"

"I know what a Gypsy is," Luca said, annoyed. Radu is not a Latin Romanian, yet she was born in our country and that makes her a citizen and a traitor. I have no interest in a debate. You have my orders."

"I say we eliminate her and be done with it," Cezar spoke for the group.

"Who is paying you and your men your substantial salaries, and who has protected you from prosecution for your previous crimes before you joined me?" Luca scowled.

"You are, Dragoş."

"Do I need to say anything more?"

The chastised Cezar replied, "No, sir. My men and I are here to serve you."

[later]

Dragoş Luca awoke at 3:15 a.m. in his suite. Having to urinate, he took care of business and was returning to his bed when a shadow sitting in a chair in the corner of his bedroom said, "Hello, Dragoş."

The startled Luca froze.

The shadow turned on a desk lamp near the chair. It was Amy Radu. Resting on her lap was a .32 caliber Walther PPK with a sound suppressor attached to the muzzle.

"I didn't think we'd see each other again so soon," Amy said. "What brings you to Casablanca?"

"I'm a fan of the movie," Luca said.

Amy laughed. "Have a seat on the bed."

He sat down.

"I know your intentions, Dragoş. You're here to kill or capture me. Those could be the only reasons. Be careful."

"Be careful of what? You and the CIA? I conduct business with some of the most wicked men on four continents, Amy. Do you think you and your little handgun will intimidate me?"

"Go back to Constanta, Dragoş, while your operation is still intact. Leave tomorrow."

"Why are you giving me this advice?" Luca asked. "Why not just shoot me right now?"

"I'm trying to give you an option."

Luca looked at her for a long moment. "Then allow me to take you to dinner tomorrow night. We'll dine at Rick's Café where you perform this weekend."

It was in Amy's Gypsy blood to know how to manipulate men.

Chapter 54

Rick's Café Americain

Canary Islands, Atlantic Ocean
Next day—Wednesday, 29 August 1951

The United States Air Force DC-3 splashed down on a wet runway at the Gran Canaria Airport at 10:20 a.m.

The only three passengers aboard disembarked. On the tarmac, a man in a black suit stood waiting for them.

"I'm Agent Bedell." He showed them his CIA identification. "I'm here at Mr. Hodge's orders. I have a car waiting to take you to your launch."

"What's the weather like in Casablanca, Agent Bedell," Erika asked. "Hot I imagine."

"Yes, during the day it's hot, but the sea breezes cool the city at night. Nighttime is actually comfortable. Rain is rare in the Sahara, but a cool morning fog from the sea is common for coastal cities like Casablanca. Unfortunately, the sun burns off the fog quickly then the temperature starts rising."

◊ ◊ ◊

The speedy launch took only three hours to get the team from the islands to the Al Meena port. The first thing the team had to do was find a hotel that was not the Sidi Maarouf Hotel where Amy and the band had rooms, or the Hotel La Casablanca where Dragoş Luca and his men were staying.

Finding a hotel took longer than Erika expected. It was late afternoon before they checked into a grungy hotel in a rough neighborhood on the Rue El Kadissa, two doors down from an opium den and brothel.

The rooms had no telephones, so Erika told the disheveled drug addict at the check-in desk that she needed to make a telephone call.

The Frenchman pointed to a wall phone nearby and said, "If the call is local, it costs three dirham a minute. Long distance is much more. "

Three dirham was the equivalent of 33 American cents.

"It's local," Erika said. She didn't quibble over the man's ridiculously high price and went to the phone. She called the desk at the Sidi Maarouf and asked for Amy Radu's room in French. There was no answer. She then asked the hotel's switchboard operator for Cici's room. The violinist was there.

"Cici, this is Erika," she said in Russian that she knew Cici understood. "I'm in Casablanca and I'm trying to get in touch with Amy."

"Erika! How delightful that you're here. I don't know where Amy is. She told me she was going to dinner tonight with someone but she didn't say who or where they were going."

[that evening—Rick's Café Americain]
Three years ago a group of investors had come together to recreate the fictional café in the 1942 movie Casablanca. They modeled the café after Humphrey Bogart's establishment down to including a black pianist referred to as "Sam" who played *As Times Go By* at least four or five times every evening. The café was a hit with American tourists and the many French who held residence in the city. Morocco was a protectorate of France.

Dragoş Luca and Amy Radu were seated by a waiter in a white tuxedo who spoke English with a French accent.

"I don't speak French, and my English is not strong," Luca said. "You'll have to help me, my dear. By the way, you look lovely tonight."

"Thank you Dragoş," Amy replied. "Your tuxedo is quite dapper. Is that Savile Row?"

"Yes. I had it hand tailored during a stop in London. And your dress?"

"Nothing as exquisite as your tuxedo. I brought this with me from Barcelona. I bought it off the rack."

"It fits you perfectly. Of course, a woman as beautiful as you would be dazzling in rags."

The waiter returned for their drink orders.

189

"What is your best Champagne?" Luca asked him. Amy translated in English.

"We have one bottle of Barons de Rothchild Brut in our wine cellar. A 1937 vintage. I will tell you that it costs 2000 dirham, sir." That was the equivalent of slightly over $200.

Dragoş looked at the man with contempt. "I didn't ask you how much it cost. Bring it to our table."

The waiter bowed and said, "Yes, Monsieur," and walked away happy. His commission on the ultra-expensive wine would be substantial.

"Thanks for agreeing to dinner, Amy," Luca said. "This is a first for me."

"What do you mean?" she asked.

"I've never had a woman show up in my hotel room with a gun one night, and then taken her out to eat the next night."

Amy smiled but didn't reply.

The waiter returned quickly with the bottle of Barons de Rothchild, popped the cork, and poured two flutes. He sat the silver ice bucket on the table.

"May I take your dinner orders?" the waiter asked. Neither Luca nor Amy had yet looked at the menu.

"Come back in ten minutes," Luca told the Frenchman.

The man bowed and left.

Luca and Amy picked up the menus. It included popular American and Moroccan entrées. One of the entrées was named the Wyoming T-bone.

"I'll have the T-bone steak," Amy said.

When the waiter returned, Luca ordered two of the steak dinners.

As they drank the French Champagne and waited for their steaks, Luca said, "There is no need for us to be at odds, Amy. I now know that you are CIA, but I can still offer you a high position in my organization. With your knowledge of international intelligence gathering, you would be my top advisor in that field with a salary much greater than what the CIA is now paying you."

Amy waited as she took a sip from her flute. "Give me a few days to think it over, Dragoş."

"Very well, but after dinner, accompany me to my suite where we can talk further."

◊ ◊ ◊

Erika called Amy's hotel room at half-hour intervals throughout the evening. She even called Cici again. It was now almost midnight and Amy still had not returned. The Shield Maiden leader went back to her seedy room after summoning Zhanna and Ryker. A mouse scampered under the bed when the lights were turned on.

"Amy still hasn't returned to her hotel. Going out to dinner shouldn't keep her out this late."

"Maybe she didn't go out to dinner," Zhanna said. "Maybe she just told Cici that and she went after Luca."

"That's what I'm afraid of," Erika replied.

"I'll go by Luca's hotel and see if he's there," Ryker offered.

"We can't do that, Axel. We have to avoid both Luca's and Amy's hotel. We don't want Luca knowing we're here so we obviously can't show up at his hotel, and he might have men watching Amy's hotel."

"Then we're going to do nothing," Ryker grouched. "I'm disappointed in you, Sonderführer."

Erika gave him an icy stare. "The band takes breakfast together. I'll call Cici in the morning. If Amy's not at breakfast, we'll go after Luca."

Chapter 55

Adapting

Casablanca, French Morocco
Next day—Thursday, 30 August 1951

At 9 a.m. the phone in Cici's room rang.

"Buna ziuna."

"Cici, this is Erika," she said in Russian. *"Have you seen Amy this morning?"*

"Da, we just had breakfast and she's here right now."

Erika breathed a sigh of relief. *"Put her on the phone, please."*

"Hello, Erika."

"Amy are you alright?"

"I'm fine."

"I know Cici doesn't understand English, but even so, we need to keep conversation over the phone brief. When is your rehearsal today?"

"Not until this afternoon."

"Good. We'll meet at the Café Tambourine in one hour. It's on the Rue Lahcen Basri a half-block north of the Boulevard Anfa. It's too far to walk from your hotel. You'll have to take a taxi. Make sure you're not followed."

[one hour later]

It was already 95 degrees in Casablanca. It would be hotter this afternoon. The turbaned taxi driver spoke only Arabic, but when Amy mentioned the café's name he knew where to go. When they arrived in front of the Café Tambourine, she paid him and walked inside. Erika, Zhanna, and Ryker where already seated at a table. Amy walked over and sat down. A carafe of Turkish coffee sat on the table. Erika poured her a cup then wasted no time.

"Where were you last night, Amy?"

"I spent the night with Dragoș Luca in his hotel room."

Everyone stared at her for a moment.

"Why?" Erika asked.

"I know why he came here. It has to be to either kill or capture me. I'm stalling him. I don't want anyone in the band to get caught up in all this and get hurt or even killed. He offered me a job if I left the CIA. I don't know if it's a ploy or not but it should give us a little time. I told him I needed time to think it over and I'd let him know before we leave Casablanca for Marrakesh next week. If he is sincere, this will give us the time we need to finish the mission we started in Romania."

"I admire the Gypsy's courage," Ryker said.

"I agree," Erika said. "However, if it is a ploy, Luca could strike at any time. I wonder how many men he has with him."

Amy replied, "I don't know. Clearly, I couldn't ask him that question."

Erika nodded. "Good work, Amy, but this changes everything. Zhanna, Axel, and I are staying in a rat trap hotel in a rundown, squalid neighborhood. Here's the phone number." Erika handed Amy a small piece of paper. "There's only one telephone in the place and it's near the check-in desk that's run by a Frenchman who's a heroin addict. The needle marks on his arm can't be missed. Hopefully he'll let one of us know that you're calling but I wouldn't bet my life on it."

Zhanna took a drag on a cigarette and asked Erika, "What do you mean when you said, 'This changes everything'?

"It means the three of us will have to be at the café the band is performing at tomorrow night."

"Last night, Luca said he'd be there," Amy said.

"With his men, surely" Erika replied. "We have to know what we're up against."

"Luca will spot you," Amy said. "Rick's Café is a much smaller venue than we normally play."

Erika said, "This is what we'll do. I'm the only one amongst us who speaks French. I'll go somewhere this afternoon and buy a wig and go to the café in disguise. Zhanna, you'd be too hard to disguise from Luca because of your height and neck scarf, and there is no way to disguise Ryker because of his size and facial scars. Both of you will remain hidden outside the café. Zhanna, take your rifle and station yourself somewhere atop a building that will give you a clear view of the café entrance. Axel, you'll stay hidden somewhere on the street."

193

"There's an alley across the street from the café," Amy said.

"That will do," Ryker said.

Amy mentioned, "Erika, I talked with Al Hodge on Sunday when he told me about Luca coming to Casablanca, and that you three were on your way. He said you're late with your scheduled check-in."

"I know I am, Amy. I'll call Al when I find the time."

Chapter 56

Undercover

Rick's Café Americain
Next day—Friday, 31 August 1951

The Barcelona Romanian Gypsy Orchestra was scheduled to take the stage at 8 p.m. Dragoş Luca and his men arrived at just after seven, taking up two tables. Because the main clientele of Rick's Café were American tourists or French locals, English or French was spoken by the mostly French waiters and other staff. This created a problem for Luca and most of his men who spoke only Romanian or Russian. A few of the French waiters spoke acceptable German they learned during the German occupation of Morocco during the war. Luckily, one of Luca's men spoke German and could communicate with a waiter who understood that language. They ordered drinks and dinner.

Unnoticed by Luca, a brunette wearing eyeglasses with tinted yellow lenses walked in and found a seat at the bar. She ordered cognac in French from one of the three bartenders.

"Mademoiselle," the bartender said. "We asked that unaccompanied ladies not sit at the bar."

"You ask," the brunette said. "Does that mean there's a law against it?"

"Ah . . . no, Mademoiselle," he replied.

"Then Monsieur, please give me my drink. Thank you."

Outside, a Russian woman wearing a neck scarf was on the flat roof of a three-story warehouse across the street loading her Mosin-Nagant. A brutish man wearing a black pork pie hat stood below in the shadows of an alley.

Eight o'clock neared. The black pianist called Sam played *As Time Goes By* then left the piano. A man appeared at the microphone on stage.

"Ladies and gentlemen," he said in English. "Tonight and tomorrow night we have performing for you a unique group. The Barcelona Romanian Gypsy Orchestra is the most popular Gypsy Flamenco band in Spain. They often tour Mediterranean cities where they perform in front of sold-out crowds in large auditoriums. Our café is much smaller than what they are used to, and we're pleased they agreed to perform here this weekend during their three-city tour in Morocco."

He paused then repeated what he said in French.

"Without further ado, Rick's Café Americain gives you the Barcelona Romanian Gypsy Orchestra!"

The band walked on stage to polite applause. Amy wore a bright green full-length dress. As always, the first thing she did was introduce her bandmates. The lights dimmed slightly in the café but left sufficient light for dining. On stage, instead of Amy starting out singing a song, the band started playing and Amy began stomping to a Gypsy Flamenco dance called *Moartea Porumbeilor*—The Death of the Doves.

◊ ◊ ◊

Four men wearing Berber headdress walked through the alleyways near Rick's Café. They did this from time to time, looking to prey on Americans who were all considered rich. In the alley across the street from the café, they spotted a large Caucasian man and walked up behind him. He turned to look at them.

All of the Berbers drew knives. One of the gang said in English a phrase he had learned. "Money. Give us your money."

Ryker quickly grabbed the knife hand of the leader, twisted it and stuck the man in the shoulder with his own knife. He then grabbed another man and snapped his arm at the elbow. All four men ran away, with the two injured ones squealing.

◊ ◊ ◊

The band had played for a half-hour when Amy left the stage for the first of her wardrobe changes. While she was gone, Cici played a solo on her violin; a Croatian song called *Cigani Ljubiat Pensnji* (Gypsy Love Song).

While Cici played, Cezar told Luca, "Let's move on this Amy Radu after she leaves this place tonight. I have a plan in place."

"I've already told you not tonight," Luca answered. "And I'll decide on the plan. I offered her a job as a ruse so she would drop her guard.

We'll capture her tomorrow night after the show. Cezar, I want nothing to happen at this café. It's too public. You and your men will follow her to her hotel, wait outside to give her a chance to get settled in her room, and then grab her in her room. This way there will be no witnesses or 'heroes' trying to interfere.

"After you have the Gypsy, pick me up at our hotel and we'll immediately drive to the ship in Rabat."

The brunette with the tinted spectacles had moved from the bar. There were no empty tables in the popular café, so she asked an American couple sitting at a table behind Luca if she could join them. This allowed Erika to overhear what he said.

To the couple she sat with, Erika excused herself for a moment and walked outside. She lit a cigarette, took one puff and dropped it in the gutter. This was the agreed upon signal to Zhanna and Ryker that they were to take no action. She then walked back into the café.

Chapter 57

Time for Amy to leave

Casablanca
Next day—Saturday, 01 September 1951

This morning, the CIA team met again at the Café Tambourine, this time for a traditional Moroccan breakfast that included a fried egg served in olive oil with a wedge of cream cheese and a couple of Dark Moroccan olives. Then 'jiben' – a sour goats' milk cheese that's eaten on its own with sweet mint tea was served.

"Unless Luca has more men he didn't bring to the performance last night," Erika said, "he has ten. They took up two tables. Luca wasn't truthful in offering you that job, Amy. Last night I overheard him tell his men that it was just a ploy to get you to drop your guard. They plan on making their move after tonight's performance when you get back to your hotel room. Then taking you to Luca's yacht in Rabat. We can't interfere at the hotel because Luca won't be with them until after they get to you. Amy, you'll have to allow yourself to be captured. Zhanna, Axel, and I will be at the dock in Rabat when you arrive."

Amy was almost relieved. "At least none of the band will get caught up in the crossfire."

[same morning]
The Som de Argint had no telephone land lines aboard the ship for obvious reasons, only short-wave radios. Because he had no practical way of contacting the captain, Dragoș Luca sent one of his men to Rabat. It was only a one-hour drive.

The message the man relayed to the captain was that Luca wanted the ship fully fueled and otherwise prepared for departure tonight. The messenger was back in Casablanca by lunchtime.

After the man left, the captain called together the eight-man crew. First he spoke to the two crewmen of the 'black gang.' These were the men in charge of the engine room. Such crewmembers were referred to as the black gang on most large ships because they were often covered with oil.

"Fire up the engines this afternoon for a testing," the captain said. "We sail tonight."

He then turned to the two cooks. "How are our provisions?"

"We have plenty, more than we need for a return voyage to Constanta," one replied.

"Good. But check them again. If there is anything else you need, you can go into Rabat this afternoon."

The other four members of the crew consisted of the captain's executive officer who manned the wheelhouse when the captain was in his quarters sleeping, the navigator, and the boatswain whose duties were many including keeping the deck clean.

The captain told the boatswain, "Make sure Mr. Luca's quarters are clean and in order."

[that evening—Rick's Café Americain]
Tonight, it was only Luca and Cezar inside the café. A carload of Luca's men waited outside. They would follow Amy Radu to her hotel. A second carload sat outside the Hotel Sidi Maarouf waiting for her to return there after the show.

Word about the Barcelona Romanian Gypsy Orchestra had spread throughout Casablanca after last night's performance and the café was crammed. Many people had to stand along the walls. Luca and Cezar had arrived early enough to get one of the last tables available.

Onstage, the band was now in it's last of three sets. As always for the last set, Amy had changed into her attire of a head scarf, a peasant blouse, and the colorful tribal skirt of her Roma clan.

Tonight the crowd was much more energetic as compared to the Friday crowd that wasn't quite sure what to expect. At one point, an American wearing a cowboy hat and boots stood up from his table and began dancing a jig and shouting. "Yee hah!" Others, mostly Americans, rose to their feet at certain points in the performance. The last song was the lively Djelem Djelem which Amy sang under a spotlight. When the

199

band finished and took its bow, everyone stood for a standing ovation and shouted either, "Bravo!" or "Encore!"

The band left the stage. The shouts of "Encore!" grew louder. The band returned to the stage to great shouting, whistling, and applause. The band played and Amy sang the energetic song *Od Ebrado do Dunava* as the crowd clapped along. That song ended the band's performances at Rick's Café Americain.

◊ ◊ ◊

A half-hour later, Amy had changed out of her performance attire and left with the rest of the band members in two sedans to return to the Hotel Sidi Maarouf. The 4-man stage crew would follow them back to the hotel a little later, after packing up all the instruments.

"I'm very tired," Amy told the band before they left Rick's Café. "Tonight I will skip the post-performance meal and go straight to bed." She said this to discourage any band members from stopping by her room that night.

Petru thought this odd. Amy had always enjoyed the after-show dinners where the band dined alone.

◊ ◊ ◊

When the band returned to the Sidi Maarouf, Amy went straight to her room. The rest of the band gathered in the hotel restaurant for their late dinner.

Amy was expecting some of Luca's men to be inside her room, but when she entered and flipped on the lights she was alone. This didn't last long.

Ten minutes later a knock came on her door. It was a waiter from room service pushing a cart. Amy let him enter. On the cart was an iced down bottle of Champagne and a bowl of strawberries. Luca's man had been taught the English words:

"Miss Radu. This is compliments of Rick's Café in appreciation of your group's performances this weekend."

200

Amy nearly grinned at Luca's man speaking English with a Romanian accent but remained pokerfaced.

"How kind," she told the man. "I'll have to send the café's manager a thank you note before we leave for Marrakesh on Monday."

He understood only the word Marrakesh. He pulled a handgun and told her in Romanian, "You're not going to Marrakesh."

Suddenly three more of Luca's men barged into her room with guns drawn.

They gave Amy five minutes to pack her bag then took her from the hotel and loaded her in one of the two cars. They drove back to the La Casablanca Hotel to pick up Dragoş Luca. Amy was transferred to a third car, a two-door Renault sedan, and placed into the back seat alongside Cezar.

In a moment, Luca emerged from the hotel and got in the front seat next to the driver.

"You checked her for weapons, of course." Luca asked Cezar in Romanian.

"Yes," Cezar answered. "She had a dagger strapped to her leg and another one in her suitcase. We found a Walther PPK in the dresser beside her bed. We collected them all. She's unarmed. Shall I handcuff her?"

"I don't think that will be necessary," Luca replied. "She's in the back seat of a two-door sedan. She can't open a door and fling herself out."

Luca signaled the driver to get moving. One car of men took the lead, the other car took up the rear. Luca's car was protected in the middle.

He then addressed Amy. "We'll have an enjoyable voyage back to Constanta, my dear. Ample good food is aboard, along with plenty of Champagne and Tuică. By the way, as in Romania, I enjoyed your performances immensely."

"What are your plans for me?" Amy asked.

"You'll be turned over to the Soviet MGB. I'm sure that will include lengthy interrogations. What happens to you after that will be up to them. But we won't dwell on that; we'll enjoy the drive to Rabat. The road is concrete the entire way thanks to the Germans who constructed it for their military vehicles during the war."

◊ ◊ ◊

The two railroad locomotive engines that powered the Som de Argint's two massive screws had to be started and warmed up for an hour before sailing. One started up, then a few minutes later the second.

In the bowels of the ship, Axel Ryker spoke to the two members of the black gang in Russian, "You will follow orders without question. Do you understand?"

Both men nodded yes nervously.

Ryker then climbed the ladder and closed and locked the hatch to the engine room sealing the men in. He returned to the wheelhouse where Erika and Zhanna had the captain and the rest of his crew under guard. The CIA team had simply walked up the gangplank and boarded the ship.

◊ ◊ ◊

Midnight approached and the dock in Rabat was lonely. The only sign of activity was taking place five piers away where men worked through the night unloading a freighter that had just arrived from Johannesburg. The three cars carrying Luca, Amy, and the drug lord's ten henchmen pulled up to the pier where the Som de Argint was docked. Everyone exited the cars and began walking up the gangway. Luca heard his yacht's engines running. He was pleased that the captain had the ship ready for a quick departure.

As soon as Luca reached the deck, the gunfire began and Luca's men started dropping, either on the deck or falling off the gangplank into the harbor waters. The men pulled their handguns and started firing blindly, not sure where the gunfire came from. Zhanna had placed herself on the top of the ship's bridge and was doing the most damage with her sniper rifle. It was easy pickings for her as she was expert at kill shots from much farther away.

Amy had no idea the attack would take place on the ship, but she knew they wanted Luca alive so she instinctively grabbed him and took him prone to the deck. This allowed Erika and Ryker to step out on the deck without worry of Luca getting killed in the crossfire. With Erika's shotgun and Ryker's Thompson machine gun, they dropped more of Luca's men. The two left alive scrambled back down the gangplank and took cover behind the cars.

Erika ran up to the wheelhouse and told the captain to sail immediately. He told the boatswain to retract the gangplank then he reached the engine room through the intercom. In a moment, the engines revved and the Som de Argint began slowly backing away from its pier. As the ship began moving, Zhanna kept firing onto the dock to ensure the two men who survived kept their heads down.

When the ship was far enough out to sea, Ryker threw the bodies of the men who died on the deck overboard.

Chapter 58

A change for the captain

Atlantic Ocean
Next day—Sunday, 02 September 1951

Through the early morning fog, the Som de Argint sailed up the African coast toward Gibraltar. Erika Lehmann entered the wheelhouse.

"Change of plans, Captain," she said. "We're not sailing through the Strait. Have your navigator set a course for Washington, D.C."

Instead of sailing to the nearby Canary Islands where a plane waited for them, Erika decided to take Luca *and* his ship to the States. Sylvania had told her that Luca's secrets were hidden on the ship, not in his villa, so she knew that delivering the ship was as important as delivering Luca.

The navigator was also in the wheelhouse. After checking his charts, he said, "Captain, that journey is 3,822 nautical miles."

The Captain told Erika, "That's five days at sea."

"That's fine," she replied. "You said last night that there were enough fuel and provisions onboard for the four-day voyage back to Constanta. This voyage is only one day longer. I know there has to be enough fuel and food onboard. No captain would take on only enough fuel and food for the exact length of a planned trip. They would make sure to have extra.

"I know that you were aware of Luca's line of business, but if you and your crew cooperate fully, I will tell my superiors that all of you were but pawns of Luca. After some questioning, you will be released. All we want is Luca and this ship. Do we have an agreement?"

The captain looked at the navigator. "Change course for Washington." Then to Erika, "At sea, my duty is first and foremost to protect the ship and my crew. We have an agreement."

"Wise decision, Captain. Luca will stay locked in his quarters and take his meals there. You won't have to deal with him. We checked his lodgings thoroughly and found only a handgun. We know there is a substantial cache of weapons onboard. Where are they?"

"Inside a hidden storage area in the bow of the ship."

"Have your executive officer show my associate, Axel Ryker, this location. He'll take an inventory. Are there any drugs onboard?"

"No. Luca would never allow that. He isn't stupid. Too easily uncovered by dogs during port inspections. All of the drugs are shipped by freighters using obscure ports with sub-standard security procedures that are run by port commanders who can be bribed."

[that afternoon—aboard the Som de Argint]

All of the Shield Maidens and Ryker had experience using a shortwave radio transmitter. Erika spent an hour encrypting a message, then entered the radio room located directly behind the wheelhouse. She shut the door and began tapping the coded message on the radio's key. It was a message for Al Hodge in Washington, but she sent it to the Canary Islands to forward to him. She didn't include the ship's radio call numbers so Hodge couldn't call her back and order her to take the ship to London or some other place. She was dead set on getting Luca and the ship to the States. This would turn a failed mission into a success *and* get them home.

[that evening]

The ship's crew and the CIA group met for a cod dinner in the galley.

Erika said to the crew. "I asked for this dinner together tonight to make sure everyone understands what the captain told you earlier about our concord. After tonight, you can all return to your normal routine. You can dine together without our supervision. My group will eat after you're done. The black gang will be released; they can come and go from the engine room as they wish. Only Dragoş Luca is our prisoner. He'll stay in his opulent room. He has restroom facilities in there and his meals will be taken down by Amy. There is no reason for him to leave his quarters."

"We know you are CIA," the executive officer said boldly. "Luca told us. The CIA is well known for its many deceits. Why should we believe you'll keep your end of the bargain?"

Ryker piped in, "You have no options, other than to disobey orders, in which case I'll personally throw you overboard. Sharks need food."

"My friend summed it up well," Erika said. "Cooperate and receive fair treatment in the United States or die. Last night you witnessed us eliminate most of Luca's experienced killers. All were armed. If you think you can do better unarmed, that's choice is yours. You need us more than we need you. If all of you are eliminated and the ship went dead in water in the middle of the Atlantic, we could radio for a U.S. Navy ship to pick us up. With the vast fleet the American Navy has in the Atlantic, we probably wouldn't have to wait more than a day for a warship to reach us. But we don't want that so you have your deal. Keep it if you want to live."

The boatswain, the lowest man on the ship's crew totem pole, spoke up, "I will keep the agreement. I want to go to America." Both of the cooks agreed. Neither of those crewmen were aware of Luca's nefarious dealings; they just knew he was rich.

The bearded Captain said, "I agreed to the proposal this morning. That means all of the crew will cooperate, including my executive officer."

[9 p.m. that evening]

The Som de Argint was now about 350 miles out to sea off the African coast, heading west-northwest. The CIA team stood outside the bridge drinking some of Dragoș Luca's Tuică. Erika, Ryker, and Zhanna smoked expensive, hand-rolled Nicaraguan cigars that Ryker had found in one of the ship's many pantries. Amy smoked a Turkish cigarette.

Unfortunately, star gazing was not possible due to a cloud-covered sky.

Zhanna had a complaint, "I can't believe that asshole Luca doesn't have any vodka onboard. Beer, wine, and this shit made out of plums is what he has. Who makes liquor out of plums?"

"Tuică is the post popular drink of my country, Zhanna," Amy said.

"Fuck Romania and the idiot who makes liquor out of plums."

Amy took no offense. She knew it was just Zhanna being Zhanna.

The humorless Ryker changed the subject. "Should we be concerned with the attitude of that executive officer? If so, we should make an example of him."

"We'll keep a close eye on him," Erika said after she blew out a waft of cigar smoke. She didn't inhale the smoke; she only puffed on the cigars. "I think he'll be okay. He's helpless and smart enough to know it."

Erika continued, "Amy, when you took Luca his dinner tonight, did he say anything?"

"Not a word. He only glared at me. I loved it."

Erika didn't insult Amy by asking if she wanted one of the team to accompany her when she took Luca his meals. She knew the Shield Maiden trained by both the Israeli Mossad and the CIA needed no help handling Luca.

"Okay," Erika said. "Starting tomorrow we'll take Luca breakfast and dinner and eliminate lunch. A guy confined to a room who gets little exercise doesn't need three squares a day."

Part 6

Chapter 59

A call to Moscow

Bucharest, Romania
Next day—Monday, 03 September 1951

Cezar was one of the two men who survived the gunfire on the Som de Argint. He now sat in General Kulikov's office at MGB headquarters.

"Take a seat," the general ordered. "My adjutant tells me you have important news about Dragoş Luca. Let's start with the basics. Who are you?"

"My name is Cezar Dalca. I am Mr. Luca's supervisor of security for his villa in Constanta."

"What's this news you have?"

"Mr. Luca has been captured and his yacht commandeered by four CIA agents."

Kulikov stared at him for a moment. "When did this happen?"

"Late Saturday night, General."

"Saturday! Why did you wait so long to report this?"

"I thought the CIA agents might take the Gypsy singer back to Barcelona so I drove to the Strait and got a ferry to the British side. I reported to the authorities in Gibraltar that the ship had been hijacked and a hostage was onboard, but the ship never showed up. It's obvious the CIA is sailing the ship somewhere else."

Kulikov buzzed his secretary. "Send in Major Dubinin. He should be at his desk."

"Mr. Cezar Dalca, you're under arrest."

"What! Why?"

An MGB major walked in.

"Major, this man is under arrest. Transport him to our stockade in Otopenia."

Cezar interrupted. "What are the charges? I have done nothing but inform you of what is taking place!"

"Get him out of here, Major."

The MGB major roughly handcuffed Cezar's hands behind his back and forced him out of the General's office.

When the major and prisoner were gone. Kulikov sat back in his chair and lit a cigarette. He knew Luca kept all his paperwork in a hidden safe on his yacht. This included all his drug distributors in several continents and possible information on weapons deals in the middle east and to warring tribes and countries in Africa. That could be damning information for the Soviet Union, as Luca served as the middleman to prevent direct contact between the weapons supplier and buyer.

He assumed the CIA agents were sailing the ship to the United States. He could not let that happen. He picked up his desk telephone and dialed a direct line to Moscow.

[same day—Washington, D.C.]

Leroy Carr returned from Korea last night. Al Hodge was in his office.

"Leroy, glad you're back. Before you get started on Korea, Lehmann's team captured Dragoş Luca."

"I thought that mission was over when they left Romania."

"It's a long story," Al said. "In a nutshell, we found out Luca was sailing his yacht to Casablanca to coincide with the times Amy and her band would be performing there. I sent Erika, Zhanna, and Ryker there to back up Amy."

"Where is Luca now?" Carr asked.

"Get this, Leroy. The hooligans not only captured Luca they pirated his ship. They're sailing the bastard to Washington on his own yacht."

Both men broke out laughing.

"Can we reach the ship with shortwave?" Carr asked.

"Are you kidding? You know Lehmann isn't going to give us the ship's call numbers in case we tell her to do something she doesn't want to do. She routed the message to me through the Canary Islands."

"Alright, Al. Let's give her some help. Go to the Pentagon and talk to the Naval Department—Admiral Doerner is in charge of the Atlantic fleet. We'll assume Erika will have the ship take the shortest route home. Tell the Admiral we'd appreciate it if he would assign a ship somewhere near that route to search for the yacht and escort it to D.C. With the recent improvements in radar, the yacht shouldn't be hard to find. You better do that now. We'll talk about Korea when you get back."

[that evening—Atlantic Ocean]
The Som de Argint was now 900 nautical miles out to sea. The CIA team had taken their dinner in the galley seating area an hour ago and they now all stood on deck. The team had spent much of the day searching the ship for Luca's safe without success. However, Ryker had found a bottle of Scotch and an expensive Ketel vodka in another pantry. Finding the vodka made Zhanna happy.

"Amy," Erika said. "How's Luca doing?"

"Defiant. When I took him his dinner, I asked him about the safe. He laughed and said we'd never find it. He said the captain doesn't even know where it is."

"Well, at least that confirms the captain's story," Erika replied.

Ryker offered, "Give me ten minutes with Luca and he will tell me where the safe is."

"Axel, you can get carried away. Our original mission was to capture Luca alive. We've finally now done that. The safe will be found. If we don't find it, when we get the ship to Washington, Hodge will have men disassemble this ship rivet by rivet and weld by weld until it's found."

Business was dropped. The group took advantage of the fresh sea air and the spectacle in the sky. The total overcast of last night was gone, shoved aside by the moon and a few wispy clouds that occasionally raced across its face as if the Heavens played hide and seek.

"I wonder what Count Lupei is doing right now?" Erika asked.

Amy, the Transylvanian Gypsy, answered. "It's a full moon. He's probably out in the forest singing to his children of the night."

Chapter 60

Red sky

Atlantic Ocean
Next day—Tuesday, 04 September 1951

The dawn revealed a brilliant red sky. This concerned the captain of
the Som de Argint. He had his executive officer, who doubled as the
ship's radio operator, see if he could reach any ships ahead for a
weather report. A Brazilian freighter 300 miles due west answered the
Morse code transmission, warning them to turn back or alter course.

Yet, radio transmissions cannot be focused in one direction. Three
hundred miles to the northeast, a Soviet corvette, the Ezhr, picked up
the signal. So did the U.S. submarine the USS Swordfish operating on
the surface 250 miles to the northwest. Lookouts with binoculars
stood on the conning tower.

[later that day]
The Som de Argint had enough fuel on board to reach Washington on a
direct course but altering that route might require a stop in the
Caribbean to take on more fuel. Erika ordered the captain to stay the
course. The afternoon rain at first was just a drizzle; it intensified to a
torrent in less than an hour. Then the wind moved in.

[Washington, D.C]
Because of the time zones differences, the message from the Swordfish
to the fleet's flagship aircraft carrier was relayed to Washington
shortly after lunchtime. The CIA was notified shortly thereafter.

"The weather report request has to be from them, Leroy," Hodge
said. "Under international maritime law, for a response to any 'calling
all ships' transmission, the ship's radio operator has to identify the
flag the ship sails under and give its coordinates. In this case it's
Romanian and we now know its latitude and longitude. We now have

212

them on radar. They're about halfway across the Atlantic and sailing directly into a helluva of a storm—25-foot waves, high winds, heavy rain."

"The sub will be okay," Carr said. "All it has to do to get out of the storm is submerge so it can stay its course to intercept Luca's yacht. The only problem with submerging is it cuts the sub's speed in half."

"Yeah, but it's by far the closest of our ships to the yacht. There's another potential problem, Leroy. The fleet's aircraft carrier picked up a ship on radar that altered its course just after the transmission—a course that will intersect the yacht's route. The fleet admiral onboard the carrier can't send up planes to identify it. They would have to fly into the storm."

[after dark that evening—Atlantic Ocean]

Everyone onboard the Som de Argint held on to whatever was handy. The captain sat in his chair in the wheelhouse with a safety harness around his waist. The waves had now reached 30 feet. The captain steered the ship directly into them which was the only option. If the ship got turned sideways and stuck in a trough between waves it would be disastrous.

The bow of the ship raised out of the water with every wave then crashed down, sending a flood over the hatched down deck. Then the stern would rise from the water and the exposed churning screws caused the entire ship to vibrate madly and put heavy stress on the engines.

Suddenly, one of the two lifeboats mounted on the deck midships broke loose and dangled over the port side rail suspended there only by its rope. With every wave the lifeboat would bang hard on the ship.

"That lifeboat has to be cut away," the captain said loudly. It was more of a yell so he could be heard over the racket of the storm.

Erika was in the wheelhouse along with Axel Ryker. Zhanna was in the engine room with the black gang and Amy stood outside Dragoş Luca's room in case the storm swamped the ship in which event she would shoot him rather than take the chance he would somehow survive.

213

"We'll cut away the lifeboat," Erika told the captain.

"Stay here, Sonderführer," Ryker said. "I will do it."

"One person can't do it. We'll both go," Erika insisted.

The wheelhouse was located on the deck, underneath the bridge. All Erika and Ryker had to do to get on deck was open a door hatch. The captain turned on the deck lights while Erika and Ryker waited until the ship crested the next wave. Then they quickly opened the watertight door and stepped out. That part was easier than getting the hatch closed which took great effort in the high wind on the tossing ship. It took Ryker, with his almost superhuman strength, to close the door.

Holding onto the rail, Erika and Ryker fought their way forward. Climbing the next wave, the ship seemed to be pointed almost straight at the sky. Then came the inevitable crashing down on the other side of the crest. The powerful flood of water almost sent Erika overboard, but Ryker grabbed her.

Drenched to the bone, it took them ten minutes and two more waves to reach the suspended lifeboat.

"Hang on to me," Erika shouted to Ryker. "I'll cut it away."

With his vice-like grip. Ryker locked onto the rail with his left hand and grabbed the back of her pants and belt with his right as Erika let go of the rail. She drew her dagger and began cutting. Even though the knife was razor sharp, it took multiple swipes to cut through the 2-inch-thick rope. Finally, the rope was severed and the lifeboat slammed into the water.

Now they had to make it back to the wheelhouse.

Chapter 61

A profitable find

Atlantic Ocean
Next day—Wednesday, 05 September 1951

Never was a new day more welcome by the Romanian crew of the Som de Argint. At breakfast time, the sea was still choppy, but the five-foot waves were a weak stepchild of the previous night's gale. Although it had proved to be a mighty struggle, Erika and Ryker eventually made it back to the wheelhouse last night.

Breakfast was delivered to the crewmen on duty by one of the ship's cooks. On duty right now were the captain and one member of the black gang down in the engine room. The rest of the crew took their meal in the galley before reporting for duty. After the crew finished their breakfast, the CIA team took their place at a galley table.

Today, breakfast was scrambled eggs, a croissant with butter, goat cheese, an apple, and olives.

"Where are we?" Amy asked. "Will we still get to Washington sometime tomorrow?"

"The storm slowed us and knocked us off course," Erika answered. "The captain told me this morning that we'll probably arrive Friday."

"Can we trust that asshole?" Zhanna mumbled with a mouthful of eggs.

"I'm not relying on trust," Erika replied. "I've been checking our coordinates at least three times a day. We're on course for Washington.

"Amy, what's your report on Luca?"

"I'm sure he's hungry. He didn't get dinner last night because of the storm. I'll take him breakfast when we're done. Other than that, there's nothing to report."

"Sonderführer," Ryker said to Erika. "I told you if you'll give me some time with Luca, I'll find out where his safe is located."

Erika had asked Ryker dozens of times to stop referring to her by her Abwehr rank, but to no avail. She had now learned to just let it flow off her back.

Erika thought about it as she ate. "Okay, Axel. But remember you're not in the Gestapo anymore. Our mission is to deliver Luca alive. Amy will be with you when you question Luca to make sure you don't go too far."

As they talked, the USS Swordfish had resurfaced to pick up speed and was heading their way. Also in pursuit was the speedy Russian corvette warship that ran at full speed ahead.

◊ ◊ ◊

An hour later, Erika dialed the combination to the safe which was cleverly hidden inside a bulkhead in the stern of the ship, just above the engine room. Ryker had not only gotten Luca to reveal the location to the safe but the combination as well. The boatswain, whose one of many duties included being the ship's medic, was called upon to apply splints to Luca's four grotesquely broken fingers and dislocated left wrist.

Everything was in the safe. Many thousands of American dollars along with Luca's 'black book' containing names of his opium transport freighters, their home ports, and names and locations of all his drug distributors. Also included were specifics of his middleman weapons dealing for the Soviets but no names of buyers were recorded. Erika put the black book back in the safe and took the money.

[later that morning—Washington, D.C.]

"Luca's yacht is still on the radar so it survived the storm," Al Hodge told Leroy Carr. "This morning the carrier was able to send up a plane to identify the bogie. It's a Russian corvette. The Swordfish was originally closer to Luca's yacht but it was slowed because it had to submerge to avoid the storm. The corvette can sail at eight knots

216

faster than our sub, even if the sub is on the surface. It's a coin flip as to which will reach the yacht first."

"Damn," was the first word that came to Carr's mind. Then, "This might end up causing an international incident, Al. I don't want to be called to appear before a private session of the Senate Intelligence Committee and answer questions again about a Shield Maiden mission."

"The only option we have is to call off the sub," Hodge said. "If we do that, we abandon four of our agents. I can't do that, Leroy."

"Neither can I," Carr replied. "I guess we're left with nothing to do but cross our fingers."

[that evening onboard the Som de Argint]
When his yacht sailed, Dragoş Luca, who was accustomed to the finer things in life, insisted on fine dining and a well-stocked pantry. Tonight the Shield Maidens and Axel Ryker sat down to a pasta dish with shrimp and mussels on a bed of linguine with a white wine sauce. Before dinner, Amy had gone below decks to the ship's wine cellar and brought back a couple of bottles of expensive French Sauvignon Blanc.

Before they began eating, Erika distributed the money she pilfered from Luca's safe. Each team member received slightly over two thousand dollars. The money, or what they would do with it, was not discussed.

Chapter 62

Warning shots

Atlantic Ocean
Next day—Thursday, 06 September 1951

By late morning, lookouts onboard the Russian corvette, the Ezhr, finally had the Romanian yacht in their binoculars. The captain was notified and the boarding party put on notice. His orders from Moscow gave him an option. First, board the ship, rescue Luca, confiscate everything in his safe, and take the CIA agents hostage. The option given him was that if for some reason boarding was not possible, the Som de Argint was to be sent to the bottom with everyone onboard, including Luca. Whatever incriminating evidence Luca had would end up in Davey Jones' Locker with him.

Onboard the Som de Argint it was Zhanna's watch. She lowered her binoculars and summoned her teammates to the bridge using the ship's intercom.

When the others got to the bridge they looked out and saw nothing.

"You need the binoculars," Zhanna said. "At eleven o'clock off our stern, a Russian corvette is heading our way. There's no way this yacht can outrun it. Once during the war, I was on Russian corvette in the Baltic Sea. Those ships can steam at over thirty knots."

"Do you have a guess when it might reach us?" Erika asked.

"Less than an hour," Zhanna answered.

"Zhanna, stay on watch. The rest of us will go below and get weapons from Luca's stash. There are a couple of Russian PPD machine guns down there along with AK-47s. Nothing Luca has is going to cause serious damage to a warship, but at least we'll go down fighting. Don't let yourself be captured. Does everyone have their L-pill?" This was a cyanide capsule; 'L' stood for lethal.

Everyone nodded.

"Before I use mine, I'll shoot Luca," Amy said. Erika gave her the go ahead.

Zhanna had done a good job estimating the time it would take the corvette to reach them. In 50 minutes, the Russian warship had drawn close enough that binoculars allowed the ship's name to be read. In 5 minutes, the Ezhr had positioned itself to allow a warning shot with one of its 6-inch guns. The shell exploded in the water about 50 yards off the Som de Argint's bow.

The ship drew even closer, then a voice speaking Russian could be heard through the ship's powerful PA system.

"This is Captain Nicolai Debrow. You've seen our flag. We will send over a boarding party. Tell your captain to cut his engines immediately."

"Amy!" Erika shouted. "Go to the wheelhouse and tell that captain to keep full steam ahead." Amy ran off.

The Russian captain waited 5 minutes. When he realized his orders were being ignored, he got back on the intercom. "If your ship does not cut its engines within one minute, we will destroy your vessel and send you to the bottom."

Just then a bubbling torpedo trail could be seen crossing directly across the bow of the Ezhr. The conning tower of an American submarine broke the surface. On the side of the conning tower was an emblem of a swordfish. The Americans had sent their own warning shot.

The sub fully surfaced, creating much froth, and it was now the American captain's time to use the ship-to-ship address system. He and two other officers appeared atop the conning tower.

"This is Captain Robert Alton of the USS Swordfish. We have orders to escort this Romanian ship to the United States. Withdraw."

The captain of the corvette had onboard a crewman assigned to his ship who could translate English.

The English-speaking crewman voiced the reply that Captain Debrow had told him to say. "These are international waters, not American waters. The ship flies a Romanian flag. Romania is in our sphere."

Alton came back. "A U.S. destroyer from the 7th Fleet is three hours away, heading here at full speed ahead. It has you locked onto its radar. I suggest you contact your superiors. Your ship cannot survive a confrontation with an American destroyer. We will give you two hours to contact your commanders and come to a decision. We will be watching from below."

The last thing Captain Alton did was aim the speakers at the Som de Argint. "Tell your captain to reduce the ship's speed to 7 knots but do not stop." Eight knots was the submarine's top speed underwater when it had to run on batteries instead of the diesel engines used when on the surface that propelled it at twice that speed.

The men on the conning tower disappeared and the Swordfish vanished into the depths.

◊ ◊ ◊

An hour later, Captain Debrow of the Ezhr had relayed a message to Moscow and waited for his orders. He included information about the American submarine that stalked them from below and the destroyer that was supposedly heading their way. A half-hour after that, the Shield Maidens, Axel Ryker, and the crew of the Som de Argint watched the Russian corvette peel off and head away.

Another half-hour passed and the Swordfish broke the surface like a breeching whale, coming to the surface less than a hundred yards off the Romanian ship's port side midships.

Erika and Amy were on deck and waved at the men who appeared on the conning tower. They didn't wave back but were all business.

The sub's captain used the PA system instead of a short-wave transmission that could be picked up for hundreds of miles. "Increase your speed to 16 knots. The Swordfish can maintain that speed on the surface while we wait for the destroyer."

Erika used a bullhorn. "Captain Alton. This is Erika Lehmann of the CIA. We invite you and your executive officers to dine with us this evening onboard the Som de Argint."

"No," the dispassionate voice came back across the sea. "Our orders are to guard you until the destroyer arrives, at which time we will return to the fleet. The destroyer will accompany you the rest of the way to your destination."

[that afternoon]

When the Canon-class destroyer, the USS Booth, appeared on the horizon in the mid-afternoon, the Swordfish waited until it grew closer then submerged, never to be seen again by the people onboard the Som de Argint.

Eventually the American warship that dwarfed the Romanian pleasure yacht pulled up alongside. Again, the powerful PA speakers were used to avoid a transmission.

"Attention Som de Argint! We are sending a boarding party. Cut your engines."

This time the captain of Luca's yacht was ordered to comply by Erika. In a few minutes, the yacht went dead in the water.

The boarding party came across in three rubber skiffs over what were now only 2-foot waves, each skiff powered by a single outboard motor. Erika told the captain to order the swimming platform just two feet above the waves be lowered to allow easy access by the U.S. seamen.

When the seamen boarded, a petty officer took charge.

"We're here to place into custody . . ." He looked down at a paper. "A Dragoş Luca. Is he onboard?"

"Yes," Erika replied. "He's below, locked in his cabin. Follow me. You're more than welcome to take him off our hands."

The petty officer and four members of the boarding party followed Erika to Luca's cabin.

"Are you Dragoş Luca?" the petty officer asked Luca.

"No. I'm Thomas Jefferson," Luca said snidely.

"That's Luca," Erika said.

The drug kingpin's hands were cuffed behind his back even though it was hard to get the cuffs around the splint on his left wrist. He was escorted to one of the skiffs and taken to the destroyer.

Somewhat to Erika's surprise, the petty officer didn't ask her about Luca's safe or what was in it. His only question was about the speed of the yacht.

"How fast can this vessel sail?"

221

"Twenty-four or five knots if there's no head wind or rough seas," she responded.

"No inclement weather is predicted for several days. Sail at full speed to Washington. The Booth will escort you. You should arrive sometime tomorrow."

"Please give my thanks to your captain," Erika said.

He nodded. "I will, and I'll say goodbye. When you are within visual of the dock in Washington our orders are to leave you."

"Where are you taking Luca?" she asked.

"I'm not privy to that information. Only the captain knows."

[that evening]

The USS Booth had moved farther away and slightly behind the Som de Argint so the destroyer's substantial wake would not rock the yacht. Still, it was within 300 yards off the yacht's starboard stern and loomed menacing for any ship that dared cross it's path.

The CIA team sat down to a steak and lobster supper. With Dragoş Luca no longer on the ship and in custody of the U.S. Navy, the team was able to relax.

"When will we get to Washington?" Ryker asked as he put a piece of bloody steak in his mouth that he had ordered rare. He was impatient to be reunited with his wife and son.

"I spoke with the navigator this afternoon," Erika said. "His estimate is around lunchtime tomorrow, Washington time."

Amy said, "I'm glad we're rid of Luca. Every time I had to look at him I felt nauseous."

"He's the property of the U.S. Navy now," Erika responded. "That means we fulfilled our original mission to capture him. All of us should feel good about that."

Zhanna, who wasn't paying attention to the conversation broke her lobster tail away from the body and said, "Where in hell is the dipping butter?"

"It's right in front of you," Amy said.

Erika asked, "Amy, I wonder how the band is handling your disappearance?"

"They'll be in Marrakesh this weekend. When we get to Washington tomorrow, I'll call Petru at their hotel and tell him I'm okay. I'll come up with some excuse. The band will be okay in Marrakesh. They played together for over two years before I joined them, and they had already become popular on their own."

Chapter 63

Luca's crew

Atlantic Ocean
Next day—Friday, 07 September 1951

When the Som de Argint drew close enough to the Eastern Coast of the United States for it to be visible to the naked eye, the USS Booth peeled off and headed south.

"I wonder where they're taking Luca," Amy asked.

"Hard to say," Erika replied. "They only thing I know is that coastline is a sight for sore eyes."

When the Romanian ship neared the port in Washington, a harbor master on a tug met the ship, boarded, and went to the wheelhouse to guide the captain to his pier. Al Hodge, who had received constant updates from the Navy, stood on the pier with six agents as everyone disembarked.

The Romanian crew was loaded into an olive drab Army bus and taken away by two agents and a couple of MPs. Two more of Hodge's men boarded the Som de Argint which would be guarded 24-hours-a-day until it was moved to a more suitable location allowing a thorough search.

Hodge had two sedans waiting to take the Maidens and Ryker to E Street.

◊ ◊ ◊

At CIA headquarters, everyone gathered in Leroy Carr's office. He seemed to be in good spirits.

"Welcome back," Carr told the team. "It looks like you all came through unscathed."

"We were extremely lucky this time as far as injuries," Erika replied.

"We'll have to talk about you going dark without permission, Erika. But I want to congratulate you all. You took a failed mission and reversed it, and without your normal mayhem that in the past has gotten me called to testify on Capitol Hill."

"Where is that destroyer taking Luca?" Amy asked.

Hodge answered. "Amy, you're trained by the Mossad and the CIA. You know the number one rule for field agents—don't ask about information you don't need to know. It protects you."

"How about the crew of Luca's yacht?" Erika asked. "Can you tell us where they were taken?"

"To the stockade in Fort Dix, New Jersey," Carr answered. "We'll send down a team to begin interrogations tomorrow."

"Leroy," Erika said. "I made a deal with the crew. I told them if they cooperated in getting us to the States, they wouldn't be imprisoned. Only the captain and his executive officer knew about Luca's business and those two worked for Luca only because it was a good job. They were not involved in any of his dealings. Luca kept no drugs on board the yacht. The rest of the crew knew nothing."

"Erika, you're not the Department of Justice. You have no authority to make deals on behalf of the U.S. government. With that said, if their interrogations reveal what you say, I'll do what I can to make sure your promise is honored."

"Axel persuaded Luca to tell us where his safe was hidden on the ship," Erika said. "Tell your men there is a fire extinguisher box mounted into a bulkhead in the stern of the ship, one deck above the engine room. The box pulls out and the safe is behind it. Everything is in there—all of Luca's partners in crime in his drug business and certain information about his weapons dealing for the Soviets."

"Axel," Carr said. "How did you get this information from Luca?"

"I reasoned with him."

Zhanna burst out laughing. "That's a good one, Axel. Give me a cigar."

Carr looked at Hodge, "Al, how badly is Luca injured."

"He had splints on several fingers and his wrist when we took him off the yacht."

"What else was in the safe?" Carr asked Erika. "Passports? Maps? Money?"

"I saw some passports, but nothing else. No money. When can we get out of here? I haven't seen Ada in two weeks."

"Since it's Friday, your debriefings will start Monday. We'll go with four-hour sessions a day but use as many days as required," Carr responded. "Axel, you may return to Philadelphia this weekend but be back here Monday morning. Amy, as soon as you complete your debriefings, we'll send you back to your band. That's a cover we can't afford to lose. If there aren't any questions, you're dismissed until Monday morning. Be here at eight o'clock."

When the team left and only Carr and Hodge were left in the office, Hodge asked, "I wonder how much money Lehmann shanghaied from that safe?"

"We'll never know, Al. Just let it go."

[Arlington, Virginia]

As soon as the team was dismissed, they crowded into one taxi and made a beeline to the Lili Marlene Café. Ryker, too large for the backseat, sat beside the driver with the three women shoulder-to-shoulder in the back.

"For more than three passengers, my company charges more," the cabbie told them.

"We don't give a shit about that," Zhanna said. "We'll pay your fee. Just get this thing moving."

Forty minutes later when the taxi pulled up and stopped in front of the café, Zhanna paid the fee from the money Erika had given her from Luca's safe. She included a $10 tip.

The driver's eyes bugged as he looked at the tip which was more than the fare. "Wow! Thank you, lady."

"Fuck you!" Zhanna said.

Erika rushed into the Lili Marlene with tunnel vision, ignoring the expansion, and found Ada in the kitchen. Mother and daughter hugged and kissed multiple times.

Angelika was nearby and eventually Erika hugged her, too.

"The addition to the café was completed a week ago, Erika. Let me show you. Is Zhanna with you?"

226

"Yes."

"Then she needs to be shown around, as well."

"Show it to all of us," Erika said. "Axel's father-in law paid for it, and I'm sure Amy will want to see it."

Angelika led the group. The original café could seat 48 people. The addition now allowed for a seating capacity of 200. A large stage two feet off the floor took up an area in the back of the addition.

Angelika then led them upstairs. Over the addition was a two-bedroom apartment for Erika and Ada, and a one-bedroom for Zhanna. Both had their own bathroom and were fully furnished with beds, dressers, sofas, and a coffee table for the small living rooms. All the furniture looked expensive. Each apartment also had a small kitchenette where coffee could be brewed, and breakfast and lunch prepared on the two-burner stove.

"The construction man said because of space limitations only a two-burner stove would fit," Angelika said.

"That's okay, Angelika. Two burners are plenty. This is wonderful. I can hardly believe it." She turned to Ryker. "Axel, we all have a lot of thanking to do to your wife and your father-in-law."

"You'll see Rose tomorrow," Ryker replied. "Instead of returning to Philadelphia for two days then having to come right back, I'll have Rose and our son fly into Washington tomorrow on the family's plane. We'll stay at a suite in the Mayflower Hotel until the briefings are finished."

"Good," Erika said. "I love Rose. She's a sweetheart."

When the group returned downstairs, they lost Amy who fell behind when she paused to inspect the stage.

Part 7

Chapter 64

Amy's idea

Norfolk Naval Facility, Virginia
Next day—Saturday, 08 September 1951

Dragoş Luca was behind bars. Last night, a Navy medical corpsman had removed the splints from his broken fingers and dislocated wrist and replaced them with a cast.

This morning, a jailer opened Luca's cell door and Al Hodge stepped in with a female translator from the CIA translator pool.

"Good morning, Mr. Luca," Hodge said. "I've heard a lot about you. I'm afraid my translator doesn't speak Romanian, but she's quite qualified in Russian, which I understand you speak. My name is Al Hodge. I work for the United States government. I'd like to ask you a few questions if I may."

The translator did her job during the conversation, which would end up lasting for two hours.

"You are holding me illegally," Luca said. "I'm a Romanian citizen in good standing. I've never been charged with a crime."

Hodge pulled Luca's 'black book' out of his jacket pocket. "That may be, Mr. Luca, but let's talk about this interesting ledger we found in a safe on your yacht. It's an impressive yacht, by the way."

[that evening]

Zhanna Rogova was now back at the one place where she was happy, as bar manager at the Lili Marlene Café. The café normally had good crowds on the weekends. Tonight was no different, and with the extra tables even more people were eating and drinking.

Erika sat at a table with Angelika, Amy, and the Rykers. Rose had brought their baby. Erika, the godmother, held the 1½-year-old boy on her lap. Ada was upstairs in their new apartment reading *Tom Sawyer* for a school assignment.

"Rose," Erika said. "I don't know how we can thank you and your father for what you've done for the café."

"We wanted to do it, Erika. I hesitated about making choices for you and Zhanna about the furnishings, but I thought it might be nice to have a place ready to move into when you returned."

"Everything is lovely, Rose."

Amy, knowing how much her bandmates wanted to perform in the United States had an idea.

"Rose, do you think your father might be interested in sponsoring the band to come to the United States? I'm not asking for money. An American citizen is needed to vouch for acts from overseas. All Mr. Bristow would have to do it sign a paper."

"I'm sure father will be glad to," Rose responded.

"Where will you play, Amy?" Erika asked.

"Here at the Lili Marlene, of course."

"Amy, your band plays in front of sold-out arenas in front two or three thousand people."

"We also enjoy playing small venues, Erika. Our home cantina in Barcelona—the Cordobes—seats only two hundred and fifty people, only slightly more than the Lili Marlene now with the expansion. Rick's Café where we played in Casablanca seats even less than the Cordobes—only about two hundred and twenty. Besides, money is not the main consideration. I know the band would gladly just break even for a trip to the States."

Rose said, "It will be hard to break even playing such a small venue with the travel and lodging expenses the band will have to pay. Two major expenses you don't have when you perform in Barcelona. I will talk to my father."

"Rose," Amy stressed. "Please make sure you tell your father that I'm not asking for money, only his signature as our American sponsor."

Erika thought about the money she had purloined from Luca's safe. Each team member received $2,200. "I agree with Amy, Rose. Your father has done too much for us already. Amy and I recently came into some money. I will give her mine, which in addition to hers, should be more than enough to pay for the band's travel and hotel."

"Yes, we have the money," Amy echoed.

"Just what we need around here," Axel said. "More Gypsies."

Everyone laughed, including Amy and Rose. Although comedy was not Ryker's intention, many of his dogmatic remarks sparked humor.

Actually, Ryker would have offered to kick in some of his own money Erika gave him but he had already spent it on a set of diamond earrings, matching choker, and bracelet for Rose from the top diamond merchant in Washington. The jewelry would be ready for pick up on Tuesday. Any enemy who had the misfortune to cross Ryker's path during a mission would be hard pressed to believe the scar-faced fiend of a man treated his wife like a queen and his son as a prince. Ryker believed Providence shined on him when Rose appeared in his life. To Ryker, nothing of importance existed outside of his wife and son.

"Alright, it's settled," Erika said. "Because of Archibald's high standing, if he is willing to sign the verification papers for the band we'll have no problems. No one will question the endorsement of Archibald Bristow. Amy and I will pay for the band's expenses."

Angelika spoke up. "Erika, with this expansion we need more waitresses. We have only one full-time and one part-time waitress now."

"You're the manager, Angelika. You take care of it. I can also help wait tables on busy nights."

"We'll also need additional help in the kitchen," Angelika added. "At least part-time. Bertha is 63 years old. Busy nights are a strain for her."

"That's fine, Angelika, but we have to find someone who knows how to prepare German dishes like Bertha. I want the Lili Marlene to keep its German-theme even though we also serve American food. We'll always have an authentic German meal on the menu every day."

Chapter 65

Hola

Marrakesh, Morocco
Next day—Sunday, 09 September 1951

Amy made the call from the Lili Marlene. It being Sunday, the café was closed in the German tradition. It took a half-hour of talking to several overseas telephone operators, but Amy was finally connected to the hotel where she knew the band was staying. She asked the hotel switchboard operator to connect her to Petru Kivac's room. Amy hit a stroke of luck. Petru and the entire band were in his room. Their North Africa contract had ended last night with their Saturday evening performance at a sold-out 2000-seat auditorium in Marrakesh.

Petru picked up the phone. "Hola," he said in Spanish.

Amy used that language.

"Petru, this is Amy."

"Where have you been, Amy! Are you alright? We've been worried."

"I'm fine, Petru. It's a long story—too long to get into now. But that's not why I'm calling. I'm in the United States. Tell the band I have us an American sponsor for a performance in America."

"Hold on," Petru said. "The bandmembers are all here."

Amy could hear Petru's announcement and the band cheering in the background. When Petru got back on the phone, Amy said. *"When the banks open tomorrow, I'll wire you the money to your hotel in Marrakesh for your flight. Fly into Washington, D.C., and check into the Mayflower Hotel. That's where I'm staying. Your rooms will be reserved for you. We will be performing next weekend so get here as quickly as possible."*

"How long is the engagement?" Petru asked.

"I don't know yet. But even it's for just the one weekend, we'll be performing in the United States. That's what everyone in the band said they wanted."

"We'll get there as soon as we can," Petru said.

"*Good,*" Amy said. "*Please ask Cici to bring with her my costumes and anything else I left behind.*"

Chapter 66

Nuns have heavy shoes

Washington, D.C.
Next day—Monday, 10 September 1951

The debriefings started today. 'Debriefings' was a euphemism for what they really were—cross-examinations. They were something every field agent dreads. It amounted to days of being asked the same questions over and over by multiple interrogators whose job it was to make the field agent slip up somewhere along the way. Each agent was separated and questioned alone.

Erika by now was expert at avoiding their traps. Amy, trained by the top two secret intelligence services in the world, the Mossad and the CIA, knew what to say and what not to say.

Zhanna merely stared at her debriefers, speaking only when she had a vulgarity to sling at her cross-examiner. Axel Ryker, who during the war was Heinrich Himmler's chief Gestapo inquisitor, knew all the tricks and more often than not would laugh at the man across the table. "I could teach you many things about interrogation," Ryker told one of his debriefers.

[that evening at the Lili Marlene]
"How does Ada like her new school?" Amy asked.

She and Erika sat at the bar talking to Zhanna.

"I think she likes it fine," Erika responded. "It's a Catholic school, and the nuns keep the kids in line. I told her she has to get all her homework completed each day before she can come down and help in the kitchen."

Zhanna smashed out her cigarette in a bar ashtray and said, "Those school nuns can be assholes. They wear heavy shoes."

Erika and Amy sat looking at her for a moment. "What do their shoes have to do with anything?" Amy asked.

"They like kicking you with them."

Erika and Amy could only shake their heads. Amy moved on. "This morning I wired the money for the band's flights and talked to Petru again. They fly out of Morocco early tomorrow morning. Their route takes them to Madrid, then to Ireland. Once across the Atlantic, there's the Newfoundland stop then on to D.C. If they don't run into any bad weather, they should be here late Wednesday night or early Thursday morning."

"It will be nice seeing them again," Erika said.

Chapter 67

Typical Shield Maiden

Washington, D.C.
Next day—Tuesday, 11 November 1951

Al Hodge had spent the entire day yesterday at the Norfolk Naval Facility stockade questioning Dragoş Luca. Little had come out of it.

Hodge was now in Leroy Carr's E Street office.

"I told Luca we know he runs his drug freighters out of Antalya, Turkey," Al said.

Erika and Zhanna had supplied the CIA this information that they had learned from Luca himself when he offered them a job working for him. Of course, he had not mentioned anything about the goods his freighters shipped.

"What was his response?" Carr asked.

"He's holding to his story that he's an honest businessman. He said if any drugs were smuggled onto his freighters, he was unaware of it."

"What did he say about the Russian weapons deals recorded in his ledger?"

"Unfortunately, he was smart enough not to write specifics about the weapons, only his contact people and money amounts. He claims those listings are not for weapons, but for humanitarian aid—medical supplies and other things—supplied by the Soviets to countries sympathetic to communist ideals. Humanitarian aid would not be illegal under any laws, international or here in the States. He knows all the angles."

"What are you saying, Al? That this guy might walk?"

"I'm saying we have to find a way to prove those are weapons deals, or that he was directly involved in drug trafficking where some of the drugs ended up here in the States if we want to present a solid case to the Department of Justice."

"Erika said she thinks Luca has a facility in Mexico City that processes the opium to heroin, right?" Carr asked.

"That's an assumption on her part, Leroy. Luca told her that she and Zhanna would be spending some time in Mexico City. In Luca's black book he lists a name and telephone number in that city. We need to send a team down there to gather evidence. Amy speaks Spanish, she's an obvious choice."

"I don't want to get the Shield Maidens involved," Carr said. "They've done their job. We have several agents that speak Spanish. All five agents on the Falcon team that work mostly in South America speak Spanish. They just returned from Venezuela so they're available. We'll send them to Mexico City. Anything else?"

"After her debriefing today, Amy came to my office to tell me her band was on its way to the States and will perform this weekend at Erika's café."

"You're kidding," Carr said.

"Nope. I told her she should have cleared this with us beforehand. It's typical Shield Maiden shit—telling us after the fact. Amy played it smart, before she told me about it, she had Rose Bristow have her father vouch for the band's entry visas."

Carr thought for a moment. "If Archibald Bristow is backing them, there's not anything we can do about it. We'll have to go to one of the performances. It won't hurt us to get more familiar with Amy's bandmates."

Chapter 68

Biscuits and gravy

Washington, D.C.
Two days later—Thursday, 13 September 1951

Since there was no clear-cut time when their plane would arrive in D.C., Amy was not at the Washington airport to greet the band when the Pan-Am DC-4 commercial flight sat down in a light fog at 7:10 a.m. After clearing customs, the group hailed taxis to take them to the Mayflower Hotel where Amy had told Petru their rooms would be waiting. In Romanian the word mayflower was the same as in English, so there was no problem telling the taxi drivers where they wanted to go. Every cabbie in Washington knew where the Mayflower Hotel was located on Connecticut Boulevard.

After the band and stagehands checked into their rooms, Petru called the hotel's switchboard operator and told her the phone number Amy had given him. There was no answer at the Lili Marlene Café. Petru didn't know the café didn't serve breakfast and didn't open until 11 a.m. The bull fiddle player then asked the switchboard girl to connect him to Amy Radu's room at the Mayflower, using the English words he had looked up in a Romanian to English dictionary, "Room Amy Radu, please."

Amy picked up the phone.

In Romanian, Petru said, "Amy, we are here at the hotel and in our rooms. I'm in room 414."

"I'm sure everyone is hungry after the long journey," Amy said. "Gather the band, Petru, and I'll meet you all in the hotel restaurant for breakfast in thirty minutes."

A half-hour later the Barcelona Romanian Gypsy Orchestra and stagehands were reunited with Amy and sitting around a long, white linen-covered oval table in the Mayflower Hotel restaurant. A waitress delivered coffee.

Everyone was still curious about why Amy disappeared after their weekend in Casablanca, but Amy spoke first. "Your rooms are paid for

238

and any meals you take here at the hotel. If you go out to eat, you have to pay for it yourselves unless you eat at the Lili Marlene Café where we'll perform this weekend."

"Where is this place?" Raval, the accordion player, asked.

"It's in Arlington in a state called Virginia, but it's not far. Arlington is just across the Potomac River. It's only about a thirty-to-forty-minute drive from this hotel if the traffic is not heavy. The café is a small venue, about the size of Rick's Café in Casablanca where we performed. But the booking was enough to secure everyone's visas."

"How long is our engagement?" Viorel, the guitar player, wanted to know.

"I told Petru over the phone that I don't know, Viorel" Amy answered. "It might be just the one weekend. But we have a booking in the United States. That's what you all wanted."

No one argued with that and since Amy did not offer an explanation on why she disappeared in Casablanca they didn't question her about it. It was not the Gypsy way to question why. Amy's caravan Gypsy culture was based around moving from place to place. They were simply happy to be here.

"Amy, I have your costumes and other things you left behind," Cici said.

"Thank you, Cici."

When the waiter came around for their orders, everyone wanted to try an American breakfast. Amy was the only one who spoke English so she ordered everyone scrambled eggs, bacon, hash browns, and biscuits and gravy.

As they waited for their meals, Petru said, "We need to see the stage, and work out a rehearsal schedule. We got sleep on the plane. We need to rehearse today and again tomorrow morning. We'll play the songs we used in Casablanca. This way we'll need only quick walk-through rehearsals while our stage crew checks out lighting and sound."

"Okay," Amy said. "I'll arrange it."

◊ ◊ ◊

[same day]
It was the early afternoon in Arlington, but it was evening in Romania when Erika's phone call to Castelul Lupului got patched through. She made the call during a lunchbreak during her last day of debriefing.

She knew her phone call would never get connected if she called from the Lili Marlene or a payphone, so she placed the call from E Street. As a CIA team leader, Erika had been assigned a small office there, although she rarely used it. But at E Street, calls to behind the Curtain were able to get through because of scramblers that made it impossible for switchboard operators to determine from where the call originated. Erika told the various Eastern bloc operators that she was calling from Sarajevo, Yugoslavia.

Finally, the phone rang at Castelul Lupului. Geofri answered.

"Hello, Geofri. This is Erika."

"Hello, Erika! It's wonderful to hear from you."

"May I speak to the Count?"

"I'm afraid he's not here. The wife of one of the shepherds who grazes his flock in the eastern area of the castle lands had a baby. A midwife delivered the child, and the Count decided to visit the family today to see if all was well and to ask them if they need anything."

Erika knew she could trust Geofri. "I called to give the Count an update about Dragoș Luca, Geofri. Please tell the Count that we located and captured Luca and he's now behind bars in the United States."

"I will tell him, Erika. The Count will be pleased."

Erika was not aware of the problems Leroy Carr and Al Hodge were experiencing with putting together evidence against Luca.

[an hour later in Arlington—early afternoon]
The band held a brief rehearsal at the Lili Marlene while the stagehands tinkered with the lighting and sounds systems. They found the sound system to be adequate, but the lighting needed more colorful spotlights. However, this was discussed only among themselves. No one complained to Angelika or asked for more colorful lighting. They would make do. Erika and Zhanna were not there during rehearsals; they were

at E Street undergoing their last day of debriefings. Amy had yet to tell her bandmates that Erika owned the café and Zhanna managed the bar. Angelika, the café manager, was the only one Amy had introduced them to.

[that evening]

Before the Lili Marlene's expansion, it had room for only twelve 4-chair tables. Now, there were many more 4-chair tables plus five 6-seaters, four 8-seaters, and a 12-seat table. Seating capacity had been increased from 48 to 200.

All seven members of the Barcelona Romanian Gypsy Orchestra plus their four-man stage crew were seated at a 12-seat table for an early dinner. They all wanted to try some American food, so Amy ordered a family-style meal of Southern fried chicken, okra, green beans and mashed potatoes with white gravy. All were served in large bowls and the diners helped themselves. For a drink, everyone wanted to try a Coca-Cola.

As the band chowed down, fascinated with the food, Erika and Zhanna walked in. Amy's bandmates spotted them and stopped chewing.

Erika and Zhanna saw the group. As they headed toward the table, Amy told the group, "Erika owns this café and Zhanna runs the liquor business."

Again, it was not the Gypsy way to question one of their own. There was only one empty chair at the table, so Erika pulled up one more chair so both women could join the band and crew.

"Hello, everyone," Erika said in Russian. "Thank you so much for agreeing to perform at the Lili Marlene Café. We'll have an exciting weekend."

Chapter 69

Change in routine

Arlington, Virginia
Next day—Friday, 14 September 1951

As promised, Archibald Bristow had paid for advertising the band's appearances at the Lili Marlene Café in the Washington Times. He also had Rose contact a couple of Washington radio stations in the Washington/Arlington area and order an advertisement that ran four times a day for three days this week.

The band was scheduled to begin performing at 8 p.m. By seven the café was full.

Members of the band used the expanded storage room upstairs as a dressing room with curtains in place for Amy and Cici to change. Cici needed only one initial change before the performance. She always wore brown pants and a white blouse with a brown leather vest. To keep her hair off the violin strings she wore a black bowler hat.

Amy, as usually, would have additional changes before the performance ended.

Zhanna and Angelika manned the bar. Bertha and Ada were in the kitchen and having a hard time keeping up with the food orders. The café's fulltime and parttime waitress were both working along with Erika and Rose taking food and drink orders.

Everyone had to hustle.

Ryker sat at one of the new six-seat tables with Archibald Bristow and his wife Bernice, Leroy Carr and his wife Kay, and Al Hodge.

When the time came for the band to perform, it fell on Erika to take a brief break from serving and bussing tables to go to the stage and announce the performance was about to start.

"Ladies and gentlemen," she said into the microphone as the crowd banter lowered. "Thank you all for coming to the Lili Marlene Café tonight. I apologize if anyone's food or drink orders are taking a few minutes longer tonight, but I think you'll find it worth your while when you see the performance tonight. The Barcelona Romanian Gypsy

242

Orchestra, Europe's most popular Flamenco orchestra is with us. They will be on stage shortly."

Erika returned to waitressing. In about ten minutes the musicians came out of a door next to the stage and took their places with their instruments. Amy was not with them. She had suggested to the band to change the normal routine tonight. The band struck up a Romanian instrumental.

When it ended, the band received applause, then the lights went out on the stage. When they came back on, Amy Radu stood on stage wearing a sultry, form fitting long canary-yellow dress. Her head was down, looking at the floor. The crowd grew quiet.

Chapter 70

Bad news

Arlington, Virginia
Next day—Saturday, 15 September 1951

The performance last night ended with a standing ovation and chants for an encore. After autographs were signed and pictures taken, the band took its traditional post-performance dinner at the Lili Marlene after the café closed.

Even though Amy was in superb shape, she was exhausted. Her performance was much more physical than the rest of the band members. She slept until ten o'clock this morning.

She returned to the Lili Marlene from her room at the Mayflower for an eleven o'clock meeting with Erika, Zhanna, and Ryker. They met at the table upstairs in the old storage room.

"We definitely need more help tonight," Erika said. "Angelika spoke with Bertha. Bertha is going to have her two daughters helping in the kitchen tonight. Karen, our fulltime waitress, has a friend who is a former waitress she thinks she can convince to help out tonight because the tips last night were so good. All that will help a lot."

"I made forty dollars in tips last night," Zhanna said. That amount was three times what she normally took in on a Friday night bartending. The waitresses had done even better.

"I made fifty-five dollars in tips last night and divided it between Karen and our parttime college student waitress," Erika said. Including their own tips, the waitresses had made two week's pay in one night.

Erika then got down to the real business for the meeting. "Al Hodge took me aside for a few minutes last night. He told me the Russian government is demanding the State Department release Dragoş Luca and that he be delivered to the Soviet embassy in Washington."

"What! Why!" Zhanna exclaimed.

"The Russians claim Luca is innocent and the CIA abducted him with no evidence of the charges against him. Luca has denied

244

everything, including being a weapons dealer. Al told me Luca's ledger doesn't supply enough evidence to take to the Department of Justice."

"What can we do about that?" Amy asked.

"Apparently nothing," Erika replied. "Leroy Carr has sent the Falcon team to Mexico City to try and dig up more evidence from Luca's opium-to-heroin operation there."

Erika paused. "I promised Count Lupei that I would keep him up to date about Luca. Now I have to call him and tell him all this stuff."

[that evening]
Word had spread and tonight's performance was standing room only with people being turned away at the door for lack of space. Rose helped again and the extra waitress Karen brought in, along with Bertha's daughters helping in the kitchen, was a godsend, but everyone was still hard-pressed to serve the crowd.

Chapter 71

Buna ziua

Transylvania, Romania
Next day—Sunday, 16 September 1951

The telephone rang at Castelul Lupului. Geofri picked up.

"Buna ziua."

"Geofri, this is Erika. Is the Count available?"

The butler switched to English. "Yes, Erika. I will tell him you're calling."

Once again, Erika was calling from her office at CIA headquarters in the E Street Complex to make use of the scramblers. It took about five minutes before she heard the Count's voice.

"Yes, Erika," he said. "How are you?"

"I'm fine Count. Thank you. I gave you my word that I would keep you informed about Dragoş Luca. I'm afraid I'm calling with some disconcerting news. The Soviet embassy ambassador here in Washington is demanding that Luca be released to them. They claim he was abducted without cause. Unfortunately, my superiors don't feel the evidence against him is sufficient enough to present to our Justice Department. That is not to say that Luca will be released. We have a team in Mexico City trying to gather more evidence."

There came a long pause from the telephone at Castelul Lupului.

Finally, the Count said, "I appreciate you keeping your word, Erika."

"Count Lupei. I feel confident that our team in Mexico City will gather the needed evidence. It's a good team."

"Very well," the Count said wearily. "Is that all?"

"Yes, Count."

Erika heard him say, "Goodbye. Take care of yourself, Erika." Then he hung up.

The butler stood nearby. "Geofri, prepare our travel trunks. You and I are going to America."

[later that day]
Zhanna was in her new apartment above the café. Erika knocked on the door and Zhanna let her in.

"I spoke with Count Lupei this morning and gave him the latest news about Luca."

"Yeah? How did that go?"

"Not good," Erika said. "It was easy to tell he wasn't happy."

"On a lighter note," the leader of the Shield Maidens continued, "I've got some news about Amy's band. Archibald Bristow invited Amy to bring the band to his estate next Saturday night for a performance to raise money for one of his wife's charities. This will extend their visas for at least another week. Her bandmates are thrilled about that."

Chapter 72

Someone from the recent past

Arlington, Virginia
Two days later—Tuesday, 18 September 1951

It was just after 7 p.m. Erika sat at the bar having a drink alongside Amy. Zhanna was making a Tom Collins for a customer seated at the other end of the bar.

"Ryker and Rose flew back to Philadelphia this morning on the Bristow's airplane," Erika told Amy, "Rose got the details about Saturday night from her mother and she called me this afternoon. Her father will have a temporary stage put up in the Grand Hall. If the band wants to fly to Philadelphia Friday morning, Rose said her father would have someone take them on a driving tour of Philadelphia that afternoon and the band can overnight at the estate Friday and Saturday night."

"Okay," Amy responded. "I'll tell Petru. I'm sure he will want to do that. They will enjoy the tour and that will give the stage crew an opportunity to check out the lighting and sound system at the estate."

It was then that Shirl Hatfield entered the café. He spotted Erika at the bar.

"Hello, Erika."

She turned and saw the handsome first lieutenant who wore civilian clothes. "Shirl, what a surprise."

"It's good to see you again, Erika. I'm glad you're back from your travels."

"Shirl, this my friend, Amy Radu. Amy, this is Shirl Hatfield."

"Hello, Amy. It's nice to meet you."

"Hello, Shirl."

Zhanna approached. "Mister, are you just standing there sightseeing or do you want a drink?"

"I'll have a Yuengling."

Erika said, "Try the Warsteiner Dunkel, Shirl. It's imported from Bavaria."

248

"Make it Warsteiner," he told Zhanna.

"Imports are a quarter more than domestic beers. That will be a dollar and a quarter. That will include the beer and my tip."

"That's fine," he replied.

When Zhanna left to pour the beer, Hatfield said, "Your bartender is a pip." Erika had told him that she owned the café.

Both Erika and Amy grinned. "That's Zhanna," Erika said. "She has her ways." Erika would have told Zhanna that the beer was on the house, but as the bar manager, Zhanna always carped when she had to give away free alcohol.

When Zhanna returned with the beer, Hatfield paid. Then Erika said, "Shirl, let's get a table. Amy, please excuse us."

After they sat down, Hatfield said, "Your manager told me you were traveling but she didn't know when you would return, so I've stopped in here once a week. I figured you were somewhere overseas working your State Department translator job."

"That's right. I was in Belgium for a while. NATO headquarters is in Brussels, as you know."

Hatfield nodded.

"How do you like the beer?" she asked.

"It's good. I've had Warsteiner before on stops in Munich, but it was the golden version, not the Dunkel." Dunkel was German for dark. The beer was black like Guinness, yet a lager.

"Shirl. Why are you here? You travel a lot and so do I. There is no future for us. I told you that you need to find a nice West Virginia girl."

"Erika, why can't we see one another when we have the opportunity?"

She paused as she looked at him.

Chapter 73

Shock

Arlington, Virginia
Three days later—Friday, 21 September 1951

Last night, Erika had gone to a movie with Shirl Hatfield.

This morning, Amy and the band left for Philadelphia on the Bristow family airplane. The twin-engine Cessna seated twelve. A net-covered shelf above the seats held baggage and the smaller instruments. Petru's bull fiddle and Mitica's cimbalom drum went into the storage hatch under the plane. It was a tight fit for the band, the stage crew, their bags and the instruments, but everyone and everything managed to get aboard.

[that evening]
Erika stood at a table talking to a couple who were regular customers when two men entered the café. Erika, who was hard to surprise, was shocked and could hardly believe what she saw. It was Count Lupei and Geofri standing just inside the door looking around.

Erika excused herself and walked over to greet the men. Both wore a suit but no tie.

"Count Lupei and Geofri," she said, "I almost doubted my eyesight."

"Hello, Erika," the Count said.

"Please let me seat you. Have you had dinner?"

"No," the Count answered.

She led them to a table and sat down with them. The Count held her chair.

"Where are you staying, Count?"

"Geofri and I arrived just this afternoon. I thought you might recommend a hotel."

"The Mayflower Hotel. It's the finest hotel in Washington, and only a thirty-five-minute drive from here. I'll drive you there when it comes time."

Geofri said, "We have two large trunks."

"Where are they now?"

"In the cab waiting outside," the butler replied.

"I'll have them brought in. Dinner and drinks tonight are on me. Heaven knows it is small repayment for your generous hospitality you have shown us at Castelul Lupului."

"Please order the food for us," the Count said.

"Our German dinner tonight is Jägerschnitzel. Will that do?"

"Anything is fine. I see Zhanna looking at us from behind the bar."

"She's in charge of our liquor business. What would you like to drink?"

The Count said, "Scotch, please."

"I'm sorry to say we don't have Laphroaig. Our best Scotch is a twelve-year-old Johnnie Walker."

"Whatever you recommend."

"Geofri?"

"I'll have the same. Thank you, Erika."

Erika went behind the bar and got an unopened bottle of the Scotch and three whiskey glasses. Zhanna had seen the Count and didn't complain this time about the free liquor.

"Zhanna, recruit a couple of guys to go outside. A taxi is out there with two travel trunks. Have them bring them into the café." Erika looked around the bar and saw two regular customers.

"Charlie and Ralph are down there. Ask them to do it. Give them a free beer."

Then Erika went into the kitchen and ordered two Jägerschnitzel dinners.

She returned to the Count's table, opened the bottle of Scotch, and poured drinks for them all. "Count, your trunks will be brought in by two men."

"Thank you, Erika," the Count said, "Geofri, go with these men and pay the driver."

Geofri saw two men walking out the door and followed them.

"Count, the meals will be delivered in about fifteen minutes. I have already eaten dinner, but I will join you for a drink. Your presence tells me that you want to talk with me."

"Any more news about Luca since you called Sunday?"

"Nothing yet," Erika said. "Count, I'm confident that our team in Mexico City will find the evidence we need. I know the men on that team. They are very good at what they do."

"Luca is a scourge on my homeland. An ancient place as beautiful as anywhere in creation. For the sake of argument, my dear, what if these men in Mexico City fail?"

Erika took a breath. "I would never lie to you, Count Lupei, and tell you there's no chance that Luca could walk free, but that's not going to happen until all resources have been exhausted regardless of the amount of time it takes. I've been ensured of this by my superior, Leroy Carr. He's the Deputy Director of the CIA."

"Luca must never be allowed to walk free," said the Count. "I would like to speak with your Mr. Carr."

"I know he would welcome that," she said. Then she thought for a moment. "Tomorrow night, Amy and the Flamenco band you and Geofri watched perform in Cluj-Napoca are giving a concert at an estate outside Philadelphia. Mr. Carr will be there along with Mr. Hodge, my CIA team's handler when we're deployed on a mission. It's a charity affair hosted by Axel Ryker's mother-in-law."

"Mr. Ryker has a wife?"

"Hard to believe, isn't it? Yet, it's true. And his wife, Rose, is a sweetheart. Rose's father is among the richest men in the United States. His wife, Bernice, often throws lavish parties to raise money for various charities. If you wish, I'll get you and Geofri an invitation. For these extravagant affairs, Bernice Bristow often hosts powerful politicians, celebrities, and the upper crust of Philadelphia and East Coast society. But I'd bet this café that she has never had a real European count attend. She'll be ecstatic. With your permission, I will call Rose later tonight."

"And you said that this Mr. Carr will be there?"

"Yes, Count."

"Very well, my child."

"Amy is already there with the band. They flew out this morning. It's only a one-hour flight. Rose is sending the family's private airplane back tomorrow to pick up Zhanna and me. You and Geofri can fly with us."

Erika was glad that Count Lupei and Leroy Carr would get the chance to talk face-to-face. Maybe Leroy would have more success at easing the Count's mind than she was apparently having.

Chapter 74

Bernice lists to starboard

Outside Philadelphia, Pennsylvania
Next day—Saturday, 22 September 1951

The Bristow Estate encompassed 8,320 acres of land—13 square miles—about a thirty-minute drive west of the Philadelphia outskirts.

Besides the enormous Bristow mansion, on the lands were a large lake (stocked well for fishing—a passion of Archibald Bristow) with a dock, boat house, and three lake houses. Rose and Axel lived in one of the lake houses. There was also a 9-hole golf course with three ponds. Farther away stood a large horse barn where racing thoroughbreds were pampered by a small but fulltime stable crew.

The Bristow's Cessna carrying Erika, Zhanna, the Count, and Geofri sat down on the Bristow's private airstrip at 5:25 p.m. They came early because of the six o'clock pre-arranged meeting Erika had set up. The early time would allow Amy to attend the meeting between the CIA, the Count, and Archibald Bristow. When the plane landed, Erika saw that Leroy Carr's CIA-issued Lockheed Hudson was already on the ground.

A shining, black Cadillac limousine awaited at the airstrip to drive the Count and those with him to the estate.

◊ ◊ ◊

Other guests were yet to arrive, so the Grand Hall was empty except for the estate's maids and hired caterers running around ensuring everything was perfect.

The count and Geofri wore expensive Gucci tuxedos. The Count had around his neck his official, brightly colored lanyard with a silver medal denoting his authoritative status as a true Romanian count. His ceremonial wolf's head cane he held in his left hand. Both Erika and Zhanna wore formal evening gowns.

Rose and her mother were waiting behind the arched, heavy oak 10-feet high double front door to greet the Count when he entered. A

254

doorman from the Alexander Hotel in Philadelphia had been hired for the night. When he opened the door and the Count stepped in, Erika thought Bernice Bristow looked like she might swoon when she laid eyes on the handsome, distinguished looking Romanian noble.

Bernice Bristow bowed. "Count Lupei. We are honored that you grace our home with your presence. My name is Bernice Bristow and this is my daughter, Rose. I will be your hostess tonight." She bowed again.

The Count took off his black stove pipe hat. He looked inquisitively at the woman who had married Axel Ryker, then turned back to her mother. "Please, Mrs. Bristow," the Count said in English but with a heavy Romanian accent. "There is no need to bow. I am a visitor to your delightful homeland." He took Bernice's hand and kissed the back of it. "I am charmed."

The Count then gazed at her with his soul-piercing green and golden eyes and said slowly, "I ... am ... your servant." Then her bowed to her.

Bernice Bristow's eyes started to slowly roll back in her head, and she began to sway from side to side. Erika saw this and caught the Bristow matriarch as she fainted.

Rose and Geofri revived Bernice quickly. Rose couldn't help laughing at what happened. Her mother had greeted many powerful and famous people to her charity soirees over the years, but Rose had never seen her faint while welcoming one to the mansion.

After everyone had made sure Bernice was okay, the Bristow's butler took the Count, Erika, and Zhanna to the library. Geofri followed but waited outside the door. Leroy Carr and Al Hodge were already there with Archibald Bristow, as were Amy and Axel Ryker. Archibald rose from his chair and greeted the Count. Everyone else also stood.

"Count Lupei. I'm Archibald Bristow. Erika has told me much about you. Welcome to my home." He then introduced Leroy. "I understand you met Mr. Hodge a couple of years ago." The men shook hands and Archibald continued, "We're meeting here in the library because it has more room than my study." Archibald invited the Count to sit down, then said, "What would you like to drink? I understand you like Laphroaig Scotch and Tuică. I have both."

The Count was surprised that Bristow had Tuică. It was usually not available outside of Romania. (Amy had gifted Archibald a bottle from the case she pilfered for the band off of Dragoș Luca's yacht.)

"Tuică will be fine. Thank you."

When everyone was seated and had their drink (and a cigar or cigarette if they wanted one), Leroy Carr was first to speak.

"Count Lupei, Mr. Bristow has influence within the top echelons of our government. He's aware that everyone in the room besides you and him is CIA. We can talk freely. I know you are concerned with Dragoș Luca. Let me assure you that what Erika told you is true. The Central Intelligence Agency is using all of its resources to gather the additional evidence on Luca we feel we need for an airtight case to present to our Department of Justice."

"Which means you do not yet have that evidence," the Count said. "I cooperated with your agency because I was led to believe that Luca would never again be a free man. Otherwise, he would have never left the grounds of Castelul Lupului alive. Even the slightest chance of Luca walking free causes me great concern. He is a blight on my beautiful homeland, Mr. Carr."

Carr replied, "Count, I am not a politician. I'm not going to sit here and lie to you or sugarcoat it. There is that slight chance, but I assure you that it is very slight. We are moving Luca from where he is now to an abandoned former German POW camp in Trinidad, Colorado. It was designed to hold 2500 prisoners but is deserted now. Luca will be the only prisoner. Troops from the Colorado National Guard, Army Military Police, and a contingent of CIA personnel will guard Luca. He will live in spartan conditions and escape will be impossible. Mr. Hodge will accompany Luca there and the level of interrogations increased while we await news from the team I assigned to gather more evidence on Luca in Mexico City."

Count Lupei didn't respond. Instead, he turned to Archibald Bristow. "Mr. Bristow. I thank you and your gracious wife for inviting me to your magnificent home. I have seen Miss Radu and her ensemble perform. I'm sure your guests will be enthralled by their repertoire."

That ended the meeting. A meeting much briefer than anyone expected.

◊ ◊ ◊

By eight o'clock all the guests had arrived and were milling about the Grand Hall chatting, eating the expensive canapés, and drinking French Champagne. Among them was the mayor of Philadelphia and his wife, the local U.S. Congressman and his wife, and other movers-and-shakers. Many rich Philadelphia socialites were there as usual. They never missed one of Bernice Bristow's charity soirees if invited, even though they knew it would cost them a substantial donation. All of them knew a newspaper photographer would be on hand. If they were lucky, their picture might appear on the society page of *The Philadelphia Inquirer*.

Bernice Bristow asked Rose to welcome everyone. Rose used the microphone on the temporary stage.

"Welcome, everyone," Rose declared. The loud banter subsided. "Thank you all for coming tonight. As you know, we're here to raise money for the Juvenile Diabetes Foundation. We have a treat for you tonight. Performing for us will be the Barcelona Romanian Gypsy Orchestra. They are the most popular Gypsy Flamenco band in Spain and several other European countries. They tour throughout the Mediterranean, and they recently concluded a tour in north Africa."

Rose acknowledged the mayor, the congressman, and a few other notables, then added, "But before the band takes the stage, I'd like to introduce our guest of honor. Count Sorin Lupei of Romania is with us tonight."

A spotlight shown on the Count, something he was not expecting nor wanted. For the sake of politeness, he bowed slightly to the applause.

"The band will take the stage in about fifteen minutes," Rose announced. "In the meantime, please continue to enjoy the food and drink."

The socialites nearly stampeded over themselves to get to Count Lupei, hoping to get a photograph taken of themselves with a European noble.

◊ ◊ ◊

None of the guests had ever seen a real Gypsy. They had heard only negative things about them—the men were thieves and the women prostituted themselves.

The Barcelona Romanian Gypsy Orchestra was on stage for only an hour, but that was enough time for the band and its striking singer/dancer to charm them. It was as if a Gypsy witch had cast a spell on the high-brow crowd.

When the performance ended it was no surprise that the socialites asked for a photograph with the band, but even the mayor and congressman and their wives requested a photograph from the *Inquirer* photographer.

After all that was taken care of, the hungry band joined the crowd for some food. Amy was still attired in her clan skirt and peasant blouse that she ended every performance wearing. Most of the of guests jockeyed around Count Lupei or band members, seeking to talk with them. This time at the Bristow event the mayor and congressman, who were normally the ones receiving most of the attention, were virtually ignored.

Chapter 75

Erika's concerns

Arlington, Virginia
Next day—Sunday, 23 September 1951

After the event at the Bristow mansion ended last night, Erika, Zhanna, the Count, and Geofri flew back to Washington. Amy spent the night at the mansion with the band. The band would arrive back at the Washington airport sometime this afternoon. Axel and Rose returned to their lake house on the estate property.

In the closed-on-Sunday Lili Marlene, Erika sat in Zhanna's apartment. Ada was in her and her mother's apartment next door. Zhanna had percolated a pot of coffee on her two-burner stove.

Something nagged at Erika.

She took a sip of coffee and said, "Zhanna, do you remember when we first approached the Count at Castelul Lupului about Luca. He was hesitant to get involved."

"I remember. He said he had to consider the families who lived and worked on his land."

"Exactly. But all that changed in a blink of an eye when one of Luca's men killed one the Castelul Lupului wolves."

"What are you getting at, Erika?"

Erika took a sip of coffee. "I think Count Lupei has come here to avenge the death of that wolf, more than any other reason."

Zhanna shrugged. "I told you in Romania when Luca was a prisoner at the Count's castle that we should let the wolves take care of Luca."

"That wasn't our mission," Erika said.

"Okay, that wasn't our mission, but look at the way things have turned out. Even Leroy Carr admits there is a chance of Luca being released."

[that afternoon]

By 4 p.m., the band members were back in their rooms at the Mayflower. Amy reported to the Lili Marlene. This time, the Shield Maidens sat at the table closest to the bar in the empty café.

Erika didn't start out talking about Count Lupei. Instead, she had news for Amy.

"Amy, last night Archibald Bristow told me that he, as the band's American promoter, can get the visas of the band members extended if you have additional bookings. We'd love to have you perform again next weekend here at the café. And for as many weekends as the band wishes to remain in the States. How do you feel about a four-weekend contract?"

"I'll tell Petru. I haven't spoken to him about future commitments in Spain or the Mediterranean. The band is under the impression that we will all return to Barcelona this week."

Erika fessed up. "I need you here in the States for a while, Amy. I think we might have a problem with Count Lupei."

"What problem? Did you tell Leroy or Al about it?"

"No. I haven't told Leroy or Al. It's only a hunch on my part, but I think the Count came here to kill Luca."

"How can he do that?" Amy asked. "Luca's heavily guarded by armed troops around the clock."

"I don't know how," Erika responded. "But you have seen the odd things that can happen when the Count is involved. I need you here. I feel an obligation to the Count, and I don't want him brought up on charges here in the United States."

There came a pause. Amy finally said, "If Petru hasn't signed any contracts for performances in Europe, I'm sure the band will be unanimous in wanting to extend its American tour. I could always stay behind, of course, but it would be less suspicious if the band had a contract for more shows here in the States. But either way, I will remain with you, Erika."

"Thank you, Amy."

Zhanna exhaled a cloud of cigarette smoke and added, "I hope the Count succeeds. This is what's wrong with America. Criminals like Luca are protected by 'rights.'"

Chapter 76

A four-week engagement

Arlington, Virginia
Next day—Monday, 24 September 1951

The Barcelona Romanian Gypsy Orchestra dined tonight at the Lili Marlene Café. Joining them at their table was Erika Lehmann. Besides supplying a plane for their transportation and putting the band up for two nights at his lavish estate, Archibald Bristow had paid them well for their performance.

"Rose Bristow told me over fifteen thousand dollars was raised for the charity," Erika said in Russian to the group.

Everyone thought that was wonderful.

Petru said, "Erika, I'm happy to tell you that we can accept your kind offer for a four-week contract to perform here at your café. Before we left Barcelona, I was contacted by a promotor in Greece, but dates had not yet been decided on, so no contract has been signed."

"That's wonderful, Petru," Erika said.

The band members and stage crew were excited and raised their glasses in a toast. Cici said, "Can you take us to an American theater this week to see a movie?

"Yes," Erika answered. "But the movies will be in English, with no Romanian or Russian subtitles."

"That doesn't matter," Cici said. "We just want to go to a Hollywood movie in America."

"We'll go tomorrow night," Erika promised. "By the way, Mr. Bristow is paying for more advertisements for your four-week engagement here at the café. I'm sure it will be standing room only every night, like it was the night of your last performance here. Angelika is working on getting more help for those weekends, but that's not your concern. I'm just glad everyone will be in the States for at least another month." She included the entire band in her comments, but she mainly referred to Amy.

Chapter 77

Extra rare

Washington, D.C.
Two days later—Wednesday, 26 September 1951

Leroy Carr had summoned Al Hodge to his office to talk about Dragoş Luca.

"When will Luca be moved to Colorado, Leroy?"

"Sometime next week. That German POW camp has been abandoned since the last prisoner was sent back to Germany in '46. The place needs a lot of clean-up, and provisions brought in for the mess hall to feed the guards. The guard barracks has to be gotten back in order— all the beds in the camp were removed and sent to military hospitals. Some of the perimeter barbed wire has to be replaced."

Hodge said, "At the meeting Saturday night at Bristow's mansion, you told that Count that the level of interrogations will be increased. You never talked to me about that. And you never explained to me why you're moving Luca to that POW camp in the first place. You know he can't escape from the Norfolk Naval stockade."

"I know he can't, Al. But the Falcon team in Mexico City is running into dead ends. I don't like doing this, but I'm going to let Ryker interrogate Luca after he's moved to the camp."

"You've always been against getting Ryker involved in interrogations of prisoners here in the States, Leroy."

"I hate to do it, Al, but a confession from Luca might be our only avenue. You'll have to go with him. Make sure Ryker doesn't kill him or make him a vegetable. That's why I'm moving Luca to that remote camp. I couldn't have Ryker do what he does best at Norfolk."

"Does Ryker know about this?" Hodge asked.

"Not yet. I would never tell anyone anything before I told you. We have to keep this quiet. Don't tell anyone, not even Erika."

◊ ◊◊

[that evening]

Erika took Count Lupei and Geofri to dinner at the Capitol Hill Steakhouse. The upscale restaurant was located only a few blocks from the capitol building and a place where one was likely to spot a congressman or senator dining with their wives, a fellow elected official, or a Supreme Court judge.

Erika had made reservations, and after they were seated, Erika said, "Count Lupei. I hope you'll allow me to pay for dinner tonight."

"No, my child. I will pay." The Count wore a dark-brown Savile Row suit with nothing to reveal his Romanian nobility in order to avoid attention. Geofri also wore an expensive suit. His was black. Erika wore a navy V-neck cotton dress with just the slightest amount of cleavage visible.

When the waiter arrived, they placed drink orders and meals orders at the same time. For the meals, Geofri ordered a New York strip cooked medium. Erika ordered a medium rare ribeye. The Count ordered the filet mignon. "Please tell your chef to make that extra rare," the Count told the waiter.

As they waited for the drinks, Erika said, "Count Lupei, what sites have you seen in Washington? I'd be happy to drive you and Geofri around tomorrow if you wish."

"That would be pleasant," the Count said.

The drinks arrived.

"Count, may I ask you a frank question?"

"Of course. I appreciate frankness."

"I think I know why you're here. It's to eliminate Dragoş Luca. Is that true?"

The Count gazed into her eyes as he took a sip of his Scotch. He then put the glass down. "You know this because you are a She-Wolf, one of few over the centuries. You are an aberration over the vastness of time. You are what you are because of your Creator. You cannot flee from it."

Their eyes never parted. He had answered her question.

Part 8

Chapter 78

Ryker accepts

Washington, D.C.
Monday, 01 October 1951

Axel Ryker sat down heavily in a chair facing Leroy Carr's desk. As always, he was wearing his black porkpie hat. Al Hodge was there.

"Ryker. Dragoş Luca will be flown to Colorado on Wednesday. The former German POW camp outside Trinidad will be ready for him by then. Al is in charge of security during transport, and he will accompany him. Luca will be shackled and as many guards as Al deems necessary will be on the plane."

Ryker looked bored. "What has this to do with me?"

"Let me finish," Carr said sternly. "I called you in because I'm sending you on a lone assignment. You'll fly to Trinidad on Thursday and begin interrogation of Luca. We need a confession of guilt from him. You are not to get carried away. Al will be there to make sure of that."

"You underestimate my time in the Gestapo, Herr Carr," Ryker responded. "I don't get carried away. With interrogations I proceed until I get the truth. That will not take long if I'm given free reign. I can tell when someone is lying to me."

"I'm not giving you total free reign. There are conditions," Carr stated firmly. "Luca is not to be killed or taken to the point he cannot speak coherently."

Ryker smiled grotesquely. "I accept those conditions."

"No one is to know about this, Ryker. Not even Erika. Tell your wife only what you tell her before any mission, that you have an assignment, and you have to travel. Am I clear?"

"I understand. I will also tell Rose that I won't be gone long. This is a simple assignment and I won't have to work with Lehmann and her women."

◊ ◊ ◊

[that evening at the Lili Marlene Café]
Last weekend's performances by the Gypsy band had been standing room only, helped by word of mouth and the advertising paid for by Archibald Bristow. Knowing it would be hectic like the last time the band performed at the café, Angelika had hired four more temporary waitresses to help out during the band's engagement, and Bertha had both of her daughters helping in the kitchen. This made things run much smoother for the staff.

Erika and Amy sat at the bar talking to Zhanna. They had already been interrupted four times by regulars who had attended the performances and sought an autograph from Amy.

Between autograph hounds, Erika said, "Amy, you and the band are making the Lili Marlene famous. Even our weekday business has picked up."

Amy smiled, "That's good."

Erika handed Amy an envelope. "Here's the money that was agreed upon for last weekend's performances."

"I'll get it to Petru."

Zhanna said, "I want permission to hire another bartender. With the added business we're now getting, Angelika won't be able to handle the bar by herself when we're away on an assignment."

"You're right, Zhanna," Erika said. "Good idea. You and Angelika can do the interviewing."

Chapter 79

Strange migration

Arlington, Virginia
Two days later—Wednesday, 03 October 1951

Erika called Count Lupei's suite at the Mayflower Hotel. Geofri picked up.

"Geofri. This is Erika. I'd like to invite you and the Count to dinner tonight at the Lili Marlene."

"I'm sorry, Erika. The Count is not here."

"That's okay. Just tell him when he returns to the hotel."

"I'm afraid that won't be today. The Count has decided to do a bit of traveling. I'm not sure when he will return."

Erika knew immediately that something was amiss. The Count never traveled without his butler.

"Where did he go?" she asked.

"Again, I'm sorry. I'm not at liberty to say."

[an hour later at the E Street Complex in Washington]
The CIA monitored daily newspapers from every major U.S. city, paying special attention to cities or states where any CIA agents were working. Officially, the CIA was prohibited by its charter from conducting operations on U.S. soil, but this was commonly ignored if the need arose. After reading a brief article in yesterday's *Rocky Mountain News,* a major daily based in Denver, Al Hodge made a beeline to Leroy Carr's office and handed him the article.

"What's this about?" Carr asked.

"Read it, Leroy. It's a small article that was on page three of a Denver daily.

Carr read it.

Strange Migration of Wolves

The Colorado Department of Wildlife Conservation reports that there has been a recent increase in the timber wolf population in the mountains surrounding Trinidad in southern Colorado. Conservation officials have no explanation for the migration. Hunters, fishermen, and mountain hikers in that area are warned to take precautions.

"Call Erika, Al. Have her come in immediately. She must have spilled the beans to the Count that we were moving Luca."

"She didn't tell him, Leroy. You did. You told Archibald Bristow that night of the charity event when we were all in his library. The Count was there."

Carr, with all his concerns, had forgotten.

"Damn!" He bellowed.

Hodge said, "We're going to have to get Erika involved. She has some sort of bond with that Count. Maybe Erika can find him. She's in the building. I saw her going down an elevator about a half hour ago. I was at the other end of the hall and was going to speak with her, but when she saw me she closed the elevator door."

"Find her, Al, and bring her to my office."

Al didn't have to. He was barely out of his chair when the intercom on his desk buzzed. It was Carr's secretary.

"Mr. Carr. Erika Lehmann is here and asking to speak with you."

"Send her in, Effie."

Erika walked in the office and sat down. She was irked. "Leroy, I went down to the transportation room and checked recent files. The records show that Al is flying out tonight to Colorado and Axel is doing the same tomorrow. Why didn't you tell me about this?"

"Because I didn't think you or the Maidens needed to get involved, but knowing you, you would have gone cowboy and went there anyway.

Simple as that. Al reminded me it's my fault the Count knows about moving Luca to that POW camp. That was certainly my mistake. Now I have a question for you. Al was at the Count's castle during your first mission there in '49. He told me about the strange things he saw, mainly concerning wolves. Why wasn't anything about that in your recent report?"

"I didn't think it was vital information about the mission."

Carr handed her the newspaper article. "Read this."

After she read it, she placed it back on his desk.

"What do have to say about it?" Carr asked her.

Erika shrugged.

"Answer me!" he demanded.

"Alright. Keep your pants on, Leroy. Yes, it must be the Count's doing. I assume the reason Al is flying out tonight is to transport Luca. Send me to Trinidad tomorrow with Axel. It won't be easy, but maybe I can find the Count. I'll go by myself. Amy needs to stay here. It will look suspicious to the band if she again disappears on them. And if I take Zhanna, she's liable to kill Luca on sight in revenge for Jaro Banik."

"That's exactly what I'm doing," Carr said. He then paused for a brief moment. "I'm sorry I snapped at you. I have no one to blame for this other than myself."

[that evening]

Erika called Amy at the Mayflower and asked her to stop by the Lili Marlene at seven. Erika, Zhanna, and Amy now sat upstairs at the storage room table.

"I have to leave town for a few days," Erika told them.

"Why?" Amy asked.

Erika was always honest with her teammates. She told them about the newspaper article. "The Count has to be somewhere in the area around Trinidad. I'm being sent to find him."

"Why aren't we going?" Zhanna asked.

Erika explained the reasons she had told Leroy Carr.

"It's not a dangerous assignment," she assured them. "I have nothing to fear from the Count or the wolves. Both of you know that.

Hopefully, I won't be gone long. Zhanna, will you stay with Ada in our apartment? It's a two-bedroom. You can sleep in my bed. I know Angelika would gladly have Ada stay in her studio apartment, but it's so small I know it has to be at least a small imposition for Angelika. Just make sure Ada gets her homework done."

Chapter 80

Meatloaf

Trinidad, Colorado
Next day—Thursday, 04 October 1951

Erika and Ryker arrived at the POW camp around dinnertime. They had
flown to Denver on a commercial airline. That plane was not totally full
and all the other passengers jockeyed around so they wouldn't have to
sit next to the daunting Ryker. In Denver they boarded a smaller plane
that had been chartered from a private company by the CIA
transportation people for the flight to Trinidad. Once in Trinidad, they
were picked up by an MP driving a Jeep, sent by Al Hodge to deliver
them to the now heavily guarded camp located about 20 miles south of
the small town.

Trinidad was 6,000 feet above sea level and the first thing Erika
noticed was the chilly October air.

When they arrived at the camp, the MP took them to Hodge's
quarters. He was reading some paperwork when they entered.

"Have you two eaten dinner yet?" he asked.

"No," Erika said.

Hodge handed them a sheet of paper. "Here's a map of the camp.
Report to the mess hall and have something to eat. It's meatloaf tonight.
The cooks close it down at seven and the mess hall is about a six or
seven-minute walk from here, so you better go now. When you're
finished, meet me back here."

Fifty minutes later, Erika and Ryker were back at the barracks
Hodge used as his quarters. He had the building to himself.

The first thing Hodge said was, "Give me your maps. Even after
housing all the security, there are still plenty of empty barracks. I've
assigned both of you one and a room was made ready for you this
morning." He wrote an X over one of the barracks on Erika's map, and
over another one on Ryker's map, then handed them back to them.

"Take a seat." Hodge said. "Ryker, you'll begin interrogating Luca
tomorrow morning. Remember the conditions Leroy laid out for you.

271

Erika, Trinidad has only 8,000 residents. There are only two small motels in town; they are motor lodges mostly for drivers who have been on the road too long and want to pull over for some sleep, or for hunters from the bigger cities like Denver, Pueblo, or Colorado Springs. Guys who are spending time in the area during bear or elk hunting season. One of these motels is located on Highway 85 on the northern edge of town. The other is on Highway 350 that heads east."

"I'll check them," she said. "I doubt I'll find the Count at any of those places. With his accent he'd be too conspicuous, but I'll go there first."

Speaking to both of them, Hodge said, "Keep in mind that the weather this time of year is much different than in Washington. It gets cold here at night because of the elevation. Last night it got down to 39 degrees. Last week, it snowed."

"I'm from Bavaria, Al," Erika reminded him.

"Where is Luca being held?" Ryker asked.

"In the camp stockade. It's where they placed German POWs who got out of line or who had tried to escape. It's the barracks next to the mess hall. They put it there so prisoner meals would be handy to deliver. There's a big red X painted on the door. It contains cells and is heavily guarded. I gave the MP first lieutenant in charge your name as an interrogator. You'll have to show I.D. every time you go there."

"I'll have to go only twice," Ryker promised. "Once tomorrow morning and again Saturday morning."

Hodge and Erika looked at Himmler's top inquisitor.

"Regardless," Hodge said. "None of us are going home until we have a signed confession from Luca. Erika, it's your job to find this Count and convince him we have things under control. He can't possibly think he can penetrate this camp and get to Luca, wolves or no."

Erika listened, but didn't reply.

When Hodge finished with them, Ryker walked back to his barracks. Erika stood outside admiring the magnificent sunset, painting a mural overtop the mountains to the west. The sky was a riot of orange, red, and pink hues. She had checked on the phases of the moon. The next full moon would appear Saturday night. In Transylvania, a full moon in October was referred to as the 'wolf moon.'

Chapter 81

Axel calls on Dragoş

Trinidad, Colorado
Next day—Friday, 05 October 1951

At 4 a.m., well before dawn, Dragoş Luca was awakened when his cell door opened. He sat up on his cot. A man stood just outside. The lighting in the corridor was brighter than in his cell, so Luca could see only a silhouette. It was a large man wearing a cocked hat.

When the shadow stepped into the cell, Luca saw his scarred face. It was Axel Ryker who Luca met at Castelul Lupului, and the same man who broke his wrist and four of his fingers on the Som de Argint. He still wore a cast.

"I hope I didn't disturb your sleep," the German Ryker said in Russian. He was born in Lithuania so Russian was actually his mother tongue.

"So, the CIA sent you to interrogate me," Luca replied. "You're wasting your time."

"Cigarette or cigar," Ryker offered. "I have both."

Luca was dying for one. "Cigarette."

Ryker shook a Chesterfield out of its pack, handed it to Luca, then held his Zippo lighter for him.

"How are the conditions here?" Ryker asked. "I know you've been here only for two nights."

"Get to the point," Luca sneered.

Ryker took an envelope from his jacket pocket and tossed it on Luca's cot. "Read these papers over carefully and then sign them. You have one day. If you don't, I will return tomorrow morning." The monstrous Ryker then glared at Luca. "Believe me, that is something you do not want. It will be in your best interest to cooperate."

"You don't scare me Ryker. When you broke my fingers and wrist we were in international waters. Now we are not. I know the Americans are prohibited from torturing prisoners by their Congress. The Soviet Embassy will gain my release. I've been arrested unjustly."

273

"As I said, sign the papers today or you will sign them tomorrow."

Luca laughed. "You better check with your superiors before you lay another hand on me. The Americans would never dare."

"I'm not American as you can tell from my accent. I was Gestapo during the war. I was the first man Reichsführer Himmler called upon to deal with 'special problems.' That was a part of my life I look back on with fondness."

[later that morning]

The MP corporal who had picked up Erika and Ryker yesterday at the grass landing strip in Trinidad drove Erika today. Showing her phony State Department identification card to the persons manning the motel desks, it didn't take her long to check the registries at both of the small lodges. She even described the Count to the clerks and told them about his accent. As she had predicted, the Count was not staying at either place.

Two hours after she left the camp that morning, she was back and having coffee in the mess hall by herself. When finished, she walked outside and scanned the horizons in all directions. To the east were the Spanish Peaks. To the west loomed the Rockies, with the foreboding, nearly 10,000-feet tall Fisher's Peak standing sentinel, jutting toward Heaven above them all.

Erika spent a couple of hours preparing for her trip. She obtained a WW II Army backpack, a heavy Army jacket, a pup tent, water canteen, matches, a flashlight, and some K-rations. She left the camp at 2 p.m. and began walking west, toward Fischer's Peak.

The foothills of the Rockies were not far from Trinidad. She reached them shortly, but still had a long journey ahead.

[later that afternoon]

Al Hodge had spent most of his day going around the camp having meetings with the chiefs of the various levels of camp security. He also had a lengthy telephone conversation with Leroy Carr back in Washington.

It was 4:30 p.m. before he returned to his quarters. He had instructed Erika and Ryker to meet him in the mess hall at five so they could fill them in on their day. When he entered his room, on the floor was a note that someone had slipped under his door.

Al, the Count is not in Trinidad. I've gone into the mountains. Erika

◊ ◊ ◊

By 5:15 p.m. Hodge and Ryker had found a table and sat down with their trays of overcooked pork chops they stood in line to get. Everything at the camp was military-style, including the mess hall.

"Okay, Ryker," Hodge said. "Give me your report."

"I delivered the confession papers to Luca this morning and gave him a day to think it over. He will sign them tomorrow."

"He said that?"

"No, but I'm confident he will. Where's Lehmann? I thought she was supposed to be here."

"She didn't find the Count in Trinidad. She's still looking."

[later that night]

Erika had crossed over the foothills and was now working her way up through the dense forests of the Rockies. She loved the sharp smell of the pines. Darkness had fallen and overhead the sky was especially brilliant at the high altitude. But it was cold for that same reason. Erika became accustomed to cold weather having experienced Bavaria winters as a child, yet still, the Bavarian Alps were not nearly as high as the Rockies and she knew it was time to make camp.

By eight o'clock, she had ascended about 1,000 feet up the slope of Fisher's Peak. She set up her one-man pup tent and started a campfire. The fire would supply warmth, and she hoped it would make her conspicuous and lure the children of the night to her camp.

After settling in, she opened one of the K-rations and sat by the fire.

Chapter 82

Howling

Rocky Mountains of Southern Colorado

It was just past midnight and Erika had settled into her tent only an hour ago. Now the howling began. It was distant but still it awoke her. She went back to sleep, knowing the Count would find her.

Four hours later, Erika awoke again. This time she wasn't sure why. Putting on her shoes and exiting the small tent, she saw that her campfire was now just a few glowing embers. Then she saw the multiple pairs of shining eyes gazing at her from the forest. They disappeared quickly.

She put some pinecones on the embers to restore the fire along with branches from a fallen spruce, then opened another K-ration and waited.

[that morning at the POW camp]

Civil daylight, the light that begins appearing just before the sunrise, had just begun to lighten the night sky. Many stars fled at the start of civil daylight, but the nearly full moon and the morning star, Venus, were still visible.

The camp's infirmary had no doctor, but it was ably manned by a crusty, experienced Army nurse who served for three years in Europe during the war in various frontline M.A.S.H. units. She cursed like a sailor, but she was expert at caring for the wounded and always began her daily routine very early in the morning—a habit that gripped her during the war. She was aided by a young Army medic.

Dragoş Luca was brought in on a stretcher by four Army privates followed by Axel Ryker. The nurse examined him quickly and said, "What in hell happened to this guy? He's all fucked up."

"He fell down," Ryker said.

Heinrich Himmler's favorite Gestapo interrogator then left and walked to Al Hodge's barrack with the signed confession.

[Fisher's Peak]
Count Lupei walked into Erika's camp as the sun, ready to command the day, started rising in the east.

"Hello, Count Lupei."

"Hello, Erika. I've been expecting you. Follow me."

The walk farther up the mountain took an hour before they came upon a small, rustic cabin in bad repair. He led her in. A small fire burned in a wood stove.

"It's odd seeing you in those clothes, Count," Erika said. He wore olive drab fatigues.

"I bought them at an Army Surplus store in Denver. Please, have a seat. I'll make coffee." He put water into the percolator then coffee into the strainer. He placed it on top of the wood burning stove and added a log. "There is a running spring just a hundred feet up the mountain. It makes for excellent coffee. It won't take long. The stove gets very hot."

"How did you find this cabin?" Erika asked.

"It was an easy task. Also in Denver, I picked up a publication for hunters and fishermen. In the back was a listing of free cabins available for them on public property throughout the state. Apparently, this state builds these small shelters for survival purposes. Many inexperienced hunters get lost in these vast, beautiful mountains. This one needs repair, as you can see, but it's sufficient and elk hunting season doesn't begin until the end of next month. The lakes for fishing are distant. I was right that this place would be abandoned."

He sat down on a rickety chair. "Are you hungry? I brought a supply of what the Americans call beef jerky."

"Thank you, Count, but I'm not hungry. I brought along some United States military meals soldiers use in the field. I ate about an hour before you found me."

The count nodded, then said, "What is it you want to tell me, my child?"

"Count Lupei, I know tonight there is a full moon—the October moon referred to in Transylvania as the wolf moon. That Army camp is heavily guarded. Men in towers have machineguns. If attacked by the children of the night, many of the wolves will lose their lives. I'm asking that you give us more time. Axel Ryker is working on getting a confession from Luca. If anyone can do it, it's Ryker." She didn't know that Luca's confession had already been signed.

"I've been given many promises by your CIA, Erika."

"Please wait, Count. Give us a few days. I will return to the POW camp and come back here Tuesday and update you."

The Count didn't reply. The coffeepot bubbled. He rose and poured two cups.

[late that afternoon]

Erika didn't get back to the camp until shortly after five o'clock. She went directly to Al Hodge's barrack. She knocked. He answered and she entered.

"Al, the camp will be attacked by wolves tonight. It will be late, probably around midnight."

"So, you found the Count? Did he tell you this?"

"I found him, or more accurately he found me. I asked him for more time. He didn't reply, so I know this will happen. Call off the guards and put Luca outside the camp. Let him get what he deserves."

"That's crazy, Erika. I know odd things have happened in Transylvania during your two assignments there, but you're telling me the Count has an army of wolves. I can't base a decision on that foolishness. Besides, Ryker got a confession out of Luca this morning. We need him alive. I'm flying him to Lowry Air Force Base in Denver tomorrow morning. They have a hospital on the base. Luca's left arm has been broken in two places and every finger on that hand broken. He also has a dislocated shoulder, a broken ankle, a ruptured eardrum, and is blind in one eye. The Army nurse in charge of the infirmary told me he needs surgery on a couple of the breaks as soon as possible. She said he could be transported as long as he has medical attention available on the trip. I'll take her with me to Lowry."

Erika had no sympathy for Luca. She said, "I wish I would have known this—about the confession, I mean."

"You had already headed to the hills."

278

"I know that Al. It's nobody's fault. It's just that I don't have enough time to get to the Count tonight."

[later]
Erika was keeping watch on her own near the western boundary of the camp that faced towards Fisher's Peak. It was about 11:30 when the moon silhouetted a long string of at least five dozen timber wolves taking their place on the top of the nearest foothill just a mile from the camp.

Erika ran to the camp gate, demanded that the guards allow her to leave, then began running toward the wolves. When she was about half-way to the wolves, the Count appeared in the middle of the large wolfpack. The wolves lowered their heads, snarled, and began trotting toward the camp. Erika tried to call them off, but she didn't have as much power over them as the Count. They ignored her and continued on. Erika's only hope was to get the Count and tell him about Luca's signed confession. She ran up the hill toward him. When the enormous wolfpack got within 500 yards of the camp, they broke into a full sprint toward the barbed wire.

Chapter 83

A call to Washington

Outside Trinidad, Colorado
Next morning—Sunday, 07 October 1951

Erika had gotten to the Count in time. After she told him about Luca's confession, the wolves stopped in their tracks just as they were about to enter the light from the camp perimeter light poles. The men in the guard towers never saw them. They began returning to the Count. This happened without any type of audible signal by Count Lupei.

Erika had told Hodge what happened. Al believed that she had found the Count but discounted the outlandish story. That was okay by her. It would save her from a lengthy report.

The Count showed up at the camp gate this morning. He now sat in Al Hodge's barrack reading over Luca's several page-long signed confession. Besides Al, Erika and Ryker were there.

When Sorin Lupei finished and gave the papers back to Hodge, Al said, "Luca will never again be a free man, Count. He has been injured. This afternoon I'm flying him to a hospital at a U.S. Air Force base in Denver. Erika and Axel will be with me. After he receives some needed surgery, we'll take him back to the Fort Dix, New Jersey, stockade and then we'll present charges against him to our Department of Justice. It will be an airtight case because of his signed confession. You are welcome to accompany us on the plane."

The Count accepted the offer. He had faith in Erika, but not the CIA. He wanted to be sure that Luca was returned to Fort Dix.

[later that morning]
Hodge was on the phone with Leroy Carr in Washington. He had called Leroy yesterday and told him about the signed confession and the shape Luca was in after being interrogated by Axel Ryker.

"Leroy. We're leaving the camp with Luca for Lowry in three hours."

"Okay, Al. Tomorrow, I'll shut down the camp and send everyone back to their normal duties."

"Don't send that Army nurse away," Hodge said. "I'm taking her with us to Denver and then keeping her until we get Luca back to Fort Dix."

"Okay."

"Erika was right about that Count being in the area. He showed up this morning. I let him read Luca's confession."

"I would have done the same thing," Carr said. *"Good work, Al."*

"How are we going to explain Luca's injuries to the Justice Department people? He's going to take months to heal. He'll probably be in a wheelchair when he's arraigned, and that Army nurse tells me he might never regain eyesight in that one eye."

Carr thought for a moment. *"I'll come up with something. The official report will state that Luca fell into a ravine during an escape attempt, or something along those lines. How long will you be in Denver?"*

"The nurse has a ton of experience with the wounded. She told me that he should be able to be transported within three or four days after the surgeries. We should have him at Fort Dix sometime next weekend."

"Oh, boy," said Carr. *"That gives Erika time in Denver. You know she's tight with the Smaldones. Make sure she doesn't get in trouble."*

"I'll do my best, Leroy. You know she doesn't give a shit when either of us tell her to stay out of trouble during her free time. I could confine her to the base."

"We can't lose the Shield Maiden team. Detaining her might make her quit the CIA again. Zhanna and Ryker can't quit, but Amy and the Fischer sisters would probably resign in support of Erika. She's an American citizen now and we no longer have a hammer over her head because of her past work for Abwehr. Nick Sparks at the State Department would take her back as a translator in a second." Erika had quit once before after a heated dispute with Carr over the CIA trying to monitor and place restrictions on her free time. *"Plus, her café is starting to do well. That gives her a second option. All we can do is keep our fingers crossed that you don't have to bail her out of jail for the umpteenth time."*

Chapter 84

Gaetano's

Denver, Colorado
Next day—Monday, 08 October 1951

The group arrived at Lowry Air Force base in Denver yesterday evening. Hodge, Erika, Ryker, and the Count had been given their separate rooms in one of the officer's barracks on the massive Air Force base.

Luca was undergoing surgery this morning while Hodge met with Erika for breakfast in one of the three mess halls.

Hodge took a sip of coffee, then said, "I wanted to talk with you privately. That's why Ryker and the Count aren't here. I feel that the best thing to do is confine you to the base while we're here."

"That's bullshit, Al. Why?"

"I won't do it if you can tell me you'll stay out of trouble and stay away from the Smaldones."

"I understand, Al."

Hodge had made his obligatory demands, but he knew she'd ignore them.

[that evening]

That afternoon, Erika called Ada. She had called her daughter every day since leaving for Trinidad. Now, she walked into Gaetano's restaurant at 6 p.m.

Gaetano's was located in what was known as Denver's Little Italy section on the northwest side of town. The restaurant was owned and run by the Smaldone family who controlled Denver's organized crime, and indeed held sway over the rackets of gambling, loansharking, and extortion in two states—Colorado and Wyoming. The Smaldones were not involved with drugs or prostitution but strong-arming someone who was late on a gambling debt or loan payment was an integral part of day-to-day business. Fat Paulie Villano headed the crew of thumb breakers (or much worse).

Erika had spent time in Denver during two previous missions. Checkers Smaldone (the don of the family), and Fat Paulie Villano (their chief enforcer and Checkers' cousin) had even visited Erika at the Lili Marlene Café once during a trip they made to the East Coast for a meeting with a New York City crime family. Erika and Zhanna had both been 'made' by the Smaldones which granted them membership in the family. Females becoming 'made men' was practically unheard of in the mafia and in fact prohibited within all the East Coast and Chicago families.

Tonight, even though it was Monday, most of the tables were already taken. Everyone in Denver knew the restaurant was the headquarters of the Smaldone family because of the numerous arrests that appeared in the two Denver daily newspapers. Nevertheless, the place enjoyed good business from customers from all over the city because it served the best Italian food in Denver, and it drew the curious who hoped to get a glimpse of a mobster.

Erika walked up to the bartender.

"Hi, Tommy."

He looked up. "Erika."

"I see you're back. Last time I was here you were doing a stretch in Canon City." (The Colorado State Penitentiary was located down state outside that small town).

"I got out four months ago. What are you drinking?"

"I'll take a Coors. I haven't had one since the last time I was in Denver. (Coors beer was brewed in Golden, Colorado, and was available only in the Rocky Mountain states).

Tommy poured the draft.

"What do I owe you?" she asked.

"Are you kidding me? Checkers would have my hide if I charged you."

"Is Checkers around?"

"No. But Chauncey and Paulie are upstairs eating." (Chauncey was Checkers' younger brother).

"I'll go up. Thanks for the beer, Tommy."

283

Upstairs over the restaurant was the nerve center for the Smaldone operations. When Erika got to the top of the stairs, she didn't recognize the guard at the door, and he didn't know her.

"My name is Erika Lehmann. Tommy told me that Chauncey and Paulie are up here. I'd like to see them. What's your name?"

"None of your damn business. What do you want to see them about?"

"I'm a friend."

"Do you have any weapons on you?"

"Yes. A handgun."

"Give it to me."

She took the Berretta out of its holster tucked inside the back of her slacks that was concealed by her untucked blouse.

"Wait here," he commanded. He entered the room and closed the door behind him. A brief moment later he re-emerged and handed the Berretta back to her. "I apologize if I was rude. My name is Dario. Chauncey told me you are a made family member."

"That's okay, Dario. You were just doing your job," she said.

"Go on in." He opened the door for her then closed it after she stepped in.

As Tommy had said, Chauncey and Fat Paulie sat at a table eating.

Fat Paulie Villano put his fork down and looked at her. "Well, fuck me bald. Look what the cat dragged in." As his nickname implied, he was a large, round man. In his late 30s, his hair already had a noticeable receding hairline. The younger Chauncey had the reputation of being a ladies' man. He was in his late-20s and good looking.

"Hello Paulie, Chauncey. I came by thinking the restaurant would be closed but hoping someone would be here. Last time I was in Denver, the restaurant was closed on Sunday and Monday."

Chauncey said, "We're still closed on Sundays, but last spring, we decided to be open on Mondays. Too much business we were passing up. Have a seat, Erika. Have you had dinner?"

"Not yet."

"What do you want?"

"Penne and mussels. Thanks, Chauncey."

Chauncey Smaldone went to the door and told the guard to go downstairs and place the order, then returned to his seat.

The Smaldones knew Erika was CIA, but they didn't find that out until after she had been made. She was still in good standing because she had never betrayed them to anyone in the government, and in fact she had once gotten a criminal charge against Checkers dropped when she told Al Hodge that if Checkers were arrested it would be a blow to her mission at that time. On that assignment, she had worked with the family in trying to find a Russian spy who was being protected by the small Russian mob located on the other side of the city.

"How's Zhanna doing?" Fat Paulie asked. "Is she still above ground?"

"She'll be here tomorrow," Erika said. She had called Zhanna from Trinidad yesterday, after she learned she would be making a stop in Denver.

"How long will you be in town?" Chauncey asked the natural question. Neither man asked her *why* she was there. That would be up to Checkers to ask if he wanted to.

"Not sure, but it looks right now that I might be here through the weekend. I see the poker tables are still up here so I'm assuming the Friday and Saturday night games for the family members are still happening."

"That's right," Chauncey said.

"Great. Zhanna and I will be here. When is Checkers returning?"

"Tomorrow. He had to go to Pueblo today on business."

Fat Paulie asked, "Where are you staying?"

"Lowry Air Force Base."

"Come here tomorrow at this same time," Paulie said. "The boss will want to talk to you about that."

"Screw you, Paulie," she said. "I'll be here, but only because I'd like to see Checkers."

Fat Paulie laughed and looked at Chauncey. "I've always liked this fucking broad. She's got balls."

285

Chapter 85

Checkers

Denver, Colorado
Next day—Tuesday, 09 October 1951

Dragos Luca had his surgeries yesterday morning and was now under guard in the base hospital. After breakfast this morning, Al Hodge summoned Erika and Ryker to a meeting in his quarters.

"The nurse's estimate about how long Luca would be here before he could be moved was pretty accurate," Hodge told them. "The doctor who operated on Luca told me he should be able to be moved next Monday. I talked to Leroy. He'll have our transportation people line us up an Air Force DC-3 for our flight that morning. We're not taking Luca back to Norfolk. He's going to the Fort Dix stockade. The crew of Luca's yacht is no longer under custody. They were deported to France. What they do, or where they go from there, is their business."

Neither Erika nor Ryker commented. Hodge then looked at Erika. "I see from the base's entrance registry that you checked out of the camp at five o'clock yesterday afternoon and returned at ten. Where did you go, Erika?"

"I got a taxi and took a drive around town."

"Baloney," Hodge replied. "I'd lay odds that you went to Gaetano's."

"I stopped by there for dinner, Al. So what?"

"I asked you not to have any contact with the Smaldones."

"You stressed that I stay out of trouble," Erika said. "I didn't get in any trouble. It's none of your business what I do during my free time. I've already had this conversation with you and Leroy."

Hodge sighed. "Lehmann, you've already taken years off my life. If you end up in jail, I'm not going to bail you out this time. Your ass can sit in the can while we return to Fort Dix."

"Oh, I forgot to tell you, Al. Zhanna will be here this afternoon. She'll need quarters."

"Dammit, Erika . . ."

She cut him off. "It's our free time, Al." She rose, kissed Hodge on his cheek and patted his head.

"Get away from me, Lehmann," Hodge said.

"I'm bored," Ryker grunted. "I'm returning to my quarters to call Rose."

[an hour later]

Ryker got the long-time butler at the Bristow estate on the line.

"Neville, this is Axel. I called our lake house and Rose didn't answer. Is she there at the mansion?"

"Yes, Mr. Ryker. I will let her know you're calling, sir."

In about a minute, Rose picked up the phone. *"Axel?"*

"Yes, it's me, my love. How is Johnny doing?"

"He's fine, but I can tell he misses his father."

Ryker cared about nothing else in the world besides his wife and son. "Rose, I will be home late next Monday evening."

"Hurry back, my darling."

When the call ended, Ryker sat back in his chair. He knew a man who had done the things he had done for Heinrich Himmler did not deserve a woman like Rose.

[that afternoon]

Not being on official CIA business, Zhanna had to pay for her own flight. She used some of the money Erika had pirated from the safe on Luca's yacht to pay for a commercial flight. She landed at Denver's Stapleton Airport at 2:35 p.m. Erika was there.

In a taxi on the way back to Lowry, Erika told her, "Al is being a prick. He's not going to get you your own quarters. He said that you'd have to bunk with me. I had a rollaway bed brought in. I tried it. It's as comfortable as my barrack's bed."

"I don't give a rat's ass," Zhanna said. "Many nights during the war, I slept in a cold, muddy foxhole with my head on a rock. I can sleep anywhere. When you called me you said we'd see the Smaldones."

"You and I will go there tonight for dinner and to see Checkers."

287

"How many of the old crew we know are not dead or in prison?" Zhanna asked.

"I don't know, but Chauncey and Fat Paulie are still around. I spoke with them last night. Also, Tommy, the bartender we met during our first mission in Denver is back from prison—out on parole. He was behind the bar last night."

"Oh, yeah? I like Tommy."

[that evening]

Erika and Zhanna walked into Gaetano's at shortly after 7:00. Erika planned to go straight upstairs, but Zhanna sat down at the bar so she joined her.

"Hello, Tommy," Zhanna said. "Do you remember me?"

"Sure, Zhanna. I was in stir the last time you and Erika were here, but I remember you. What are you ladies drinking? It's on the house."

"Double vodka—straight," Zhanna replied. Erika ordered a Coors.

After they finished that round, they ordered another, left the bar, then ascended the steps at the back of the restaurant.

Eugene "Checkers" Smaldone was two-inches shorter than his taller, younger brother Clyde "Chauncey" Smaldone. Nevertheless, Checkers didn't need size to intimidate. He could do that by simply taking off his black, horned-rimmed, tinted glasses and gaze at a delinquent gambler, or anyone late with a high-interest loan shark debt who needed a wakeup call. If that didn't work, he'd assign Paul Villano to deliver a sterner message.

When Erika and Zhanna were let in by the guard, Checkers sat at the table with Chauncey, Fat Paulie Villano, and Frank "Blackie" Mazza. Blackie was a captain in the family with his own crew that raised a lot of money for the family. Besides that, he frequently did enforcer work for Paulie.

"Hello, Erika and Zhanna," Checkers said.

"Hi, Checkers," Erika said. She then looked at Mazza. "Blackie, it's nice to see you."

Mazza nodded.

"Have you eaten?" Checkers asked.

"No," Erika said.

"There's lasagna over there on the wall table with plates and silverware. It's still warm. Help yourselves."

The women filled their plates and returned to sit down at the table. Neither Erika nor Zhanna had had anything to eat today since breakfast and they shoveled the food into their mouths.

Fat Paulie said, "Nothing has changed. Both of you dames still eat like Billy goats."

Zhanna flipped him the finger and continued to eat. This amused Checkers, who smiled.

"So, are you two on a mission for the feds?" Checkers asked.

Erika's mouth was full. She shook her head, swallowed, then said, "No, we're in Denver on free time. We'll be here through the weekend. We'll be at the poker games Friday and Saturday nights."

"Good," Checkers said. "In the meantime, I have a job that the two of you are perfect for. You'll work with Blackie."

Checkers went on to explain the 'job.'

After he finished, Zhanna said, "We'll get it done. I'm going downstairs to talk with Tommy."

Chapter 86

The Day the Earth Stood Still

Denver, Colorado
Next day—Wednesday, 10 October 1951

Erika was again at Gaetano's having dinner upstairs. Zhanna was not there. She had invited Tommy to a movie.

[same time]

Zhanna and Tommy sat in Denver's Loew's Theater with their popcorn and Orange Crush soft drinks. The movie was a popular new release, *The Day the Earth Stood Still,* starring Michael Rennie and Patricia O'Neal. It was about an alien flying saucer, commanded by Rennie, that landed in Washington, D.C. to deliver a dire message to the earth's inhabitants.

At one point as the movie played, Tommy said, "Zhanna, I have never seen you without a neck scarf. You must really like them."

In the dim light of the theater, Zhanna removed her scarf. "Here is my reason. I must wear them to avoid attention."

Tommy looked at the hideous wound that encompassed her neck.

Chapter 87

La Casa Roja

Denver, Colorado
Next day—Thursday, 11 October 1951

Zhanna didn't return to Lowry until four o'clock in the morning, so she had gotten less than four hours sleep when she and Erika walked to the nearest mess hall for breakfast. Erika didn't ask her about last night, figuring it was none of her business. They first got some coffee and sat down.

"We have to meet Blackie at Gaetano's tomorrow morning at nine. He'll have a driver take the three of us to Kittredge."

"What is that place and where is it?"

"It's a small mountain town about a forty-minute drive west of Denver."

Their job was to collect on a delinquent $2,200 college football gambling debt that had been run up by pair of brothers who lost the money to a Smaldone bookie. They were a week late paying up.

"I'm thinking of inviting the Count out to dinner tonight," Erika said. "Al and Axel can come along if they want. What do you think?"

Zhanna shrugged. "Okay by me."

"We won't go to Gaetano's. Paulie doesn't like Ryker. There might be trouble and I don't want the Count to get mixed up in that, especially if Al is with us. We'll go to a nice little family-run Mexican restaurant I stumbled upon during our last assignment here. I'm sure the Count has never had Mexican food."

[that evening]

It took two taxis. The Count and Hodge in one. Erika, Zhanna, and Ryker rode in another cab that led the way. Because Erika's cabbie had been robbed twice, he didn't allow anyone to sit in the front seat next to him. All passengers had to ride in the back, behind a heavy wire screen. The massive Ryker sat in the middle, crushing Erika and Zhanna against the back doors.

Zhanna elbowed him. "Move over you big fucking palooka."

"Don't make him move my way," Erika emphasized. "I already feel like canned sardine."

From the outside, the La Casa Roja was not impressive. Actually, it was an old shotgun house that a small Mexican family had converted to a restaurant. Mom and the oldest daughter did the cooking. The father ran the bar and the younger daughter waited tables. One waitress was enough to take care of the eight tables.

After the two cabbies were paid, the group walked in and was seated at a six-person table and given menus by the teenage daughter.

"Have you ever had Mexican food, Count?" Erika asked.

"I must admit I have not. I will rely on your suggestions."

"I ate here more than once during my last trip to Denver. Everything I tried was good. I especially enjoyed the cheese enchiladas."

"Then I'll ask you to order for me."

The waitress showed up to take their drink orders. Erika ordered Margaritas for herself and the Count. "It's a drink made from a liquor called tequila," she told him. Zhanna ordered her usually double vodka shooter, Hodge and Ryker a Scotch.

When the drinks were delivered, they placed their food orders.

"Count what do you think about this area of America?" Hodge asked.

"The mountainous regions are very impressive, both here and around Trinidad. Nevertheless, I look forward to returning to Castelul Lupului."

Erika said, "I hope you'll stay in Washington for a few days, Count, and visit us at my café."

"Your invitation is kind, my child. But I will return to my home after Dragoş Luca reaches his destination at your Fort Dix."

292

Chapter 88

Kittredge

By 9:30 a.m., Erika and Zhanna sat in the backseat of a sedan heading west into the mountains. Frank "Blackie" Mazza sat in the front alongside his driver.

Blackie told the women. "These two pricks live on a small farm with their father just outside Kittredge. It's a hick mountain town and it takes the local cops forever to respond to a call out in the boonies like where this farm is located, so we're good to go there. I'll go to the front door to make the collection. You two cover the back door in case these assholes try to hightail it out the back. You have your heaters, right?"

"We have them," Zhanna said.

"If they come out the back door, shoot them in the leg. We don't want these cocksuckers dead until we collect. Got that?"

"We've got it," Erika said.

The driver coiled around the hairpin mountain road curves until he stopped the car a couple of hundred yards from the farmhouse where it could not be seen.

"Let's go," Blackie said to Erika and Zhanna. "Gino, stay with the car."

When they neared the small, rustic farmhouse, Blackie waited for Erika and Zhanna to circle through the pine forest and take their positions behind the house. He then went to the front door and knocked vigorously. In a moment, an old man opened the door. He held a double-barrel shotgun.

"Who are you and what do you want?" the wizened old man asked.

"I'm here to collect a debt from your two prick sons, old man. Send them out here."

The old man said, "Don't call my sons that." He raised his shotgun and pointed it at Blackie. "Get your ass off my property."

"I'll stick that gun up your ass, you old coot. Send your sons out here."

The old man fired a blast over Blackie's head. This made the Smaldone captain duck from the concussion.

Erika and Zhanna heard the shotgun blast but continued covering the back. "Stay here," Erika told Zhanna. "I'll see what's going on."

Back at the front door, Blackie said. "You're making a big mistake, you old cocksucker!" His ears were ringing. "Do you know who I'm with? I'm a member of the Smaldone family."

"I have one shot left," the defiant old man replied. "You have thirty seconds to get off my property." The old man started counting.

"Watch your back, old man. I'll return." Blackie left the porch and began walking away. His plan was to assemble Erika and Zhanna. The three of them would rush the house.

When Blackie was about thirty yards away when the old man stepped out on the porch and pulled the trigger on his last shell. Most of the birdshot pellets missed Blackie but three or four penetrated the back of his pants.

"Eoww!" Blankie yelled and headed for cover.

Erika reached the front of the house. She saw the old man's gun was a double barrel and knew he was out of shells. As he started to reload, she rushed him and took the gun away.

From behind a tree, Blackie shouted. "Shoot that sonuvabitch! He shot me in the ass!"

Erika started laughing. She ignored the order, but still she barged into the house looking for the brothers. The old man had told the truth. His sons were not there.

She ran back outside and fired a round in the air. She knew Zhanna would recognize the sound of her Beretta Brevetatta. She gave the shotgun back to the old man and said, "I salute you, but tell your sons to pay their debt. This won't end for them for them until they do. And tell them to stop gambling. Apparently, they're not good at it."

Zhanna arrived from the back and they followed the hobbling Blackie Mazza back to the car, the two Shield Maidens laughed at him all the way.

"What are you two laughing at?" he said. "Erika, I told you to shoot that bastard."

"It's not my fault you underestimated the old man," Erika replied. "I'm not going to shoot a man for standing his ground on his own property. He's not the one who owes the family. I told him to make sure his sons pay up."

"Yeah, fuck you, Blackie," Zhanna added. "What food will we have at the poker game tonight?"

[that evening]

The Smaldone family didn't send anyone to a local hospital for a gunshot wound, knowing the doctors were required by law to report such wounds to the Denver police. Instead, they had a doctor who was well paid to treat such wounds in his office and keep his mouth shut.

This afternoon, the four small birdshot pellets were removed from Blackie Mazza's buttocks. He was upstairs at Gaetano's when the weekend poker games for family members was about to start. There were 18 made members taking up the three poker tables. Right now the tables were covered by tablecloths as everyone was eating Mostaccioli with sweet Italian sausage and marinara sauce. Bottles of red wine sat on the tables. Erika and Zhanna, as usual, were shoveling the food into their mouths.

Erika had filled Checkers and Fat Paulie in on what happened in Kittredge. Paulie was the first to tell the rest of the men.

"Blackie was shot in the ass by a hick farmer today."

All the men roared in laughter.

"Fuck all of youze," Blackie said. He sat on a pillow he brought for his wooden chair.

Checkers wasn't pleased with Blackie. "You should have made sure the brothers were there before you went. And leave the old man alone. He's a civilian. I want that money by Wednesday. Ya got that ya dumbass?"

"I got it," Blackie said. "I'm sorry boss; I'll collect."

"Add two points to the total for them being late," Checkers added.

When everyone finished eating, the tables were cleared and the linen removed. The high stakes games began.

Erika had given her share of the money she filched from Luca's safe on the Som de Argint to Amy to help pay for the band's expenses to come to the States. She had $185 on her. Zhanna had used only enough of her money to pay for her flight to Denver, so she still had the bulk of her share. Knowing Erika was a much better poker player than her, Zhanna give Erika an extra $500.

Erika and Zhanna sat at a table with Fat Paulie, Bobby LaSasso, and brothers Roger and Johnny Russomano—all made men.

Games of Tute Erika had recently played in Europe had seen her break even at best. Poker she was much more skilled at and tonight she was back in form. An hour into the game she was up $240. Zhanna was losing. The Russian took too many chances trying to hit inside straights and would keep calling bets with poor hands. Erika had warned her about these faulty strategies in the past, but that advice fell on deaf ears.

The games were dealer's choice and when the cards came around to Erika she said, "Kansas City stud, gentlemen and lady."

"Ante up," she said. Everyone threw a $5 chip to the middle of the table. She shuffled then offered the pack to Bobby LaSasso for a cut. He sat on her right. Then she dealt each player five cards.

Everyone looked at their hand. A player could ask to replace three of his cards. Everyone did this except Paulie. He wanted only one. This told Erika he was going for an outside straight, or he had two pair and was going for a full house.

"I'll bet," Paulie said. "Ten bucks." He threw the chip on the pile.

"I'll raise it $10," one of the Russomano brothers said. The other brother folded, as did LaSasso. Every else called. Then Erika said, "I'll call and raise another ten."

Fat Paulie looked at her. "This dame's bluffing."

"Quit calling me or Zhanna 'dames' or 'broads,' Paulie. Zhanna and I are members of this family like everyone else in here. You were there the night Zhanna and I were made. We insist on that respect. Call us by our names."

Chauncey, who played poker at another table overheard. He said, "She's got a point, Paulie."

Paulie didn't respond to Chauncey. He actually liked Erika and Zhanna but hated losing at poker or at the track. At those times his dark side surfaced.

"Everybody just show your hand." He laid down his cards. He had two pair. "Kings over nines."

The Russomano brother who had stayed the course also had two pair, but his tens over fives was lower than Paulie's. Zhanna had one pair of Jacks.

Erika showed her hand. "Three boxcars." ('boxcars' was Smaldone slang for eights).

"Fuck me!" Paulie said, and in anger he threw his cigar against the wall. Jimmy, the teenage nephew of LaSasso, served as the gofer for these games—getting player's drinks, more food if they wanted it, etc. He ran over and picked up the burning cigar, put it an ashtray, then grabbed a broom and dustpan and swept up the ashes while Erika swept the $150 worth of chips toward her.

"Give me one of your cigars, fat man," Zhanna said.

"I'll take one, too," Erika said.

"Fuck the both of youze," he said.

Checkers stepped in. "Give them a cigar, Paulie."

Paulie glared at the women, but eventually took two cigars out of his jacket pocket and tossed them across the table.

Chapter 89

The Falcon team

Denver, Colorado
Next day—Saturday, 13 October 1951

This morning, Al Hodge was awakened by a ringing phone. He sat up on the edge of his bed and looked at his wristwatch laying on the nightstand. It was 4 a.m. Thinking he knew who was calling, he cursed and picked up the receiver. "Yes," he said groggily.

"Al, this is Leroy."

"Leroy? I figured this was a call from Erika and Zhanna from the Denver jail. It's 6 a.m. in Washington. This must be important. What's up?"

"The Falcon team got the goods on Luca's Mexico City operation. They have evidence that Luca's opium was converted to heroin there and that some of it ended up in the United States. With this linked together with his journal and confession we're on Easy Street. He'll never be a free man again. The Russian embassy will have to back off."

"Great news, Leroy!"

"Is Luca still on schedule to be transported to Fort Dix on Monday?"

"Yeah, nothing's changed there."

"Okay, I know you won't get to Fort Dix until late. Meet me in my office Tuesday morning with Erika, Zhanna, and Ryker."

"Alright, Leroy. We'll be there."

"Tell Count Lupei and Erika about this development, Al."

"I will."

[that evening]

Erika and Zhanna arrived at Gaetano's an hour before the poker games were to start. Zhanna had asked for the early arrival so she had some time to talk to Tommy. Both women found seats at the bar.

Fat Paulie Villano sat at a special 8-chair table in the back of the restaurant reserved for Smaldone family members. Zhanna never got the chance to talk to Tommy. A young waitress walked up to them and told them Paulie invited them to join him at his table.

"Take a seat," Paulie told the women. He then waved over the same waitress. "Take their drinks orders sweetie." Also at the table sat Chauncey, Blackie Mazza, and Bobby LaSasso.

Villano said to Erika and Zhanna, "I want to apologize to both of you for my behavior last night. You are made. I have a problem with losing. It's my cross to bear."

"We know that Paulie," Erika said. "Last night wasn't the first time we played cards upstairs. The matter is over as far as Zhanna and I are concerned."

"How much did you leave with last night, Erika?"

"Just over $1,100."

"Jesus!" LaSasso said. "You're not leaving tonight until you lose that money back."

"Don't threaten me, Bobby," she replied. "I'll leave when I want to leave."

That wasn't enough for Zhanna. She jumped up quickly and placed her dagger to LaSasso's throat. "If you bother my friend I'll give your throat a smile from ear to ear." Her Russian accent was prominent.

"And I'll let her do it, Bobby," Checkers said. "These women are friends of mine and made family members. Show them the same respect you're entitled to as a made member."

LaSasso held up his hands. "Alright, alright! I get the message. Get this crazy Russian off me."

◊ ◊ ◊

When the card games began, Fat Paulie placed Bobby LaSasso at another table. Taking LaSasso's seat at Villano's table was Blackie Mazza's driver, Gino. Tonight's food that had been sent up from the kitchen was meatball sandwiches with fried green and red bell peppers on the side. The gofer, Jimmy, rushed around delivering drinks.

The games were about to start but Erika and Zhanna were still attacking the meatball sandwiches that sat on a small table next to them so sauce or cheese would not be dribbled onto the felt poker tables.

Paulie tried to be patient. "Are you two about ready to play cards or are you going to stuff your faces all night?"

Erika nodded and said something unintelligible because her mouth was full of food.

"Okay," Paulie said. "This is my table. I'll be the first dealer."

Two hours into the game, Erika's lucky streak continued but her winnings were token, having only increased the chips before her by $40. That was true until she won another nice pot. Erika had nothing but got Paulie and the other men to fold by her bluffing. She scraped in $90 from that pot.

Erika ended the weekend poker games at Gaetano's by walking away with $1,450. Zhanna had lost almost $300, but Erika gave her friend back the $500 stake Zhanna had given her. This left Erika $950 in the black. Three hundred dollars more than her monthly salary from the CIA.

Chapter 90

A sad Fat Paulie

Denver, Colorado
Next day—Sunday, 14 October 1951

Erika Lehmann, Zhanna Rogova, and Axel Ryker sat in Al Hodge's quarters on the Lowry Air Force Base. It was late morning.

"I have good news from Leroy," Hodge said to them all. "The Falcon team established a direct connection from Luca and heroin being smuggled into the States. With Luca's confession about his gun running that Ryker got out of him, he's screwed. I told the Count about this earlier today."

Erika was especially relieved.

Hodge continued, "Everything is on schedule as far as Luca is concerned. We fly out of here at nine o'clock tomorrow morning. Tuesday morning, Leroy wants all of us in his office at ten."

[that afternoon]
Erika wanted to say her goodbyes to the Smaldones. She took Zhanna with her. Erika knew the restaurant was closed on Sundays. Yet, she also knew many of the boys would be around. Running Denver's most powerful organized crime syndicate was a seven-day-a-week job.

The two women arrived at the restaurant in the late morning as a light snow fluttered down. The Smaldones were expecting more arrivals to a sit-down Checkers had called for, so the front door was unlocked.

Checkers, Chauncey, and Fat Paulie sat at the Smaldone table at the back of the restaurant waiting for the others.

"What are you doing here?" Paulie asked Erika. "Did you come to rub it in because of your lucky streak. How much did you walk away with?"

"After I paid Zhanna back the money she staked me, I won $950."

"Fuck me in the ear!" Paulie bellowed.

301

Checkers took over. "What brings you and Zhanna here?"

"I told you we were leaving Denver tomorrow, Checkers. Zhanna and I just stopped in to say goodbye."

Checkers gave both women a hug. So did Fat Paulie and Chauncey. Of all the three mobsters, surprisingly it was Paulie who looked the saddest that they were leaving. "Don't be gone so long next time," he said.

"We'll try not to be, Paulie," Erika said and kissed him on the cheek.

"Goodbye," Erika said to them all. As they walked through the door, Zhanna turned back and waved.

Part 9

Chapter 91

Baloney

Denver, Colorado
Next day—Monday, 15 October 1951

Two inches of snow had fallen on Denver overnight. This was small potatoes for this city—a poor stepchild to much more massive snows the area would experience during the winter. The airport maintenance crews were accustomed to clearing snow off the runaways from as early as mid-September until late April—some of those snows two or three feet deep. The trucks plowed and the deicing crews used chemicals to defrost the aircraft wings.

The Air Force DC-3 took off on time. Onboard were Al Hodge, Dragoş Luca, Erika, Zhanna, and Ryker. Three CIA security agents were also onboard as was the hard-boiled Army nurse from the Trinidad operation, there to monitor Luca's wellbeing.

Since handcuffs would not fit over the thick cast on Luca's left hand and forearm, Hodge locked Luca's right hand to the arm of his seat. The drug kingpin also wore a cast on his left leg to help heal the ankle Ryker had snapped, a white cotton patch over his blinded eye, and a similar patch over his shattered eardrum.

Luca, his nurse, and the security detail were positioned in seats near the front of the fuselage. Erika, Zhanna, and Ryker sat in the back. The tires of the DC-3 left the terra firma of the Mile High City at 9:15 a.m.

By 1:00 p.m. the plane was over Missouri. "Is anyone hungry?" Erika asked. Zhanna and Ryker said yes. Erika walked to the front and retrieved from a cooler six baloney sandwiches and three bottles of RC Cola. She returned and gave everyone two sandwiches and a drink.

As they ate the sandwiches, Erika said, "At least we'll get back in time to see the band's final performances at the Lili Marlene. Their four-week contract ends after this coming weekend."

"All I want to do is see my wife and son," Ryker stated strongly.

"Zhanna," Erika said. "How about you?"

"As long as I get back behind the bar, I'll be satisfied. And I look forward to sleeping in my own bed."

[that evening]

The DC-3 did not require a refueling stop for the 2,000-mile flight. It skidded down on a dry runway at Andrews Air Force Base at 8:20 p.m.

While they disembarked, Hodge told the Maidens and Ryker, "I have a car here to take you two back to Arlington and Ryker to the Mayflower. Be in my office at nine o'clock tomorrow morning."

Luca, Hodge, the nurse, and the three CIA bodyguards loaded into a small Army bus and road off. Erika, Zhanna, and Ryker piled into the sedan driven by an Army MP.

"Axel, come with Zhanna and me to the café and eat something. You can take a taxi back to the Mayflower later."

"Very well, Sonderführer. I assume all of us will be coming and going from E Street for a few days for debriefing. I will call Rose from your café and ask her to come to the hotel tomorrow and bring our son."

Again, Ryker had used Erika's WW II Nazi spy rank. She ignored it.

Chapter 92

Another She-Wolf

Washington, D.C.
Next day—Tuesday, 16 October 1951

"What's going on with Count Lupei?" Hodge asked Erika.

She and Ryker sat in his E Street office.

"He and Geofri flew back to Washington on a commercial flight," she said. "They're leaving tomorrow to return to Romania. I invited him to stay for a while, but he wants to get back. He said he will stop by the café tonight to say his goodbyes."

"It's my understanding that this coming weekend is the last for Amy's Gypsy band. Is that right?"

"That's when the contract ends," Erika replied.

"Don't extend it," Hodge ordered. "I'm happy for the band members that they got to spend some time in the States, but they need to return to Barcelona. We'll all miss Amy, but she needs to be in Europe with her cover. I spoke about all this with Amy on the phone last night. I'm just telling you, Erika, so you don't throw a monkey wrench in the works by going to Petru with another contract."

Hodge then addressed both Erika and Ryker. "Leroy has decided you two will not undergo debriefings about Trinidad. He doesn't want it on the official record that we allowed Axel to interrogate Luca. The official transcripts to the Senate Oversight Committee and the Justice Department will show that Luca suffered his injuries during an escape attempt.

"Axel, you're free to return to Philadelphia."

"Rose is already on her way here," Ryker said. "I thought there would be debriefings. We'll stay at the Mayflower tonight and return to Philadelphia tomorrow."

"Okay," Hodge said. "The mission is officially over. I'll try and give you more down time than you had before this assignment. Erika, I'll be at your café Saturday evening for Amy's final performance."

305

[that evening]

Erika and Amy sat at the Lili Marlene Café bar talking to Zhanna.

"Zhanna," Erika said. "Any luck with prospects for an additional bartender? I know you were looking for one before I left for Colorado. I meant to ask you in Denver but there was so much going on it slipped my mind."

"Not yet," Zhanna answered.

Erika turned to Amy. "Al said he spoke with you last night."

"Yes. We're to return to Barcelona after our shows here this weekend. It's for the best, Erika. Luca's money that you and I pooled to pay for the band and stage crews flights and hotel rooms is getting low. Putting up eleven people at the Mayflower for several weeks is expensive. And we still have the flights back to Spain."

Axel Ryker and Rose walked in.

Zhanna, from her place behind the bar, faced the door and saw them first. "The gorilla just walked in."

Axel and Rose sat down at a table and Erika and Amy joined them.

"It's nice to see you again, Erika," Rose said.

"Thank you, Rose. I bet you're glad Axel is back."

"Yes, our son and I missed him terribly."

"Where is my godson?" Erika asked.

"Back at the hotel with the nanny. Erika, I wanted to ask you something. My parents are flying in on Saturday to see Amy and her band's final performance. I know how hard it is to get a table. I was wondering if you could reserve us one."

"Rose, it's always an honor to have the Bristow family at the Lili Marlene. Al Hodge told me he's also coming on Saturday. Do you think your parents would mind if Al sat with you?"

"Of course not. That would be nice. Wouldn't it be Axel."

Ryker grunted, "I'd rather not."

"Don't be rude, my dear," Rose told him.

"Then I'll reserve a six-person table for you," Erika said. "Would you like some dinner tonight?"

"We've already eaten," Rose replied. "Axel took me to the Capitol Hill Steakhouse. We can't stay long. We might have one drink before we leave."

◊ ◊ ◊

Ryker and Rose left the café about a half-hour before Count Lupei and Geofri walked in. Erika saw them, walked over to greet them, and led them to a table. Amy joined them. Angelika was working the bar with Zhanna and told her that she would cover for a while, so Zhanna also joined the table.

"We'll miss you Count," Erika said. "And you, too, Geofri."

Both men wore casual blazers, the top link of their shirt collars unbuttoned.

"I just came by to wish you all well," said the Count. "And extend to you all an open invitation to visit Castelul Lupului any time you wish."

Zhanna said, "That would be great if I don't have to drink any of that stuff made from apricots."

"I've told you a dozen times that Tuică is made from plums, Zhanna," Amy corrected her.

"Count," Erika said. "Thank you for your kind invitation, and it would certainly be wonderful to visit you again, but you know the difficulties we face when we have to go behind the Iron Curtain. That problem was made easy this time because Amy's band was invited by the Romanian government. Otherwise, we're forced to sneak in."

"Erika," the Count said. "I understand your daughter lives here with you. Would you introduce us, please?"

"Surely, Count. Ada is in the kitchen doing dishes."

"I'll get her," Amy volunteered.

When Amy returned with Ada, Erika said, "Count Lupei and Geofri, this is my daughter Adelaide. Adelaide, this is Count Sorin Lupei and Geofri."

The ten-year-old looked at both men. "Hello."

The Count looked into the child's eyes for a long moment. He then looked at Erika before returning his gaze to her daughter. He took Ada's hand. "Adelaide, it is my honor to meet you. It is my hope that I will see you again someday, my child."

Erika was unnerved. "Ada, you may return to the kitchen now. Thank you, my darling."

"Yes, Mutti."

As soon as Ada left, Erika said, "Count Lupei, is this the real reason you came here tonight? I don't want my daughter following me into the life I lead. I want something better for her."

"Occasionally, the gift is passed to the next generation," the Count said. "Adelaide has inherited your gift. Rest your mind, Erika. This does not mean Adelaide has to follow you in your life. She can pursue any life she chooses. She might never know of her gift."

Chapter 93

Not wanting to talk

Arlington, Virginia
Next day—Wednesday, 17 October 1951

Amy was not at the café tonight. Erika sat at the bar talking with Zhanna between her drink orders for customers. Erika noticed that Zhanna was wearing the wolf's head pendant given to her by Jaro Banik, but Erika didn't mention it.

"Did the Count get off okay? Zhanna asked.

Erika nodded. "I went to the airport with him and Geofri this morning."

"What do you think about all that stuff the Count said about Ada last night."

"I don't want to talk about it."

Count Lupei's words about her daughter had brought to mind an incident last year when she and Ada were walking through a nearby Arlington park. It wasn't long after she returned from her first mission in Romania where see met the Count for the first time.

A huge Doberman Pincher was being walked on a leash by its owner who seemed to take humor in his beast of a dog snarling and barking aggressively—scaring children, other dogs, and even adults.

Erika and Ada sat down on a bench. When the Doberman and its master passed them, the dog quit snarling and looked frightened. Erika thought it was because of her, but when, without fear, Ada rose from the bench and approached the dog to pet it, it whimpered and cowered behind its master.

Ada returned to her mother's side and asked, "Why doesn't the doggie like me, Mutti?"

Chapter 94

Amarisi

Arlington, Virginia
Two days later—Saturday, 20 October 1951

Friday night's performance by the Barcelona Romanian Gypsy Orchestra was exactly what everyone expected—a hectic standing room only sellout. Tonight, the band would perform for the last time at the Lili Marlene.

It was still an hour before showtime, and the café overflowed. Manning the kitchen were Bertha and her two daughters. Ada was in charge of keeping up with the dirty dishes. Behind the bar, Angelika, Zhanna, and a moonlighting bartender from the Mayflower that Amy recruited all worked to keep up. The café's fulltime and parttime waitresses had recruited five temporary waitresses for the weekends the band played. Four local high school boys had been hired to bus tables so the busy waitresses wouldn't have that additional chore.

Erika sat at a table with Archibald and Bernice Bristow, Rose, Ryker, and Al Hodge.

"Are you going to have to work tonight, Erika?" Rose asked.

"We should have enough help tonight, but I'll help out if I'm needed."

"I will, too," Rose said. "I enjoy doing it."

Erika smiled. "You're a treasure, Rose."

"I'm glad these performance weekends have been successful for your café, Erika," Archibald said.

"All the thanks go to you, Mr. Bristow. The expansion of the café, and the advertising for the band that you, in your generosity, paid for."

"I think the band has much more to do with its popularity than the advertising," he said. "People seemed to be fascinated with a Gypsy band, and let's face it, the performances are outstanding. Miss Radu can certainly mesmerize a crowd. If there had been no advertising, word-of-mouth alone would have ensured a sold-out crowd. If the band members would like to stay longer in the United States, I'm confident that I can get their visas extended."

Hodge stepped in quickly with a lie. "I'm afraid the band is under contract to perform in Greece, Mr. Bristow. They begin that tour in two weeks."

"I see," Bristow said. "Well, contracts have to be honored. But if they ever want to return to America, let me know, Erika."

"I will. Thank you, sir."

"Will the Count be joining us tonight?" Bernice Bristow asked.

Rose smiled and interjected. "My mother has a crush on the Count."

Bernice's face turned crimson. "I certainly do not! You speak out of place, young lady, and with your father sitting right here."

Everyone smiled, including Archibald and even Axel Ryker, who enjoyed the spunk his wife displayed on occasion.

Erika said, "I'm afraid the Count and his butler left for home on Wednesday, Mrs. Bristow. I'm sure they're back in Romania by now."

"I hope their journey went well," Bernice said, covering her tracks. She then shot her daughter a disapproving look.

◊ ◊ ◊

When eight o'clock rolled around, Erika took to the stage and spoke into the microphone.

"Ladies and gentlemen." The loud crowd banter lessened. "Tonight, appearing at the Lili Marlene Café for their last appearance during their current visit to America, please welcome the Barcelona Romanian Gypsy Orchestra!"

The crowd delivered up loud clapping and whistling. The lights on stage went out. When they came back on the bandmembers stood with their instruments and struck up the lively Gypsy tune called *Cigani Ljubiat Pesnji.* Amy was not on stage but as the band played, a spotlight came on and showned on Amy standing at the back of the crowd. Everyone turned in their seats.

She wore a colorful peasant dress and a head scarf with her long hair flowing down her back. She began singing and dancing as she made her way through the tables toward the stage, pausing often to flirt with the men by tickling them under their chins. The reaction of the women sitting with the men varied from smiling to frowning. Amy made sure she did this to Al Hodge. Erika and Rose laughed.

The band members were determined to make their last performance in America a memorable one, pulling out all the stops. The concert lasted nearly two hours as they played all of their most popular songs used in Barcelona and throughout Europe. Cici played a solo violin medley during one of Amy's costume changes. Mitica played a tune on his cimbalom during another time Amy was off stage changing.

When the time came for the last song of the night, Amy and the band had done their job spellbinding the onlookers. Amy was now wearing her tribal clan skirt.

She spoke into the microphone. "Thank you all for welcoming us to your country so warmly. We will forever hold in our hearts your kindness and our time in your beautiful land. I hope you have all been entertained."

The crowd roared with applause, shouting, and whistling.

"Our final song tonight will be *Lule Lule.* It's a favorite among the patrons of our home cantina in Barcelona."

After *Lule Lule,* the band joined hands and took a bow to a standing ovation. When they left the stage, deafening chants for an encore wouldn't subside until that band came back out. Loud cheering followed.

The band played *Amarisi,* a high tempo Gypsy caravan song that lent itself more to dancing than to singing. Amy removed her hair scarf, flipped out her flowing raven locks and whirled and whirled, as she had done in her carefree days as a fifteen-year-old teenager around the campfires in Transylvania.

Books by Mike Whicker

The Erika Lehmann Spy Series

Book 1: *Invitation to Valhalla*
Book 2: *Blood of the Reich*
Book 3: *Return to Valhalla*
Book 4: *Fall from Valhalla*
Book 5: *Operation Shield Maidens*
Book 6: *Hope for Valhalla*
Book 7: *Search for Valhalla*
Book 8: *A New Valhalla*
Book 9: *Shield Maidens Return*
Book 10: *Valhalla Won*
Book 11: *Cliffs of Valhalla*
Book 12: *Smoketown Legend*
Book 13: *Farewell Valhalla*
Book 14: *Singing with Wolves*
Book 15: *Upstairs at Gaetano's*
Book 16: *Nighttime in Berlin*
Book 17: *Dancing for the Gestapo*
Book 18: *Intrigue at the Lili Marlene Café*
Book 19: *American She-Wolf*

Other books by Mike Whicker:

Krozel (a novel) and *Proper Suda* (a novel)
and
Flowers for Hitler: The Extraordinary Life of Ilse Dorsch
(a true-life biography)

Books are available in print copy from Amazon.com, bn.com,
Walmart.com, and as e-books from Kindle.

Author welcomes reader comments.
Email: **mikewhicker@hotmail.com**

Acknowledgements

A grateful thanks to Susan Wedeking Gregory for all her help with proofreading, editing, and her always dependable good advice.

And what can I say about my gift from Heaven, my wife, Sandy? She believed in me and encouraged me from day one—back 26 years ago when I hesitantly, and with little confidence, went to work on my first book, *Invitation to Valhalla.* A novel that took me six years to write. Twenty-two books later, she's still there for me.

Made in the USA
Las Vegas, NV
21 September 2021